76

SPRING SONG

Joyce Cary, one of the foremost English novelists of the last thirty years, intended to publish his short stories in book form under this title. During the winter of 1956–7 he revised some stories, and wrote four new ones, but he had not completed the preparation of the volumes when he died in March 1957. *Spring Song* contains all his finished short stories including five which have not been published before. However various their themes and techniques, all of them are constant in revealing the author's love and compassion for men, his deep awareness of good and evil, his strange personal mixture of irony, simplicity and fun, and his joy of life.

Joyce Cary

SPRING SONG
and other stories

London
MICHAEL JOSEPH

First published by
MICHAEL JOSEPH LTD
26 Bloomsbury Street
London, W.C.1
1960

© *copyright 1960 by executors for the estate of Joyce Cary*

Set and printed in Great Britain by Tonbridge Printers Ltd, Peach
Hall Works, Tonbridge, Kent, in Bembo eleven on twelve point, on
paper made by Henry Bruce at Currie, Midlothian, and bound by
James Burn at Esher, Surrey

CONTENTS

This volume contains all Joyce Cary's short stories published under his own name. (I have not included any of the ten early stories published under the pseudonym Thomas Joyce.) The dates of publication, which are not necessarily the dates of composition, are given in the table of contents. The last five pieces in the volume are hitherto unpublished. They cannot as yet be precisely dated. But the dates given are the earliest at which they are known to have existed. I have followed Joyce Cary's own titles both for the volume and for the individual stories.

WINIFRED DAVIN
Oxford, 1959

BUSH RIVER

A BLACK pony, tied by one leg to the stump of a tree, was eating corn from a wooden bowl. A little brown soldier groomed it furiously, prancing round it in poses of dramatic violence, and twisting his face, like his body, every moment into some unexpected form. Sweat poured down his cheeks and bare chest, on which an identity disc and a leather amulet, on separate cords, performed a kind of African minuet. After every few strokes, he fell back a yard, passing his quivering hand, as small and nervous as a child's upwards over his whole face and cried loudly in Hausa, 'Oh—beautiful—oh, the lovely one. Oh, God bless him. See how he shines.'

A young officer with an eyeglass in his right eye walked slowly round pony and groom. Now and then he glanced severely upon both. Everything about him, his clipped hair which left him almost bald, his clipped moustache, even his eyeglass increased this air of severity, of an austere and critical aloofness.

'Now then, Mamadu,' he said impatiently, 'get on with it. What about the tail?'

'Oh, what a tail. Did you ever see such a tail?'

'I never saw such a dirty one.'

The little soldier pulled his face into a long, dolorous oval and sent his eyebrows to the top of his skull. But the officer did not notice this performance. He had walked down to the river bank.

The river was an African river never yet banked up, tamed, dredged, canalised; a river still wild. It poured along in tan-coloured flood, carrying with it whole trees, and every part of its surface showed a different agitation. Here it was all in foaming breakers, suddenly cut off by a spear-shaped eddy like pulled brown silk; beyond the eddy was a dark sea, with crisp waves jumping, like a

9

wind flaw; and over on the far side, long manila ropes of water which seemed to turn upon themselves as they were dragged under the banks. This savage river not only moved with agile power; it worked. One saw it at work, digging out its own bed, eating at its banks. Every moment some bluff crumbled; stones, bushes fell and vanished.

The young officer, like most people, found a certain attraction in all rivers and moving waters. But African rivers fascinated him. Looking at them he understood that old phrase 'the devouring element.' He asked himself how Africa survived against such destruction. At the same time, he thought, how magnificent was the gesture with which Africa abandoned herself to be torn, like a lioness who stretches herself in the sun while her cubs bite at her.

A thin old sergeant, with extremely bandy legs, marched up, gave a sketchy war-time salute, and said in a grumbling voice, 'Captain Corner, sir.'

'Yes, sergeant?'

'Germans, sir. They come.'

Young Corner withdrew his eyes slowly from the fascinating river and looked once more at the pony, which had taken its nose from the bowl to nibble at the orderly's legs. He said severely, 'Don't forget the tail, Mamadu.'

And once more he walked slowly round, frowning through his eyeglass at the pony.

It was a Barbary stallion, jet black except beneath the belly, which showed a tinge of bronze. It had legs which looked too fine for its body, a crest like the Parthenon chargers and a forelock swinging to its nose. The little head, with full round eyes and tilted nostrils, was like a stag's. The ears were small and pointed, curled like the husks of an almond.

Corner had never before owned a pony of such quality and he was obsessed with the creature. Indeed he had already committed a great folly for its sake. A week before he had received a command regarded by himself and most of his brother officers as a special distinction, a step to promotion. He was to take charge of a sticky and dangerous operation, the planning of a route through the heart of enemy country, by which a heavy gun could be dragged, in secret, to Mora mountain, a German stronghold that had held out against two assaults. It was thought that the fire of this gun, taking the Germans by surprise, would not only smash their defences on the mountain-top but break the morale of their local troops, who could have no experience of high explosive.

This was the year 1915, before the days of bombing by planes. The Cameroons campaign of 1914–16, against the German army of occupation, was a war of raids, ambushes, sieges, enormous marches, and especially surprises. There was no reconnaissance by air, no radio, and intelligence could only be got by scouts and spies. Whole columns would disappear for weeks together, to burst out, a thousand miles away, upon a panic-stricken capital. Two patrols would stumble upon each other by accident in high jungle and stare with amazement for a few seconds before grabbing their rifles.

The strategy of such a war was that of the old bush fighters who knew the jungle, who did not expect a field of fire in order to secure a position, who understood how to place a listening sentry in a tree, who could distinguish between the cough of a leopard and a husky, bored Negro *hauptmann* wandering from his post to look for a chicken, who could take a thousand men in line through thick scrub without losing touch and change front without their shooting each other.

Corner's instructions were to avoid anything like a road or even a used track. They were likely to be watched. He was not even to cross a road by daylight. He was to plot his line as far as possible through untouched bush, to avoid any indication that might put the enemy patrols on the alert, and to hide by night.

Officers in that campaign were allowed their horses, but only in the main column—never on scout, point or patrol duty. For one thing, Nigerian horses in use are all stallions; they will scream at the most distant scent of a mare. For another, a man on a horse can be seen above the top of all but the tallest grass. Corner's assignment was actually that of a man on scout duty all the way. But he had not been able to persuade himself to leave his darling pony behind in some horse lines to be neglected by strangers, starved by thieving camp orderlies, or borrowed by some subaltern for a forced march, to be left dying in a swamp. Few men who parted from their horses in that war ever saw them again. Corner knew his duty, but he said to himself that most of his course lay through high bush where a horse would be as easily hidden as a man. 'And as for mares, there won't be any about—the villages are empty.' But already twice Satan had imagined mares and sent out a trumpet as good as a bugle call for every German within a mile.

Each of these tremendous neighs had scattered the men, diving for cover, and startled the young man out of himself. Each time, in the awful silence which followed, he had sat waiting for a shot, and thinking with amazement, 'My God, what a goddam bloody fool I was to bring this bloody pony. What a hell-fired ass I am.' And the amazement was even stronger than the anger. It was as though he discovered for the first time his own folly, his own mysterious power to forget, simply to abolish common sense and walk gravely, with the most reasonable, dignified air, into impossible situations.

The men creeping back from the scrub would look sulkily at the barb still walking on his toes with ears cocked and nostrils flared. They hated Satan for these alarums. And that was why the young man now said to the sergeant, 'After all the row you've been making down there.' He was defending his darling. He was saying, 'You complain of my pony, but what about your chatter?' And even while he said it, he was ashamed of himself, he was amazed at his own small-mindedness. 'Not like that, Mamadu—don't tear at it.' He took the comb out of the man's hands.

'Captain, sir. Captain Corner, sir.' The sergeant made another war-time salute, and cried in a voice unexpectedly shrill, 'We see 'em, sir.'

Corner, understanding these words at last, looked with surprise at the sergeant and said, 'Who see who, Sargy?'

'Germans, sir. We see 'em, over the river. And the river too big. He too big.'

'That's the style,' Corner murmured to the orderly. He took the excuse of stroking the pony's croup, as if to test the grooming. He did not like to show too openly his passion before Mamadu in case of provoking the latter's admiring outcries, which, for some reason, got on his nerves. His severe air was in fact a defence against this noisy and exaggerated praise. 'Gently does it,' he said, and Mamadu cried, 'Oh, what hair—what a tail. God save us, it touches the ground.'

Corner carefully unravelled the tail; Satan, having ground up every bit of corn in the bowl, turned his delicate nose and began to eat the tree stump. His tail switched in the young man's hand, and he glanced sideways at his master. The large black eyes, more brilliant under the thick short lashes than any woman's, expressed something which always gave Corner acute pleasure, though he could scarcely have described it, except by the words, 'The little bastard don't give a damn for me or anybody else.'

He frowned and said, 'Eating still—this horse would eat anything.' The sergeant turned and walked off, humping his right shoulder in a peculiar manner.

'Oh, a lovely eater—it's a marvel how he eats. Why, he'll eat a desert round himself wherever he is.'

The orderly quite understood that Corner's critical look was simply the outward manner of his obsession; a lover's constraint. Like a lady's maid, he easily penetrated his master's mind. And Corner, like a lady, slightly resented it. He said illogically, 'Then why don't you groom him properly? Look at that mane—look at the dust in the roots.'

'But, sir, it's too thick—just see how thick. Holy God, a wonder for thickness.'

The sergeant reappeared under the huge trees which surrounded the little mud flat. His shoulder was now almost at his ear and he had also begun to limp. He said flatly, 'We no cross here, sir—he too bad place.'

'But we have to cross here; it's the only good place for the gun.'

The duty of the party was to discover if it were practicable to drag a French 75 a hundred miles through the unmapped bush to a certain rendezvous. The idea was to surprise the Germans with this gun, which ranked, in Africa, as heavy artillery.

'The men, they say they no fit to cross.'

'Why?' Corner was startled. He looked thoughtfully at the sergeant. 'There's nobody there, you're not afraid of demons, are you?' he asked.

Sergeant Umaru had, in fact, a great terror of demons, especially in strange bush, and his fear sometimes infected his men. But the men were already frightened of the river, the Germans or demons. Corner found them huddled in a group on the bank, staring through the scrub across the roaring stream. Their faces had the look of panic,

a loosened appearance as if the flesh had turned soft and sagged a
little from the bone. Mouths were hanging slack; one young soldier
was showing his lower teeth.

'What's the trouble?' Corner was saying. 'There's no Germans
within miles. And this river is too fast for crocodiles or water
spirits.'

He was fond of his men and knew them well—brave and cool in
action, but subject to unexpected and mysterious panics.

'It's a bad place,' a lance corporal muttered, rolling his eyes about
like a child in a cellar.

'Nonsense, it's a very good place. Mamadu, saddle up. Where are
the swimmers for the loads?'

On the evening before, there had been eight volunteers eager to
take charge of the loads—rifles, ammunition and rations floated on
gourds—but now there were none. Corner looked round him with
an air of surprise, which was purely formal. His mind was scarcely
interested in this crisis. He was preoccupied with the river. 'A very
good place,' he murmured. 'Where's the guide for the ford?'

'No guide, sir—he no come.'

'No guide.' He was startled. And then at once he felt a peculiar
sense of anticipation. Not of pleasure, scarcely of excitement. It was
as if an opportunity had opened itself before the young man, a gate
in the wall of his routine, through which his mind already began to
flow. Or rather the force which poured eagerly through this gap
was not his at all but that peculiar energy which had possessed him
for days; the energy of his passion for Satan, for the wild bush,
especially for the wild river. The different streams rushed together
at the same gap, and their joined forces were overwhelming. They
swept away the whole bank, the whole wall. Young Corner looked
severely upon his men and said in a voice of resignation, 'I suppose
you want me to give you a lead. Bring Satan, Mamadu.'

Satan was brought. He stretched out his shining neck and nibbled
the tassel on the sergeant's fez. But no one laughed. The men were
quite dissolved in panic. While Corner mounted, they gazed at him
with round eyes which seemed to be liquefying with fear.

The little sergeant alone had his surly veteran's composure. He
hitched up his whole right arm and muttered, 'Very bad river, sir.
Them crocodiles live, sir. Them Germans live other side. I see 'em.'

But Corner did not even listen to him. He had been carried far away from any notion of Germans, of crocodiles. He had no mind for anything but the river and Satan beneath him, who, by means of the magnificent river, was going to achieve a triumph. He held out each leg in turn to Mamadu to pull off his boots. Bare-legged, he hooked his big toes through the sides of the stirrup irons, gave his eyeglass an additional screw, and jammed on his hat, a disreputable terai. Then, for the first time, he examined the river, not as a fascinating object, but as an obstacle. He measured the weight of the current and the direction of the eddies.

He had swum horses before, but only for a few yards; once on a road after a storm, once in a river pool; never in flood water.

It was not a thing one set out to do. On an ordinary journey, the groom took horses across unbridged rivers from a boat, holding them short by head ropes to keep their noses up. A man who chose to swim his own horse when a boat or a ford was available would have seemed quite mad; and if he managed to drown himself or his horse, he would also seem irresponsible.

Corner, at twenty-six, was an extremely conventional young officer, a little bit of a dandy, a good deal of a coxcomb. He had a strong prejudice against the unusual. It seemed to him affected and he hated affectation. And what gave him a calm personal delight in this opportunity seized upon so eagerly by the forces which possessed him was the knowledge that he *had* to swim this river. He had a first-class excuse for doing what he had often wanted to do. He told himself that he was not his own master, not in any sense of the word.

Satan stepped into the water, moving as usual with the precise muscular liveliness of a dancer, and obeying signals that his rider had not consciously given, the shade of a leg pressure, the very beginning of a wrist turn.

A corporal called out suddenly, 'Don't go there, sir—we find them ford, sir.'

Satan's breast was already under water. He lifted his head; he was swimming within five yards of the bank.

Corner, up to the neck as Satan's hindquarters sank beneath him, took his feet out of the stirrups, hooked his right hand into the pommel of the saddle and floated over it. He found at once that he had no control over the pony. He could only talk to him in Hausa, 'Keep at it, friend—straight ahead.'

And when he spoke, he felt an affection for the little horse, an exultant pride in his courage, so different in quality from anything he had known before that it could not be described. It was more than sympathy, more than the bantering love of a friend; it was a feeling so strong that it seemed to have its own life, full of delight and worship; laughing at Satan and rejoicing in all devotion and courage; the mysterious greatness of the spirit. He wanted to laugh, to call out, like Mamadu. But again, as if constrained by decorum or a sense of what was proper to his responsibilities, he merely looked severe and repeated, this time in English, 'Keep it up, old boy—that's the stuff.'

They were now in mid-current. At this level, the river seemed a mile wide and the waves a little ocean storm. The far bank was a mere line on the horizon. A tree trunk, turning its branches like an enormous screw, went swinging past, three yards from Satan's nose. Satan turned an ear back as if expecting some remark, but his nose never deviated an inch from the course. It pointed like a compass at the opposite bank, now passing at a speed which seemed like a train's.

Once only he showed some emotion, when a wave splashed into his nose. He then gave a snort, not the short loud snort of indignation or surprise, but the longer exhalation which means inquiry and suspended judgment. The bank was now close and it proved to be extremely high and steep—what's more, the eddy under the bank was like a millstream. Satan seemed to be deeper in the water. Another wave struck him in the nose and he snorted loud and sharp. Corner thought, 'If he turns back, we're done.'

But Satan obviously had no notion of turning back. Possibly he was too stupid to think of it; or perhaps wise enough to know its danger. Perhaps it was not in the habit of his mind and breeding to turn back. He struck with his forefeet at the clay, now flying past at the rate of four miles an hour. But it was as hard as brick above water level, and his unshod hoofs brought down only small shoots of dust. Corner murmured, 'That's it, old boy, go at it.' But he did not see exactly what was to be gone at. They whirled along the bank and Satan continued to stab at it furiously; he sank suddenly over his nose and, coming up again with a terrific snort, again stabbed and again sank.

They were carried round a point and struck a snag, itself caught against a stump. The cliff behind was breached by some recent avalanche which was heaped among the roots of the stump. Corner threw himself on the snag and backed up the slope, hauling on the reins. Satan made a powerful effort and heaved himself out of the river. In a moment both were on the level ground ten feet above, among short bushes.

Corner felt as if he too had swum a river. He was tired as only a swimmer can be. He chose a patch of young grass and lay flat on his back, holding Satan by the loose rein.

Suddenly he heard a click and turned his head towards it. Over a bush, not ten yards away, he saw the outline of a head in a German soldier's cap and a rifle barrel.

'The Germans,' he thought, or rather the realisation exploded inside his brain like a bomb on a time fuse, illuminating a whole landscape of the mind. He was stupefied again by the spectacle of his own enormous folly, but also by something incomprehensible behind it and about it. And it was with a kind of despair that he said to himself, 'You've done it at last, you fool. You asked for it. But why, why——'

He hadn't even a revolver, so he lay quite still, fatalistic, but not resigned. For he was resentful. He detested this monster of his own stupidity.

At the same time, he was in great terror, the calm helpless terror of the condemned. He was holding his breath for the shot. He had a queer sensation so vivid that he still remembered it twenty years after, of floating lightly off the ground.

Nothing happened. There was a deep silence. And then suddenly a cold touch on his bare calf made him shiver. But he perceived at once that it was Satan's nose. The pony wanted a tuft of grass that was just under his leg.

The young man jumped up and looked angrily at the bushes. But no German fired.

'Captain.' The sergeant's voice behind was full of exultation. Dripping, he saluted almost well enough for a recruit on parade.

'Oh, you've got over at last.' Corner turned upon the man.

'All present, sir.' And he saluted again. 'We find them ford—dem guide come.'

'I suppose he was there all the time. We stop here. We'll have to ramp this bank. Put out two pickets at once. And tell the men to keep on the alert.'

The men, shouting and laughing in triumph as they climbed the bank, were annoyed to be put on picket. They were quite sure that there were no Germans within miles. As the sergeant said in Hausa, 'If the Germans were here, they would have fired before this.'

Corner, with a brisk efficient air, marched up and down, inspected the pickets, pegged out a section of bank to be cut away. He could hear the orderly's voice raised in a song of praise loud enough to reach his ear, and intended to do so.

'Oh, the marvellous swimmer. Oh, the brave horse. Oh, princely horse—the worthy son of kings among horses. Look at him, my brothers. How nobly he moves his lovely ears. Oh, wise horse, he's as wise as a clerk. God bless him in his bravery—in his beauty. Oh, God bless him in his eating.'

Corner frowned and walked further away, as if from contagion. Why had that German not fired—orders to give no alarms?—panic at the sudden appearance of his own men coming up the bank in force? But what was the good of wondering at chance, at luck, here in Africa? Next time it would be different.

He turned his thought from the event, from Satan—he would not even look at the river. But all the more, they were present to his feeling, the feeling of one appointed to a special fate, to gratitude.

UMARU

IT had been raining for two days, the drizzling mountain rain of the Cameroons. The detachment, on special duty behind the German lines, was under strict orders not to be noticed. That was its duty as well as its only security. Fires could not be lit except in brightest day. No tents were carried. But the subaltern in charge, young Corner, had brought a tent-fly with him; an old fly looted from some German camp. Camouflage had not yet reached these remote parts, except in practice, but this big oblong of canvas, once green, had withered to shades of dun and olive which matched perfectly the sparse northern bush.

At sundown the drizzle became only more varied in texture. The wind was rising and the sky, till that moment one weeping bank of water-grey mist, so low that at a little distance it could be seen tangled in the thorns, began to break into enormous clouds, or not yet clouds, shapeless drifts. Corner looking at his men, huddled in their cloaks while they ate their cold porridge, and feeling the rain trickle down his own back, thought that no creature in the world could be more miserable than a wet soldier. He called the old sergeant. 'We'll sleep under the fly, sergeant. There's room for all of us with our feet in the middle.'

Sergeant Umaru, thirty-year veteran, called often Father Umaru by the men, heard with customary wooden disdain; and answered only with a sketchy war-salute. But the men were shy. When the party went to bed, in a well-drained sandy hollow among low scrub, Corner and the sergeant found themselves alone at one edge, while the men's heads, pretty close together, stuck out on the other three sides.

The arrangement, no doubt, would have looked comic to an

observer in a balloon; it would have seemed like a vast family bed
with one white and nineteen black faces sticking out all round a
large patchwork quilt. But it did not strike the family as comic. The
clouds, as they were lifted higher on the strong wind and rolled into
thicker lumps, let fall a much thicker rain, in splashes as if from
buckets carelessly tipped about. The family was glad of its
cover.

The men murmured together in their high voices, very like sleepy
children. Corner, with his head on a rolled macintosh, tried to sleep,
but he kept on being waked by some bit of talk in a familiar voice,
as a man, even asleep, catches anything said by one of his own
household. A certain Salé, a thin gangling lad with a balky eye,
remarked that for his part he'd rather be a horseboy. And Corner's
ear noted, That was meant for me. So Salé has ambitions—he wants
to be in the horse-lines, and I thought he was hostile. That eye
probably meant only that he was wondering how to make an
approach. A moment later he was brought awake again by the
deeper voice of one Adamu, a tall and powerful river pagan,
renowned for his savage temper, who was talking about his village.
'A good place—good land—plenty of water. You never saw such
onions. And the fish—aiee! Women too. Now up here women are
no good. The north is bad for women. In the sun they burn up and
go hard. You want to come down our way for women. But it's
what they always say, Women and fish, if good you would wish,
seek where shady groves by rivers flourish. Yes, a moist folk.' All
this in a soft chant like a man repeating someone else's poem. 'Yes,
a good land in all ways—we have a lovely place—aiee!'

'A rotten place, I know it well.' This was from a little bandy-
legged hill pagan, called officially Moma Gombe, and unofficially
Shoot-Monkey. 'Now Kano—that is the place—a real city.'

'No, it isn't very good, perhaps,' Adamu agreed unexpectedly in
the same dreamy voice. 'Yes, it has its faults—too many floods—
too far from the big markets——'

One of the others suddenly uttered a loud yawn and exclaimed,
'Ow, my bottom,' and the young corporal at the top left-
hand corner reproved him, 'Shut up, you'll wake Three-
Eyes.'

Three-Eyes was Corner, who was therefore obliged to lie still and try to sleep. In a few minutes he was actually going to sleep, but at the last moment of half-consciousness, just as he was congratulating himself, 'I really am nearly asleep,' he became so instantly and feverishly awake that it was hopeless even to think of sleeping. His legs ached, every nerve twitched, lights jumped in front of his shut eyes, and all the cells in his brain seemed to be darting about and banging together like bubbles in soda water.

The men were already asleep. There were snores and grunts. One of them muttered a few words, 'But it's so high—I don't——'

Corner gave it up; he could no longer stand the commotion inside. The rain had stopped some time before, abruptly, after five minutes' quick fire; he turned on his back and opened his eyes, to be startled by a commotion overhead even more wild and much more grand. There were now at least three levels of cloud all moving in different directions. The old round clouds, now once more joined in masses, but masses of enormous size and sharp outline, moved slowly with a vast piled dignity almost due east; a second layer, much lower, was made up of fantastic torn shapes, swimming fast like the debris of a flood. One saw something like a drowned bullock, swollen and limp, with twisted body and its legs pointing opposite ways, and a haycock just breaking up into wafts of straw. Or it was more like the ruins of some immense jig-saw map— Germany, France, Italy, England, Scotland, with their jagged coast-lines and frontiers, caught up in some furious gale of time, and being stretched, squeezed, joined and divided in the process; not by sudden jerks, but by a smooth continuous deformation, which was much more expressive of the powers at work.

And below all, moving faster still, as fast as a horse could gallop, and in a third direction, white fragments, wisps trailing their filmy skirts not much higher than the trees, seemed like ghosts of clouds, lost benighted creatures rushing through the dark transparent space below the tumult in the desperate anxious hurry of all lost creatures trying to find out where they are, and what they are, and where they ought to be.

A sudden movement beside him made Corner turn his head. Old Umaru, also on his back, with open eyes, had just scratched the calf of one leg with the toe-nails of the other. Corner spoke without meditation. It was as if the vivacity of his nerves was glad to find a tongue. 'How would you like to be back in Bauchi, Sargy, in a nice warm house?'

Umaru said in his driest tone, 'I don't live in Bauchi.'

'Then why are you called Umaru Bauchi?'

'That's just a Company name.'

'Where do you come from, then?'

'Nowhere. I don't belong anywhere.'

'But where were you born?'

'On war.' He used the word used by the old Emirs to mean an army in being, on the move. 'I go where the Company goes,' and he added severely, as if instructing a small boy, 'that's the best way.'

'But the Company has a home, it was stationed at Bauchi. That's where it has its wives and its friends.'

'Friends. I don't have friends. Friends are no good.'

Corner was now quite content to lie awake and to enjoy the sky and the talk. He was extremely awake but the commotion inside had suddenly vanished, as if drawn out of him by that of the sky, that was, the lower sky. For in the upper layer, that region of cold majestic forms, the moon, which had for a long time, itself out of sight, been throwing a brilliant greenish light on the precipices of the top clouds, as on a range of Himalayas, was now very slowly projecting one edge of itself into a small triangle of blue already so full of white glitter that it was scarcely blue at all.

Suddenly in a different tone, abrupt and reluctant, but undoubtedly curious, such as Corner had never before heard from the old man, he asked, 'In your country, Caftin, among the water, do you keep friends?'

'Of course, plenty.'

The sergeant pondered. At last he exclaimed, 'Plenty. I have friends too—like that.' His tone abolished this promiscuous relation as something casual and frivolous. But his voice ended on a high note; it seemed that he was about to make further confidences. The young man waited with an expectation which seemed to have occupied all the place of those restless cells, a feeling not only of curiosity but discovery. He had taken the sergeant for a good stolid Hausa, a sun-dried old soldier without an idea beyond his trade, and now it seemed that he had reflections of his own. He had always liked

Umaru for his honesty and his courage, but now he felt, especially at the point where his elbow touched the old man's back, a warmth of sympathy.

The moon, but half disclosed, was cut off as by a shutter. A vast black cloud below, a ragged tormented thing shaped like Greece, but with an immensely stretched out isthmus at Corinth, had come rushing across the middle darkness. It was hustled by in a few minutes, but as its distorted Peloponnese was dragged away by the neck, a volley of big rain, cold heavy drops, widely spaced, came smacking down as out of clear space. They made a quite surprisingly loud report on the hollow canvas and stung the face. But the young man did not pull in his head. He was still preoccupied with Umaru's last remark.

'But Umaru, it isn't good for a man to be lonely.'

'Yes, it is very good.' This was with great conviction. Umaru was lying rigid with his little grey beard aimed truculently at the moon, now once more in sight, and with her full face. She had proceeded at least another half-inch upon her way during that interruption. 'Very, very good. That's the way to live—like a Haji.' (A Haji is a pilgrim.)

'Ah then, God is your friend.'

'No—no, no—no,' with all the explosive violence of the Hausa negative. 'God is——' He paused, trying to find an adequate word. Then he said in a mild tone, 'He is our great One.'

'Yes, that's true.' The young man certainly felt the greatness at that moment, but not with any reverence, only elation. Simply because he began to admire the scene as beauty, it seemed to him more extraordinary. He said to Umaru, carrying on the conversation, 'It's a grand night now—look at those clouds.'

'A bad night,' Umaru said. 'Very bad. More storms coming. A bad, bad night. God help us.'

'But good to look at.'

'To look at.' Umaru said this with wondering contempt. Again there was a long silence. Then suddenly he muttered in a grumbling tone, 'Time for sleep—God bless you with it.'

'And you, Father.'

'And health.'

'And much health.'

'God prolong us,' in a growl. He turned on his side. But the young man lay on his back for another hour, and still at the place where his elbow touched Umaru's back he was aware of a certain activity of feeling at work as if by itself; an affectionate concern which did not stop. At least, it was still there when he noticed it some time later. It was laughing, too, by itself, but not at Umaru. It was quite independent, a serene enjoyment.

A SPECIAL OCCASION

THE nursery door opened and Nurse's voice said in the sugary tone which she used to little girl guests, 'Here you are, darling, and Tommy will show you all his toys.' A little brown-haired girl, in a silk party frock sticking out all round her legs like a lampshade, came in at the door, stopped, and stared at her host. Tom, a dark little boy, aged five, also in a party suit, blue linen knickers, and a silk shirt, stared back at the girl. Nurse had gone into the night nursery, next door, on her private affairs.

Tom, having stared at the girl for a long time as one would study a curiosity, rare and valuable, but extremely surprising, put his feet together, made three jumps forward and said, 'Hullo.'

The little girl turned her head over one shoulder and slowly revolved on one heel, as if trying to examine the back of her own frock. She then stooped suddenly, brushed the hem with her hand, and said, 'Hullo.'

Tom made another jump, turned round, pointed out of the window, and said in a loud voice something like 'twanky tweedle.' Both knew that neither the gesture nor the phrase was meant to convey a meaning. They simply expressed the fact that for Tom this was an important and exciting, a very special occasion.

The little girl took a step forward, caught her frock in both hands as if about to make a curtsy, rose upon her toes, and said in a prim voice, 'I beg your pardon.'

They both gazed at each other for some minutes with sparkling eyes. Neither smiled, but it seemed that both were about to smile.

Tom then gave another incomprehensible shout, ran round the table, sat down on the floor and began to play with a clockwork engine on a circular track. The little girl climbed on a tricycle and pedalled round the floor. 'I can ride your bike,' she said.

Tom paid no attention. He was trying how fast the engine could go without falling off the track.

The little girl took a picture book, sat down under the table with her back to Tom, and slowly, carefully, examined each page. 'It's got a crooked wheel,' Tom said, 'that's what it is.' The little girl made no answer. She was staring at the book with round eyes and a small pursed mouth—the expression of a nervous child at the zoo when the lions are just going to roar. Slowly and carefully she turned the next page. As it opened, her eyes became larger, her mouth more tightly pursed, as if she expected some creature to jump out at her.

'Tom.' Nurse, having completed her private business, came bustling in with the air of one restored to life after a dangerous illness. 'Tom, you naughty boy, is this the way you entertain your guests? Poor little Jenny, all by herself under the table.' The nurse was plump and middle-aged; an old-fashioned nanny.

'She's not by herself,' Tom said.

'Oh Tom, that really is naughty of you. Where are all your nice manners? Get up, my dear, and play with her like a good boy.'

'I am playing with her,' Tom said, in a surly tone, and he gave Nurse a sidelong glance of anger.

'Now Tom, if you go on telling such stories, I shall know you are trying to be naughty. Get up now when I ask you.' She stooped, took Tom by the arm, and lifted him up. 'Come now, you must be polite, after you've asked her yourself and pestered for her all the week.'

At this public disclosure, Tom instantly lost his temper and yelled, 'I didn't—I didn't—I won't—I won't.'

'Then I'll have to take poor little Jenny downstairs again to her mummy.'

'No—no—no.'

'Will you play with her, then?'

'No, I hate her—I never wanted her.'

At this the little girl rose and said, in precise indignant tones, 'He is naughty, isn't he?'

Tom flew at her, and seized her by the hair; the little girl at once uttered a loud scream, kicked him on the leg, and bit his arm. She was carried screaming to the door by Nurse, who, from there, issued sentence on Tom, 'I'm going straight to your father, as soon as he comes in.' Then she went out, banging the door.

Tom ran at the door and kicked it, rushed at the engine, picked it up and flung it against the wall. Then he howled at the top of his voice for five minutes. He intended to howl all day. He was suffering from a large and complicated grievance.

All at once the door opened and the little girl walked in. She had an air of immense self-satisfaction as if she had just done something very clever. She said in a tone demanding congratulation, 'I've come back.'

Tom gazed at her through his tears and gave a loud sob. Then he picked up the engine, sat down by the track. But the engine fell off at the first push. He gave another sob, looked at the wheels, and bent one of them straight.

The little girl lifted her party frock behind in order not to crush it, sat down under the table, and drew the book on to her knee.

Tom tried the engine at high speed. His face was still set in the form of anger and bitterness, but he forgot to sob. He exclaimed with surprise and pleased excitement, 'It's the lines too—where I trod on 'em.'

The little girl did not reply. Slowly, carefully, she opened the book in the middle and gazed at an elephant. Her eyes became immense, her lips minute. But suddenly, and, as it were, accidentally, she gave an enormous sigh of relief, of very special happiness.

SUCCESS STORY

A n old man in a brown bowler walked slowly along the path. His narrow trousers, in a pale brown whipcord, were cut in the style of the 'nineties. The sleeves of his long-waisted coat were so tight that one wondered how his great yellow hands could pass through them. He was like an old grasshopper, left over from last year to shuffle when it could not leap. He reached a bench, stared at it a long moment, tapped it with his stick as if to require something of it. Then he turned himself carefully round; bringing into the spring sunlight, pale as a primrose, his dun face, hollow-cheeked and dry; the great orbits of his sunk eyes; the long nose fallen at the tip; his white moustache, of thin separate hairs like glass threads. This face expressed resolution and some alarm. A string of muscle jerked in the shadow of the cheekbone. Suddenly he swung forward from the hips, placed both hands upon the knob of his stick, and broke at the knees. His look of alarm became intense, his long flat feet jerked upwards, he collapsed upon the seat as if his body had telescoped into itself, like a picnic beaker. But in a moment it began to rise again; the clothes to fill. The old man straightened his back, raised his chin; until, upright at last, he pulled down his waistcoat, settled his hat, and looked about him. He had now the air of success. His attitude declared, 'Good for you, old man; that was well done.'

A small child, a boy of about three, came running along the path with a wooden truck on a string. He carried a whip with which he whipped the truck; at the same time, he pranced up and down and snorted. He was the horse as well as the driver. He passed the old man on the bench; then turned back and made two circles in front of it.

The old man did not notice the small boy. He was still enjoying himself and he had no time to enjoy anything else. He twitched one side of his moustache, spread his knees, stretched out his long thin arms, and pressed down upon the stick so hard that it slipped a fraction of an inch upon the gravel. This startled him; he frowned at the stick. But at once, ignoring such a trifling accident, he raised his head again and looked defiantly into the air over the small boy's head.

The child, attracted perhaps by the desire for an audience, was making another circle in front of the bench, whipping and prancing. He paused within a foot of the old man's knob-jointed legs in their shining cloth. The old man noticed the boy, looked at him for a moment with surprise, and then gradually began to smile. A slight flush appeared on the hard dry skin of the cheekbone. He stooped forward and said, 'Gee, gee.'

'Gee gee, gee gee,' the child shouted.

'Gee up,' the old man said.

'Gee up, gee up.'

The old man was surprised by his success with the child. He smiled broadly; his moustache rose; his eyes sparkled; he looked round to see if anyone had noticed this triumph. But there was no one within twenty yards.

'Gee up, gee up,' the child shouted, whipping the cart. At each stroke of the whip, he raised his knees higher.

'Gee up, Dobbin,' the old man cried. He laughed, showing rows of china teeth, and swayed his whole body in a circular movement. It was a sitting-down dance of pleasure, a spring ballet. He called in loud confident tones, 'Gee up, gee gee. Gee up, Dobbin.'

'Gee up, gee——' The child stopped close to the old man's knees and looked up at him with piercing inquiry.

The old man smiled down at him and put out a knotty finger to touch the round rosy cheek. But at the last moment he hesitated, as if fearing to take a liberty. 'Gee gee,' he said, 'gee up, gee gee.'

The child suddenly dived for the truck and held it up to show the old man, who, startled, as by an unexpected condescension, jerked his whole body forward in order to examine it. He nodded. 'Nice gee gee.'

'It's a lorry,' the child said in a loud clear voice.

'Yes, yes, nice lorry.'

Suddenly the child planted the lorry on the old man's knees, and scrambled upon the bench beside him. He had fallen in love with his admirer.

The old man was astonished. He still smiled and there was still in his eyes the look of success; but apprehension had appeared in the middle of his forehead. He said in a mild hopeful voice, 'Gee up, gee gee.'

But the boy had abandoned that game. He put one hand on the old man's shoulder and shouted, 'Iss a lorry—a lorry.' Then, fixing his bright keen eyes on the old man's face, he began to jump up and down on the bench. Each jump became more energetic and more affectionate, that is to say, closer to the old man's legs and body. At the same time, he burst out laughing and shouted something incomprehensible. The old man's smile was now full of alarm and deprecation—it was the grimace with which the humble, everywhere, seek mercy from the strong.

The boy, uttering another loud and incomprehensible speech, tripped against the old man's leg and lurched into his lap on top of the lorry. One foot was planted on his thigh, one hand grabbed him by the lapel. He gave another jump, using the lapel as a lever, and roared with laughter.

The old man's smile had gone. His mouth fell open. He looked round in terror and despair; but no one was within call. His body began to sink; his waistcoat to sag.

Suddenly a small thickset girl came running across the grass, picked up the truck from the old man's knee, put her arms round the boy's stomach, and lifted him to the ground. She said nothing but her round, rather pale face expressed the most formidable calmness.

The boy uttered a yell and grabbed the old man by the trousers. The girl set in her heels and tugged. Neither looked at the old man, who, for his part, was too far gone even to move. His only sign of life was a feeble wave, as if to brush the boy's hand from his trouser leg. But he did not actually touch the child's hand. He was too diffident, too polite. His hand performed the gesture of removal and at the same moment, disowned it.

The girl gave another heave and tore the boy away. She bent herself back at an angle of at least forty degrees, to keep his kicking heels from her shins, and staggered across the path on to the grass. She opened her fingers, dropped the truck, and then with a powerful jerk forward planted the child on the ground as a navvy might ram a pavement, with ferocity rather than indignation.

The child's legs crumpled like macaroni. He rolled over backwards. His screech was ear-piercing, heart-broken. It called on heaven for justice and revenge. The little girl picked up the truck, put it beside his left ear and trotted away to some unseen nurse among the trees. The boy suddenly rolled over and scrambled to his feet. His action was full of vindictive purpose. He rushed at the truck and kicked it over on its back. Then he uttered another howl, longer, louder, but more musical. It was a repeat howl, an encore, with little passion but much recollected artistry.

The old man paid no attention either to his friend or his rescuer. Probably he could not have told, off-hand, by whom or what he had been saved. He lay broken in, ravaged like a pie after a birthday party. His very clothes, hat, trousers, waistcoat, seemed in ruins; a little broken heap, from which projected the long insect legs and flattened feet; his mouth hung open; his filmed eyes, pale as fish bones, gazed forward without expression. It appeared that the grasshopper was dead. Only the finger-muscles twitched from time to time, fumbling on the knob of the stick.

The small boy was now forty yards away. He was aiming another kick at the truck, which had already lost a wheel. He had stopped howling. He was laughing so heartily at the new game that when at last he kicked, he missed the truck altogether and staggered sideways with shouts of laughter. He was drunk with laughter.

The old man's hands had closed upon the stick. His chin gradually rose from his chest. His neck tilted back. His eyelids blinked, his brows frowned, and he shifted his feet on the gravel.

Suddenly, as if to take an enemy by surprise, he made a plunge forward, swinging his head downwards almost to the knob of the stick. His long thin buttocks rose three inches from the seat and hung suspended. The battle was joined. The issue was in the balance. The hands pressed, the stick swayed, the old man's face was creased with alarm, appeal, desperate resolve. Then slowly he swayed forward, head, stick, thighs. He was on his feet. Gradually his knees straightened.

At last he stood upright. He raised his chin, a trembling hand went up to set the hat straight. For a moment he stood. Then all at once he lifted his stick about two inches and struck its iron ferrule hard upon the gravel. He had done it again.

ROMANCE

THE sun came out, a spring sun, primrose colour; not yet too warm in the springtime park, not yet burnt out. The nurse put down a rug and on the rug a baby of about a year old. Then she returned to a seat, well sheltered by some laurel bushes from the spring breeze, still cool, and opened a book. The baby lay on its back for some minutes, gazing with calm wonder at a sky like a forget-me-not with small thin clouds like puffs of frosty breath. No doubt it had forgotten the sky in the last few minutes and was interested to rediscover it. But at last it grew bored, and tried to roll over. To do this, it held its arms and legs as rigid as those of a Dutch doll and jerked them violently in the air. These exertions produced only a slight rocking movement in its perfectly round body, of which the proportion to its limbs was about that of a tortoise. But the baby continued its struggles until, by accident, it kicked both legs and arms in the same direction, and toppled slowly over on to its face. It then began to crawl off the rug.

The nurse, without taking her eyes off the book, said 'Naughty.'

The baby, with one hand in the air, paused. Its attitude was that of Colleoni's majestic charger in Venice or George III's famous 'copper horse' at Windsor, and it seemed to enjoy cutting a dash. When it had crawled another two quick steps, it ended in the same grand pose. The nurse made ready to turn a page and again cried 'Naughty' with keenest indignation. She turned the page. Her eyes and sharp little nose were directed at the next sentence on the top of the new page even before she had turned it. 'Naughty, come back at once.' The baby, still in mid-prance, even curving one wrist in an affected manner which horse-sculptors could only envy, looked back over its shoulder at the nurse. Its face, rosy and polished, had

no more expression than an apple. Then it crawled straight off
the rug.

The nurse looked up from her book and gave a shrill cry of anger.
Two spots of red appeared in her white cheeks. But she still held the
book open before her at reading level; she was hoping, with all her
might, that something would save her from breaking off in the
middle of this wonderful chapter.

Her hope was lucky. A small girl of about five, in blue linen
trousers with cross-over braces behind and a bib in front, had just
come to inspect the laurel bushes. She squatted down and peered
into them, probably in search of a hidy-hole. Her expression was,
however, disinterested, even bored. She seemed to be performing a
duty rather than a pleasure. Now, hearing the cry of 'naughty,' she
started up, looked round the corner of the bush and saw the baby.
At once she started forward and, repeating 'Naughty! naughty!
naughty!' all the way in exactly the nurse's tone but with a rising
pitch, caught the baby by the thighs and dragged it to the rug. She
then retreated backwards, at first quickly, as from the too-near
presence of a strange nurse, but then more and more slowly. Her
eyes, fixed on the baby, expressed both desire and regret. The same
expression can be seen on the faces of polite children who, at a
birthday party, too quickly refuse a second slice of cake.

The nurse's eyes had already darted back to her book. The baby,
as soon as it felt solid ground beneath it, crawled off again, this time
towards the path. The little girl gave a cry and rushed to the rescue.
But now another little girl, dark-headed, in a short red frock, who
was running along the path, also noticed the baby's escape. She
turned to head it off from the gravel. 'Dirty! dirty!'

She reached it first, caught it and tried to lift it bodily into the air.
She was a strong child and by a great effort she succeeded in raising
its forepart from the ground so that it hung suspended. Its face, in
this position, was still perfectly calm. 'Dirty, dirty,' the dark little
girl scolded.

The blue girl now reached the spot and caught the baby round
the legs. 'Naughty, naughty.' She dragged it towards the rug.

But the other, perhaps not having noticed the rug, half hidden by
the shrubs, dragged it in a different direction so that its woollen
coat rose over its ears. 'Dirty, dirty,' she cried.

'*Naught-y*,' cried the other, tugging at the legs. She did not look at the dark girl, who, for her part, ignored this interloper. Each pulled with all her might. The baby's clothes came apart in the middle, showing several inches of its round white body. But it made no sound. Its arms, sticking straight out like pegs, were obviously waiting to crawl again as soon as this interruption came to an end.

The dark little girl gave a sudden angry scream, whereupon blue trousers shouted, 'It's mine, it's mine—I had it first.' Her voice shook with tears.

In the distance, the nurse turned a page. Her nose jumped up six inches ready for the next sentence; but her eyes moved a little further, and saw the struggle. She cried in a tone of impatient despair, 'Naughty boy.'

'Let it alone,' shouted the dark girl. 'Leave go—go away.'

'Mummy, Mummy,' cried the other in tears.

A plump young woman, strolling along the path in the sun, with a face of such tranquil, unreflecting enjoyment that she seemed like one of those drunks who, at the end of the party, do not even need to smile from their trance, stopped, gazed, gradually took in the scene and at last, with a look of such conscious wisdom that it seemed to say to itself 'Ain't I a clever responsible person?', rescued the baby, carried it to the rug, and carefully, maternally laid it flat on its back.

The baby at once made a desperate attempt to turn over. Since it had forgotten the trick and jerked its arms and legs in different directions, it succeeded as before only in rocking itself slightly from side to side. But it continued its efforts with Chinese resolution. The nurse turned a page. The two little girls, who had followed the plump young woman to the rug, looked longingly at the baby; the plump young woman shooed them away with the gestures of one driving sheep. They retreated slowly and reluctantly, on divergent routes, glancing backwards. The dark one frowned and bridled; blue trousers sobbed. The plump young woman gazed round as if for the owner of the baby, but since the nurse, her face now completely hidden by the book as she sat forward in her chair, like a stall-holder at the crisis of the fifth act, gave no sign of attention, she moved away. A slight bend of her short neck sideways, a certain motion of the hips, at once decorous and undulating, seemed to say, 'After all, virtue *is* its own reward.'

Blue trousers flew at the baby, gave it two sharp smacks in the face and ran as if for her life. The baby uttered yells of astonishing loudness, each yell different from the last and expressive of a new species of disgust.

The nurse looked over the top of her book. Her mouth opened to call reproof. But she closed it again without speech. She saw that this time there was no help for her. She jumped up from her seat. The book was still open in her right hand—instinctively she was keeping the place. But suddenly, with a movement of fury, she banged it shut and threw it hard upon the ground. She wanted to hurt that book.

EVANGELIST

JOHN PRATT, fifty-five, on holiday at the sea, gets up one sunny morning, looks from the window, says, 'It won't last,' and picks from his seven suits the only dark one. He dresses himself with care, and eats for breakfast one piece of dry toast.

'A touch of liver,' he says to himself, takes his umbrella and a bowler, and goes for his morning walk along the Parade.

'Why the bowler?' he asks himself. 'I'm not going back to town.' And suddenly it strikes him that he is bored. 'Impossible,' he says; 'I've only been here a week and my regular time is always a fortnight.'

He looks about him to discover some usual source of pleasure in this charming old place; and immediately he is seized, possessed, overwhelmed with boredom, with the most malignant and hopeless of all boredoms, holiday boredom. It rises from his stomach, it falls from the lukewarm air. Everything in sight is instantly perceived as squalid, mercenary, debased by mean use and vulgar motives. The Regency façades whose delicate taste he has so much admired, which bring him year after year to a place neither smart nor quiet, seem to leer at him with the sly, false primness of old kept women on the look out for some city lecher, willing to set off cracked plaster against lewd dexterity.

He looks at the sea for freshness. But it appears thick, greasy: he murmurs with horror, 'The cesspool of the whole earth.' He sees the drains discharging from a million towns, the rubbish unbucketed from ten thousand years of ships, wrecks full of corpses; the splash of glitter beyond the pier is like the explosion of some hidden corruption. The ozone comes to his nose like a stench.

He sees from the distance a friend, the Colonel in his light-grey suit, stepping briskly. He is whirling his stick—it is plain that he is in his usual high spirits.

Pratt crosses the road to avoid him. A taxi hoots in an angry and distracted manner, but he does not hurry, he would rather be killed than betray the dignity of his despair. The taxi's brakes squawk like Donald Duck—it comes to a stop at his elbow—a furious young man with upstanding black hair and red-rimmed eyes thrusts out his neck and bawls insults. Bystanders laugh and stare. Pratt does not turn his head or quicken his walk. He accepts these humiliations as appropriate to such a morning in such a world.

The shopping housewives with their predatory eyes and anxious wrinkled foreheads fill him with a lofty and scornful pity, as for insects generated by a conspiracy of gases and instinct to toil in blind necessity for the production of more insects.

Yes, he thinks, humanity is like the maggots on a perishing carcass. Its history is the history of maggots; the fly, the buzz, the coupling of flies, the dropping of their poison on every clean thing, the hunt for some ordure, some corpse, the laying of eggs, and another generation of maggots. Foulness upon foulness. Tides of disgust and scorn rise in his soul; he stalks more grandly; he has become a giant for whom all history is meaner than the dust on his boot soles.

Suddenly he is accosted by a red-faced man, an hotel acquaintance, who starts out of a shop and seizes him by the hand—impossible to avoid this person. The red-faced man is in a fluster. Has Mr Pratt seen the news? Is there going to be a war, is this it? Should he sell out his investments and pay his debts; should he fetch back his family from abroad?

Pratt draws himself up and out of mere wrath at this intrusion, utters in severe tones such banalities as amaze his own ears. If war comes, he says, it will come, and if not, then not. There are good arguments on both sides of the question. If we believe our freedom is worth defending, then we should be ready to defend it at all costs. For faith is not faith, not what we truly believe, unless we are prepared to die for it. And in a conflict of faith those alone who are prepared to die for what they believe deserve to win. As for bombs, one can die but once. One will die anyhow and possibly much worse than by a bomb.

And all these panic-mongers, are they not more than foolish? Panic is not only useless, it is a treachery—a defeat—an invitation to the enemy within as well as without.

The red-faced man is taken aback by this rigmarole of eloquence. He listens with surprised attention in his green eyes—then with respect. Pratt's unmoved solemnity, his severe tone born of scornful indifference, impress him. He ejaculates murmurs of approval. He says that this is just what he himself has always thought. And this is probably true. He could scarcely have escaped such reflections.

At last he is greatly moved. He turns even redder, his gooseberry eyes shine. He grasps Pratt's hand with fervour and a glance that means, 'This is an important, a solemn occasion. You are a bigger man than I took you for. Men of sense and courage, like ourselves, should be better acquainted.' He departs exalted.

Pratt walks on alone, his step is still majestic but full of spring. He is exhilarated; he looks at the sea and it appears to him noble in its vastness, transcendent in its unconcern, venerable in its intimation of glorious deeds. The houses are like veteran soldiers in line, meeting with stoic pride the injuries of time. The housewives, striving, saving for their families, wear the brows of angels; the battered angels roughly carved on some primitive church. He salutes with heroic elation a world made for heroes. He perceives with joy that it is going to be a fine day, that he is hungry. He whirls his umbrella.

BABES IN THE WOOD

IT was market day. The narrow pavements were full of window gazers, shoppers, push-cars containing bored, patient children, prams, walled in by cars, vans, bicycles. At short intervals all the way along, the deep river could be seen to break back upon itself in a foam of bobbing hats and caps, eddying in wide slow whirlpools, which were quite as effective in damming up its stream.

Anyone who could force his way to a block would find there two push-cars abreast; or at the centre of each whirlpool, a pram with a baby. In the deepest and most turbulent by Woolworth's door, a very small brown baby, with a bald head fringed by a light ginger fluff, sat alone in a vast flat-bottomed pram. No one paid any more attention to it than to the lamp-posts or other natural obstacles of the countryside, and it was as totally indifferent to the tall surrounding crowd as if they had been rocks or trees, a wood of human trunks, cutting it off from all others of its kind and hiding it from the sky.

In one hand it grasped its mother's bag, upside-down, in the other a half-chewed biscuit. It was trying with all its strength to put the biscuit into the bag, by forcing it through the bottom.

A small thin woman pushed out from the shop, seized the pram and thrust it forward, twisted it to the right to avoid another pram, projected it under a bus's nose to cross a side street, tilted it again to climb the opposite pavement, and once more using it like a battering ram, charged the opposing crowd. She had to put forth all her contrivance, as well as her whole muscular energy, to make any progress at all. She was barely five feet high, a mere atomy, worn to bones and skin. It was impossible to tell her age; she might have been fifty, or twenty-five. Her yellow face was deeply lined, but her hair which flew in wisps about her face was a greenish yellow. Her expression, her gestures, were those of a refugee among machine-guns. Her eyes had the wild stare seen only in animals which turn at bay, and nervously exhausted women. One would have said, when some other pram blocked her path or some passer, with eyes fixed on the shop fronts, ran into her, that she would scream or fall down in a fit.

Each turn of the pram tossed the baby like a ball on a racket. The jerk to the right sent its skull against the folded stays of the hood; the jerk up in front, to surmount the kerb, sent it rolling back against the rim of the body; a sudden jolt as the pram caught in some submerged obstacle caused it to strike its button nose against the bag in its own hand. But in the actual moment of contact, which visibly brought water to its eyes, it made another determined effort to push the biscuit through the bag.

The jolt was caused by the wheel of another pram, coming from the opposite direction. It contained a very fat baby of two or so, in a woollen cap. This baby was asleep, its face shone with heat. Its mother, also fat, was pushing with one hand and looking at a shop window.

The little woman, enraged by this opposing force, glared and screamed in a voice which seemed also tearful, 'Can't you look where you're going?' But in the same moment, as the fat woman turned, she recognised a friend, and shrieked in an even louder voice, 'Maggie.'

Maggie, too, though her hair was neatly brushed underneath a man's cap, had a mad look, but not of a desperate madness. Rather she seemed lost and terrified, sure of disaster and misery but not able to imagine what new form it might take. And though she had such powerful arms, such swelling cheeks, yet all her flesh was displaced as if some impatient fate had battered on it at random. The cheeks were dented under the eyes as by heavy fists. The forehead over the thick drooping nose had a great irregular hole among its perplexed wrinkles like the mark of a hammer. The little chin was thrust to one side under the crooked lip and cleft as by a kick. And the flesh displaced by these careless blows hung loose on the neck, the lobes of the ears, the jowl, and under the chin. The little pale green eyes lay at the bottom of brown cavities like old rain-water in the shell-pits of some battlefield.

The friends greeted each other with outcries, drew up the two prams side by side, and over the crash and boom of the traffic, the grinding of feet, within which the voices all round sounded only like the twittering of wrens in a hedge, one heard their screams of protest and complaint.

'Worse and worse,' from the little one.

'Can't get nothing done.'

'It's more than a woman can stand.'

'All these cards and rations and then this.'

The baby was growing annoyed with the bag. It banged it on its legs and waved the biscuit up and down with its other hand. Then, no doubt hoping that these violent actions had changed the situation, and changing its own tactics, it slowly, cautiously, even stealthily, laid the biscuit against the leather.

An errand boy rode up on his box-bicycle. The sweat was running down his nose. His lips were formed as if to whistle but no sound came. He had no wind left. He dismounted, propped the bicycle against the kerb and smoothed his hair with both hands. Already a faint whistle was coming from his lips, which strengthened and took form as 'Run, Rabbit, Run.' He took a basket full of soda-water bottles from the box and turned. The basket pulled him so crooked that he seemed to be deformed. His face expressed a calm self-confidence, except the lips, which, pushed forward for a difficult passage, had a certain artistic defiance as if they challenged public criticism. As this boy, by a sudden complicated movement which seemed to involve a dislocation of the right shoulder as well as the spine, swung the basket through the narrow space between the outside pram and the row of bicycles, he put out his left hand, took the bag from the baby, dropped it in the pram, caught it again right side up, and before the baby had time to do more than part its lips for a cry, planted it between its legs and twisted the catch so that it fell open. With no change of expression, and still whistling the difficult passage, he then made another desperate swing which carried him past the obstruction.

The baby's lips were already closed again. It did not even look at the boy or enquire what providence had intervened in its career. It dived into the bag the hand holding the biscuit. Its face was as grave as a Prime Minister at a cabinet meeting.

The two friends had noticed nothing. They were lost in their community of despair.

'My old man in the 'ospital.'

'Keep you 'anging about and then they don't *tell* you nothing.'

The baby, having dived the biscuit into the bag some fifteen times, lost it or battered it to pieces. It then continued the diving action once or twice without the biscuit, but stopped with its hand deep in the bag. It was asking itself, 'What am I doing this for—what's the sense of my proceedings?'

The fat woman was in the middle of her lamentation. Her voice was heard bawling her special grief. The crowds grew worse and worse. How was she expected to get her shopping done and do her washing and be on time with the kids' dinner. 'Why,' she shouted, 'you can't get *in* the shops.'

The baby drew out its hand grasping a crumpled piece of paper and tossed it away. At once, it knew what it was doing. It dived again and flung out a comb, another piece of paper screwed up, several pennies. Its actions were full of energy and purpose; the air was filled with money, letters, keys and safety pins.

Suddenly the little woman turned and saw what was happening to her bag. Her face twisted itself into a look of the utmost exasperation, a fury of despair. It seemed to say, 'This is the last straw.'

The fat woman gave a hoarse cry of sympathetic dismay.

The baby looked up at the two women. Its expression did not change, but as its hand flung another penny into the air, almost against its own nose, it blinked. The women cried out together.

'Ducky.'

'Little pet.'

Both were smiling in the same expression of delight; self-forgetful, innocent, foolish, fond.

The two prams, locked wheel to wheel, block the whole width of the pavement; a man with a sample case, forced to take his chance among the traffic, mutters as he skips past, just in time to dodge a van. And fifteen yards away on either side in the steaming mass rise despairing cries. Mothers and wives already late with their shopping, already agonised by the thought of hungry families and broken time-tables, thrust bags and prams against prams and backs. Their faces set in fierce resolution, their eyes glaring at anyone who dares even a murmur of protest, are those of soldiers in the front line who know that they fight for a good, a righteous cause; that their hearts are pure.

RED LETTER DAY

The old man, the well-off uncle, arrived early to tea—it was the first of the month, his regular day. But just before his coming the young couple had themselves been invited to a party for that same afternoon—a 'good' party. They stood now in the hall wondering how it would be possible, even at this late hour, to escape from their guest.

'After all, any afternoon does for him,' said the wife, laying her hand on the drawing-room door.

'But, darling, do remember—this is quite a red letter day for the old boy, he gets out so seldom.'

'Exactly; that's what I say, it's all the same to him when he comes.'

'It would be idiotic to offend him.'

'It would be idiotic to refuse the Goodwins—it's just luck our being asked at all, and if we refuse they'll never think of us again. They have such hundreds of friends already.'

'But it's four o'clock *now*. What excuse can we give? And you know how touchy and suspicious these old men are. They get so wrapped up in themselves. He'll see in half a second that you're putting him off and never forgive it. I shouldn't blame him. I shouldn't exactly enjoy it myself.'

They argued savagely, nose to nose, in furious whispers which sounded like the hissing of snakes roused from a summer nap in some warm garden heap.

In the drawing-room, sunk in the deepest armchair, the old man waited, gazing absently through the open glass door at a freshly watered lawn. His ears were good except in a crowd—he heard the whispering but gave it no attention. It was none of his business, and he was too old and tired to waste time on other people's business.

So he continued to look at the garden. And it seemed to him now that the smell of the wet grass was coming to him—and perhaps a whiff of sweet-briar from the hedge. His wide, thin nostrils twitched. Yes, no doubt of it. And a faint but distinct current of pleasure vibrated in his old dry nerves. How nice that was. He'd forgotten how nice—something he missed in that flat of his. How easy it was to lose touch with simple ordinary enjoyments, and how precious they were.

He had hesitated about his visit today—his nurse had been all against it, she had kept on reminding him of his bad nights, and that last attack which had so nearly finished him—she was certainly an excellent woman, most devoted and reliable. But he had insisted that he had family duties. He was expected. He must go. How glad he was now that he had taken the trouble and the risk.

Suddenly his grand-niece, aged six, dashed into the room from the garden. She was carrying an immense doll of black stuff with a round face, goggle-eyes made of pearl shirt buttons and enormous teeth. At the sight of the visitor, she stopped abruptly, stared and blushed. She was startled by his thin yellow cheeks and deep wrinkles.

The old man moved only his large pale eyes towards the child. He could not afford to waste energy.

At last, aware of the child's silence and supposing her embarrassed, he murmured, 'Is that your best dolly?' But the question expected no answer, the glance had that appreciation seen only in the very young and the very old whose pleasure is unmixed with reflection, without any overtone of idea. The old man did not seek even to placate the child, he enjoyed her as he had enjoyed the garden, that whiff of grass and briar brought to him by an accident of time and place.

The child ignored a remark which, as she perceived at once, was merely polite. She put the doll behind her back, and walked slowly up to the old man, staring at him with an intent piercing curiosity. Then she said, 'Are you *very* old?'

He looked at her with the permanently raised eyebrows of his age, and echoed placidly: 'Very old.'

'Very, very old?'

'Very, very old.'

'You're going to die soon.'

'Yes, I suppose so.' His eyes, bright with pleasure in spite of the eyebrows fixed in their record of old griefs, gazed at her with absent-minded wonder. He was thinking 'Yes, how charming they are, children—how nice she is.'

'You only have two years more.'

'Two years?'

'That's what it says in the almanack.'

'Two years.' He repeated the phrase as a child turns over words without troubling to consider them. 'The almanack.'

'Yes, Mummy's almanack.'

'Your mother's almanack,' he murmured. It did not interest him to discover in this way that his niece had been looking into *Whitaker* to calculate his expectation of life. He felt nothing about it at all. He had no time for such boring considerations. He said dreamily, as if the words were prompted by some part of his brain which, being set in motion, continued in the same direction quite apart from his thoughts, 'And what is dolly's name?'

The whispering outside had come to an end. The young couple entered the room from the side door behind his chair. They both had that air of hardly restrained impatience which belongs to young healthy creatures everywhere: colts, kittens; the girl, buxom and a little too rosy, the man lean, with a soft thick mouth. Their bodies seemed to bring with them that atmosphere of a snug private room, over-curtained and rather stuffy, which belongs to happily married couples in the youth of their pleasure.

And like others who enjoy much happiness, they hated the least interruption of it. They hated and resented this quarrel. As they came towards the old man, their faces expressed the highest degree of exasperation.

When he turned his eyes towards them and made a gesture as if to get up, both smiled the same smile, one that did not even affect pleasure but only politeness.

'Don't, don't get up,' the woman cried, and kissed his forehead, gently pushing him back into the chair. 'Uncle dear, it's such a nuisance——' and she began an elaborate story, plainly a construction of lies, about a telephone call from a friend who was suddenly taken ill. But if he would not mind amusing himself for half an hour —an hour at the very most—they would hurry back. Or perhaps he would rather come another day when they would be free to enjoy his visit.

The old man seemed to reflect, and said, 'Thank you.' Then, after another pause, as if for deeper reflection, he added, 'I'm afraid I'm rather early, aren't I?'

The couple exchanged furious glances. What enraged them was that he did not trouble even to examine their hint. He was too vague, too gaga. The woman tried again—'The only thing that worries us, Uncle, is that we might be kept—it's always so uncertain, when people are ill.'

'Don't trouble about me, my dear—I'll be quite all right.'

They looked enquiry at each other. The wife pushed out her cupid's mouth, too small for her round cheeks, and half closed her eyes as if to say, 'You see—I told you he was going to spoil everything.' The husband frowned from her to the uncle, unable to decide which was the chief cause of his enormous disgust.

'Two years,' the little girl exclaimed loudly. She had never taken her eyes off the visitor. 'In two years you'll be dead.' She gave a little skip. 'In two years.'

The couple were horrified. They looked blank, senseless, shocked —as if someone had let off a bomb and blown out all the windows. The husband, very red, said in a voice of foolish surprise: 'Really— that's hardly—ah . . .'

The young woman took the child by the arm and said, 'That's enough, Susan. Come, it's time for you to go upstairs.' At the same moment she gave the uncle a glance full of guilty anger, which meant, 'Yes, I'm wicked, but it's all your fault.'

Susan jerked away from her mother and said angrily, 'No, I don't want to——' The old man slowly unfolded his long thin arm towards her as if in sympathy. He murmured, 'I haven't seen the dolly, have I?'

The little girl gazed at him. She was still fascinated by the idea of his age. She said, 'Two years, and then you'll be dead.'

'Susan, be quiet.'

The little girl's eyelids flickered. She was feeling what death meant. Suddenly she went to her mother and put her arms round her skirts, as if for protection. The old man's eyebrows rose a little more; a colour, almost youthful, came into his cheeks, and he smiled. He was charmed by this picture, so spontaneous, so unexpected. He thought, 'How pretty that is. How nice they are.'

BUYING A HORSE

THE Horse Marines, as they were called in Africa, otherwise the Mounted Infantry, took a knock charging the Germans in high grass. All their officers were killed or wounded and their ponies were left in a bush station where two or three died every week—most of the grooms had run away or gone for soldiers. In the confusion of war, just started, no one remembered the ponies or could have known where they were.

Young Corner, Staff officer and galloper to the Commandant, was much surprised one morning to come upon the remnant tethered to their pegs. He saw at once that half should be shot and the rest, those fit to travel, sent to the rear; and sorted them out, pointing with his short riding-stick, 'That one is finished—that one can go.'

He had just condemned a black pony, a tottering skeleton covered with dirt, when the creature put out his nose and nibbled his shirt. His orderly tapped the pony on the nose and said, 'Now then, you son of a female.'

But Corner was touched. He had a weakness for good-natured horses of which he was quite aware. He told himself often that the creatures were merely greedy and extremely stupid animals whose patience and courage had no more merit than the colour and scent of a plant, but without the least effect on his secret passion.

'This one no good,' said the orderly. 'He die.' He walked round the pony and disdainfully pointed out its various defects. Corner fixed his eyeglass as if for an impartial estimate and said severely, 'Yes—yes—I see. But it has good blood too—look at that head, like a deer.'

The orderly, quite understanding his master's weakness, looked at him demurely and said, 'Yes, Caftin—a lovely horse—an Azben.'

An Azben is a type of small Arab, often black. It is much prized in
Africa.

'Do you know who it belongs to?'

'Major Long-hump—he got bullet for belly.'

Corner knew Major Long-hump—actually Major McA., late of
a Dragoon Regiment, a singularly thin and tall Scotsman with a
sudden stoop high in his back. McA., in leading the rather mad
charge of the Horse Marines on infantry hidden in grass, had received
three bullets through the body, and was due to be invalided home.

'I'll have to see the Major about it,' said Corner. 'Give it a feed
now—though I doubt if it will eat. It's obviously done for.'

'Oh, sir, he soon strong again. Azben too brave to die. I think we
buy him, sir.'

Corner frowned as at an absurd suggestion. But he went to the
Major that afternoon at the evacuation hospital and asked if he would
sell the pony, 'as a gamble.' The Major answered promptly that
nothing would induce him to part with his beloved Satan, 'the finest
polo pony in Nigeria' and a 'true-bred Barrb.'

McA. was just out of bed, in pyjamas, creeping about the hospital
on two sticks, the picture of a veteran broken in his country's wars.
Now, as soon as Corner's back was turned, he dressed, sent for an
ambulance and, sweeping aside the feeble objections of the hospital
orderlies, had himself conveyed to the bush station. But the whisper
of a horse deal is enough for an African camp: within ten minutes
Corner had news of the Major's disappearance from three different
sources, and followed at speed.

He found McA. on his legs beside the pony, orating to half a
dozen bush pagans and three worried-looking women, with full
water-pots on their heads, about mankind's responsibility for dumb
animals. He had forgotten his sticks and pains—he was now the old
grognard who puts his horse's comfort before his own.

McA. was a Highlander, famous throughout the country for his
reckless dash, and above all for a certain magnificence of speech and
gesture. Life for him was a series of dramatic events which required
of every feeling man a worthy response. Young Corner, like most
of the young officers, admired him as a hero, and what's more a hero
who knew how to act and speak like a hero; and, therefore, was
inclined to make fun of him.

'Good afternoon, sir,' he saluted with a slightly exaggerated smartness. 'What do you think of the patient?'

McA. was a hero but he was also a dyed-in-the-wool horse-coper. What horseman is not? He turned slowly about to examine Satan, raised his formidable nose and drew down his immense grey eyebrows. His expression was that of a Lord Chancellor preparing to sum up the evidence in a State trial. After a pause of at least a minute (the women staring with guilty terror as if expecting instant execution) he pronounced slowly, 'Give 'm a warm mash and r-rub down and he'd carry the Lord Mayor.'

'But, sir, he can hardly stand up. Look at his knees. They are trembling all the time.' And the faithful orderly cried loudly and passionately that the pony was dying. 'Only look at him—Allah, food for the birds.'

McA. fixed Corner with his small blue eye and stretched out a long thin arm. 'Young man,' he said, in the tone of a prophet denouncing the youth of the world, 'if you were better acquented with me and this horse you would not utter such freevolity. It is a characterristic of Satan to stand so, as if, indeed, he might fall down. It is well known that a high-bred Azben a wee bit out of condeetion has that very trembling at the knees. It is due to his high breeding—his nairvous constitution.'

'Well, sir, according to the best advice,' Corner referred thus to his orderly, 'he won't last another twenty-four hours. But if you're willing to let him go I'll take a chance.'

'To let him go.' McA. sunk down his chin upon his chest and looked out of the top of his eyes, actually through his eyebrows. The coper was in strong conflict with the hero. The glance was heroic, but the coper seemed to hesitate in the question—'Young man, are you making me a serious proposition?'

'How much would you ask?'

'Ye mean, if there was any question of a deal? Upon such an hypothesis, Corner, the Emir of Sokotoo would give—yes—fifty pounds for a Barrb like Satan—yes, only for his sairvice at stud. Look at that shoulder.' McA. gave the pony a slap on the shoulder. It was not a hard slap but the poor creature reeled. For a moment all thought it would fall. The orderly uttered an exclamation, a woman cried out, 'Take care.'

McA.'s arm stiffened against the shoulder in a powerful effort to hold the pony up. At the same time he looked the other way, towards some distant horizon of the spirit. His expression was dreamy, poetic—it reminded one of that celebrated portrait of Edmund Kean resting his elbow on a skull.

'But, as I say, that's purely hypothetical.' He meditated aloud. 'To sell Satan, I couldn't forgeeve myself—though indeed the puir beastie could do with a home—ye might say I owe it to me old friend.'

He cautiously relaxed the arm—it appeared that Satan had recovered his balance. McA. carelessly swept away the hand and turned to Corner with a gesture of heroic pathos, arms bent, palms outward, forehead wrinkled, his eyes bright with grief. For the moment the hero had mastered the coper. 'The biggest hearrted horrse I ever rode—and I may never see 'm again.' His voice shook —he was deeply moved by this eloquence.

And so was Corner. He answered therefore in his briskest tone, 'I tell you what, sir, I'll give you ten shillings a leg—tomorrow. If the pony lives so long.'

McA.'s pose had not changed, but the raised hands, the wide eyes, by some subtle transition now expressed horror and amazement. 'Ten shillings a laig,' he interrupted, 'I never haird of buying horses by the laig.'

'In Ireland,' said Corner, inventing freely, 'it's quite the usual thing.'

'Ten shillings a laig,' McA. exclaimed loudly. The coper was now ascendant. 'Two pounds.' It is impossible to describe the scorn and injury expressed in the two pounds.

'Excuse me, sir, what I meant was thirty shillings.'

McA. stared for a moment in silence, then uttered in the deepest tone of his considerable range, 'Thairty shillings. Did you say thairty?'

Corner, who had remembered in time the orderly's expert criticism, pointed with his stick at the pony's off foreleg. Three diagonal burn-scars below the knee showed that the leg had been fired, at some time, to cure a sprain.

'Ah, that off-fore,' McA. recollected himself, 'a pairfectly sound laig—I rode that pony when we won the polo cup from the

Gunners and he galloped everything else off the ground.'

'Well, sir, it may move free, but it's a swinger. There's no nerve in it. It might let you down any minute.'

'Thairty shillings,' said McA. Suddenly he threw back his head, clapped his elbows to his side and, raising his eyes towards the sky, uttered a laugh which could only be described as hollow. The hero had once more found his stage. 'Thairty shillings—for Satan. Dahm it, boy, if ye have the nairve to offer such a sum, I'll take ye.' He turned towards the ambulance with head sunk down like one that has received a mortal stroke. He took three long, slow strides and sank down on the stretcher; then beckoned the young man with a long knotty finger. Corner bent down to his lips.

'Cash,' he whispered, hoarsely, brokenly—'today.'

'Certainly, sir.' Corner was surprised by this sudden relapse into the coper and perhaps his feeling showed in his face. He may have allowed himself to smile.

McA. seized his hand. 'My boy,' he sighed, 'I trrust ye with that grrand wee horse. For I know ye have a good hearrt. Take care of him for my sake. Cherish him as he desairves.'

'I'll do my best, sir. Rely upon it.'

'God bless you.' The hero fell back on his pillow with a wave which dismissed the world to oblivion and was borne away as to slow music. His eyes were closed. In his own imagination he was on his way to a soldier's grave.

Corner, standing alone in the deserted camp beside the shaking pony and the discreet orderly, felt that—after all—McA. had had the best of it; he hoped especially that he had not smiled. Yes, he felt small, young and cheap—perhaps, he thought, as he looked at the foundering pony, he had even been cheated.

SPRING SONG

SPRING in the park with an east wind and a sky as blue as winter milk, an obvious duty day for children to be given the first sunshine of the year. A tall girl in spectacles is in charge of a small brother and sister. Her nose is magenta; her mouth and forehead, the stoop of her neck, express a resignation not so much virtuous as necessary. She stops for the third time in five minutes to let her charges catch up. 'Oh, do come on, Mag.'

The little girl in the blue cap is pushing a doll's perambulator which has lost a wheel. She balances and propels it with immense muscular effort and, at the same time, pours out a long story in successive bursts.

'And when he went into the castle, he called out three times, "Tooboody, tooboody, tooboody," but of course he was an akkerpeetie man.'

'What say?' with a patience that grieves for itself.

'He was an akkerpeetie man.'

'That's nothing, Maggie.'

'Yes, it is.' The little girl with an adroit unexpected twist drives the perambulator over the iron edging of the path, on to the worn grass. Tall daffodils, florists' daffodils, wave in the fenced-off beds; but the grass is still wintry. Empty cigarette-cartons lie about the children's feet.

'It's the akkerpeetie,' the little girl pants in a loud voice. 'The akkerpeetie man—he was made of fish-bones.'

'Oh well, go on if you won't talk sense.'

'And the tooboody came skinking along the collidor.'

'Corridor, you mean.'

'No I don't, it wasn't a corridor. It was a collidor, with a round top—and the akkerpeetie man let down his beard to the ground and

55

said, "I'm not afraid of *anybody*." He had a toople too.' And with
the rising note that goes with rising inspiration, she chants, 'He had
a toople too—with bla-ck whiskers—on a sil-ver chain. And it was
shaved all down the back—once every Friday.'

'Oh, a poodle, like your Uncle John's.'

'No, a toople—because it had such a long face.'

'A dog, then.'

'It wasn't a dog—it was a singum—because—because—it came
from Baffrica where all the dogs are scats.'

'Oh well, go on,' with a sigh from the very heart of over-
burdened teenage.

The little girl is silent. There is a pause.

'Go on, what's next?'

'But you never believe nothing I say.' Suddenly she lets go the
perambulator, which at once falls over, spilling a large rag doll on
the brittle grass, and rushes at the brother walking on the other flank
of the party. This brother, aged about five, is wearing a pair of blue
corduroy shorts which obviously give him great pleasure. He carries
both hands in his pockets, and doubling his fists pushes them out
sideways forming two large bumps over his hips. As he walks he
looks down at the effect and throws out his legs in a swaggering
gait. He is studying swagger in all its details, including the proper
way to hold the hands in the pockets. When Margaret suddenly
appears before him, he stops and looks at her with a totally blank
expression, as if he has never seen anything like her before.

'Tom, Tom, did you be-lieve my story?'

'Yes, I did.'

'Oh Tommy, how can you?' says the tall sister. 'You weren't even
listening.'

'Yes, I was, it was a very nice story.'

'What's it about, then?'

'I don't know.'

'There you are!'

'But I liked it,' Tom says. 'I liked it *very* much.' And he looks
down again at his hands, pushes them still further apart and kicks
out his right leg in a kind of embryo goose-step. Margaret has,
meanwhile, circled twice round Tom in a series of skips, performed
sideways so that her face is always directed to him as a centre. She

is examining him with the greatest interest and a growing pleasure. Now, stopping right in front of him, she pushes her face close to his, and says, 'A toople.' Suddenly she bumps into him and shouts, 'A toople—a toople—is a singum.' She utters a loud triumphant laugh.

The boy gazes at her in amazement. She begins to explain, between shouts of laughter. 'Glad said, "What's an akkerpeetie man?" and I said, "He had a toople too." So Glad said, "What's a toople?" and I said, "A toople is a singum,"—I said, "He had a toople too." '

Tom bursts into shouts of laughter. The tall girl, surprised and irritated by this senseless explosion, calls out, 'That's enough.'

'A toople—a toople—he had a toople too.' And the children reel about as if they are drunk; running into each other, bumping each other. They are crowing with delight. 'An akkerpeetie man—and he had a toople too.'

Two soldiers in battle-dress, strolling by, look round at the children and grin. One of them lifts his forage-cap back from his forehead as if to say, 'Yes, it's almost warm—it's really spring.' But the tall girl is furious. She turns crimson and rushes at the children. 'Stop that, you hear. I won't have it.' Her voice quivers; one would have said that she is frightened.

The children dodge her—'An akkerpeetie man—and he had—he had,' they choke with laughter, 'a toople too.'

She springs upon them and tears them apart. 'You want slapping, that's what you do.' The little girl, jerked and shaken, turns also red. She says in a high offended voice, 'But I didn't do nothing.'

The boy has already forgotten the episode. With his hands once more in his pockets, he glances downwards to adjust the bumps at the correct angle. Margaret turns down her lips, as if about to cry, but thinks better of it. She rights the perambulator, stoops for the doll, and in the same movement, with an acrobatic whisk of her whole body, catches the perambulator, before it can fall over again, on her left buttock.

'Oh, do come on, Maggie—you make me tired.' Gladys is indeed tired. Her whole form droops; her voice mourns to Heaven a cruel injustice, a neglected fate. The little girl frowns. Then she puts the doll into the perambulator and says in a low determined voice, 'Lie down, Vera, or I'll give you such a smack on your poly.'

THE LIMIT

IT is a shopping street with lights at intervals. As they change, traffic is turned on and off as by a tap. First there is vacancy from pavement to pavement, then a rush from both sides—solid blocks of traffic charging like tanks and, like tanks at the charge, getting quickly out of line.

At this time in the morning young men and women are at work and the pavements are crowded with parents and grandparents doing their household shopping—serious and anxious people in serious clothes. They meet only briefly, for a few short pregnant words on grave matters, children and prices. The children are all young, below school age—they weave in and out of the slow, dark streams of shoppers. They are meeting friends on their own eye level, chasing each other, carrying out various experiments in locomotion such as hopping on one leg, swinging around a lamp-post, pacing carefully on the joints between kerbstones, or walking backwards.

The dogs, at the lowest level, are also paying attention chiefly to each other: their noses point warily about, enquiring, seeking, recording; they sidle out of doorways as if from ambush; absorbed in a lamp-post they do not even notice feet, they dodge away at the very last moment; they catch sight of a strange nose that has suddenly projected itself from behind a string bag full of potatoes, and stand with rigid tail and every muscle taut in the question, friend or enemy; they dash wildly off down side streets on some private recollection of the most urgent importance.

The relation between the three levels is one of responsible authority mixed with affection: parents hastily snatch up a child's hand to steer it in the right direction; their gestures say plainly that this is no world to wander in. Children shout peremptory advice at dogs or drag them by the collar from dangerous acquaintances.

A small boy of about four in a red and white jersey stands at the kerb holding a black mongrel puppy by a piece of string tied to its collar. The puppy has a singularly large head and feet which seem too heavy for its insignificant body. As it tosses its head and tries to bite its string, two children, girl and boy, rather smaller than its owner, desert a perambulator to play with it. Greatly flattered, it twists its neck sideways and turns up its eyes in an affected manner, then throws its front legs about and cavorts like the lion in the royal arms. The children try to tickle it; it pretends to bite them and they squeal. The boy in the striped jersey looks down with watchful but benevolent condescension.

The puppy, growing more excited and still more anxious to please, attempts a more brilliant romp, falls over its own tail and breaks the string. It wriggles upright again and runs backwards into the road, fortunately empty.

The boy with the jersey dives to catch the loose end of the string. The puppy gambols further off, the lights change and the traffic comes on with a rush—a lorry and a car hoot together. The boy tries to shoo the puppy towards the opposite pavement, but it cavorts sideways. The child makes a sharp turn to head it off and this brings him back in front of the traffic from the nearest light. A sports model, renowned in all the advertisements for its acceleration, has come away with a rush. It strikes the boy somewhere in the back, whirls him around and picks him up on the mudguard.

He makes no sound at all; it is as though a small bundle of coloured clothes has suddenly appeared in the trough of the guard. Brakes and tyres scream, the car stops, shuddering against the kerb, and the bundle slides off and collapses into itself on the roadway exactly like empty garments—limp and soft. In a moment there is a crowd, a policeman holding the ring. A young doctor, or perhaps medical student, kneels down to examine the child—he is quite dead.

The neighbourhood is poor, the car expensive—the crowd is hostile. The women are especially angry. A powerful matron at the back, her bare arms red with work, a man's felt hat balanced on her thick grey hair as if to express her mastery in life, is shouting something about bloody murderers—don't let 'em get away with it.

The motorist is well aware of his danger. At each new shout he looks round nervously; his round, plump face is shining with sweat, his hands fidget with his cap and coat, both of the gayest check. First he takes off his cap as if feeling that this is only proper in the presence of death. Then, when the policeman questions him, he puts it on again as if to show that he has no reason to humble himself before the law.

The policeman, a tall, bottle-shouldered man, also very young, with a singularly blank face, the face of authority exaggerated by a sense of the occasion, writes carefully and slowly in his notebook. He might be filling in a census form.

At last he turns to the crowd and asks for witnesses—but it appears that no one present has seen the accident. And the question seems only to make the women more angry; they are tired of these slow preliminaries, they are shouting for immediate vengeance.

The young man is terrified, his shaking fingers button and unbutton his coat—the confused idea of making it less conspicuous is followed by a fear that he may seem to be preparing for flight. He looks round the circle of muttering and screaming women and tries to make them understand that he could not have avoided the accident, but not a word can be heard, and his fear, his apologetic grimaces, his fumbling hands also enrage the crowd. It makes a surge forward at some new pressure from behind, and actually touches him. He shrinks against the policeman who stretches out his arm in a commanding and protective manner. But even as he does so he too receives a push in the back which nearly unseats his helmet.

Another wave of pressure goes through the mass and now someone at the back of the ring is shouting, 'Make way there.' The ring opens and a small, pale woman, perhaps forty, perhaps fifty years old, is thrust forward by the woman in the hat. Her triumphant gesture says plainly, 'Here you are—this will finish the talk.' The clamour falters for a moment and the young man's rapid urgent speech breaks through, 'But I couldn't help it—I was just——'

The pale little woman, now also in front of the crowd, interrupts him. 'That's right.'

This produces a complete silence. The policeman puts his helmet straight and so recovers his dignity. He turns with his notebook at the ready. 'Yes, ma'am?'

'It wasn't his fault—it wasn't anybody's fault,' the little woman said in a high thin voice.

'You saw it, did you?'

She shakes her head and says, 'No, I was in the shop—I couldn't see anything.'

'Then how do you know it wasn't anybody's fault?'

'He was my boy.'

Everybody stares at her with amazement and confusion—it is as though she has spoken in Chinese. But she is not at all disconcerted. For the first time she looks at the child's body huddled in the dust, and she says even more loudly, 'No, it wasn't nobody's fault.'

The policeman and the motorist gaze at her still as if she is mad. But the women are already going away. They understand why she doesn't want to blame anybody—she can't take any more bitterness.

A GOOD INVESTMENT

OLD Mrs Bill of Hunter's Green had three daughters, Daisy, Letty, and Francie, the youngest. Daisy is a spinster of fifty who travels round the world from one friend's house to another on cargo boats, buses, hitch-hikes, and has, she says, a gorgeous time. She drinks a good deal when she can get it free, eats enormously, and loves a noise. Letty is married to a lawyer called Gordon Todd with a taste for archæology which, it is said, has damaged his practice. They have two children, boy and girl, and Letty complains very much of their wildness, of all her housekeeping troubles and expenses. She spends much of her time in bed, and whenever the children or the husband are too much for her nerves, she telephones to her mother for Francie, who duly rushes over and takes charge of house, husband, and children for as long as Letty can keep her, that is, as long as her mother is ready to spare her. This is usually four days at the most.

Letty complains bitterly of her mother's selfishness when she recalls Francie even after a week. 'What does she want with Francie —she has Mrs Jones, and there's only herself to look after. And after all, Mother is a good deal stronger than I am.'

Mrs Bill says that Letty is a poor spoiled lily and that she preys on Francie. But she does not excuse Francie for deserting her because she blames Francie for having spoiled Letty at the beginning. 'There's no need for Francie to rush away at a word from Letty and it's very bad for Letty. But it's Francie's affair. I never interfere.'

Francie says nothing. She has no time between her various duties of keeping Mrs Jones the housekeeper in a good temper, managing her mother's parties; and she knows too that anything she said would only irritate Letty and bring from her mother the remark, 'But why all the fuss? I never fuss, life is too short.'

Francie Bill is a very small woman, about thirty-five years of age, with a big round forehead, deeply lined, small grey eyes, and a rather prominent round chin. Her mouth is good and it has a very serious expression, except when she laughs. She laughs with her whole face, causing her eyes to disappear and her wrinkles to deepen.

Some time ago Francie had a love affair, but for months no one even realised it except the lover. He was a widower with a daughter of nine. His name was Catto, aged forty-eight, partner in a printing firm, moderately well off, and, as he considered, good at life. That is to say, he knew how to make a success of most things. His marriage had been successful, but he was not at all afraid, like so many prudent citizens who have had lucky marriages, of taking another chance. He realised very well how much luck had gone to his first choice—his wife, actually on the honeymoon, had changed into a different woman with exceedingly strong views on such delicate questions as where to live, how to decorate and manage a house, and which of her husband's friends were worth keeping up with. It was pure luck that he had agreed with her.

But he considered that a man of his age and experience would have more foresight in a second choice. He began to look round almost as soon as his wife was buried. He wanted above all a good housekeeper and a companion for his daughter—he was accustomed to good housekeeping and he distrusted nurses, even the most expensive. And he told himself that even from a financial point of view, the plan was justified. 'With wages at their highest and service at its worst, a competent wife is actually a first-class investment.'

And one day, by good luck, as he said afterwards, he met Daisy Bill at Wimbledon. He had barely settled himself on his stool in the morning queue, when a tall brown girl in a man's shirt, about three yards further down the row, called out loudly, 'Bill, Bill,' and then, 'Daisy.'

Catto as a small boy had known the Bill family very well. For three summers running they had shared the same lodgings at the seaside, and he had got on very well with Daisy especially, nearest to him in age. He had even fallen a good deal in love with Daisy at fifteen, during their last holiday together.

He thought, even before he identified the girl, 'Daisy Bill, could it be the old Daisy, and not married? If Daisy really isn't married, then what about her? The right age, too old for babies. I don't want a rival to poor little Jean, and Daisy was really a very nice girl in a very nice way—good-natured, healthy, and she would probably have money too. As far as I can remember all the Bill girls had something coming from the aunt who married into toothpaste.'

He looked round him, half stood up, and after a moment recognised Daisy. 'She must be that huge red-faced woman with the cigarette-holder shaped like a pipe. She couldn't be anyone else with that nose and those eyes. Yes, there she is waving to her friend.'

He excused himself to the neighbours and edged past them to present himself. Daisy knew him at once. She cried out in a voice to be heard ten yards away, 'Good Lord, Tommy, Tom Cat!' and wrung his fingers in a powerful clasp. 'But how wonderful, you haven't changed a bit. How extraordinary. What a bit of luck. You must join us.' The neighbours in the queue, discreetly interested and pleased, with that almost family feeling which belongs to the Wimbledon queue, made way for his stool, and he joined the Bill party. It consisted now of Daisy, a little, thin, sharp woman who turned out to be a celebrated authoress, and the brown girl in the man's shirt who was a tennis star, a county champion.

Catto had been shocked by the change in Daisy's looks, but her greeting reassured him. He was reminded again of his old love, her easy good nature, her freedom from all those airs which in a girl of sixteen he most detested, touchiness and sudden changes of mood. He had told himself then that, with all her charm, she was as reliable a friend as any of the boys at school.

'Good heavens,' Daisy said, breathing tobacco in his face, 'do you remember those walks along the shore? And how you hated the kids for trailing after us?' She gave a loud laugh and then, dropping his hand, turned to the champion and exclaimed in a serious tone, as one who takes up again the more important affairs of life, 'So you don't think much of Seixas' service?'

And the pair continued their tennis gossip with enthusiasm. Catto might not have existed for either of them.

The authoress, having glared at the champion for some time, dismissed Catto with a single glance, and then, with a twist of her little pursed mouth and a droop of her eyelids, fell into a gloomy meditation which made her all at once ten years older and gave her a sad but distinguished beauty.

Catto had no recollection of his jealousy; Daisy seemed to have a more accurate memory of their affair. But he was already sorry that he had so impulsively presented himself. He observed his old friend with a rueful amusement. 'Yes, steady as a boy and now a regular fellow.' He recoiled from this bluff Daisy. It was obvious why she had never married. And neither of her sisters, even if they were unmarried, had ever attracted him. The languid, fragile, lovely Letty, always being rescued from crabs and wrapped up from the cold; the rat-tailed Francie, at six, with her red button of a nose, hurling herself into the seas and making love to the very fishermen.

But just before the party, having obtained its tickets, dispersed for lunch, Daisy recalled her manners and became even more hearty, asked after his family, expressed a manly sympathy for his loss, and told of her own father's death. But her mother was still at the old place, she would so like to see him again. Why not come out next week-end? There was to be quite an amusing party to dinner.

Catto accepted these attentions in their own spirit and resolved not to go to dinner on any account. Why waste time on the Bills if Daisy was not a suitable prospect? He was put out when Mrs Bill wrote to him. She also expressed her sympathy, a cheerful sympathy: 'These things must happen, one has to take them,' and she pressed him to come to dinner. 'You remember Hunter's? It's just the same, and Daisy tells me so are you. Isn't that nice? It's quite encouraging in these days when everything else seems to get worse and worse, including the people. But poor things, I suppose they can't be blamed for being so flat when the newspapers are so full of bombs. Though I can't imagine why everyone should go off so terribly before the bombs even tick, or whatever they do when they drop.'

And in a postscript she wrote, 'Quite a small party, about eight, don't dress. Mrs Mair is coming, who lost her husband last year in that plane crash, and the Offer girl who used to be so fond of you.'

Catto seemed to hear a voice, a rattling little voice like a cracked dinner bell. He had not heard it for thirty years, in fact since his last holiday with the Bills, before he had gone to the university and they had gone to Switzerland for Letty's health. He had not paid much attention to it then. Mrs Bill had not talked much with boys of his age, nor, indeed, with her own children. She had been preoccupied with her handsome husband and the half-dozen other men, much older than herself, who frequented the house. Even at the seaside her life had been a series of parties, chiefly on yachts. The Bills had taken rooms at Clarksfoot, small and remote, unfashionable and even uncouth, with its mining workers, its Welsh Bethels singing hymns on the beach, because of her friend, Lord S., who kept his big yacht there.

S. asked her to his parties in harbour but did not expect her to go cruising. Mrs Bill was a very bad sailor. Her stories of her own feelings on the sea were among her most amusing. The voice tinkled with laughter in the background of Catto's mind. But now that it came back to him in the cadences of the note, so neatly written in a minute, precise hand, he found, to his surprise, that he liked his memory of Mrs Bill, as of someone always gay, lively, good-tempered, and tolerant. 'Perhaps she did not trouble much with us children, but she never worried us either. She understood how to make things pleasant and comfortable. And then this widow, Mrs Mair? I know Mrs Bill was a bit of a match-maker. But why not— a widow might be the answer for me. She'd know the ropes and wouldn't have fantastic expectations, and yet she would appreciate the solid advantages of a husband and being on good terms with him. And this Offer girl too, she must be somewhere near my age if she was fond of me thirty years ago.'

He accepted Mrs Bill's invitation; and it was true that the house had not changed. But the neighbourhood had. The place had been a farm, and Theodore Bill had even kept it as a farm, without a bailiff, losing money every year. Now the farm-house with its garden stood incongruously in a vast new suburb which was actually named after it, Hunter's Green.

Catto, opening the old wooden gate, a farm gate still, had the sense of one who finds an unexpected treasure and, at the same moment, sees it fall into the dust, as the bodies of the old saints are said to do when you dig them up. He had loved Hunter's Green where he had ridden his first pony, and had his first passionate love, with the slim, lovely girl who had put him over the jumps. With

Daisy, in short. And where was that Daisy now? She was less than an existence, for the actual Daisy was already making faint and unreliable even that sweet memory that had been a vivid existence. And now Hunter's Green, the old Hunter's Green, the solid bricks, the immense elms, the coach-house with its dovecot, mysteriously disintegrated before his very eyes.

Hunter's Green had never pretended to beauty. It had always been a plain house—square, three-storied, with a slate roof a little too small, and a long lean-to conservatory.

In the farm among its trees, with the cows grazing opposite the windows, this plainness had been a charm. It seemed to say, 'I am the unpretending home of plain country people.' True, Theodore and Tottie Bill were anything but plain country people. But for that very reason, they had appreciated Hunter's Green, and carefully preserved its honest want of make-up.

But now the rough five-bar gate, the coarse grass in the lawn which was much too small for a paddock, a minute haycock in one corner of it, and the rusty pump at the angle of the wall, looked false, stagy. They had indeed become false by being preserved into a different age.

Catto went in expecting more disappointment of the same kind, relics of the past that spoiled and obscured the past by their meretricious survival. He was delighted, therefore, by Mrs Bill. The little woman seemed no older. She was the same—pretty, vivacious, with her fine thin nose, her dead white skin, her black eyes that sparkled all the more for the contrast of her cheeks, her cracked voice, her high Edwardian handshake.

'Ah, but this is an occasion—don't you feel the sand between your toes? Don't you smell the stairs on the *Naiad*? I have never been able to use rubber since poor S. died. It makes me cry and it makes me seasick, and those are two things that simply can't go together. Some people drink claret with oysters, yes I know, I met such a man and he wasn't a character part. In fact, it was old Roger Kent.' And turning to another guest, 'Do you remember Roger in *Mrs Tanqueray?*'

She had turned from Catto, as Daisy had turned from him, to a more responsive audience, and seeing her white curly head from behind, he reflected, 'But she was dark then—she must be seventy.

I think she hasn't changed because I've been getting old too. And certainly she's kept her features.'

The dinner was quite good, the company distinguished, if not of the first distinction. A well-known Shakespearian actor, scholarly and earnest like all those who have never been stars; an ugly, amusing old critic with a broken nose, like a boxer's nose; and the vicar, a big red-faced man, full of good stories, and, Catto would have said, old port, a type that he had not met for years, and enjoyed. 'A sensible stout fellow,' he thought, 'and probably a fine preacher. I wish we had more of them in the Church. Good fellows with their feet on the ground.'

Mrs Mair, a well-known women's editor under her maiden name, arrived late with a new husband, and the Offer girl, a thin pale creature of about seventeen, enthusiastic about ballet, had never even heard of Catto. He remembered that Mrs Bill was celebrated for her inconsequence. It had been one of her charms and, because it had been a charm, he enjoyed it again.

Francie was the eighth at the table. That is to say, she did not appear till after the soup, when, flushed, hot, with damp hair and red shiny nose, she slipped into her place between the young bride-groom and the critic's wife.

As the vicar sat opposite Mrs Bill it was impossible to alternate the sexes, and Catto, on her left, sat next to the critic. No one explained Francie, or her sudden appearance. Catto was left to infer, after some reflection, that this thick-set woman, with grey streaks in her hair, must be the youngest Bill daughter, Frank, Frankie, Francie. He could not recognise her at all. But when she disappeared again with the chickens, and came in soon after the ice pudding, he perceived that she was acting as cook. The maid who waited was no doubt a daily woman, possibly a waiter hired only for the party. And when the party moved to the veranda, overlooking the bogus paddock and the decorator's haycock, he noticed that Francie not only arranged her mother's cushions but mixed the vicar's whisky and fetched the actor's pipe from his room.

The actor, Maxton, was staying in the house. He seemed like an old family friend, and when Francie, noticing that he fumbled in his pocket, silently disappeared and brought the pipe, he did not interrupt his description of Bernhardt's absurd masterpiece in L'Aiglon, he received the pipe with his fingers as a man at table who has dropped a fork takes a new one from the waiter.

'Or a father from a daughter,' Catto thought. 'But she calls him Mr Maxton. He can't be so familiar. Yet she knew what he wanted and where to find it.'

And suddenly he had a new recollection of the old Francie, the child of six who had always been so dirty, noisy, always falling into the water, tearing her frocks, so often in the way when he had wanted to be alone with the lovely, so friendly Daisy. He recalled a general cry of, 'Frankie, Frankie,' and the small girl with flying tangled hair tearing madly along the corridor; his brain lighted up a snapshot of Mrs Bill at her prettiest in a white serge frock, standing on the stairs above a group of men and saying with a charming bend of her head, 'But don't bother, I'm absolutely fated to lose things. Frankie will find it for me,' and then again, 'Frankie is the practical one, aren't you, Frankie?'

And again he saw, at forty-eight, an angle of his old friends that, at eighteen, had made only an impression on his memory, none on his observation. Daisy had been so easy, so friendly, yes, and Mrs Bill's tinkling voice had usually been heard by the children in these cheerful laments. She was always needing something fetched or found. Her good-humour confessed, 'I'm a nuisance, I know, but you'll forgive me because I forgive everyone else.'

And Frankie had been the practical one. Had they given her the character and made her a family slave, was she really fit for nothing else? And looking at the girl's face as she sat, silent as usual, half hidden behind her mother's chair, listening to the actor and the critic discussing Bernhardt, he thought, amused by the recollection, 'Yes, how she trailed after me—after anything in trousers. How she would throw herself into my arms and say, "But Tom, you haven't kissed me good night." And I should think she's a real woman still—rather shy and dull perhaps but the tomboy has quite disappeared.' And suddenly he thought, 'Why not Francie, could I do better? A kind soul, modest, simple, pretty capable, too, if she cooked that dinner. Of course, she's a bit young—she can't be more than thirty-six. There could be a baby, and that's a complication I particularly wanted to avoid. Of course, one could make a bargain—babies barred. It's common enough in second marriages.'

He reflected a moment on this tricky point. But like many steady, careful fellows who look for a fair deal in life, he had also a strong sense of what is fair in dealing with others. 'No,' he thought, 'if she wanted a baby I should have to give her one. On the other hand, youth does have some advantages. She'd stand up better to the job.'

He looked again at Francie, and caught her at a plainer moment. The lamp shone on her nose and the prominent forehead, a strand of damp hair, well steamed from the kitchen, was lying limp against her cheek. But Catto rallied. 'Damn it, I'm not a boy. What do looks matter? What I need is a good home-maker—someone to take an interest in Jean—domestic competence and peace.'

He sought some private talk with her, but this was difficult to manage. Rain was falling in thick heavy lines and the cars could not come down to the door because, at Hunter's Green, as in a proper farm-house, there was a little front garden full of old-fashioned flowers, with a narrow brick path to the front porch. The party stood crowded in the hall, looking out disgustedly, while Francie was busy with hats and coats.

When she brought him his coat he turned smiling and said, 'Frances, Frankie, do you remember Clarksfoot?'

But Mrs Bill interrupted with a remark to the world, 'Dear me, there used to be a carriage umbrella in the hall. But it seems to have lost itself. Everything in this house gets itself lost.'

Francie, still silent, ran for the carriage umbrella in the back passage and escorted the guests to their cars.

Catto, who had come by train and taxi, had a lift in the critic's car. He made one more attempt to speak to Francie from the back window. 'Thank you, Francie, do you remember how you used to go round at bedtime and wish us all good night?'

The girl had turned away at a call from the house. Someone had dropped a scarf. She did not even hear him. But Catto was a determined man. He wrote to Mrs Bill, thanking her for a delightful evening, and asked her to the theatre 'with my old friend Francie.'

And when Mrs Bill refused on account of an engagement, he took the train again to Hunter's Green and called.

He was lucky. Mrs Bill was out, and Frances was weeding the garden. In an old pair of trousers, gardening boots, a plaid shirt, and a handkerchief tied over her hair, she looked like a picture of slave labour in a Soviet camp. But she received Catto with something of Daisy's frankness. 'I'm sorry Mother's out, but she'll be in at six. Do wait. She'll be so upset to miss you.'

'Thanks, I should like to. And how are you, Francie? I didn't really see you last week.'

'Do you mind if I finish this border—I've got so behind with the weeds.'

'No—let me help you.'

'Oh, you couldn't—you'll get filthy.'

'I can wash.'

'Are you sure you know which are weeds?'

'I see you're still practical.'

The woman looked at him in surprise. He explained his point, as a joke, but she did not smile. She reflected and said at last, 'I wonder——'

'You were a quaint little thing at six.'

But she was weeding again, he saw only the short broad back.

'You don't remember me at all.'

'Not really.' She stood up again and looked at him intently. She was obviously curious, she felt that his visit had some purpose beyond a mere call.

She shook her head, 'Mother says that you were Daisy's great friend.'

'I liked to think I was yours too. You never let me leave the house without a kiss.'

'Oh well, at six.' She dismissed this carelessly. She was not at all embarrassed, as Catto had expected. She showed no shyness. Indeed, now that he had been able to talk to her, he felt that she had grown up with something of the Bill poise. She asked him abruptly, 'What do you do, Mr Catto? Tell me about yourself.'

'That's a very dull story. I'm a printer, a widower, with a young daughter—forty-eight years old. Really, there's nothing more to tell.'

'Is it long since you——' she hesitated.

'Lost my wife? No, eighteen months. But it seems a very long time indeed. We were very happy—I am a lonely man, Francie—a very lonely man. Men like me who have been happily married and then widowed, suffer a very special kind of loneliness.'

The woman looked at him and the wrinkles in her forehead were very noticeable. 'Yes, I can imagine it. I'm sorry. But then you did have all that happiness.'

'It's a danger.'

'Yes, it's a danger. But worth it. Or don't you think so? Perhaps now——'

'Oh yes, tremendously worth it.'

'In fact, in spite of everything, you've been——'

'Yes, I've been lucky. I was always rather lucky. I was lucky to know you when I was a boy.'

'Me——'

'I mean the family as a whole. Yes, you too. You were rather an important part of the experience.'

The woman looked at him and her expression was critical. She was taking a new view of this middle-aged man who made such rapid advances. Then she said that she must really get the weeding done, and set to work. No word was said for twenty minutes and the silence itself was expressive. It said plainly that there was a situation.

'I've been too sudden,' Catto said to himself. 'She doesn't seem shy—at thirty-six, she knows how to manage her feelings. But she's timid and wary.'

The bed finished, they straightened up together face to face, and the girl smiled in a broad and frank manner. Her whole face expressed a personal interest. She had settled something with herself. 'Come, Mr Catto, you need tea, or a drink.'

'Why Mr Catto?'

'Well, what did I call you?'

'I was Tom to you all.'

'Come, Tom, we'll have tea.' She blushed as she spoke and stooped to gather her basket.

For the moment, Catto was afraid that he had been too enterprising. He did not want to commit himself to the girl before he knew her better. He had, as we have seen, as well as prudence, a strong sense of responsibility.

But the woman at once recovered her practical air. She had placed Catto to her satisfaction as a nice middle-aged man eager to renew his childhood memories. They talked of the days at Clarksfoot, they exchanged news. She told how Mrs Bill after her husband's death had lost most of her money and sold the land, how Daisy loved travelling and seldom appeared at home, how Letty needed special treatment and how much it cost.

He told her about his marriage, about Jean, and how hard he thought it for a girl of nine to lose her mother. That he had seriously considered marrying again, on her account alone.

'I'm sure you're right,' Francie said, 'if you can find the right person.'

'That's the problem.'

'A widow perhaps, without children, who wanted a child to care for.'

'I'm not so sure. A younger woman might be a better companion.'

'A widow could be quite young. There are lots of young widows. What about war widows?'

'It's the person that matters. I don't see why she need be a widow.'

'Oh no, of course.'

'Or why I shouldn't have another baby if she were young enough.'

There was a pause, and Catto again thought that he had been indiscreet. But the woman was only reflecting. 'You'd have to discuss that with the new wife.' In fact, it was not till three months later, when Catto actually proposed in so many words that Francie understood him.

'You really want to marry me?'

'Yes, yes. I've been trying to tell you so for the last fortnight.'

'Well, I did wonder sometimes but I didn't like to think——'

'But you haven't answered me yet.'

'But don't you see?'

'What?'

'Why I didn't like to think. Why, Tom,' and she laughed that tomboyish broad laugh which brought all her wrinkles and made her little eyes disappear, 'of course I'll marry you.'

The laugh disappeared and she looked suddenly very serious. All at once Catto understood that the headlong Francie of thirty years before was still there. He was much startled. He had not expected so passionate a kiss, so eager an embrace.

Mrs Bill was greatly amused by the news. She congratulated Catto and said, laughing, 'Sir Galahad to the rescue, or is it Perseus? But I'm not really a monster, you know, and Francie loves her chains. She adores a fuss.' Catto, taken by surprise, found himself turning red. He did not know what to answer. But Mrs Bill had dashed on at once, 'Letty will hate you, but it won't do Letty any harm to take a little exercise.'

He received a most friendly letter from Daisy in Venezuela, who said how glad she was to see that her darling Francie was to get away from home at last and have some life of her own. She wanted Catto to 'keep mother at bay, for Francie's sake, or you'll have no peace.'

The wedding was quiet. Mrs Bill forgot to provide linen and Francie bought her own wedding dress, but Catto presented his bride with the latest refrigerator, freezer, enamelled stove, and double sink in a completely remodelled kitchen, and all Mrs Bill's old friends sent autographed copies of their works—published twenty or thirty years before, period sensations now wearing as strange a look as the hats and skirts of that ancient world in which they had achieved their distinction.

Catto had already arranged for a honeymoon in Paris. His first honeymoon had been in Paris. Francie had hoped for Italy, but she enjoyed Paris enormously as a bride. And she was deeply apologetic when the month they had planned was cut a week short because Daisy came back from Jamaica, in a banana boat, with a mysterious illness called Daisy's fever, and the Cattos had to hurry home to look after her. But Catto could not complain that Daisy looked upon his home as a refuge in time of trouble.

Francie nursed her for six weeks before Catto got a hint, from Mrs Bill, that Daisy's fever came on only when she was broke. 'Don't let her kill Francie,' she wrote. 'Daisy has always treated Francie as her private and personal slave. Have you tried the gold cure for the fever? A cheque, I've found, is far the best prescription.'

Daisy had been complaining every day of all the wonderful holidays she was missing by this unlucky illness, and Catto now offered her a loan of twenty pounds to take advantage of an invitation to Finland. She left the next morning by milk-float to catch a trawler whose captain was an old Bombay friend. Catto, relieved, told himself that Daisy would not come very often. But he protested when Francie confessed that she had engaged herself to stay three days at Hunter's Green in order to cook for her mother's traditional Easter party. He wrote to Mrs Bill suggesting that he should advertise for a temporary cook. But she answered none was required.

'Francie seems to think she ought to come but it's quite unnecessary—Mrs Jones is quite lazy enough as it is. She does just as little as she dares.' She addressed the note to Galahad Catto Esq., and signed herself 'the monster.'

Catto took it to Francie and said, 'You see, your mother doesn't even want you.'

'But it was Mummie told me that Mrs Jones threatened to give notice if she asked five people to stay. And now she's asked seven people. And you know if we lose Mrs Jones we'll never get another up to Mummy's standards.'

'Then she'll have to change her standards—like other people.'

Francie was silent, as usual, in these arguments. But a certain obstinate desperation in her forehead and chin seemed to ask, 'How? It's easy to say, but how do you do it?' And she went to the work— Mrs Bill's celebrated party was again a great success, for which she received much praise, even a graceful notice in a Sunday newspaper. And for three months afterwards she did not send for Francie; either she did not need her or she had been offended by Catto's note.

Francie believed that she was offended, and it worried her. 'Mummy is so sensitive about being a nuisance,' she said. 'And of course she'll never tell you when she's hurt.'

'She's no right to be hurt.'

Francie's wrinkles deepened. 'It's not very nice for her, living alone. I should hate it.'

Catto did not answer that Francie was off the point. He told himself that women have their own methods of argument and that, above all, he must not start a quarrel with Francie about her mother. That situation was too foolish as well as too vulgar. How easy for a sensible man to avoid it. And it seemed that Mrs Bill, hurt or not, meant to leave Francie alone.

Francie's first baby was born in December, a very cold December; and on the day before she got up there was a note from Letty asking if she could take the elder girl to school, she herself had a migraine; and on the day after she got up, Mrs Bill telephoned. She did not ask for help. Mrs Bill's claim that she never sought Francie's help, was perfectly justified. Her method was to send news of trouble, as a joke, or to ask advice. This time she did both.

'I've got three people for the week-end and of course Mrs Jones has sprained her ankle. You can rely on Mrs Jones's ankle, it's never failed her yet when there's some real work to do. But meanwhile I have to find an experienced daily. Should I advertise? I'm so bad at these things. And I simply must get someone by this evening.'

Catto, running in from the works in the mid-morning, to have a glimpse of his wife, finds her up and dressed. She is at the telephone, nursing the baby through her opened coat and arguing with Letty about school clothes. Jean, with an expression of reserved disapproval which comically reproduces her father's look in the same kind of crisis, stands looking on. Jean, a sensible Catto, is already devoted, in her sensible way, to her stepmother. She knows how to value her practical good nature, and quite agrees with her father about the Bill relations.

'But Letty,' Francie's voice implores her sister to be reasonable. 'She simply must have four face towels. It may be ridiculous but you know there was trouble last time when she went with only two, and it upsets a child so much to be different.'

Catto, furious, tries to take the telephone out of Francie's hands. Startled, she turns crimson and fights him.

'No—what are you doing?'

And he, equally surprised by this strong resistance, gives way. She says hastily to Letty, 'It's all right, darling. Nothing. I'll be round in ten minutes,' and hangs up. She smiles nervously at Catto and says, 'I can do Letty on the way to Mother's. How lucky that I was going anyhow.'

'You're not going to do Letty, or your mother either. This is where we stop. You're not fit.' And seeing the obstinate look in her face, he begins to storm. Her mother and Letty are two of the most selfish people on earth. And has she no consideration for her baby, not to speak of her husband?

Francie, flustered, tries to interrupt. Suddenly she bursts into tears. Catto, alarmed by her violent agitation, sits down beside her and puts an arm around her.

'My darling, you see how it is. Someone has to make a stand. Let me do it for you if you're afraid.'

'But you can't, you can't. No one can.'

'But that's nonsense.'

'You don't understand. Letty would simply let that poor child go off again with all the wrong things, and of course Mother won't get a daily in time for dinner this evening. There isn't a hope. She'll leave everything to settle itself, and Mrs Jones will limp about and get up a grievance till she gives notice. She loves a real grievance. And if Mother loses Mrs Jones I'd have to go every day. Either that or Mother would have to live with us. And you'd hate that. Oh dear, there's Gordon in the car.' And still nursing, while her brother-in-law, chattering about Letty's headache, gathers her bag, she hurries out.

Six months later Mrs Bill did lose Mrs Jones, and she has failed to keep another housekeeper. She is very cheerful and says that on the whole she prefers to manage without Mrs Jones who had no humour.

Francie has her second baby, and she lives a still more distracted life, dashing over three times a week to manage her mother's household. It has been proposed that Mrs Bill should live with the Cattos, but she absolutely refuses to give up her dear old house, with its glorious memories of William Archer, E. F. Benson, and George Alexander. And as for the proposal that the Cattos should live with her, taking half the house for their separate apartment, which is Mrs Bill's solution to the problem, Catto can't bring himself to leave his home. He points out that the kitchen was especially designed for Francie's convenience.

So that he too lives a distracted life. See him now at ten o'clock at night waiting at Hunter's Green to take Francie home. It is raining but he is so angry that he won't leave the car to go into the house. This, of course, is stupid, for Mrs Bill is always good-natured with him and says, 'My dear Tom, I don't ask Francie to run my show, it's Francie who insists on it. She's so practical—she hates a muddle. Now, I don't mind muddle a bit.'

For Mrs Bill has never suffered from a muddle—Francie sees to that. And Catto thinks bitterly, 'Practical and affectionate—how true that was—and is.'

Suddenly the house door opens and Francie comes running

through the rain. He starts the engine, before he realises that she has neither hat nor coat. She comes to the driver's side, pulls open the door, and puts her arms round his neck. 'Darling, only ten more minutes, I swear.'

'But you're getting wet.'

'Yes, I saw the car from the window and I knew how you were feeling. Only ten more minutes. And then we'll be off. And I am so longing——'

She kisses him again and again, there is a cry from the house, 'Francie,' and she runs.

Catto falls back in his seat. He is excited, his heart is beating fast, there are tears in his eyes. For he adores his wife, it is an agony for him to see Francie used, worn out by people that, to him, are worthless beside her. And it seems that there is no cure. He suffers, he grumbles, he quarrels with the amused Mrs Bill, he makes a fool of himself, he does not know if he is more happy or more wretched. All he knows is this passionate love, a thing he has never imagined before—that devours him with anxiety, with anger, with despair.

CARMAGNOLE

THE boy, about six years old, fair and brown eyed in blue silk trousers, was projected slowly into the drawing-room by the long arm of an unseen mother. When the arm had reached its full stretch, it gave him a last little push and then withdrew from sight. The boy stopped at once and looked round at half a dozen other children ranged about the room in silent watchfulness.

It was a party from which, by request, mothers and nurses were excluded. Their voices could be heard in the hall; in every female timbre from oboe-soprano to viola-baritone; like the tuning up of an orchestra; and as in such tuning, certain phrases could be heard repeated over and over again.

'It's Mary's first real party, so of course.'

'Rather shy, I'm afraid.'

'At six o'clock, then.'

'They do rather cling together at first.'

In the drawing-room there was dead silence. Half a dozen children with their backs set against the wall or the more solid pieces of furniture, stood on guard.

The boy in blue trousers, finding himself alone on the vast empty plain of pink carpet, hastily backed against the wall and took a small girl by the hand. The girl was attached by the other hand to a taller child in spectacles. They were obviously one family.

Another arm stretched from the door; an arm in blue linen; a nurse's arm; pushing forward a very small toddling baby with close-cropped hair like the bloom on a nectarine. His round pink face had the absorbed gravity of one accustomed to solitude and his own ideas. His little legs, still curly as if but half unfolded from the womb seemed about to collapse under him at every step.

When the blue arm had reached its full length, a contralto voice, gilded and thickened with that treacle which nurses use for cajoling, said, 'Look after baby-brother Philip—you'd better take his hand.'

The boy in blue stretched forward and accepted the baby's hand, who at once made for the middle of the floor towing his brother and staggering by some extraordinary means, at an angle of forty-five degrees with the carpet; like a skater changing feet on his edges. He then stopped, drew himself up and stood in a peculiar attitude of suspense like one who feels a suspicion and expects he knows not what. Philip looked patiently down at his brother. The two sisters gazed with mingled anxiety and hostility. The other children stared blankly. Suddenly a pool of water appeared on the floor next to the baby's left foot. It grew, spreading a dark stain on the pink carpet. The baby let go of Philip's hand, and sat down abruptly next the pool. His face was still grave, aloof, absorbed.

The boy in blue was horror-struck. He glanced round him with a look of despair. He was afraid even to run away from the scene of the family crime. His sisters turned scarlet and drew suddenly together. The same stir passed through all the children. All grasped the horror of such a crime, at a party, in a strange drawing-room, on a new pink carpet. Some grew also pink; others rounded their eyes in dismay; a small very fat boy with bristling fair hair, over-come by collective guilt, tried to force himself out of sight behind the piano.

The baby, noticing the pool apparently for the first time, stooped over it with an enquiring air and took aim at it with one short tapered forefinger. He did not touch it; and he was not indicating it. The finger served apparently as a kind of antenna; an exploring member.

A voice outside, an ocharina contralto with a bubble in it, called, 'Oh Bridget.'

The children started and some grew pinker. This was the voice of the hostess. An Irish voice like a small muted fiddle answered.

'Yiss, Mahdam.'

'On the piano, I think, and my bureau.'

A tall buxom parlourmaid with a very flat back came gliding rapidly into the room. Her pointed face, pointed nose, pointed lips, expressed a religious decorum which was somehow increased by her rapid silent smooth movement. In spite of her grenadier carriage, her head with its white cap was bent slightly forwards from the neck; as of one approaching an altar; not with reverence since the face expressed none, but with an habitual courtesy.

In her hands she carried two glass dishes full of chocolates. One she placed on the piano, then turned to cross the room to the bureau.

A wave of panic passed through the children fluttering them like reeds. The sisters pressed tight together; Philip turned round as if to fly; but then, suddenly arrested by some opposing force, stood on one leg; the fat child disappeared altogether between the piano and the wall; a little girl in the corner gazing upwards at the maid, suddenly drooped her lips as if about to cry.

The maid began again her hieratic passage across the pink carpet. Her mouth with its pointed lips was like that of an old priest, neither sad nor smiling; but willing and submissive. She directed her course to pass the baby. But suddenly she stopped, and looked down. The baby, still pointing his finger, looked up at her as one might glance upwards at the sky to notice a change of weather.

Suddenly the maid broke into giggles. Her face turned pink; her blue eyes sparkled; she put her left hand to her cap, as if fearing that it would slide off, and giggled helplessly, loudly.

The children stared at her; then all at once they broke into shouts of laughter; the little tearful girl was so intoxicated with joy that she uttered a loud shriek. The boy in the blue trousers reeled to and fro, lolling his head almost to his shoulders; then suddenly began to jump round in circles.

The baby is gazing round him with astonishment. Two little girls dart upon him simultaneously and seize him from opposite sides. They are full of excitement; and it overflows upon the baby. They want to drag him somewhere; to caress him; perhaps to undress him. He fights them strongly; makes himself as rigid as a starfish. Suddenly he utters yells of indignation.

The maid is still in fits of giggles. The chocolate dish sways to and fro and threatens to spill. Philip pulls her by the apron and jumps up and down. The others crowd round her, prancing, romping, grasping at her skirts, her arms; the little fat boy has tumbled on his back and is kicking his legs in the air. They cannot express their delight; in their antics, their shouts, there is something violent and rebellious. One looking suddenly in, might have been reminded of those old

French prints in which revolutionary mobs dance in the grand hall of Versailles, battering its polished floor with their brass-bound shoes.

Philip is leaping as high as he can, grasping at the maid's bodice and trying to catch her eyes. His flushed face, sparkling eyes and wide laughing mouth seem to say, 'We're all together in this, aren't we?'

A GLORY OF THE MOON

THE children were playing funerals. A small dark boy of about six was lying in an orange-box at the edge of the leaf-pit. His eyes were closed; his hands crossed on his breast. The box was too short for him and he had to draw up his knees, but he held them sideways in the effort to make himself as flat and dead as possible.

A square-shouldered girl of about ten, with a very round brown face, was holding one end of a skipping rope which was passed under the box. The other end was in the hand of the parson, a thin fair boy, the same height as the girl, with a singularly long thin nose and large grey eyes which seemed to bulge with impatience. A maid's apron, pinned to the shoulders of his jersey, made a surplice. He was holding a piece of folded newspaper from which he was pretending to read, using such striking phrases as he had picked up in church or from broadcasts. He intoned these words in High Church style with a peculiar quivering intensity, excited both by their quality and his own success as a parson.

'We are like the grass. It is green in the morning but in the evening it is cut and withered—and worms will eat our body.'

The little boy in the orange-box fluttered his long lashes and blinked. A smaller, very fair little girl, standing beside the box as mourner, did not look at him, but stared with round fascinated eyes at the speaker. Her lips moved now and then as she tried to repeat the words after him.

The parson, after a moment's pause for recollection, shrilled with the same dramatic emphasis, 'The last enemy is death for he puts everything under his feet—come on, Mag.'

This was to the brown-faced girl who had been attending with a nervous frown, and kept her eyes fixed anxiously on the boy in the coffin.

'Come on, Mag,' the parson repeated sharply, jerking his end of the rope. 'Wake up.'

The girl started and pulled on the rope. The head of the box was lifted slightly and together they dragged it down the ramp of the pit until it was resting among the dead leaves and yellowed grass cuttings, withered flowers and bracken, which filled the hole.

The brown girl said to the little boy, 'You all right, David?' whereupon the parson turned upon her and exclaimed angrily, 'Do shut up, Mag.'

'But I only——'

'He's dead—he's dead, I tell you—how can he talk to you? And he's absolutely all right if you'd only let him alone. He doesn't mind a bit.'

At this David pressed his lips together more tightly. The parson said loudly, 'In the midst of life we are in death.'

Suddenly the corpse scrambled out of the box. The parson threw down the paper and shouted in disgust. 'Oh, what's the good.'

The little boy was climbing up the ramp. He thrust out his lower lip and glanced sideways at his elders with that look which, in small children, means, 'Kill me if you like—but I'm through.'

'He's frightened,' Mag said. 'I said he would be.'

'Oh well, let's chuck it—I thought you wanted to do the thing properly. But of course if you're going to go fussing about the kids——'

'I'm not fussing about the kids. I only said that David——'

'All right, I've chucked it. It's chucked,' and he threw his newspaper on the ground in all the rage of a frustrated artist. Mag, indignant, turned to the small girl. 'Kate wouldn't mind, would you, Kate?' Kate answered in a high dreamy voice as if her ideas were far away, 'No, I wouldn't mind.'

'Oh let's chuck it, it's no good.'

'You always say that,' Mag was still indignant. 'Here, I'll bury her myself if you won't. Get in, Kate.' The little girl at once lay down in the box which she just fitted, crossed her hands on her breast and shut her eyes. Mag dived for the newspaper but the parson got it first. 'All right, Kate—only don't forget you're dead. Absolutely dead.'

The little girl's lips moved. She was accepting this condition, but in a whisper appropriate to someone in another state of existence.

The service continued. 'Man that is born of woman has but a short time to live. He goes like a shadow—he is cut down like a flower——'

Kate silently repeated after him and her cheeks turned slowly pink.

The parson picked up a handful of leaves and scattered them over her. One dead aspen leaf, with its long stem attached, fell on her neck, but she lay like stone. 'Dust to dust—ashes to ashes.' He paused to examine the excellent corpse—then in a triumph of realisation, and more and more excited by the sound of his own voice, broke into full song. 'There is a glo-ory of the sun, and a glo-ory of the stars, and a glo-o-ory of the moon.'

The child's lips moved again to follow the words. Suddenly her face crinkled and shortened. She gave a sob. A line of moisture glistened between her closed lids.

The parson stopped and said furiously, 'Dash it all, what's wrong now?'

'N-nothing.'

'Oh get up, for goodness sake. I said you kids would ruin everything.'

'But I don't want to get up. I like it.'

'Then what are you crying for?'

The little girl looked wondering from the box. The withered leaves shook on the breast of her frock while she tried to catch her sobs.

'I don't know.'

OUT OF HAND

THE six young cousins, two Corners and four Evelyns, were together in Ireland for the whole summer, three months. They were considered a delicate lot by their parents who did not, either, set much store by school. But the Evelyn grandmother always engaged a governess to give them morning lessons. This year she was a little, thin, fierce-looking woman, very young, with that kind of shining brown hair which looks as if it had meant to be gold. But her eyes were very dark. Her name, they said, was Miss Farrell.

She seemed very efficient and produced at the first lesson a black book in which, she said, she would enter marks, good marks for good conduct, bad marks for bad conduct. And then there would be prizes every Saturday for good children; but those with bad marks would be reported to Mr Evelyn for punishment.

Lessons were given in a little parlour which looked towards the shore not thirty yards away. People from the village passed continually along the shore by a path; there was nothing between the path and the house grounds but a wire fence. Thus the children, by turning their heads, could see the people passing, fishermen with nets, Miss McGinty from the sweet-shop in a new blue frock, two strange children in red stocking caps with extraordinary tassels, large yellow tassels; and behind the people was the great sea loch, Foyle, full of small jumping waves throwing up such a glitter of sparks that it made your eyes blink.

Why were Tom and Willy taking out their nets now? It wasn't full tide for two hours. Were the herring in? What on earth was Miss McGinty doing on the shore at this hour of a Monday morning? Where had those queer children come from and what were they doing?

'Look at your book, Harry,' said the governess in a sharp tone which made Harry jump and blush. And a moment later, it was, 'Tommy, if you look out of the window again, I'll have to give you a bad mark.' And Tommy, aged six, with a round brown face and hair like teased lint, started so violently that he knocked his book on the floor. No one had ever talked to him like that before. But all were startled by the woman's angry tone. It was alarming. What would she do next? The cousins were agreed in hating trouble.

Subdued and nervous, they sat now with their eyes on their books, while Miss Farrell instructed the youngest girl, Bunty, in her letters. Felix Corner, aged eight, who behind his book had been doing a full-rigged ship on the edge of the table with a pin, did not dare, for more than five minutes, to put on the dolphin striker, his favourite spar. But when he could bear no longer to see the naked bowsprit, and tried very cautiously to give the one necessary scratch, his hand was seized and the pin whisked out of it. She had caught him; but how?

The boy sat horrified while he received a bad mark. What was a bad mark? What did it look like? All were horrified. Bunty gazed at Miss Farrell with open mouth.

And then slapping shut this terrifying book, she said to them, 'I know what you did to poor Miss Taggert. But you needn't think you're going to do it to me. The truth is you're thoroughly out of hand. But I know how to deal with bad children.'

All were amazed by these words, 'out of hand.' Tommy blinked as if he would cry, Felix's green eyes gazed at Harry, fair and blue-eyed, with enquiring wonder; his brows were raised to their highest. Harry's sharp clever face expressed guilt and confusion; and his sister, Molly, with her thick braids of straw-coloured hair, her freckled cheeks and nose, blushed deep pink and sent an appealing glance at the angry Miss Farrell, whose black eyes seemed enormous with rage.

But who was Miss Taggert and what had they done to her?

Felix Corner, pondering this fascinating question for a long time, was almost giving it up when suddenly there started up before his fancy, as from a trap-door, a tall bony woman with rather untidy grey hair and pince-nez hooked on by a little gold chain over one ear. What a surprise. Yes, it was Miss Taggert. How had he forgotten that chain and the way it swung and sparkled in a ray of sunlight? How nice she had been, Miss Taggert. She told them stories and gave them sweets, and played the piano to them. She had been especially nice to him, Felix. Yes, it was certainly Miss Taggert who had given him those lessons last year, and then she had stopped giving them lessons. And he remembered now that his Grandfather Evelyn had said of Miss Taggert that she was no good, her bark was even worse than her bite.

But what had they done to Miss Taggert, with her gentle voice, her understanding smile? He had loved her, they had all loved dear Miss Taggert. What fun they had had with her during lessons. And suddenly another vision sprang up before his eyes, the vision of a face, not Miss Taggert's face, but Molly's, that morning when Harry put the cartridge on the fire. How Molly had jumped.

They had all been surprised by that bang; and rather angry with Harry afterwards. Harry had been much too young last year to play with cartridges. He had been only six then; he had no sense. He might have killed somebody. Some of the shot had actually hit the ceiling and made marks there, like stabs with a pencil.

His eyes flew up. Yes, they were there still. And suddenly, to his own surprise and horror, he uttered a crow of laughter.

'What was I saying, Felix?'

'You were saying—that we were bad.'

The governess turned scarlet and said, 'Go and stand in the corner —you're the worst. I was warned about you. No, not a word.'

The boy, quite downcast at this unexpected catastrophe, slid off his chair and went slowly to the corner. He perceived now that the woman had been talking to Harry and Molly about islands and peninsulas. Ireland was an island; Inishowen was a peninsula. But he knew all that. He had been listening all the time. How unfair not to let him explain. Obviously this woman had a bad temper, she was dangerous. They would have to be careful or she would spoil the whole summer.

He stood very still, therefore, in the corner. Luckily, by turning his head very slightly and his eyes as far as they would go, he could see edgeways out of the window. And suddenly he remembered a picture in the *Wide World Magazine* of a burglar hanging by his hands from a window-sill. He was just about to drop forty feet into a shrubbery.

The sill of the window was eight feet from the ground because the ground floor of the house was raised above the level of the garden. But it struck the boy that there was a garden bed straight below and that it would be possible for even a small child to get out of the window, let himself down to the full stretch of his arms, and drop safely into the soft earth.

What an idea for the next game of robbers, or hide-and-seek, on a wet afternoon. He would run to this room and they would all be sure of catching him. Then they would come in and find that he had disappeared. They would be absolutely astonished.

A voice, his grandmother's, called outside the door. The governess said, 'Yes, Mrs Evelyn,' and went out of the room, leaving the door ajar. Felix darted to the table. 'I say,' he whispered, 'what about the window?'

'What about it?'

'You could get out.'

'No, you don't,' Molly said severely. 'I won't have you breaking your legs.' Molly was nine, the eldest, and when she remembered this superiority, she mothered the party.

'Bet you I will.'

'Bet you you can't,' Harry said.

'All right, just watch.'

'No, let me first.'

'No, you don't, Harry.'

The clever Harry was already across the sill. But when Felix tried to follow, Molly flew and caught him back. Molly had already organised the affair. 'No, Fee, you'll have to help Jack and Tommy down, and me Bunty. She'll never dare by herself. Stop Tommy—wait.'

Tommy, a quiet, reserved but quite fearless child of six, had already hurled himself into mid-air. He landed face down, partly in a fuchsia bush, partly on the grass verge.

Miss Farrell's voice from somewhere down the passage called, 'Stop talking, children—don't think I can't hear you.' This caused a panic. What would happen now if that rude and violent woman came in and caught them? The very idea was terrifying. Felix and

Molly snatched up the two youngest, bundled them through the window simultaneously and let them down with clasped hands as far as they could reach. Unluckily, Molly's hair, escaping from its braid, suddenly tumbled in a canopy over Bunty's face so that the child could not see. She called out shrilly, 'Don't let go—don't let go.'

Molly at once let go and jumped after her sister with such desperate abandon that she tore her pinafore on the trellis and landed on her back among the fuchsias. But terror, increased by the ruin of her pinafore, gave her extraordinary agility. She rolled over in a moment, jumped up and grabbed the breathless Tommy, still prone.

Already the governess was in the room; she darted round the table and caught Felix's arm. The boy did not try to escape. He was paralysed by this fearful situation. And he was left to face it, to explain it, all by himself. The children outside had already rushed into the wood close behind the house.

Felix stared with wide eyes at the woman, whose grip hurt his arm. She jerked his arm violently but said nothing; she was choking with rage. He tried desperately to think of some explanation, some excuse. But what could he say? He could not remember even why they had been getting out of the window, or who had suggested such an extraordinary thing.

'Oh Miss——' he could not remember her name. 'Really, I didn't mean to——' he stammered in his anxiety and fright. But suddenly the governess let go of his arm, sat down in a chair, put her hands over her face and broke into loud helpless sobs.

The child could not believe his eyes and ears. Gazing, he turned deeply red. Then slowly he got out of the window, dropped to the ground, and followed the others into the wood. They surrounded him. 'Did she catch you? What did she say—will she tell Grandy?'

Felix gazed round at them as if he had seen a ghost and could not yet accustom himself to the everyday solid world. At last he said, 'She's crying.'

'Crying?'

'Not really *crying?*'

'You're making it up,' Molly said in a severe maternal tone.

'Yes, she was.' Felix was gravely certain of the fact. 'Crying.' His voice, his look expressed the same amazement, that a governess, a grown-up, so powerful, so free, should cry because of anything that children might do. He walked slowly away. He couldn't get over it.

A MYSTERIOUS AFFAIR

Every now and then my friend Ned Simpson would say he was sick of the city; he would get out of it before it killed him. We did not pay much attention to these outbursts, all of us hated the city, that is to say, work, worry, noise. And most of us found our holidays too long. After a fortnight we wanted to get back to work, worry and noise, to life. And when we grumbled at the city our wives would smile wisely or sadly and say nothing. But Ned's wife would cry, 'Then why don't you leave it? Why do you stay? You say yourself there's no need. And you're nearly sixty. In another year or two, it will be too late.'

As our friend Grain, the tea man, says, Nell is a headlong woman, it's no good telling her. 'Women,' he says, 'are the everlasting Bourbons of the world. They never forget anything and they never learn. All the experience in the world is no good to 'em, they start new from the beginning every day.'

We had to agree that this was true, of Nell at least. But we excused her. She was so devoted. She had that special devotion for Ned seen only in childless wives. Ned was her child, her only one, as well as her husband, and for years she had complained that she never saw the real Ned. Before work he was simply a concentrated train catcher in such a fury at the time-table that he would not speak to her; and at night, he came back so tired that he would say at the very door, 'For God's sake, don't tell me things—I'm all in.'

And when Nell spoke of retirement, he would answer, to our alarm, 'Yes, why don't I chuck my hand in? Why don't I put my damned umbrella through that damned old station clock? I tell you why—because I've lost my guts. Because I've nothing left inside but a comptometer and a lot of ticker tape. And what's it all for? The city is just a habit—a bad habit. And not so good as dope. That makes you feel good for a minute or two. You get something for your bargain.' And he swore he would leave that half year.

But three years later, he was still cursing the city, that old vampire, still swearing this was his last month. But was still catching the 9.20 from Wimbledon every morning. And we had stopped being alarmed. We smiled when Nell said, 'Ned is longing to go but he's had such bad luck. Always some new crisis at the office. It's absolutely extraordinary.'

Grain remarked dryly that all offices were extraordinary in this way. But Nell assured us that Ned's office was quite a special case. Ned had never known such a lot of trouble, what with the change of government and the wild behaviour of commodities.

'I've never known a tame one,' Grain said. 'My God, Ned and his copper. I wish I could shut him in a cage for an hour or two with tea. He'd know something about commodities then—if he came out alive.'

Then one morning, a very wet morning, during a bus strike, Ned resigned. He had to give six months' notice, according to his contract, but he would not stay another hour. The partners, sons of the men who had started the firm, with Ned's able assistance, were much alarmed. Ned had practically run Ackbee Electrical since old Ackbee died, just before the war. He had kept it going during the war and reconstructed it afterwards. They said they had not expected their managing director to leave them at sixty-two. They begged him to reconsider—he was indispensable for another five years at least, until the new overseas branches were in full operation.

They even went to Nell, and begged her to use her influence. Money was no object. They would give Ned anything he asked for, on top of his directorship. But Nell laughed at them. She had never liked the Ackbee brothers. She considered that they had exploited Ned.

And she was already looking for a country cottage. All they wanted, she said, was a simple little place with electricity and water, in an established garden with some good trees and a southern slope. Both Ned and Nell were keen gardeners, that is to say, Nell would work at their patch all the week and on Sundays Ned would criticize it and tell her how much better it would be if it were twice the size and had better soil. And if he could do it himself.

Nell had to have a good garden, for Ned's sake. But she was not particular about the house. Except that Ned could not bear Tudor or Queen Anne and she hated modern. All they wanted was a quiet little place without any fake or phoney and no suggestion whatever of a city land agency's window, a tourist folder, or an architect's review. It must look, according to Ned, as if it had grown there, among the flowers, as if its bricks and tiles were made of garden earth, and matured, of course. But a hundred years old would be enough. And it must be in first-class order. An old house in bad order can ruin a chartered accountant. Yes, and perhaps a little glass, just one good house. And, yes, no view unless it was absolutely unspoilable; over the green belt, or national trust land. And, oh yes, it must be within ten miles of Town for Covent Garden. Nell wanted her operas.

We told each other the tale at the golf club and laughed at Nell. We agreed that this catalogue was just like Nell, she always demanded the earth, especially for Ned.

But Grain took a deeper, more subtle view. Had Ned got cold feet and set Nell on an impossible quest? 'We've got to remember Ned will never admit he's made a mistake. This house-hunt is a get-out.'

We agreed that there was something in this. Nell would never find a place to suit them both, not in Ned's lifetime. We all knew something about house-hunting, especially for simple little places, in good order.

And neither did Nell find her simple little place. After months of search, she was desperate, and amazed. 'It's absolutely extraordinary,' she said, 'what people, quite nice people, will put in advertisements about houses. You wouldn't believe it. I went forty miles yesterday to see what they called a little gem, just redecorated, all conveniences, in large garden with a view over the Thames Valley. And do you know what it was?' We couldn't imagine. But we had difficulty in affecting surprise when we heard that the little gem had twenty-five rooms, in Victorian Gothic, that it overlooked a gas works, and backed on a goods yard.

She did find a nice little house, in a brick-field; and she saw a wonderful garden too, with what was called a gentleman's desirable residence which turned out to be a wooden shack attached to an enormous vinery, rotten as a sleepy pear.

The six months was up. There was no house to go to, and Ned asked what the hell a man was to do in this goddam century. There was no place left for a Christian to have some peace. He supposed the idea was that the goddam city had got him and didn't mean to let go till it had sucked the last drop of his blood. But he'd show it. And he told the worried young partners, neither of them much over forty, that he could only stay from month to month until his arrangements were made. 'I'm sorry,' he said, 'but you've had four-fifths of my life and I want a fraction for myself—just to feel what real life is like.'

He was much excited by his own boldness of decision. 'I'm sorry to let these chaps down, but damn it all, it's now or never for me. And what was I born for? What have I got to show for my life? A lot of dirty paper. No, I want to *do* something, create something, if it's only a rockery. I have ideas about rockeries.' And he pulled out an advertisement about garden stone work, alpines. He wanted us to say, 'Wonderful,' but we were too worried. Things were rather dicky in the markets just then and we would miss Ned and his enthusiasms, his feuds, especially his rage against the city.

But six months later, he was still the prop of Ackbee's. And his retirement had become a joke. Nell was still looking. She had discovered, indeed, a very nice place, with a good house and garden, in a pretty valley with no view except of fine trees. Its only fault was that it was twenty-five miles from town and rather expensive. And Ned would not dream of it. 'It's not the money—it's the distance and the train service. I'm not going to let Nell cut herself off from her music. She'd wither away—she'd be impossible to live with. Nell needs Wagner as a cow needs oil-cake. No, no, no—ten miles from Town is the limit.'

'What did I tell you?' Grain asked us; and though we did not want to acknowledge his superior acuteness, we had to agree that he had been right. Jokes were made about Ned's plans even in his own hearing. He was asked if he had ordered the rock for that rock garden—rocks were going up every day. Ned would smile at this or simply contradict. Rocks were still cheap if you knew the right man.

Then one afternoon, we had a large party at the golf club. There was a lot of chaff before lunch. Some stockbrokers had joined us in the bar and were in a rollicking mood.

Commodity men like to pretend that stockbrokers are a frivolous race, who never come in contact with the harsh realities of life, say, in the corn or hide markets. This, of course, is itself hardly a serious statement, but it is a well-known fact that brokers do sometimes, on 'change itself, indulge in horse-play such as would be quite out of place among base-metal dealers, and it is true, too, that the brokers had had a bad week, and were looking forward to a worse. They were therefore full of jokes, of the elementary kind we used to make in the trenches of the first war, before a big attack. 'Where's Simpson?' one of them cried. 'The great retirer.'

This was a jobber, and he was answered by a jobber.

'Retired.'

'My God. You don't mean it? Hold me up.'

'For the moment,' said the other, a little dried-up fellow who, they say, has been in the city since the jubilee of '97.

The first one, a bald, fat fellow of about sixty, notoriously facing bankruptcy, tipped the second one's cap off and shouted, 'Forward, the reds.' The rest at once joined in with shouts of 'Up, the Arsenal,' 'Manchester United,' and played football with the cap, so that Ned coming back into the room could not get at the bar.

'Hi,' he called, 'this isn't 'change.'

The fat jobber kicked the cap out of the window and shouted, 'Goal.' There were yells of 'Foul,' 'Offside,' and someone blew a whistle.

Ned had now gone to the bar and was brooding over a double whisky; he growled to me, 'Look at fatty—do you know he's got a heart. He might drop dead any minute.' I said perhaps that was what he wanted.

The crowd, having argued for two minutes and proposed throwing the little old man out of the window to find his cap, closed in for drinks. The bald one, crimson and panting for breath, so that he could hardly speak, slapped Ned hard on the back and croaked, 'The copper king is offended by the dead-end kids.'

'To Hell with copper,' Ned said, 'and you too.'

'That's where we live,' said the mummy, laughing and showing a row of china teeth like tombstones, 'it's been a bit hot this month.'

'Five to one,' gasped the fat man, 'that Ned Simpson is here next year, and still retiring. In quids.'

Ned was astonished. He turned red. 'What the hell do you mean?' Then suddenly understanding the chap, 'Taken. Where's your fiver?' 'No, old boy. Not till you've retired. I mean really retired. Gone. Skedaddled. Vanished. Left the city.'

Ned said to the barman, 'Tom, put it down. If I'm still at Ackbee's at the end of this year, I pay Mr James one pound. And if not, he pays me five.'

We were all quiet now. We realised the possible consequences of such a challenge. Even the jobber was quiet for a moment. But, as I say, he was in a don't-care mood. He didn't cry off. And in fact, he nearly won. It wasn't for another eleven months that Ned left Ackbee's. One of the partners had been ill, and the other got married. In sheer decency, Ned explained, he had to stand by the firm in these difficult circumstances.

But that bet had sunk home. He kept cursing at that jobber, even after he went broke that autumn, and took too much sleeping pill about a week later. He subscribed for the widow, but declared that he would claim the bet from the fund.

Of course he did not do so. But Grain was convinced that he had retired simply to score off that brash jobber. 'And that's pretty stupid—to commit suicide because another suicide has challenged you to do it. Because it is suicide. You'll see. Ned won't last two years in retirement.'

Grain, a bluff, honest fellow without much tact, who, I think, rather despises tact, told Ned himself, after a business lunch at the Savoy, one of those nice expensive lunches you get on an expense account, that he was a fool. He was making the old mistake of all such fools. 'If anyone was ever city, Ned, you're city. Back, belly and sides. The only flowers you really care about are stocks. Your finest view is St Paul's, your native heath is the pavement and your proper atmosphere is smog. Country air and oxygen will rot your lungs in a year, and as for peace and quiet, you will lie awake all night praying to hear one lorry—only one heavy lorry—change gear only once and tell you that there's still some business going on somewhere.'

This was within a week of Ned's retiring date, which was, in any case, fixed and irrevocable. It's not surprising that Ned who loves good eating and drinking, who was savouring his cigar and his

D

brandy, glared furiously at his old friend, during this speech. But all at once, his brow cleared. The cigar, the brandy was having the right effect, the effect it is meant to have at a business lunch. And he answered mildly, 'I'll see you all underground in your smog.'

Actually he stayed three weeks even beyond the date fixed. There was an unexpected crisis. A creditor defaulted. The firm that was building the North German branch had a quarrel with the local council and threw up the contract. The Ackbees, in a panic, appealed to Ned and he went on a tour through all the branches to make a general report on progress and prospects.

But in that same month, Nell found the ideal place. It had not been advertised at all. It belonged to an old lady who was going to retire; that is to say, to live in an hotel. She had vaguely thought of shutting the cottage up and meanwhile gave her housekeeper notice. The housekeeper had a sister in a shoe shop where Nell took Ned's shoes to be mended. And the sister heard her tell the proprietress that perhaps she would not be leaving the neighbourhood that September, she could not find a house in the country.

The sister said nothing till Nell had gone home. She was a woman of slow reactions. But the proprietress happened to meet Nell in a fish shop and told her of the cottage. Nell drove down at once. And the place was exactly what she had, so wildly, demanded. A sober box of a house, built about 1840, like any estate cottage of that time, whitewashed over brick, with the narrow entrance passage thrown into the parlour to make a hall, and a patched-on living-room at one end opening on the garden. A modest house that said only, 'I have no pretensions, I am here to be used—a place simply for shelter and warmth.' A house like a faithful cook.

And all in perfect order, rich old lady's order. The ancient glass-house built against the kitchen wall, so that it needed no heat, had just been completely restored. The old lady did not grow pot plants; but she liked to take breakfast in the sun.

Nell, indeed, hesitated when she found that the magnificent view was not, as the old lady had said, over the green belt, but over a ducal estate, one of the finest in the country, and therefore almost certain to be cut to pieces and turned into building land as soon as the Duke died. And the Duke was eighty.

But Ned, when he saw the garden, the southern slopes, the rich deep earth in the borders, clinched the bargain. Nell was a donkey, he said, she never knew when she was well off. To hell with safe views. No view was safe in this world. Your green belts were fly-traps. The damned old spider of a government was always hovering around ready to tie you up in a fever hospital or an aerodrome at any moment. Governments love to break the law—it makes them feel good—it makes them feel like somebody. And that's what all governments were after.

And he hurled himself into planning, digging, planting before the carpets were down. For that autumn, winter and spring, he and Nell might have retired to Kamchatka for all we knew of them. They did not even fulfil a promise to ask us to stay. They did not answer invitations. Someone saw Nell at *Götterdämmerung*, blissfully asleep in a stall. But I did not set eyes on her for a whole year, not till the next May, when I ran upon her, with sunburnt cheeks and shiny crimson nose, coming out of a store in Victoria Street. She had been inspecting a new motor mower. Nell had been a smart woman, Ned liked her to dress well. Now she was wearing a broken felt hat, a corduroy skirt bagged at the knees, an old tweed coat that might have been Ned's oldest. She looked like someone playing the country duchess, except that she was obviously not only indifferent to her appearance, but to her situation. She was not flaunting country clothes in town, she was treating town as a county capital where one went to buy agricultural machinery.

She beamed upon me and apologized for not answering my last letter. They had been so busy. They simply worked all day and at night they were too tired to write letters. Ned often fell asleep in his chair. What a marvellous life. How wonderfully lucky they had been in that place. It was perfect—perfect. And Ned was planning an orchard. Their own fruit. The latest bush apples. After all, as Ned said, even he could count on ten or fifteen years, so why not grow trees. Even in five they would have apples for market—enough to pay for the garden.

Those were the only times any of us met Nell. And we did not see Ned at all till next winter. He had a touch of arthritis and came up twice a week for massage. Luckily, he said, it was a slack time in the garden. And all his new apple trees were in. He and Nell were having a bit of a rest and, by Jove, they'd earned it. Yes, he would have just time to come in for lunch at my club and meet some of the crowd.

In fact it became a regular thing to lunch with Ned twice a week at the club. Ned obviously looked forward to it. He liked to tell us how wonderful, how exceptional his masseur was, he would shake his head over the price of zinc and copper and let us know in confidence that he had had news of the firm. These young chaps were doing everything wrong, taking fearful chances. He understood they were deep in the red already. Typical of the young—they never follow advice.

And when he had gone, Grain would say, 'He's hankering. He's sick of his damned apple trees, now they're in. Nothing to do but watch 'em grow. The trouble is Ned will never admit he's tired of retiring.'

I admit we did not give much attention to Grain's wisdom. There was a bit of a crisis on. My own firm, which had gone rather too deep into cement just before the '45 election, was now trying to hedge on bricks. And the financial outlook generally did not help. It was distinctly gloomy.

But though things were not much better next winter, we were rather struck to hear that Ned's country place was up for sale. The garden was too big for him in his bad state of health. It appeared that he had been taking a cure, without any good results. Nell suddenly turned up in a small city hotel. She called me and we had a conference, one of those long serious conferences that Nell had always held with Ned's friends, about Ned's troubles. 'It's extraordinary,' she said, 'how he's changed. Lost all his energy—takes no interest even in the new trees. And I can't persuade him to go to a specialist. As for an X-ray—not that it could be anything serious.'

We skirted round this dangerous subject. Of course, I said, X-ray was simply routine nowadays. 'Yes, of course. But if I told Ned that, he'd suspect something. He's so extraordinarily quick, he'd go up in the air. He'd think me crazy.'

It was pathetic to see the big woman's worry. Like all women, in such a place, she was suspecting cancer. Because that was the biggest disaster she could imagine.

But that too was why she could not mention it as a possibility and why I had to suggest every other possibility. Such as suppressed 'flu, a virus infection. I did not know if there was such a thing as suppressed 'flu, but Nell jumped at it. Ned had had several bad colds, and he was, by nature, a very strong man. If he had 'flu, his constitution would certainly suppress it. 'But if you want an X-ray,' I said, 'the best thing would be a painless ulcer.'

'Can you have a painless ulcer?'

'I don't see why not. If your local G.P. agrees. And I think he would.'

'You do notice that Ned is not himself?'

'Yes, I noticed he was a bit piano. But of course Ned has always been up and down. He goes in for everything with so much enthusiasm.'

Nell did not smile. But she warmly agreed that Ned went up and down. She went away clinging to this idea, but determined to arrange the X-ray. In fact, all of us were alarmed. Ned had suddenly become an old man, tottering along on a stick, groaning about the weather.

Nell sold most of her very good and much cherished furniture and took a minute two-room service flat in a vast warren near Richmond. She couldn't afford anything better. The ideal property had fetched a miserable price on re-sale, because the bill-discounter who had bought it—retiring to die there of thrombosis and ulcers—discovered by divination that the roof was full of dry rot. It was a marvel it had not fallen on Ned's head. Old ladies don't worry about roofs, and the surveyor employed by Ned to report on the place had not, apparently, worried much either. He was not buying, and besides, his torch lamp had failed before he reached the roof.

Ned said only, 'My own fault—never trust an expert.' Which meant that it was not his fault. It was the fault of a world run by slap-stick authorities. But Nell was haggard with guilt. 'I really ought to have been more careful—I was too keen to get Ned settled.'

'She was indeed,' Grain said. 'And she's pretty well settled him for good.' Grain did not actually say to Ned, 'I told you so,' but he looked it. Luckily Ned was so depressed, and so ill that he did not even notice his old friend's looks. He would say with amazement, 'Really, I have the damnedest luck—to get ill like this the moment I retire.'

'It's been noticed before,' Grain said.

'What's been noticed?'

'That men who retire get these mysterious illnesses and go to pieces.'

'Oh, that old tale,' Ned said, 'of course they do and serve 'em right if they don't face the facts. A chap wants a purpose in life—a real job.'

We were all silent for a moment, partly appalled by Grain's remark, partly at a loss to retrieve it. And Ned, perhaps noticing the embarrassment and grasping what it meant, said in a mild tone, 'But my illness isn't mysterious, Bob, I've got arthritis. And luckily they're beginning to know something about arthritis. I really think these injections are doing some good.'

In fact, Ned was picking up. Nell had failed to contrive the X-ray, with heavy casualties, but in another month, even she agreed that there was no necessity for it. Ned was putting on weight and his language about the government was so bad that it was an embarrassment to have him at the club. But, of course, he was there almost every day now. He had nothing else to do and nowhere else where he could get what he called sensible conversation.

It was a piece of luck when he met an old school friend in the train, who was a volunteer helper at the European Consolidated Welfare Central Office. It appeared that there was a great rush of work there, on account of earthquakes in Greece and floods in Italy, a wave of refugees in West Berlin and drought in Spain. The job was unpaid, but it was only for two hours a morning. And, of course, you could always stop off if you liked.

Ned, who speaks Spanish and writes German, agreed on these terms, to do some translating three days a week, and went along. And continued to go along, while the rush continued. Four old gentlemen sat in an unheated cellar with rugs round their feet, handling correspondence in German, French, Italian, Finnish, Danish, Turkish, Greek and Armenian.

'It's a scandal,' Ned said, 'but there's no doubt about the rush. And next month I'll have a holiday. Italy this time. Never seen the Italian gardens. Fountains, we've never done enough with fountains in England.'

But next month, by some extraordinary chance, the rush was

worse than ever. There were earthquakes in Italy, a drought in Greece, locusts in Spain, floods in Bavaria, and a new wave of refugees from Czechoslovakia. Ned was in charge of his room, and spent every morning there. He had recruited a lieutenant-colonel of Engineers who understood files, and an ex-Under-Secretary of Mines who knew a little Italian and made excellent coffee. Also they had put down a worn but still entire rubber carpet in the cellar, procured by the colonel from the anteroom of his old mess, by collusion with the quarter-master. All were sworn to secrecy about this racket, but it was a popular story in all the Service clubs.

Ned was getting very lame again, and this attack did not seem to yield to treatment. Nell, bold as a tigress who sees her cub in danger, went to the Ackbee firm and proposed they should take Ned back. She would guarantee that her influence would be decisive with him; he was reading the metal market review every day at breakfast. But the Ackbees were alarmed at the very suggestion. They were polite but they made it plain they had no room for Ned, not at any price. In fact, the young men, having started on their own policy, however reckless, were going to carry it through. They were enjoying themselves, and to hell with experience. If they did crash, well, they would have had a go. And a crash, nowadays, is not the end of everything. It is often the beginning of a merger, of still more expansion.

That was a year ago. Ned is now a head of department at the European Centre. He has all Southern Europe on his shoulders. He catches the 8.10 every morning, which is an hour earlier than his old morning train from Wimbledon, and he limps home, more dead than alive, about seven, to be cherished and nursed into bed, by a wife who dare not open her lips.

His work is exhausting, an endless worry, he curses it. His amateur helpers are keen but not very competent and they insist on taking sudden holidays at short notice. He himself refused a holiday altogether, he said he couldn't afford it. Things would get out of hand and he would never get them straight again.

But Nell and the doctor intervened. He took a fortnight, in June, and made a tour of Italian gardens. I was at Rome with my wife and we arranged a joint visit to Tivoli. But the Simpsons phoned that they would meet us there; they had to make an early start because they were flying to Milan that afternoon.

This is how we saw them from the terrace walking hand-in-hand along the upper alley of fountains. We went down to meet them, and they looked startled as if they had not expected us—probably they had forgotten our arrangement.

'Isn't it marvellous,' my wife said, 'and always more marvellous every time you see it.'

'Yes, yes,' Ned looked round at the landscape spread out below. 'Yes, marvellous.' And you could see him trying to gobble this view, to possess it, in thirty seconds. He looked at his watch, then at the fountains, the hundreds of fountains, running, turning, springing, doing everything with water that can be done, and then again at his watch.

'Oh, Ned—but we needn't go yet,' Nell said.

' 'Fraid so, darling. It's going to be a rush as it is. And you know how you hate a rush.'

They made their apologies and went off, limping together. For Nell, as she supported Ned, was swaying with him. She was clinging too tight. They had only four more days and this was all Ned would get before Christmas. Ned shifted his stick to look at his watch again; and put on the pace. His limp became a kind of grotesque dance, in which Nell was obliged to join.

'It's like a honeymoon,' my wife said.

'Yes, I'm afraid so.'

'That's what I meant. But not everyone has even honeymoons at that age.' And I did not pursue the subject.

Nell does not complain now that she sees only a cross husband all the working year and that her holidays are a fever, she is too pleased to see him well. For he eats like a shark and sleeps like a log.

Grain delights in what he calls his cautionary tale. And we were inclined to agree that he had been wise in foreseeing the event. But somehow it reached Nell and she was very angry. One day in the lady's annexe at the city club she tackled Grain. She said that it was all nonsense about Ned getting bored in his retirement. He'd never been bored in his life. What happened was that he got ill. He got arthritis. Perhaps that was due to a change of address from a centrally-heated house to a rather damp cottage, but it wasn't Ned's fault.

Grain said, 'Yes, of course—it was a special case, not at all typical.' But he said it in such a way as to show us that he was not by any means repentant. And when Nell went away at last, with my wife, to their concert, he explained to us that arthritis can be a nervous disease. But we were silent. Nell, after all, had spoken the truth. Ned is not a man to get bored even with young apple trees. The whole affair, in fact, now we really looked at it, appeared rather complicated and confusing. And the more you thought of Ned and Nell, the more mysterious it became. It was really impossible, we agreed, to come to any definite conclusion.

Is Ned really, as Grain says, so city that he can't live anywhere else? And yet hates the city. Almost all real city men do hate the city. They hate and they love. And then, one might not be bored in retirement, but one might, all the same, suffer some unexpected degeneration, like an old horse which is taken to the next county for a change of grass. But there were thousands of possibilities.

Besides, though Grain treats us all as if he were our oldest friend, we all detest him. He's bluff because he's conceited and he's conceited because he has the cheapest kind of mind, a reach-me-down set of ideas. He is never in doubt about anything because he never sees the insides of anything; he's a closed file. Neither is he the man, like poor old Ned, to take a chance, to bet his life, to follow his dream. In short, as my wife says, he is city to the core. But we have to remember that my wife is prejudiced. She wants me to retire.

GROWING UP

ROBERT QUICK, coming home after a business trip, found a note from his wife. She would be back at four, but the children were in the garden. He tossed down his hat, and still in his dark business suit, which he disliked very much, made at once for the garden.

He had missed his two small girls and looked forward eagerly to their greeting. He had hoped indeed that they might, as often before, have been waiting at the corner of the road, to flag the car, and drive home with him.

The Quicks' garden was a wilderness. Except for a small vegetable patch near the pond, and one bed where Mrs Quick grew flowers for the house, it had not been touched for years. Old apple trees tottered over seedy laurels, unpruned roses. Tall ruins of dahlias and delphiniums hung from broken sticks.

The original excuse for this neglect was that the garden was for the children. They should do what they liked there. The original truth was that neither of the Quicks cared for gardening. Besides, Mrs Quick was too busy with family, council, and parish affairs, Quick with his office, to give time to a hobby that bored them both.

But the excuse had become true. The garden belonged to the children, and Quick was even proud of it. He would boast of his wild garden, so different from any neighbour's shaved grass and combed beds. It had come to seem, for him, a triumph of imagination; and this afternoon, once more, he found it charming in its wildness, an original masterpiece among gardens.

And, in fact, with the sun just warming up in mid-May, slanting steeply past the trees, and making even old weeds shine red and gold, it had the special beauty of untouched woods, where there is still, even among closely farmed lands, a little piece of free nature left, a suggestion of the frontier, primeval forests.

'A bit of real wild country,' thought Quick, a townsman for whom the country was a place for picnics. And he felt at once released, escaped. He shouted, 'Hullo, hullo, children.'

There was no answer. And he stopped, in surprise. Then he thought, 'They've gone to meet me—I've missed them.' And this gave him both pleasure and dismay. The last time the children had missed him, two years before, having gone a mile down the road and lain in ambush behind a hedge, there had been tears. They had resented being searched for, and brought home; they had hated the humiliating failure of their surprise.

But even as he turned back towards the house, and dodged a tree, he caught sight of Jenny, lying on her stomach by the pond, with a book under her nose. Jenny was twelve and had lately taken furiously to reading.

Quick made for the pond with long steps, calling, 'Hullo, hullo, Jenny, hullo,' waving. But Jenny merely turned her head slightly and peered at him through her hair. Then she dropped her cheek on the book as if to say, 'Excuse me, it's really too hot.'

And now he saw Kate, a year older. She was sitting on the swing, leaning sideways against a rope, with her head down, apparently in deep thought. Her bare legs, blotched with mud, lay along the ground, one foot hooked over the other. Her whole air was one of languor and concentration. To her father's 'Hullo,' she answered only in a faint muffled voice, 'Hullo, Daddy.'

'Hullo, Kate.' But he said no more and did not go near. Quick never asked for affection from his girls. He despised fathers who flirted with their daughters, who encouraged them to love. It would have been especially wrong, he thought, with these two. They were naturally impulsive and affectionate—Jenny had moods of passionate devotion, especially in the last months. She was growing up, he thought, more quickly than Kate and she was going to be an exciting woman, strong in all her feelings, intelligent, reflective. 'Well, Jenny,' he said, 'what are you reading now?' But the child answered only by a slight wriggle of her behind.

Quick was amused at his own disappointment. He said to himself, 'Children have no manners but at least they're honest—they never pretend.' He fetched himself a deck chair and the morning paper, which he had hardly looked at before his early start on the road. He would make the best of things. At fifty-two, having lost most of his illusions, he was good at making the best of things. 'It's a lovely day,' he thought, 'and I'm free till Sunday night.' He looked round him as he opened the paper and felt again the pleasure of the garden. What a joy, at last, to be at peace. And the mere presence of the children was a pleasure. Nothing could deprive him of that. He was home again.

Jenny had got up and wandered away among the trees; her legs too were bare and dirty, and her dress had a large green stain at the side. She had been in the pond. And now Kate allowed herself to collapse slowly out of the swing and lay on her back with her hair tousled in the dirt, her arms thrown apart, her small dirty hands with black nails turned palm upwards to the sky. Her cocker bitch, Snort, came loping and sniffing, uttered one short bark and rooted at her mistress' legs. Kate raised one foot and tickled her stomach, then rolled over and buried her face in her arms. When Snort tried to push her nose under Kate's thigh as if to turn her over, she made a half kick and murmured, 'Go away, Snort.'

'Stop it, Snort,' Jenny echoed in the same meditative tone. The sisters adored each other and one always came to the other's help. But Snort only stopped a moment to gaze at Jenny, then tugged at Kate's dress. Kate made another more energetic kick and said, 'Oh, do go away, Snort.'

Jenny stopped in her languid stroll, snatched a bamboo from the border, and hurled it at Snort like a spear.

The bitch, startled, uttered a loud uncertain bark and approached, wagging her behind so vigorously that she curled her body sideways at each wag. She was not sure if this was a new game, or if she had committed some grave crime. Jenny gave a yell and rushed at her. She fled yelping. At once Kate jumped up, seized another bamboo and threw it, shouting, 'Tiger, tiger.'

The two children dashed after the bitch, laughing, bumping together, falling over each other and snatching up anything they could find to throw at the fugitive, pebbles, dead daffodils, bits of flower-pots, lumps of earth. Snort, horrified, overwhelmed, dodged to and fro, barked hysterically, crazily, wagged her tail in desperate submission; finally put it between her legs and crept whining between a broken shed and the wall.

Robert was shocked. He was fond of the sentimental foolish Snort, and he saw her acute misery. He called to the children urgently, 'Hi, Jenny—don't do that. Don't do that, Kate. She's frightened—you might put her eye out. Hi, stop—stop.'

This last cry expressed real indignation. Jenny had got hold of a rake and was trying to hook Snort by the collar. Robert began to struggle out of his chair. But suddenly Kate turned round, aimed a pea-stick at him and shouted at the top of her voice, 'Yield, Paleface.' Jenny at once turned and cried, 'Yes, yes—Paleface, yield.' She burst into a shout of laughter and could not speak, but rushed at the man with the rake carried like a lance.

The two girls, staggering with laughter, threw themselves upon their father. 'Paleface—Paleface Robbie. Kill him—scalp him. Torture him.'

They tore at the man and suddenly he was frightened. It seemed to him that both the children, usually so gentle, so affectionate, had gone completely mad, vindictive. They were hurting him, and he did not know how to defend himself without hurting them, without breaking their skinny bones, which seemed as fragile as a bird's legs. He dared not even push too hard against the thin ribs which seemed to bend under his hand. Snort, suddenly recovering confidence, rushed barking from cover and seized this new victim by the sleeve, grunting and tugging.

'Hi,' he shouted, trying to catch at the bitch. 'Call her off, Kate. Don't, don't, children.' But they battered at him, Kate was jumping on his stomach, Jenny had seized him by the collar as if to strangle him. Her face, close to his own, was that of a homicidal maniac; her eyes were wide and glaring, her lips were curled back to show all her teeth. And he was really strangling. He made a violent effort to throw the child off, but her hands were firmly twined in his collar. He felt his ears sing. Then suddenly the chair gave way—all three fell with a crash. Snort, startled, and perhaps pinched, gave a yelp, and snapped at the man's face.

Kate was lying across his legs, Jenny on his chest; she still held his collar in both hands. But now, gazing down at him, her expression changed. She cried, 'Oh, she's bitten you. Look, Kate.' Kate, rolling off his legs, came to her knees. 'So she has, bad Snort.'

The girls were still panting, flushed, struggling with laughter. But

Jenny reproached her sister, 'It's not a joke. It might be poisoned.'

'I know,' Kate was indignant. But burst out again into helpless giggles.

Robert picked himself up and dusted his coat. He did not utter any reproaches. He avoided even looking at the girls in case they should see his anger and surprise. He was deeply shocked. He could not forget Jenny's face, crazy, murderous; he thought, 'Not much affection there—she wanted to hurt. It was as if she hated me.'

It seemed to him that something new had broken into his old simple and happy relation with his daughters; that they had suddenly receded from him into a world of their own in which he had no standing, a primitive, brutal world.

He straightened his tie. Kate had disappeared; Jenny was gazing at his forehead and trying to suppress her own giggles. But when he turned away, she caught his arm, 'Oh Daddy, where are you going?'

'To meet your mother—she must be on her way.'

'Oh, but you can't go like that—we've got to wash your bite.'

'That's all right, Jenny. It doesn't matter.'

'But Kate is getting the water—and it might be quite bad.'

And now, Kate, coming from the kitchen with a bowl of water, called out indignantly, 'Sit down, Daddy—sit down—how dare you get up.'

She was playing the stern nurse. And in fact, Robert, though still in a mood of disgust, found himself obliged to submit to this new game. At least it was more like a game. It was not murderous. And a man so plump and bald could not allow himself even to appear upset by the roughness of children. Even though the children would not understand why he was upset, why he was shocked.

'Sit down at once, man,' Jenny said. 'Kate, put up the chair.'

Kate put up the chair, the two girls made him sit down, washed the cut, painted it with iodine, stuck a piece of plaster on it. Mrs Quick, handsome, rosy, good-natured, practical, arrived in the middle of this ceremony, with her friend Jane Martin, Chairman of the Welfare Committee. Both were much amused by the scene, and the history of the afternoon. Their air said plainly to Robert, 'All you children—amusing yourselves while we run the world.'

Kate and Jenny were sent to wash and change their dirty frocks. The committee was coming to tea. And at tea, the two girls, dressed in smart clean frocks, handed round cake and bread and butter with demure and reserved looks. They knew how to behave at tea, at a party. They were enjoying the dignity of their own performance. Their eyes passed over their father as if he did not exist, or rather as if he existed only as another guest, to be waited on.

And now, seeking as it were a new if lower level of security, of resignation, he said to himself, 'Heavens, but what did I expect? In a year or two more I shan't count at all. Young men will come prowling, like the dogs after Snort—I shall be an old buffer, useful only to pay bills.'

The ladies were talking together about a case—the case of a boy of fourteen, a nice respectable boy, most regular at Sunday school, who had suddenly robbed his mother's till and gone off in a stolen car. Jenny, seated at her mother's feet, was listening intently, Kate was feeding chocolate roll to Snort, and tickling her chin.

Quick felt all at once a sense of stuffiness. He wanted urgently to get away, to escape. Yes, he needed some male society. He would go to the club. Probably no one would be there but the card-room crowd, and he could not bear cards. But he might find old Wilkins in the billiard room. Wilkins at seventy was a crashing, a dreary bore, who spent half his life at the club; who was always telling you how he had foreseen the slump, and how clever he was at investing his money. What good was money to old Wilkins? But, Quick thought, he could get up a game with Wilkins, pass an hour or two with him, till dinner-time, even dine with him. He could phone his wife. She would not mind. She rather liked a free evening for her various accounts. And he need not go home till the children were in bed.

And when, after tea, the committee members pulled out their agenda, he stole away. Suddenly, as he turned by the corner house, skirting its front garden wall, he heard running steps and a breathless call. He turned, it was Jenny. She arrived, panting, holding herself by the chest. 'Oh, I couldn't catch you.'

'What is it now, Jenny?'

'I wanted to look—at the cut.'

Robert began to stoop. But she cried, 'No, I'll get on the wall. Put me up.'

He lifted her on the garden wall which made her about a foot taller than himself. Having reached this superior position, she poked the plaster.

'I just wanted to make sure it was sticking. Yes, it's all right.'

She looked down at him with an expression he did not recognise. What was the game, medical, maternal? Was she going to laugh? But the child frowned. She was also struck by something new and unexpected.

Then she tossed back her hair. 'Good-bye.' She jumped down and ran off. The man walked slowly towards the club. 'No,' he thought, 'not quite a game—not for half a second. She's growing up—and so am I.'

A HOT DAY

MOTHER, father, a small boy, aged four, are walking along the road. The little boy has to trot to keep up. At last he cries out, 'Oh Mummy, I'm so thirsty.' The mother, plump, red, sweating freely, answers patiently, 'But, darling, you just had a drink.' The father is a thin, sad little man. He protests mildly, 'Well, Nelly—he really didn't take much for tea.'

'Are we going to catch that bus or aren't we?'

'We got ten minutes.'

'Oh, all right—you always give way to Tom—that's why he acts up like this with you.'

They go into a roadside café and Tom is given a lemonade with a straw. He gazes at the straw. 'What a funny straw—it's pink.'

'Yes, it's a pink straw—now drink up, my dear.'

'But, Daddy—is it a real straw?'

'Yes, Tommy. Well, no, not exactly. It's made of something—paper.'

Tom gazes at this surprising straw and laughs, 'What, paper?'

'Yes, Tommy, paper. With something on it—wax or something. Now drink up, old man.'

Tom gazes at the straw and pinches it to see how strong it is. 'It's quite strong, Daddy, isn't it?'

'Yes. Go on, Tommy. We haven't time to waste.'

Tom pinches the straw again and then blows down it to see if it still works. This makes bubbles in his glass and he calls on his father to admire. He can be sure of his father's admiration.

The mother mops her face and says in a resigned voice, 'There, I told you it was all nonsense about him being thirsty.'

'But I *am* thirsty,' Tom says.

'Then why aren't you drinking?'

Tom blows more bubbles. The bus passes; it will go to the next village, turn round and come back on the upper road. They have fifteen minutes to walk to the next stopping place.

The mother exclaims, 'Oh, so you're going to play with it,' and takes the glass away. Tom, subdued and guilty, says, 'May I keep the straw?'

The father takes the straw and gives it to him. They set out along the road. Tom carries the straw carefully and observes it from end to end. This causes him to fall behind. And then he is seized with a strange discomfort which causes him to forget the straw. It crumples in his hand. He drops it.

It is a mile to the bus stop and the parents call to him.

'Come on, Tommy dear.'

'Don't drag, Tom.'

Tom now identifies his new discomfort and says, 'I'm so thirsty.'

And indeed he has a fearful, an overwhelming thirst. His throat is burning.

'Come on, do.'

'I'm so thirsty, Mum.'

The mother finally loses her temper and jerks his arm. 'That's enough of you today—do you want me to smack you?'

Tom breaks into tears and wails, 'But I *am* thirsty—I'm too thirsty.'

He sits down in the road. He's in despair. What can he do if people won't believe him. He'd rather die than move another step.

YOU'RE ONLY YOUNG ONCE

I T was fair time—about four o'clock on a hot September day, and warming up every minute. In the market-place twenty round-abouts were blasting out different tunes, dust rose sixty feet in the air like a thick yellow smoke, so that the crowd seemed to be smouldering with heat and excitement. A continual tremor passed through it as through a banked-down fire. At first glance it was a dark and impacted crowd—country people in their Sunday clothes massed together before the booths. But as you watched, the mass was agitated, as by a sudden flame among its ashes, and half a dozen girls or youths came bursting through. Everywhere these groups of youngsters, laughing, shouting at each other, were pushing through the crowds, choosing the densest and most resistant for each charge.

And the heavy mothers of families, the sweating farm labourers, gave way before them without change of expression. Even by the church at the far end of the fair, behind the market cross, traditional resting place, the young were tacitly allowed their privilege of Fair Day.

In the alley between church and graveyard where low walls afforded seats for worn-out parents and exhausted old people, two small, very dirty boys were blowing whistles with all their might; it was obvious in the way they trampled over the old people's feet and cannoned into their knees, that they were deliberately making nuisances of themselves. And the grandmothers and grandfathers seated along the wall looked at the boys with resignation and drew back their trampled feet, hastily, painfully, but without protest. The gipsy woman, near the church porch, who through a narrow open-ing about three inches long, in her black bodice, was nursing her baby, paid no attention to them. When at last she was bumped into, indeed, she gave them a ferocious glance. But she did not speak, she only moved her elbow to protect the baby's head and followed the pair with her furious eyes. Her gipsy rage against all the world accepted a blow, on this day, from children.

All these resigned critical faces swivelled again when three girls came rushing in from the side—three girls of about sixteen, in frocks cut far down on bare shoulders, with bright-painted lips and towers of hair, curled like Indian temples.

They were linked together in chain, and looking back over their shoulders as if pursued. All wore pink paper hats labelled on the crown in large black letters, 'KISS ME QUICK.' A little blonde who brought up the tail, very young, with a short pug nose and immense protruding lips, carried also on her braced-up breasts, round as cricket balls, a blue sash from shoulder to waist, with the legend in gold 'LOVE ME.'

They were all talking at once between shrieks of laughter, and in their headlong rush they nearly fell over a middle-aged man in brown tweeds and labourer's boots who was holding out a small girl over the gutter. He hastily moved out of their way, but though they had not even glanced at him, they were checked, and suddenly, as by a common inspiration, they sat down on the wall, and began to fan themselves, panting and crying, 'Ooh, isn't it hot,' 'Ooh, I'm thirsty.'

They preened themselves like sparrows after a dust bath and sang out their words to be heard. It was a performance, and as they now let their defiant eyes pass carelessly over their neighbours, they acted disdain and surprise.

'Ooh,' cried the blonde, at the top of her voice, 'where've we got to?'

All three broke into wild giggles and clung together. The old people, the gipsy, the row of tired middle-aged women, the farm labourer waiting patiently for the child to finish, gazed at them in a trance of patience. So they might have looked at a house on fire or a flooded meadow.

The blonde darted off and returned with three large ices in cardboard buckets; the three girls began carefully and delicately, with their wooden spoons, to eat their ices in the smallest possible scrapings. The contrast between the careful precision of these movements and the animation of their bodies, their wriggles and wagglings as they talked, perpetually pressing closer and emphasising their words with nods, tosses of their heads, reminded one of kittens or puppies at play.

The discussion was loud—it was part of the performance, meant to shock, impress, defy. The leader, a dark-haired girl, broad-chested, short-necked, with bare legs, scorched pink in the sun, was telling some story. 'So she said to me, it's not good enough. And I said to her, it's good enough for me. Well, I ask you, if you're going with a boy——'

The other two agreed so vigorously that the rest of the story was drowned in comments and illustrations.

Suddenly four youths appeared, and came along the alley. The first, in a bright blue suit, with a red rose in his button-hole, a tickler in his right hand, and a paper policeman's helmet cocked over his right eye, was swaggering in every joint. His head rocked, his elbows jerked, his legs struck out sideways, and at the same time, his face wore an expression of triumphant delight. It was just such an expression as one sees upon some hero of the day, who, after receptions, cheers, flags, deputations, and a ceremonial lunch, comes down into the street between rows of admirers, and reveals on his face, flushed with adulation and champagne, a certain vain, innocent, undisciplined expression which says plainly, 'Yes, I am a great man, a perfect hero, and how nice that is.' You see that he has forgotten all reserve, all precaution, he is feeling how nice everyone is, how good, how kind, what a nice world it is after all, where no one is ashamed of the finest, the noblest emotions, and no hero need be ashamed of admitting to heroism.

And just as behind such tennis or film star, one sees two or three enthusiasts who, having broken through the police cordon and eluded the secretaries, the organisers, crowd on the great man's heels, beaming on him from ear to ear with a fascinated, astonished joy, so after this champion in the blue suit came three other youths, literally staggering with admiration. They were holding each other by the arms, for support, reeling with laughter, and between these fits, uttering loud cries, 'Good old Bert.'

They brushed past the gipsy, who again moved her elbow to protect her baby, and glared; they bumped into the farm labourer, who was buttoning up his little girl's pants, and he said 'Hi!' in a fierce tone; they received from the old couple next door that calm level stare with which responsible persons estimate the degrees of hysteria.

The 'Hi' of the labourer was not indignant, it was merely a warning; the stare of the old couple was no less resigned than before; the grandmothers and grandfathers removed their feet in silence. But for some reason, the youths were disconcerted by their reception in this backwater. Apparently they had expected appreciation. The hero, at the labourer's shout, visibly jumped, and gave him a surprised nervous glance—his fans, even while they staggered against the gipsy's knees, turned away their faces from her black glare. Their shouts became affected, self-conscious, and much louder. The joyful parade became an invasion as of enemy troops.

Also it slowed down. The leader, coming past the church door and finding himself close to the end of the alley, halted. He perceived that merely to go away would give the effect of escape, of humiliating flight.

He looked round and saw just at his elbow the three kiss-me girls. He struck a gallant attitude before them; the three followers, crowding together, came to a halt and gazed at him with broad grins of anticipation.

The girls were still deep in their conversation. The little blonde at the far end, wooden spoon in hand, looked up at the youth with vague enquiry.

He touched her hat with his tickler, and stooping down with a swaggering bow, gave her a loud kiss. The girl, leaving her spoon in the ice-cream, jumped up and dealt him a slap in the face, so well-aimed, so expert, that it cracked like a laundry-bat on wet linen. It caused the policeman's helmet to fly into the air and sail into the graveyard, where it lay sideways on a tomb.

The three admirers took a step back; the hero, astonished, with one crimson cheek, and looking strangely diminished by the loss of his helmet, made a desperate, a swaggering attempt to carry the thing off. He cried loudly, 'Here—what's this?' and tried to snatch the girl's hat.

She, holding her ice-cream sideways at the full stretch of her left arm, flew at him, smacking him on each cheek in turn, first with the palm, then with the knuckles of her right hand, in a succession of stinging blows that went off like rapid fire. He cringed down, and she gave him a kick, delivered with the flat of her high-heeled shoe, that sent him whirling into the crowd beyond. The three followers, crouching, covering their heads with their hands, and yelling in terror that was not altogether mock, vaulted over the wall and scattered among the graves.

The blonde had already returned to her place. She inspected the inside of her ice-cream barrel which she had so skilfully preserved, spoon and all, unspilt, scraped it round, and crooking her little finger in a refined movement, put it between her lips. Her eyes were already fixed eagerly on her companions, who had not so much as looked up during the battle. Neither could lose a chance of breaking in with her own latest triumph over the mysterious, the powerful she. 'Yes, and what I said to her——' 'Well, I said if she's going to make all that trouble——' 'And then she had the nerve——'

The blonde dived forward, nose to nose. 'You know what she said to me——' and the three voices rose louder and louder in a dramatic chorus, 'She—she—she——'

A PRIVATE GHOST

As soon as he waked in the morning, Peter, aged eight, felt a difference. Then he remembered that his father and mother were away—they had gone to Dublin very suddenly for the week-end—and that Grand-aunt was also away. His grand-aunt lived close by, and always when his parents had been away she had come to stay and watch over the children. But now she was in a Dublin hospital. No one had come to hear his prayers last night. This was why, he thought, he felt a difference.

His sister Noni, in the next bed, did not notice a difference. As soon as she waked, she proposed to come into his bed, as usual; but he refused her firmly. He was devoted to Noni, and she adored him, but at the moment he did not want adoration. He was preoccupied, listening intently to the household. Noni at six was too young to notice the difference.

Certainly, the household *was* different. It was so different that he could hardly recognise it. The cat next door in the day nursery was miaowing loudly in a despairing voice; it had not been let out yet. Down in the kitchen, below the night-nursery window, someone with a very deep hoarse voice, some old beggar, perhaps, was talking to a dog. And this strange dog was padding round the floor, rattling its claws on the linoleum, and uttering now and then a little whine.

What was stranger still on this strange day was that when Annie the nurse came in five minutes later to get the children up, Lizzie the housemaid came with her. Lizzie and Annie had not been speaking for weeks past. But now they came in laughing, and Lizzie whispered something. Then she ran out of the nursery and shouted down the well of the stairs to the cook, 'I told Annie on you, Maggie.' Even her voice was a new voice, more like Maggie's when she was drunk. But Lizzie didn't drink.

Breakfast in the day nursery was delayed, and Noni grew impatient. She climbed into her chair and beat on the table with a spoon. Annie, however, was down in the kitchen telling some tale to the beggar, and what was still queerer, she had left the nursery doors wide open. The nurseries, usually so jealously kept aloof, now seemed as public as the back stairs, through which all these peculiar noises were piped direct to the children. Peter sat at the table listening. He frowned. He did not like the difference in the house. He felt a certain nervousness, and he also felt a certain responsibility, but for what, he did not know.

Suddenly he took the spoon out of Noni's hand and said, 'Don't do that—it's rude.' This was unexpected to Noni. Peter was usually kind to her. She flushed with pain and surprise. Her forehead crinkled and the corners of her mouth turned down; she was about to cry. But Peter's glance daunted her. He said severely, 'You're not a baby any more.'

Lizzie came in again when Annie brought the tray. The two were giggling together again at something that had happened in the kitchen. And then Lizzie shouted from the window at Mrs Conor, the gardener's wife, slopping past in the rain with a sack over her head and her skirt turned up to the knees. Mrs Conor answered with cheerful yells, and soon she, too, came up to the nursery. She spent the whole morning there, drinking tea and telling stories that made the usually dignified Annie explode through her nose with protesting cries, 'Oh, Mrs Conor, you're killing me!'

Mrs Conor stayed all day. After the children's dinner, at noon, all the staff gathered in the day nursery, and there was great laughter when Lizzie was persuaded to ride the rocking-horse—not that Lizzie needed much persuading. She was a pale, high-breasted girl, with big grey eyes and a little round mouth, who was dancing mad, and even when the family were there she would go bouncing through the rooms as if she were late for a ball. When she was on the horse, she laughed so much that she nearly fell off. Then Maggie pushed the horse to make it rock harder, and Lizzie gave a shriek like an engine and began to be angry. But when they all laughed she stopped being angry and proposed a dance.

So Annie played the gramophone. They did not dance, however; they were tired of the idea already. And they began to make much of the children. All of them were devoted to Peter and Noni, and now in the exuberance of their holiday, they were demonstrative, they competed in affection. Lizzie tickled Noni till she laughed herself crimson, and this almost provoked a scene. For Annie, the nurse, taken suddenly jealous, snatched the child away and said, 'That's enough.' Lizzie turned upon her and laughed in her nose, saying, 'You, Annie——' At that moment, Mrs Conor, the hanger-on, who was not quite of the inner household but earned her cups of tea by her good stories and her flattery, made a quick diversion. She lifted Peter to her lap and stroked his hair, which was as pale as flax. 'Oh, the pet—the spit of his grandda. And do you know, my prince, that I've seen him? I've seen your grandda with my own eyes.'

The maids gazed at her. Annie's breast was still heaving, and Lizzie's little mouth was still pushed out in scorn, but they were attentive. They knew that Mrs Conor had some trick in hand.

'Come now, Mrs Conor,' said Annie in her downright way. 'The old master is dead this forty years.'

'Wasn't that the one that drowned himself in the river?' Lizzie asked.

'Forty-three years,' said Mrs Conor, 'and that was before I was born, but I've seen him.' And looking at the child, she said to him, 'And how do you think that was, my pet? How do you think I saw him that was dead?' Peter gazed earnestly at Mrs Conor, and Noni, who had come to lean against her brother, made big eyes round his arm. They knew the question was not meant to be answered; it was simply an introduction to Mrs Conor's story. 'It was when I was eight—just your age, my pet—that I saw him walk. He was all in white, and while he walked he kept shaking his hands and the water was dripping from him. And, bless you, I didn't know who he was then, or what it meant. But I was frightened, and I ran to my mother, and it was then she told me about the old master. And she said if I was to see him again I must cross myself.'

There was a short silence. All four of the servants were gazing at the two children to see the effect of this tale.

'And they say,' said Mrs Conor, 'they say that it's only a child has ever seen the old master walk.'

'Was it a ghost?' Noni asked in a loud voice.

'Yes, indeed. You wouldn't see him living when he w
would you, pet?'

'Ghosts are only stories,' Noni said. 'Pappy told me.'

Peter opened his mouth to say the same thing. But as he glanced
up he caught the maids' eyes fixed upon him, and suddenly he was
not so sure that they were playing a trick upon him. When Annie
or Maggie codded him about potatoes that grew on trees or the
man in the moon, they had a laugh in them. They might look grave,
but you could feel the laugh. But now there was no laugh, and their
grave faces had a different gravity. All at once, he was not so confident of his father's assurances, even about ghosts. Did his father
know that things could be so different at home when he was away?

'There aren't such things,' Noni said indignantly. But Peter looked
at her severely, and she turned red.

'Well, now,' Mrs Conor said, 'do you tell me I'm telling you lies?'

The children looked at her, and Peter said, 'Grandda fell in when
he was fishing.'

'I wouldn't know that,' Mrs Conor said. 'But if he only fell in,
why would he walk?'

'Why, indeed?' Lizzie said. 'And why only for children?'

'Well now,' Mrs Conor said, 'I wouldn't know that either, but
isn't it the same with the fairies? They say it's only children and
naturals can see the wee folk. And so you never saw the like of him,
Master Peter?'

Peter shook his head, and Mrs Conor looked round at her
audience. 'If anyone were to see the old master, it would be this one
that's so like him.' And suddenly she winked. Mrs Conor was a
good winker; she could close either eye without the slightest change
of expression on the other side of her face. That's why Peter saw
only her grave good-natured countenance, while Maggie and Lizzie
and Annie had a glimpse of enormous slyness. Mrs Conor once more
turned her grave mild face towards Peter. 'Yes, my dear, you would
be the one, for aren't you the spit of him? It's a wonder that you
haven't seen him yet, for it's my belief he crosses that back-yard
every day of the week on his way from the water to the cemetery.'

'What, Mrs Conor?' Lizzie said. 'Every day of the week? I
wouldn't like to think that.'

'No, indeed,' said Maggie, coming into the game. Maggie was old and tired, and slow in her mind, but still she was ready to take her part in a good game. 'No, indeed,' she said. 'Why, I'd be afraid to go into the yard if I thought that.'

'But then you wouldn't see him,' Annie said. 'It would be only Master Peter here that would see him.'

'It was about six o'clock in the evening that I saw him,' said Mrs Conor. 'And they said that was the time that he went into the water.'

There was another long pause, and then Lizzie said, 'Well now, I wonder, would Master Peter see him if he looked at six o'clock?'

'It'd be a bit dark at six,' Maggie said.

'It'd have to be,' said Mrs Conor. 'You don't think that ghosts will walk in daylight? But there, I'm not saying that Master Peter would see his grandda on any day of the week, dark as it might be.'

'No,' Maggie said. 'It's only that he might take a look some evening if he wouldn't be afraid.'

'It's well he might be,' Lizzie said. She gave a deep sigh and gazed into the air with her big grey eyes, imagining the terror of ghosts.

'He would not!' Annie cried. 'Would you, my darling? Would you now?'

Peter made no answer to this. He understood the challenge. He had been challenged before, and usually in a trick, as when Maggie had dared him to open a parcel, which, so she said, might have a bomb in it, and it had let out a jumping jack, which hit him on the nose. But he had not really believed that there would be a bomb in a parcel. Who would put bombs in parcels? Ghosts were quite another thing. And it was true that his grandfather had died young, and tragically.

'Oh, he's the brave boy always,' Mrs Conor said, and Maggie came in hastily, 'Sure. There never was any of the family afraid of anything.'

'Would you look for your grandda?' Lizzie asked, staring at the boy with her big eyes.

Peter, staring back and wondering at this strange excited Lizzie, answered, 'You mean in the yard?'

'You wouldn't have to go in the yard,' said Mrs Conor. 'You could see from the kitchen window. Aye, it would be better from the window.'

'And what better day than today, when themselves is out of it?' Lizzie said.

'It's stopped raining,' Peter said, as if he had not noticed Lizzie's suggestion. 'Can I go to Willy?' Willy was the garden boy, a close friend of Peter's, but Annie did not always approve of their meetings which, she considered, were often too exciting for Peter and kept him wakeful at night.

'There now,' Lizzie muttered. 'I knew he'd get out of it.'

'Of course you can go to Willy,' Mrs Conor said quickly. 'He'd be in the cabbages this minute. And I tell you, why wouldn't ye have supper in the kitchen, too—for a treat? I'm sure Annie wouldn't mind just for today.'

'Oh, yes!' cried Noni. 'Oh, yes, yes please.'

And even Peter, disturbed as he was by the confusion in the house, was pleased by this suggestion. 'Oh, do, Annie. I'd like that very much,' he said,

'Sure, my pet,' Annie said.

'Indeed, and ye shall,' said Maggie, winking at Mrs Conor, but so clumsily that Noni noticed and stared at her eye. Maggie was very red, and seemed about to burst.

'And as for ghosts, Miss Noni,' said Mrs Conor, 'sure your pappy may be right after all. Why, I wouldn't be too sure myself. It's so long since I saw one that indeed your grandda mightn't have been one at all. There now, Maggie, don't I hear your kettle?' And the four rushed suddenly out of the room so violently that they jammed on the narrow back stairs and Lizzie gave a squeak of laughter. Then, below, the kitchen door banged shut behind them.

Peter paid no more attention to their nonsense. He was too pleased with himself for eluding Mrs Conor's embarrassing proposal. Joyfully he hurried off to see Willy in the garden. He even allowed Noni to take his hand and go with him, stipulating only that she should not speak to Willy.

Noni was perfectly satisfied to be beside her darling and listen to his conversation with Willy, while the party moved from the cabbages to the byre, the byre to the pigsty, the pigsty to the pump, where Willy completed his last duty by filling the house tanks, so that, as he said thoughtfully, 'You wains can have your baths the night.'

Peter provided most of the talk, giving, for instance, a full account of the mammoth found in Russia under the ice and explaining that whales were really animals, and had milk. He hadn't had so good a day with Willy for a week, and he started back to the kitchen in the highest spirits. The reason the children loved supper in the kitchen was that the maids, and especially Lizzie, were such good company with their gossip and their jokes. They were always playing some trick on each other and laughing. Last time, Lizzie had pulled Annie's chair away and caused her to sit down hard on the floor. The children had laughed until they could not eat, and Lizzie herself had had to say that they must behave themselves better or they would not be asked again.

They were laughing in recollection of this performance when they came into the kitchen. But what a surprise! There was no one there but old Maggie, and the table was not by the stove, but pushed into the window embrasure, close against the window itself. And when Maggie had placed them in their chairs, at opposite ends of the table, she made for the door.

'Oh, Maggie,' Noni wailed, 'I want to have supper with you all.' But Maggie muttered something about the storeroom, and went out, shutting the door after her.

Almost at the same moment, there was a moaning cry from the yard, and Peter, who had been put facing the yard gate that led from the front lawn and the river, looked up and saw the ghost. It was just coming through the gate.

The lamp in the kitchen was turned low, and the yard was lighted only by the sky, which was a pale-green colour. The yard, surrounded by barns and stables, by the byre and garage, all in dark-reddish bricks, was paved with dark-blue cinders; these dark buildings and the dark cinders soaked up the light from above. The air in the yard seemed to be without light, so that the whiteness of the ghost was as bright as a swan's feathers on a dark evening. The ghost was all in white; a short thick figure in a sheet, which was pulled over its forehead in front, and which covered its body and fell to the ground so that the creature did not seem to have feet.

When it passed the gardener's shed, it turned towards the kitchen window. And now Peter could see, under the white fold of the sheet, a face as white, except that its eyes were like enormous black holes, and its mouth was grey. This mouth was moving all the time as if crying.

Peter was fixed in such fear, such horror, that he could not take his eyes off this face with its weeping mouth. He got down slowly from his chair and retreated a pace backwards; but this brought him up against the end of the embrasure. And he stood there, fixed, helpless, unable to move, speak, or think.

'What are you doing, Peter?' Noni said, surprised at his getting down from his chair. Then the ghost moaned again, more loudly. Noni looked round, gave a shriek, and ran to her brother. Peter held her tight and drew her to one side—she hid her face against his ribs.

The ghost was now four or five yards from the window. Peter could see long leaves of river weed glistening wet on its shoulders and the water pouring down the white folds to the ground—the eyes were shining palely in the middle of their great black holes. It was staring at him and shaking its hands all the time as if in grief. He thought, 'It's crying—it wants to tell me something.' He was shivering in terror that the creature would speak to him, and yet he could not run away. He felt he had to wait for the message.

The ghost took one more step towards him and gave another long deep heartbreaking moan. Noni gripped Peter convulsively and uttered shriek after shriek. But the ghost's next move was to its right. With a wavering, wobbling motion, it glided slowly towards the back corner of the house, where it suddenly vanished behind the porch of the scullery.

Almost at the same moment, Annie, Lizzie, and Maggie burst into the kitchen. Peter, mechanically patting and stroking Noni, gazed at them with wide vague eyes as if he had forgotten their existence. Noni stopped screaming and ran towards Annie. 'It came —it came—we saw it!' she cried. But the maids were staring at Peter, with eyes nearly as wide as his own—half curious, half alarmed at the child's fearfully white face and crazy expression.

'What—what happened then?' said Annie in a stammering voice.

And now Mrs Conor, rather breathless, came darting into the kitchen from the scullery. She still had some burnt cork under her right eye, but she covered it with her hand, so that the children could not see it. 'What's wrong?' she said. 'Was that Miss Noni I heard?'

'They saw him, Mrs Conor!' Lizzie exclaimed. 'They saw the old master in the yard—did you ever hear the like of that?'

Peter came to himself, walked out of his corner, and took Noni's hand. 'It was nothing,' he said. And his face turned very red.

'A ghost, nothing?' said Mrs Conor. 'Weren't you afeared?'

'We didn't see anything,' he said. 'It was only Noni being silly. You didn't see anything, did you, Noni?'

Noni stared at him. Then she slowly shook her head. She didn't know why Peter was telling this enormous lie, but she was glad to support him.

He then walked her slowly and with great dignity towards the hall door. The maids parted and let him go. Even Mrs Conor was taken aback by this strangely aloof Peter. He led Noni through the hall into the drawing-room. He seldom went to the drawing-room except on state occasions, in his best clothes. For him, it was a place of ceremony, where grown-up persons of distinction conferred together in quiet tones and a reserved manner upon important matters—births, deaths, marriages, money, family affairs.

As soon as they entered the room, Noni protested that it was a ghost. 'I *saw* it.' Peter shut the door firmly behind them and cut off the excited chatter of the maids. Then he led Noni to the middle of the carpet and explained to her, kindly but gravely, 'Yes, it was grandpapa. But don't talk to them about it. They'd only laugh and he's our own grandpapa.'

THE BREAKOUT

TOM SPONSON, at fifty-three, was a thoroughly successful man. He had worked up a first-class business, married a charming wife, and built himself a good house in the London suburbs that was neither so modern as to be pretentious nor so conventional as to be dull. He had good taste. His son, Bob, nineteen, was doing well at Oxford; his daughter, April, aged sixteen, who was at a good school, had no wish to use make-up, to wear low frocks, or to flirt. She still regarded herself as too young for these trifling amusements. Yet she was gay, affectionate, and thoroughly enjoyed life. All the same, for some time Tom had been aware that he was working very hard for very little. His wife, Louie, gave him a peck in the morning when he left for the office and, if she were not at a party, a peck in the evening when he came home. And it was obvious that her life was completely filled with the children, with her clothes, with keeping her figure slim, with keeping the house clean and smart, with her charities, her bridge, her tennis, her friends, and her parties.

The children were even more preoccupied—the boy with his own work and his own friends, the girl with hers. They were polite to Tom, but if he came into the room when they were entertaining a friend, there was at once a feeling of constraint. Even if they were alone together, he perceived that when he came upon them they were slightly embarrassed, and changed the subject of their conversation, whatever it was. Yet they did not seem to do this when they were with their mother. He would find them all three, for instance, laughing at something and when he came in they would stop laughing and gaze at him as if he had shot up through the floor. In fact, if he asked what the joke was his wife would say, 'You wouldn't understand' or 'Nothing' or 'I'll tell you afterwards,' but she never did tell him afterwards; she would put him off with some remark like, 'Oh, it's perfectly silly, about something April said.'

He said to himself, 'It isn't only that they don't need me, but I'm a nuisance to them. I'm in the way. I'm superfluous.' One morning when he was just going to get into his car and his wife had come out to say good-bye, he suddenly made an excuse, saying, 'Just a moment, I've left a letter,' and went back to his desk, and then dashed out to the car and drove off, pretending to forget that good-bye had not been said.

Immediately he felt that he could not stand any more of this existence; it was nonsense. It was not as though his wife and children were depending any more on the business; he could sell it to a combine tomorrow, and it would support all of them in comfort. Actually he would miss the business; it was his chief interest. But if he had to give it up for the sake of freedom, of a break in this senseless life, he could do even that. Yes, joyfully.

As he circled Trafalgar Square, that is to say, as he came within the last few hundred yards from his office, he told himself that he could not go on. It was as though that moment when he dodged the customary good-bye had broken a contact. The conveyor belt on which his life had been caught up had stopped as if at a short circuit, a break in a switch. No, he could not go on. So, instead of turning down the Strand out of the Square, he drove straight on to a West End garage.

An hour later, he was in the train for Westford, a seaside place where he had once spent a summer holiday before his marriage, with three friends from college. On the luggage rack was a new suitcase containing new pyjamas, shoes, a new kit, as for a holiday by the sea—even new paperbacks for a wet day.

It was February, but when he reached Westford he was surprised, for a moment, to find that both its hotels were closed. Only the village pub, *The Case Is Altered*, was still open for visitors, and as he sat in the coffee-room, he appeared to be the only visitor, except for a commercial traveller, one Sims, a dignified young man who addressed him with the most formal politeness and showed a strong tendency to talk politics—politics on what he called the 'highest level.'

In his view, he said, what parliaments did and what dictators talked about did not really matter; what mattered was population statistics and economics. 'You can put over anything with the wire-less and the telly—that's the way these dictators do it—but you can't feed people on words. They'll swallow all the lies you like, but they can't live on hot air. Sooner or later most of these chaps have to face facts.'

'Yes,' said Tom. 'A lot later—generally too late. Look at what Hitler did with his little yarn—and called it the Big Lie all the time. Look at all the people eating lies now and getting poison all the time. What can they do, poor devils? So long as the big noise has a really tough police.'

Tom was a Liberal, a strong supporter of the United Nations. A week before, he had been saying just the same things as Mr Sims; probably they had come out of the same papers. But now all at once he was revolted, quite furious with Mr Sims, with all those nice chaps at the club and the golf course, who had been so ready to talk this nonsense with him, who simply refused to face facts, especially the enormous, obvious fact that civilisation was going to smash just because of all this cant, this wangling, this political gabble, this nonsense.

Mr Sims shook his head and remarked that the police hadn't saved the Czar.

'No,' Tom said. 'What knocked him out was a superior brand of cant. He thought the people loved him, and sent his Guards to the front. But the Bolshies told the people they'd bring in the golden age right off. And they won. They had a bigger lie and they were smarter swindlers. The poor old Czar only cheated himself; they cheated everybody.'

Suddenly Tom caught Mr Sims' eye fixed upon him with a speculative alarm. The man was shocked. He was so used to the regular nonsense, to the old, worn records grinding out the same old popular tune, that he was bewildered by this contradiction.

'Quite a new idea,' Mr Sims murmured. 'Very interesting.' He was growing more and more alarmed.

'Excuse me,' Tom muttered, and hurried out into the front hall. It was almost a run. He was afraid of losing his temper with Mr Sims, who was obviously a nice chap, a very nice chap, who read all the best papers, the best nonsense.

What especially angered him in Mr Sims was that Mr Sims'

nonsense was his own nonsense of a week before. Sims was a looking-glass in which he saw his own silly face. And it made it no better that, as he now perceived, he had always known his nonsense to be nonsense. All that time when he had been talking it at business luncheons, at the club, in the train, at breakfast to his own family, he had had the same deep feeling: My God, what nonsense!

For years he had been hiding this knowledge, just as he had always pretended that he enjoyed nothing so much as his family life. How often had he boasted of the sympathetic devotion of his wife and children, saying how lucky he was compared with so many others, who found themselves ciphers in their own homes. Why, why had he gone on telling himself these lies, living a life of hypocrisy? It was as if he had been drugged—or was it simply that the air was so thick with nonsense, with cant, that it was almost impossible for any man to see the truth, even the biggest, the most obvious truth? Wasn't it simply by a stroke of luck that he had broken out into clear air? And as if the words themselves demanded the action, he put on his mackintosh and went out.

It was raining still, but the opposite side of the bay was sharp and clear, as though seen through a lens. The grey sky was brilliant with diffused light, and the breeze had a taste of sea salt. The whole world seemed washed as clean as the pebbles on the beach.

He walked along the front. Westford's great charm in the old days had been its smallness, its lack of enterprise. Apart from the two hotels, both old-fashioned, and even forbidding to strangers, there were only a dozen or so boarding-houses along the front, and almost the entire town was in the twenty or so buildings facing the sea, and in the main street of the old village branching off at right angles. There was what was called a Marine Parade, but it was simply a paved path along the front road with, on the seaward side, a strip of rough grass where half a dozen seats had been provided. Below, the magnificent beach had neither pier nor bathing huts. The great landlord who owned Westford was against huts, and summer visitors were expected to use tents that they could hire from the town council. There were no municipal gardens, bandstands, putting courses, or sideshows to vulgarise the place, which, apart from the absence of bathing machines, might have been existing still in the eighteen-sixties.

The wind was rising and big waves were thumping on the beach. The sea turned almost black and the wet fronts of the houses, in spite of their gay colours, began to have a dreary look. The town seemed absolutely empty; not a human being was in sight. The only living creature to be seen was a dog with its nose in the gutter—as Tom appeared from around a corner, it jumped and looked at him, uttered one sharp bark, and cantered away, completely shocked by the intrusion. But the very dreariness of the scene, the monotonous pounding of the waves, the hiss of the rain in the pools gave Tom the kind of pleasure that one gets from the defiance of an enemy. He was stimulated, excited. He felt his strength; he felt that he had done well. He had made a big decision and saved his life, and he went down to the beach and walked up and down close to the waves until the rain grew heavy. His shoes filled with sand and he remembered that he had only one suit with him. He turned back to the pub, intending to read one of his new crime novels.

In the little hall of the private entrance, the clerk, who was also the barman, was waiting for him with the register, and, upon an impulse that, for the moment, he did not understand and did not examine, he hesitated and then wrote down the name Charles Stone and gave a false address. He was surprised at himself—he detested such trickery—but it was only twenty minutes later that, lying upstairs on his bed with his book, he realised how necessary it had been, how wisely he had followed his impulse. 'In the first excitement,' he said to himself, 'they might well ask the B.B.C. or the newspapers to start a hunt; the last thing I want is any publicity. I'll write to Louie at once and get things settled in a sensible manner.'

That evening—in fact, as soon as he could, with decent politeness, separate himself from Mr Sims, who was anxious to make him realise that if you can fool the people, you can't fool population statistics, so long, of course, as they are reliable—he slipped off to his room to write to Louie. There was no writing-table in the room, or any provision for writing, so he set his new suitcase on his knee and proceeded to draft a letter on the flyleaf of his paper-back.

'Darling Louie,' he began, but stopped immediately. He had always written 'Darling Louie,' but how could he begin a letter of farewell, an ultimatum proposing an end to their marriage, with 'Darling Louie'? He crossed it out and wrote 'My dear Louie.' This also struck him as false. She was not his dear Louie. And was he going to start a new life of truth, of sincerity, by writing this criminal lie? 'Dear So-and-So.' What hundreds of letters to total strangers, to touts, to frauds and crooks, to people who were, in fact, absolutely detestable to him, he had started with this lying formula, this stereotyped nonsense. Louie was simply the woman who lived in his house, like a creature dropped from Mars, more strange to him than any stranger. A woman whom he supported and who had no real contact with him at all, who did not even speak the same language. He began again, without preamble: 'I dare say you wonder where I am, but it does not really matter. As far as you and the children are concerned, I have not existed any-where for a long time. I'm not blaming anyone for this state of affairs. I imagine it's a very common one for married couples in our situation. The children are practically grown up and don't need us any more; they certainly have not needed me for years past and your life is entirely full of your own private interests. For a long time, I have been aware that I was only in the way. You would be much happier, much freer, as a widow. You could make one of those marriages that women in their forties do make after their children cease to need them, a marriage with a man suited to the new woman you have become. There is something to be said for a change of partners at our age. After all, people don't stop growing and changing simply because they are married. I agree that they have a duty to their children, but when that duty has been discharged it is absurd to make them waste the rest of their lives in pretending to a community of interests which they no longer possess. It's even bad for the children, now they are old enough to think for themselves, to live in this atmosphere of fake and hypocrisy. They get infected, too, and so the nonsense goes on to another generation.' It was a good letter; he was surprised how good it was. He realised that it expressed for him feelings that had been present for years, and that he had been, unnoticed by himself, collecting all kinds of information bearing on his argument. It was a good letter, but he did not send it that evening. He had no notepaper or envelopes with him. He could not make a fair copy and he was not sure that he had not said too much. The whole thing, as read through, had a some-what professorial air. It lacked the conviction that moved him so strongly. It gave no hint of the bitterness that he felt to be justifiable. He had been a good husband, a good father, and he could not help feeling that he had been treated with ingratitude. He lay awake half the night thinking of new things that he could put in this letter. Once he even turned on the light to write a phrase in another of his crime novels.

Next day he rewrote the letter. It was not till Thursday, three days after his flight, that he went out in the town to seek notepaper and envelopes. Then he found that the one stationer's had nothing to his taste—only stationery sets done up in ribbon and containing deckle-edged paper of the most vulgar type, or the cheapest blocks. Both, he felt, were quite impossible for his letter. He had always been particular about notepaper. However, Westford was only ten miles from the large seaside town of Lilmouth, and he would enjoy a visit there, too. He and his college friends had spent a very happy afternoon and evening at Lilmouth at the annual fair. He called, therefore, at the garage, to hire a car, and found that there was one that would be available the next day. He gave the order and returned to the pub. He was in no hurry to write his letter. Why, Louie knew that he was all right. He had phoned the office to tell them that he had to go away for a while, that he would send his address in due course, and he had asked them to inform his wife.

A letter from or to Louie would start all sorts of trouble, and meanwhile he was only just beginning to enjoy his new life. He had found out how to dodge Mr Sims—simply by having his meals earlier. And time was passing far more quickly than he had expected. It was astonishing how this lounging, thoughtful, careless existence had already fallen into a routine. A late breakfast, a stroll along the front, coffee at eleven in a little café that remained open apparently for the use of unemployed landladies, who came there to discuss their bookings for the next season. Then to the stationer's for the London papers, then early luncheon with the papers to read. After luncheon, a doze in his room. Then another stroll along the front, or, if it were fine, over the headland and along the coast for a mile or two. The sea breeze was unequalled for giving one an appetite. He had not for years so much enjoyed either the prospect of dinner or dinner itself. *The Case Is Altered* did not attempt French cooking. All the better. It provided excellent meat, beer, and cheese, and plenty of them. After dinner he was ready for a pipe and another look at the papers, and then to bed, where he read himself to sleep in a few minutes. Even for luncheon he found that he had an appetite, and he was sniffing the smell of chops in the hall, the smell that not many months before would have turned him away from such a place in the first moment, when a large, dark figure, which seemed to have been waiting in the coffee-room doorway, stepped out and said, 'Mr Sponson?'

Tom, without thought, answered, 'My name is Stone,' and then, indignant to see himself confronted by a policeman, went on, 'What do you want here? Why should I answer your questions?'

The policeman, a large West Country man with a red face, answered, in a deprecating manner, as if to say 'Excuse me,' that he had not asked any questions. He was holding his helmet in front of his stomach in the manner of a shy man who wants to occupy his hands. Tom saw at once that this polite, apologetic manner was merely assumed. It was hypocritical nonsense.

He said shortly, 'Well, don't, because I don't intend to answer any.'

'That's all right, sir,' said the policeman. 'No offence, I hope.' And he went out. Even his gesture, as, turning the corner, he threw up his chin and replaced his helmet on his head, annoyed Tom. It seemed to carry all that confidence of authority, that calm superiority of power, that is so offensive to the private citizen.

He went upstairs to his room in a rage and began to pack. He must get away at once. What enraged him was the thought that he had been followed, spied upon. Louie must have gone to the police. What right had they to pursue him like this? He had done no wrong; in fact, he was trying to do the right thing, the sensible thing. No doubt, Louie felt offended; perhaps she was hurt in her pride. She didn't want her friends to know that her marriage had failed. But if there were any publicity now it would be entirely her own fault. He had done everything to avoid publicity. He rang the bell for his bill before he remembered that it did not ring; none of the bells rang. But almost at once a maid, as if summoned by telepathy, appeared. She looked with surprise at his suitcase, half packed, and said that luncheon was ready and that someone was waiting for him.

'Someone waiting?' he demanded. 'Who's waiting?'

'In the coffee-room, sir—a gentleman.'

'What gentleman?'

The maid did not know, and seemed startled by the question. She hurried away almost at a run, and he realised that he had been shouting at her.

Tom banged his suitcase shut. The maid was obviously a spy, just as Mr Sims had certainly been a spy, and all barmen like to keep in with the police. That policeman had certainly talked to the barman, and how had the police got to know about him except from spies in the place? All at once Westford seemed to him almost as loathsome as his own suburb at home, full of people making demands upon him, thinking about him, discussing him. Certainly everyone in the pub would be discussing him—this mysterious affair, Mr Sponson's disappearance.

And who was this gentleman? Probably a detective. It must be a detective. He took his suitcase with him down the back stairs. He would escape by the yard. But the barman was at the bottom of the stairs, looking up at him with a thoughtful air, and when he turned towards the front hall, there was his brother, Fred. Fred was shaking hands with him before he realised who he was.

'Hullo, old chap, how are you? This is a bit of luck, to find you here,' Fred said.

'What do you mean, find me here? What do you take me for? You've come after me—I suppose Louie sent you?'

'My dear old chap, that's none of my business. It's only that— there's one or two small points about our own family affairs—about some of our father's things.'

Fred was in the Army, a major. Tom and he had always been good friends, but they had no family interests in common except their memories. Fred was married, with three children, the paternal estate had been divided long ago, and Tom suddenly lost his temper. 'Look, Fred,' he said. 'I don't know how you got on my tracks—I suppose I'm being spied on all the time—but it's no good coming after me like this. You won't get me to go back.'

'My dear chap, I wouldn't dream of it. In fact, I'm all for this idea of taking a holiday, a real holiday. You've not had a real holiday for years. Why not come ski-ing with me in Norway?' He slapped

Tom on the shoulder with a smile that was just a little too hearty, too brotherly.

Tom pushed the hand from his shoulder. 'Don't talk nonsense,' he said. 'The thing is to humour the lunatic, isn't it? Go along with the poor chap in his wildest fantods.'

'Good heavens, no, old boy. I never saw you looking better.'

'Because the fact is that I've just got sane—for the first time in years. I've just waked up to the kind of imbecile nonsense that my life had become.'

'Exactly. I couldn't agree more. All work and no play—a real holiday——'

'Of course I want a holiday—for the rest of my life. You think this is a breakdown. It isn't. It's a breakout. What do you suppose my life is like at home—as they call it? Bob and April stopped being my children years ago when they went away to school, and as for Louie, I often wonder whether she ever has been my real wife. Certainly I've never known just what she was after or what she thought of me. And these last two years I've simply been a nuisance to her. This is a break, in fact, for her as well as for me. It isn't so much a new life we need as a real life. As it is, we just carry on this marriage by habit. It's just an imitation marriage, a robot marriage. We go through the gestures because we've been wound up and can't stop the machinery. Well, now I *have* stopped the machinery and I'm going to have some life on my own and give Louie some life, too. She needn't be afraid she will be left flat. There's plenty of money for both of us.'

Fred made a face as if to say, 'Really, I don't want all this talk,' and said, 'Quite. I quite see your point, old chap, though, in fact, I gather she's upset, quite ill, they say—— But what about some lunch? I'm hungry.' He sat down at a table in the coffee-room and called the waiter.

But Tom was not going to be wangled in this manner. He wasn't going to have Fred go on pretending that this act of justice and sincerity was a trifle. He would not even sit down at the table. He bent over it towards Fred and said, 'So she's made herself ill. She would, but why? Because she's upset at what people will say. Because she may have to give up a few parties. Because her routine is changed

—like someone who's knocked off cigarettes and doesn't know how to pass the time.'

The waiter had arrived with Fred's chop, mashed potato, and Brussels sprouts, the standard lunch at the pub. Fred took a mouthful and then shouted, 'Waiter, half a can of old and mild!'

This affectation of ease still more irritated Tom. 'You don't believe me,' he said. 'But what do you know about it? I tell you I'm nothing to Louie but a provider and I'm going on providing. That's to say, she'll get exactly the same income as before.'

The waiter came with the beer. Fred took a sip and said, 'Might be worse,' and then, sticking his fork in the chop, remarked, 'The children.'

'Yes, the children. And if I'm nothing much to Louie, I'm still less to the children. They have their own lives, they've had 'em for years.' And when Fred went on eating his chop, Tom, now very exasperated, began a long speech about the children. He wasn't blaming them, he said. They were nice children. It was, in fact, quite right that they should be having their own lives. What was wrong and perfectly stupid was this pretence that he was needed any more —this hypocrisy, which was just as bad for them as for him, and all for nothing. His own life was simply being wasted for nothing.

Fred still went on eating, and Tom, leaning across the table on his knuckles, felt like some village orator addressing a meeting so bored that it cannot even listen. Abruptly he stopped. He was so angry that for a moment he had an impulse to take up Fred's beer and throw it in his face. The impulse was so strong that he hastily turned away and went out of the room, and, catching up his suitcase, hat and coat, made for the door. But before he could escape, the barman popped out from the saloon bar. 'Your bill, sir.' When he had paid the bill, Fred had picked up the suitcase and was saying, 'Let me give you a hand, old chap. What about the old heart?' Fred carried the suitcase all the way to the bus. He talked of their childhood. Some old album of photographs had turned up in his attic. Would Tom like to see them? There ought to be a share-out.

Tom said nothing; he could not speak for fear of screaming his rage at Fred. He knew that if he began to speak, if he said a word to him, it would be a shriek, and he dared not shriek.

The bus was standing in front of *The Lobster Pot*, the village beer-house, but it was not to leave for half an hour yet. Fred proposed that they should go in for a parting glass, but Tom hastily climbed into the empty bus and took his seat. For a moment he was afraid, he was terrified, that Fred would sit down beside him and go on talking, go on trying to smooth him down, to make him feel that nothing was really wrong, that all this that had happened was quite an ordinary event.

But Fred apparently had more sense, or possibly better instructions. He put down the suitcase beside Tom and held out his hand. 'Well, old chap, I suppose you don't want me here, but if there's anything I can do, I hope you'll send along and let me know.' Tom did not take the hand. He wanted to do so, he was fond of Fred, but it seemed to him now that if he touched his hand he would be acknowledging that Fred's mission was not completely nonsense, that after all there was something in the conventional shibboleth of family unity that had sent him to Westford. He could not touch his hand, and after a moment Fred said good-bye again and went off. What a relief. Tom felt such a sense of release that he was full of gratitude to his brother. He thought, I must write to him, I must tell him that I didn't want to be rude. It wasn't a personal matter; it was just a question of principle.

That night he was in Liverpool, at a quiet back-street hotel, a commercial hotel. His plan was to go abroad, to Eire or Europe. He had sent to the office for a letter of credit, addressed Poste Restante. But when he called at the Central Post Office, there was only a note from his chief clerk saying the credit was on its way. When it had not arrived by next morning, he wrote again, with some indignation. And on the next day, the fourth, as he came from the hotel to go to the post office, Louie stepped out of a taxi that had been waiting at the kerb. She threw her arms round his neck and broke into tears. She said nothing—after that warm embrace she only stood gazing at him with an anxious and embarrassed smile. Louie's smile through her tears struck Tom as especially artificial and disgusting. How ridiculous to try to get round him in this manner. As if he were a child to be wangled by caresses and 'darlings'.

'What exactly do you want?' he demanded. 'Didn't you get my letter?' Just then he remembered that he'd never sent that letter. He'd never quite decided how to finish it. So he added quickly and impatiently, 'What's the point of chasing me about like this? *That* can't do any good to anybody.'

Louie only continued to gaze with the same tearful and exasperating look of grief.

Another person had now descended from the taxi—Tom's family doctor, Bewley, an earnest young man, whose long, solemn face had caused Tom to say that he was more fitted to be an undertaker. He was much valued by all those valuable private patients who like to have their kinks taken seriously. Tom did not care for him, and shouted, 'Good God, and what do *you* think you're doing here?'

Bewley did not seem to hear. He did not even look at Tom but addressed himself to a stranger standing a couple of paces behind Louie—a man with very large and very black horn-rims, and very high, square shoulders. His face was square, too, with a pug nose and a large mouth, which was fixed in that habitual, professional smile that marks a floor manager in a store or the master of ceremonies at a palais de danse.

Tom had hardly wondered who the fellow was and where he had come from before he noticed, just behind, as if to take cover from his broad back, both the children. And a little to their right, he suddenly recognised, in a mysterious skulker with an immense coat collar turned up almost to the brim of a bowler hat, the long white nose and little steel goggles of his chief clerk. His whole life seemed to have gathered about him again in this back street—all those ties that had gradually bound him and wrapped him round in that cocoon of dead matter, that dusty nonsense, which, if he could not break through it now, once for all, would smother him.

'What on earth is all this about?' he asked Louie.

She opened her mouth to speak, and then lost courage and looked round at the stranger. It was he, with a slight extension of that professional smile, who answered, 'It's all right, Mr Sponson. We don't want to bother you in any way. We're just going.'

'The sooner the better,' Tom said, and, with a sudden conviction, added, 'So you're the private eye that's been spying on me.'

'Not at all, Mr Sponson.' The man stepped forward with outstretched hand. 'I don't suppose you remember me.'

'No, I'm damned if I do. Who the devil are you?'

The stranger did not answer, and for some reason Tom did not press him for an answer. He was too angry, too infuriated by that professional, confident grin. What had the brute got to be pleased about? He wanted to hit him, to knock that grin off his pug face. But he saw that this would be a giveaway; it would be just what the brute wanted. To see him rattled. He ignored the fellow, and said to Louie, with an easy, nonchalant air, 'Now, Louie, you're a sensible woman. You know perfectly well that all this fuss is completely unnecessary. It's not helping either of us to see straight. Do realise,' he went on, in a sympathetic tone, 'that I'm not accusing you of any *conscious* hypocrisy, of putting on an act. Not at all. I realise perfectly well that you *think* you're doing the right thing. For instance, I'm prepared to bet that you *think* you need me at home. Don't you?' Louie didn't answer. She only gazed sadly, anxiously. Tom thought, 'She's not even listening,' and he became more urgent. 'But don't you *see* all this is simply because you won't stop to ask yourself what you're *really* doing—what we're all playing at?'

His voice rose, and he wanted to wave his hands. But he kept them firmly under control. He smiled in a nonchalant, lazy manner. 'My dear old girl, really, you know——'

At this moment, he noticed that the party had closed on him. As the stranger had moved in, they had followed, as if drawn by some magnetic centre of attraction. The children were within a yard; the clerk, on the other side, was at his elbow. All at once he lost the thread of his calm discussion with Louie. He started back. He had actually been on the brink of running away, declaring himself a fugitive. And what from? Nonsense? To run away from nonsense, just pretence, a made-up delusion—that would be simply madness. And what enraged him as he looked round at all these nonsense-mongers was their nonsense looks. The children seemed even more terrified than Louie—the self-confident Bob, the popular and rather too successful freshman, now wore the face of a child who has seen a spectre, and April, a plump girl, whose cheeks were normally round and rather too rosy, seemed lank and pale. The lugubrious Bewley had a ferocious glare, as if affronted, and the chief clerk, a highly respectable and rather timid person whose favourite recreation was dominoes, had that desperate frown of resolution that one sees in dentists' parlours.

Tom waved one hand and muttered, 'But it's perfectly stupid,' then turned on the girl. 'Why aren't you at school?'

The girl looked frightened, as if she were going to cry, and all the rest turned their faces towards her, as if imploring her to do the wise, the intelligent thing. And obviously, she felt her responsibility but hadn't an idea of what was expected of her. Then abruptly she stepped forward, gave her father a timid peck on the cheek, quite unlike her usual vigorous embrace, and said, 'I was so worried about you, Daddy.'

'But why, why, why?' He appealed to this child of whom he was so fond. 'Look at me—I'm all right.' He laughed gaily. 'It's you who are worried, darling, it's you who are running about with looks of horror simply because I've told the truth for once.' He laughed again, and now both his arms were waving, but he didn't care. Why care? Why pretend? What hypocrisy, what nonsense! 'It's so f-funny,' he said. 'Look at you. Chasing me all over England—and why? You don't want me, you know—you haven't wanted me for years.'

Suddenly he grew disgusted. What was the good of talking? They absolutely refused to understand. They had simply sold themselves to nonsense. They simply didn't want to understand truth any more. Talking to them was like talking to Chinese. They were so completely foreign that they could not interpret even his looks, his tone.

'I'm so so-sorry,' said the girl, and she gave a sob.

The sob had a kind of echo in Tom's breast, a physical echo. He took a long breath. He wanted to console the poor child, but he didn't know how. She was too strange, too cut off from him.

And then, catching the stranger's eye, noting again his smile, he saw that the fellow quite understood the situation. He was a brute but not a fool. Tom found himself smiling at him in a confidential manner.

The stranger at once stepped forward and opened the taxi door. Tom, perceiving at once how right he had been about the fellow's intelligence, climbed in and joyfully took his seat. He was surprised for only a moment when the stranger followed him; he saw at once that this, too, was an intelligent act. He had a lot to say to him—he wanted to explain the whole ridiculous affair. As the taxi drove off, he said with a cheerful and knowing air, 'I spotted you at once—one of Louie's psychiatrists.' The stranger simply smiled, in fact, beamed at him. He now looked like a floor manager who has made a good sale. 'But all the same,' said Tom, 'I'm not having a breakdown. I'm simply fed up with nonsense.'

'I know. I know. So am I. So's everybody. You just want to get away.'

'Get away from the nonsense,' Tom said. 'But it comes after you all the time. And it won't even listen when you tell it it's nonsense. It won't even believe it's nonsense. It's so absolutely soaked in its own nonsense that it can't take in anything else. Like fish.' He didn't stop to explain this point; he was quite sure that the stranger understood. He smiled hastily to show this confidence. 'Or whisky. If you cut it off, they'd get the shakes, they couldn't breathe.'

The stranger's very spectacles were full of understanding, and Tom waved his hands and leaned towards him. 'Words,' he said. 'It's all words, words, words. They live on words—they can't understand anything but words. They think words. You talk to them, but you might as well be burbling in a madhouse to a lot of tape recorders—they only get a lot of noises. You saw that poor child—all the family in tears—for nothing. For absolute nonsense. For words. It makes you laugh.' And to his horror, he began to cry.

The stranger patted his shoulder and said, 'All over now,' in a professional but understanding tone.

The taxi drove up in front of a large, discreet building standing back from the road in a suburban street.

'Is this an asylum?' Tom asked.

The stranger actually laughed. 'No, no, no. What nonsense. It's just a place where you *can* get away. That's all you need—to get away.'

Twenty minutes later, Tom was in bed; the stranger was giving instructions to a nurse. Tom had had an injection and was sinking happily into a doze. What joy, what peace. At last he had got away. But just as he closed his eyes, he muttered again, in protest, 'This isn't a breakdown, you know. It's only—I got fed up with all the words, the nonsense.'

The stranger laid a large, cool hand on his head. 'I know. I know.' And he really seemed to know.

That was six weeks ago. Tom is now back at work, back with his family. He has been back a fortnight and already life is exactly the same as before. Louie no longer hovers about him with anxious affection; the children no longer come into the room on tiptoe and try to talk sympathetically about his long day at the office. He has found it especially trying to keep up this absurd kind of conversation. With the arrears at the office, he has been far too busy to want anything at home but peace. And why should Louie tell him about her day's amusements or the children pretend to take an interest in a business of which they have never comprehended a detail? What nonsense. Thank God they've got over it. That first week back at home had almost driven him *really* mad.

And suddenly, at the club, talking to an old friend, he hears himself say, 'Yes, I've been lucky, it's been a wonderful marriage. Well, you know Louie, and the children *stay* so nice, so affectionate. You couldn't find nicer, more affectionate children. After all, family life is everything, and mine has been a marvellous success.' He stops, startled by some echo from that holiday, now almost forgotten. The word 'nonsense' has jumped into his brain.

Neither Tom nor his family has ever admitted that he has had a breakdown—it is called a holiday, a rest cure. And no nonsense about it. But if that wasn't nonsense, what is this—all these words that he is uttering with such earnestness? But no, *not* nonsense—God forbid. More like a prayer.

NEW BOOTS

Two small girls in blue school uniforms and gum-boots stood on the pavement looking into the gutter. The snow had been piled along the short road in two long mounds and between these miniature Andes and the kerb, brown rivers were pouring towards the drains.

The road was new with bright concrete pavements. In thirty yards it stopped abruptly and became a muddy lane between tall ragged hedges. The lane and the fields beyond were covered with old grey snow through which the cabbage stalks thrust their rotting brown stems. But in the street everything was clean and new. The six villas, three on each side, were only just built; each a little different but all with the same bright red roofs, lime-washed rough cast and glittering chromium door handles. It was hard to believe that objects so bright and clean were meant for the open air. Against such roofs and walls the green-blue sky also looked quite new; as if it had just been created, only for an appropriate background to the villas. Little thin clouds were melting in this radiant sky like snow-flakes on water.

From a top window in the second villa, with bright grass-green paint, a fair-haired woman with a pale madonna face was gazing at the sky. She had a look of grave enjoyment. One sees such expressions at a concert of sacred music. She turned her eyes, with a deliberate pleasure, from the sky to the gardens, to the other villas; only passing quickly, with half-dropped lids, over the wretched-looking fields and tattered hedges. Suddenly she smiled and called out to someone in the next garden, hidden behind a trellis, 'Yes, isn't it glorious? Oh, a real thaw. Isn't it lucky I gave way about the boots? And really very cheap considering.'

Her smile was unexpectedly childish and gay; her voice too was lively; its tone rather deep. But all at once the smile disappeared; her expression became responsible and anxious. She called across the road, 'Milly, Milly, Susy, don't do that, darlings—it's too deep.'

Two small girls were standing in the brown river. With bent heads they gazed at the water as it poured round their ankles; they were absorbed in the battle between the fierce current and the strong shining boots. They did not even notice the warning from above. But the fair-haired madonna was again answering some remark from behind the trellis. 'Yes, she *is* good, Milly—and of course she's been pestering for weeks ever since she saw your Susan's. They all seem to adore gum-boots. But really, as she says herself, they're so useful. Well, it hardly seems fair to call them a present.'

The little girls were now walking upstream dragging their feet. They were tearing the water apart, flinging back the waves, breaking it into drops. They were so deeply interested in the triumphant progress of the boots, that they did not see where they were going and bumped together. One, the smaller, staggered and gave a cry. The woman called out in soft indignation, 'Milly *darling*, didn't you hear me?'

She left the window.

The little girls clasped each other and were saved. They looked up and seeing the fair-haired woman come flying out of the door, gazed in surprise. Then one, the taller, suddenly taking alarm, darted round the corner. The woman caught the smaller by the arm and propelled her gently towards the shiny villa. 'Run along Milly, darling, and change them.' Her tone was caressing and mildly bored, that of an old-established mother.

'But I'm not a *bit* wet, Mummy,' the child cried. She looked at the boots and raised the toes to make the sun sparkle on the wet creases, 'They didn't let in a single drop.'

'I should hope not—on the very first day.'

'I needn't take them off, need I?'

'Of course you must—run along, dearest—I've no time.'

The little girl went slowly into the house, raising her knees high and trampling the ground. The woman called out gaily at the trellis, 'I've collected mine—but your Susy escaped.' And then, 'Oh no, Susy is a darling.'

A sound like muffled gunfire came from the villa, where Milly was climbing the stairs, trampling on each with all her force. It was wonderful how much noise the new boots could make. She pounded across the landing to the nursery and banged open the door. Then she marched in, kicking up the boots as high as possible in order to make them conspicuous. The effect was like a goose-step. A small boy of six, with hair like barley straw, was squatting in the middle of the floor among bricks. He did not look up. He was gazing anxiously at a lop-sided tower which stood among a complicated system of buildings and walls. The tower swayed, and he quickly put out his hand to save it. The little girl marched right round the floor, with her new discovered goose-step. Then she stopped, looked at the little boy and said, 'Hullo, Tom.'

'Hullo,' the boy murmured. He took the top brick off the tower.

'Have you seen my new gum-boots?'

'Yes.' He put back the brick.

'They're pretty good, you know—they didn't let in a single drop.'

Tom made no answer. The little girl gazed down at the boots and wrinkled the toes; but only once. She had done that before. She stooped quickly to look at a speck of mud on one shiny toe, then wetting her forefinger from time to time in her mouth, she carefully rubbed it off. The tower swayed and Tom hastily removed the top brick. He examined the brick with a puzzled frown. He obviously suspected it of some hidden weakness, or treachery.

Milly walked up the room again, lifting her knees high; but stopped suddenly. She had already performed that march. She looked down at her feet enquiringly, then round the nursery. She was at a loss. What could she do next with the boots? Tom gave a sigh and put the brick back. But he kept his eye on it with a warning frown. He was not going to stand any nonsense from it. Milly began to shuffle across the floor, jerking each boot only a foot's length in front of the other. In this manner she shuffled directly towards Tom's outside wall. Tom, feeling danger, looked round and said, 'Mind—don't kick it.'

Milly stopped. Tom turned his eyes quickly towards the tower to make sure that the top brick was still behaving itself. Milly at once made another shuffle and pushed the wall with her toes.

The wall was of long narrow bricks, two deep. It opened silently without catching Tom's attention. Milly looked at her brother for a moment with a fixed gaze; she was smiling and pursing up her lips, pushing out her jaw in an expression of contempt and defiance. She made another shuffle, sweeping away a whole corner of the wall and touching the edge of the first building within, the garage. Tom gave a loud cry and clutched the nearest boot in both hands. Milly said with impatient contempt, 'How could I help it—if you will cover the whole floor with your silly bricks?'

'Go back, go back.' He squeezed the boot and tried to push it backwards.

'I can't even feel you,' Milly said. 'Not in these boots.'

'Go away,' Tom shouted tearfully. 'What did you come for?'

'Try and pinch me, Tom—try and pinch my leg—you couldn't you know. You couldn't do anything to me in these boots.'

She smiled at him and then looked down at the boots. Tom put his hand on top of the tower to prevent it from being knocked down and cried, 'I'll call Mummy, I'll call Mummy.'

Milly stood on her heels and raised her toes. But she had done that many times before. She straightened herself with an impatient jerk. She stood for twenty seconds, then made another shuffle and down came the garage. Tom uttered a scream, 'Mummy—Mummy.' Milly, with one magnificent kick, demolished the tower. Tom jumped up and threw himself upon her, hitting, clutching and kicking. Milly cried, 'All right, kick away, you can't hurt me.'

But unexpectedly, he threw her off her balance. She stepped back and tripped over a chair. Both children rolled on the floor.

Milly bumped her head on the chair. But she was still full of triumph and easily kept her presence of mind. She was not frightened, not even angry. Laughing, she jerked her face away from Tom's hooked fingers trying to seize her mouth or eye, then with a quick wriggle escaped from beneath him and jumped to her feet. Tom, roaring, lay on his back among the ruined brickwork.

From below stairs came a cry, 'Milly, what are you doing—have you taken off the boots yet?' The stairs creaked. Milly looked down at the boots, soon to be lost to her, and then at Tom. She gave him a push with a toe; then raised her foot and pressed it lightly on his body. The child uttered a louder yell and grabbed at the foot. Milly raised it into the air above his grasping fingers. Her mother's voice came from the stairs, close by, in a tone of urgent grief.

'Milly—Milly.'

Milly planted the boot deliberately and firmly on her brother's face. His roar became a shriek. Milly lifted the boot again and saw blood running from the child's nose. She blushed deeply and thrust out her lips in a tremor of excitement and triumph; she stooped forward hastily to look once more at the boots. She frowned with admiration and curiosity, as if she had never before fully appreciated them.

'Darlings, darlings—what on earth——'

The little girl was already flying to the door, 'Oh Mummy, I don't know *what's* the matter with Tom—he won't let me do *anything*.' As her voice rose in protest, she stood on tiptoe, as if to prove to herself the lightness of her conscience.

PSYCHOLOGIST

Robert G., at forty-six, a nervous little man, and especially afraid of women, suddenly fell in love with a girl of eighteen and, goodness knows how, proposed to her. That is to say, it's not quite certain that he did propose. She always declared that he did nothing of the kind. It happened at a friend's house, or rather at the house of a business acquaintance. G. had no friends. But he was a keen man of business and believed in keeping in touch with anybody who might be useful to it. He did nearly all his own buying, and sometimes even acted as one of his own salesmen. He had practised salesmanship as an art—he called it an art—in his father's day, and now, as head of the firm, he would still go out on tour. And not only among wholesalers, but even to shops. He would go even to small village shops with his leaflets and samples, and try to get an order for two yards of matting or a rug for the drapery side. He would point out that all proper drapery shops were carpeted, and that even if only half a counter were reserved for drapery it ought to have a carpet in front of it. 'It's a matter,' he would say, 'of psychology. Customers don't feel like buying stuffs or even tape without a carpet.'

Some old woman in charge, some grandfather, the son of half a dozen grandfathers before him in the same shop, would answer that no one had ever noticed the want of a carpet.

'No,' G. would say, 'because they don't know what they're missing. How should they? It's a matter of psychology. But just you try a carpet and you'll see the difference in your trade.'

'But you couldn't have a carpet in a shop like this. What about the flour and the butter, not to speak of the lamp oil and the tin tacks?'

'Not an ordinary carpet,' G. would argue, 'but my washable reversible Persianap is designed just exactly for a mixed trade.'

And so on. And it was surprising how often he did sell a rug.

Of course, this made no real difference to his turnover. He was a rich man. He toured in a Rolls, but he would leave it round the corner when he did his selling in the village. And he carried his own bag of samples. It was said, indeed, that his chauffeur, late head-driver to the Duke of B., had refused to carry them. But this was not true. G. would have sacked the man on the spot for such a refusal. Not that he was an inconsiderate employer. Far from it. But he felt that a chauffeur, in undertaking the job, undertook a certain social responsibility. And that social responsibility ought to be maintained. He carried his samples himself because he considered that a chauffeur would be out of place in such transactions.

'A salesman, a real salesman,' he said, 'doesn't want to have too good a car—he doesn't want to seem too sure of himself. Shopkeepers like to feel a bit superior, well—in a position to grant favours. I believe in choosing small men to sell, five foot six is a good height. Of course, I don't make too much of it—it's a minor point. One of the best men I ever had was six foot two. But then he was consumptive, poor fellow. Anyone could see he was a doomed man. It had a lot of appeal. I used to be surprised by this chap's sales, and one day I surprised him at the job. That's to say, I observed him. I didn't go along with him, of course—a salesman must always be alone. Sort of unprotected—and out on a limb. And I saw at once how poor N. made his sales, by the way the buyer looked at him. And then he would cough a bit too—a cough in the right place would often clinch the deal. But, of course, I'm not suggesting sending out a lot of consumptives. It would be wrong. In all the dust of a drapery trade. But short men, and not too broad, or good-looking—and bald as you like—but well turned out, of course, especially good hats, really good hats, London hats, and good ties, and first-class sample cases—it's psychology.'

G. himself was about five foot five and extremely bald. Neither was he good-looking, far from it. And when he went to stay at the

W.'s, where the proposal took place or did not take place, he had, poor fellow, a boil on his nose. This boil had begun to show itself two days before the visit, but G. had never had a boil before, any-where, and so he assured himself that the redness and pain on the end of his nose were due to a severe cold infection. He was going to have a cold. This was bad enough because W. had a wife and three daughters; not only that, but a sister, a quite fashionable sister from Mayfair, often stayed with him. G. always approached W.'s with a special nervousness. Probably he would not have gone at all if it had not been that he went as a buyer. At W.'s he was in the superior position, and, in fact, W. took a good deal of trouble to entertain him. W. was a very rich man, much richer than G., but he always made a great deal of G. as a buyer. He would give him the No. 1 bedroom with its own bath *en suite*, and in summer he would take him yachting. W. hated the sea, but he lived not far from a fine yachting harbour and he kept a yacht there, for buyers. And in October he would give a pheasant shoot. He was no sportsman, but he knew buyers would expect to be asked to a shoot, even if they themselves did not shoot, and only went out with the ladies to see one beat before luncheon.

W. always gave a shoot for G. who certainly expected it. For he was a good shot. And a shoot took him out of the house in the morning, when he was particularly alarmed by ladies. His experience was that they tried to entertain you in the mornings, by taking you for a walk or showing you the garden and stables. In the afternoons you could slink away by yourself, after tea you could play billiards, after dinner, bridge, but in the mornings you had to be entertained, amused. Unless, of course, you could get away to shoot. But W. always did give G. a shoot in October.

But even then, at W.'s, he was much exposed to ladies, and worse, to girls. Mrs W., a charming woman, would insist on at least one intimate conversation. She would talk about the hazards of life, especially in the carpet business, and the passing years. How long it was since they had known each other. And she had been a bride, almost a bride, at G.'s first visit. She would never forget it. She had been nervous then of her husband's important friends, but how nice he had been. He had quite reassured her.

In fact, she had been married at least eight years at G.'s first visit, and G. dreaded such conversations more than bankruptcy lists. He never knew what to say or where to look, especially when Mrs W., as she was wont to do, in an evening frock, leant towards him. And the girls would suddenly come upon him when he thought himself safe, in the gun-room or the byre, and ask him some extraordinary question. Would he like a game of badminton in the barn? Had he ever seen the queer epitaphs in the local churchyard? Did crayfish agree with him? Could he bear music after dinner, that's to say, it was only Tchaikowsky? Questions to which he had no answers, at least without some consideration of what they might let him in for. And girls of that age never allowed you a moment. They were off at once on another tack. If not badminton, what about a run with the dogs, or a village auction? So amusing.

What's more, he knew very well that these girls were capable of laughing at buyers. He had caught them at it, on his very last visit, all three of them including the youngest, still in pigtails. He had come into the hall, a large staircase hall, from the back passage, and there they were at the far end in front of the fire, watching a performance by Etta, the middle one, aged eighteen. Etta was thrusting out her stomach and elevating her nose, stroking an imaginary moustache and laying down the law about what the government ought to do, in an extraordinary accent, between Cockney and Yorkshire, and the other two girls were laughing. Not only the youngest, who, at fifteen, laughed at everything, but the eldest, Nora, who was twenty-two, decidedly plain, and helped her mother with the housekeeping. He had thought Nora, at least, a responsible person, but here she was laughing at a buyer. In fact, when Etta herself broke into laughter all three girls giggled themselves into a state approaching catalepsy.

G., standing under the stairs in his dark corner, had not known whether he was more struck by Nora's treacherous conduct, or the brilliant art of the mimic, or disturbed by both. There was something infinitely delightful in Etta's gaiety, the liveliness of her inspiration, but there was also something wild, reckless, in her very gestures. He was a sensible man, and he knew that buyers could be self-important and vulgar to a degree. Why shouldn't they be laughed at if they were laughable? Perhaps he was growing middle-aged before his time and losing his sense of humour. He was on the whole a lonely man and didn't see enough of young and lively people.

All the same, he was relieved when Mrs W. came in from the porch, saw what was going on and reproved all the girls in rather a severe tone. G. felt then that he had had a certain right to be shocked. Mrs W., too, had seen a certain impropriety, quite slight but still definite, in this derision of a guest, and not only a guest but a responsible man, a man of substance, who had come to the house on business, important business. It was not so bad as the bad manners of tourists who pester a sentry on duty, but it was in the same class. Mrs W. was a lady, a thoroughly civilised person, an admirable wife and mother, and had her daughters well in hand, but he could not avoid the suspicion that some day Etta would take him off too. He felt her eyes upon him and was suddenly aware of a certain weakness about his legs. They weren't bandy, but, from some aspects, they seemed bandy. And once, when he was talking to W. about the psychology of carpet buyers, he surprised a look between Etta and Nora which stopped him dead. There was quite an awkward moment. But Mrs W. saved the situation with a story about her own first drawing-room carpet bought, so she said, from G.'s, and why she had chosen a pattern of roses on grass green. G. was so right, she said, about young couples' taste in furnishing. It was a brilliant diversion.

But G. asked himself why he ever went to the W.'s. Obviously he was a bore to the children and he did not enjoy himself either. It was nobody's fault. He did not blame Mrs W. for being so intimate, it was her duty; nor the girls for their giddy irresponsibility, girls were like that. You couldn't depend on them for any sort of consistency in behaviour. They were too thoughtless, too much at the mercy of the passing impulse, to acknowledge any regular social obligations—and bless them, too innocent. They didn't realise the terrible insecurity of civilisation, even such civilisation as existed in this cruel world. They were always ready to dance on the powder barrel and make faces at the lions. Especially Etta. He remembered her as a child, always in mischief—the family plague, a scraggy little girl with a very loud voice and appalling manners. She was kept away from him. But once, nine years ago, just when he was saying good-bye, she appeared suddenly from the yard in a state of filth remarkable even for her. When her mother exclaimed, she replied with a grin, showing two teeth missing in front, and turned to run. Her mother caught her and said, 'At least you can say good-bye properly to Mr G.' Etta then threw her arms round his neck and kissed him hastily on the chin. So he had seen her kissing the grey pony, her dog, the second housemaid, and her dolls, Blackface one and Blackface two—it was a gesture expressing half a dozen different emotions, from condescension to boredom. It was also experimental, to find out what kissing was worth as a grown-up occupation.

G. quite understood this. All the same it was the first and last time he had been embraced by any female since his mother's death, twenty-seven years before. And the event remained with him as an experience. He was a sensible man, he did not make too much of a child's careless peck, but yet he felt there was a relationship. Etta was in a different relation with him from all the other children who had never so much as pecked him.

However, he had not seen her again for another nine years. She was always away at school in October. And it was in those years that G. first began to ask himself why he continued to go to the W.'s. It wasn't necessary. He always gave them the same order, the shooting was not as good as his own at home. And now, after he had realised Etta's power of mimicry, especially after he had inter-cepted that glance at dinner, he decided finally that this was his last visit. It took him some time to come to this rather critical decision, but as the months passed Etta's conduct and the girls' laughter began to seem more and more sinister. He began to wonder how far they had gone in ridicule. He wondered if Etta took off all buyers, if she had taken him off already. It did not seem to him possible that she could find any reasonable excuse for mimicry in his figure, features, or manner. He was a most ordinary person and took care to be ordinary. He had a horror of eccentrics. As an old public school man and Oxford graduate (3rd Class in Greats) he desired above all to be inconspicuous. And he flattered himself that he was so. All the same, his feeling grew that Etta might, perhaps had taken him off. And this upset him in an extraordinary manner.

As a sensible man he was prepared for anything from girls. So why did he mind so much the idea that Etta might be taking him off? And he had to acknowledge that it was because of, yes, a certain relationship. Not, of course, that peck. But something that had happened since. Yes, he had got into a habit of thinking of Etta now and then as an attractive child, affectionate, frank. He had compared other children with her, to their disadvantage. He had wondered how she was growing up. And she had grown up into a lovely girl. He was a level-headed sort of fellow, had to be, in his job, a very competitive line indeed—but he could fairly use the word lovely. It was just what he had expected. And such a nice frank manner. So the scene of mimicry had startled him very much. He realised all at once that he did not know a great deal about Etta— he might have acquired quite the wrong idea. She might be a regular minx, a tartar.

No, he would never go to the W.'s again. And here he was, going to the W.'s again in October, and not only that, but going in spite of a ridiculously red nose.

Why? He asked himself as he looked at the glass and told himself that it could not be a boil. Impossible. He'd never had a boil in his life and if he was to have one, why on his nose, before a visit to the W.'s? Fate couldn't play him such a trick as that. Fate was cruel. It had made this dirty world. It had made his legs too short and removed most of his hair before he was thirty, but surely it could not give him a boil on his nose, the first in his life, not before a visit to the W.'s and a house full of derisive girls. There was one good sign. The colour was not right at the tip but slightly to one side. A red tip would be absolutely intolerable. He would look like a clown. Fate had spared him that ignominy.

But on the next day, the morning of his visit, the tip was red. Red and swollen. And very painful. It certainly seemed like a boil. And yet here he was driving up to W.'s avenue. Why? And the answer rose to his lips. Psychology. It must be psychology. But at once he contradicted himself. 'No,' he said, 'dash it all, I'm one of his biggest buyers. And I never come for more than five days. No, it's not psychology. If it wasn't for the girls, I shouldn't mind even a boil. As a buyer I don't need to mind, certainly as a buyer who buys so much, I could come with two boils.'

And there was a certain new resolution, a certain new confidence, even over-confidence, in G.'s manner when he entered the hall and shook hands with his host and hostess. He was almost brusque—he had something of that brash air which he despised so much in some of the cruder buyers whom it was his fate to entertain in his own home. Exhibitionist ruffians who, because they were buyers, considered themselves entitled to strut about his house and give orders to his servants as if they owned both.

G. found himself strutting, caught in his voice a tone of condescension, and wondered at himself. But when, in his room, he went at once to the glass to assure himself that he was not to have a boil, he saw the reason at once. His nose was hideously swollen—it resembled an overripe strawberry—his cheeks were yellow. And he felt such rage that he could have broken the furniture. A boil. And now. Here at the W.'s. What had he done to deserve so cruel a stroke of injustice?

For a moment he thought of staying in his room, sending for the doctor. He imagined the girls' eyes upon him. They had not been present to receive him in the hall—only another proof of their general irresponsibility towards even the most important buyers, men whose custom put the clothes on their backs. But he could hear their voices now, chattering on the stairs, laughing at something or somebody. He imagined their eyes fixed upon his nose, Etta's eyes. And suddenly he thought with rage, 'To hell with them,' he absolutely scorned the whole female crew. Let them cackle, let them laugh. 'By Jove, they don't realise how W. would feel if I gave my order to Z. And Z. would quote as good a price, better. Of course, I couldn't do such a thing. I'm not that sort of man. I don't allow such petty feelings to affect my conduct. And the proof is this boil. I know those girls will laugh but I don't give a damn.'

And he went down to luncheon and glowered at Etta in such a manner that the girl had to leave the room before the pudding. She was bursting. And it needed all her mother's authority to bring her to tea. 'But Mummy, I know I shall laugh if he looks at me like that. No one could stand it. Especially with that nose. What do you think is wrong with him? What have I done?'

'Well, my dear—he has a great admiration for you. You remember last year.'

'No, I don't. I didn't notice anything last year. I didn't even speak to him, so far as I remember—well, only as a duty. You all say he was so terribly smitten but I don't see how he could be, and, at any rate, it's none of my business if he is. I can't help it.'

But here Mrs W. became severe. She pointed out that G. was much the best of the buyers. That, though somewhat shy and provincial, a trifle uncouth, he was a gentleman. And he was very well off, in fact, almost rich. She was not suggesting that Etta should encourage him—certainly not. He was much too old for her and much too serious, not her type at all, but it was time she began to have some sense of responsibility and to discriminate between men who were worthy of respect—solid, dependable men in first-class business—and flashy youngsters, footling away their time and other people's time in borrowed sports cars.

Etta reflected that her mother had quite detestable ideas about love and marriage. But she came to tea and handed G. the scones not only with a straight face but a certain benevolent curiosity.

She was, of course, very well aware that G., last year, had looked at her with admiration, even adoration. Girls of eighteen can detect such a look with the backs of their heads. But she had not thought of him before as a possible husband, a rich husband, and a gentleman. As for her mother saying that he was not her type, that was typical of her mother's detestable ideas about men, and especially about Etta. What she was hinting at was Etta's supposed passion for her cousin Bill, a subaltern of twenty. But she was completely wrong about that affair. Etta could amuse herself with Bill but she knew perfectly well that Bill was a lightweight, the last man to choose for a husband. And it wasn't true that Billy had borrowed that car. It was his own—and paid for—he had paid at least three instalments. Above all, why did her mother think that a man like G. would be too serious for her? Why didn't her mother realise that she was grown up and had quite as serious interests as, for instance, Nora, who had just married a shipowner, a widower with three children, and what's more, a Primitive Methodist. Everyone was delighted with Nora's marriage. And Etta quite agreed that Nora had shown good sense in accepting him—he was, taken all round, rather better than Nora might have expected, with her dumpy figure. Nora was a darling, but millionaires could get plenty of darlings who were also beautiful. The shipowner, in fact, would probably have done just that if he had not been a Primitive Methodist. And Nora knew that very well. She had balanced the man's personal suitability, his excellent manners, good temper and health, against the age, the children and the evangelism, and her own figure and rather small eyes. No one was surprised at Nora's good sense, why then should they expect Etta to behave like a fool? She was, if they only knew, the very last person to be caught by any of your Bills, however amusing for an afternoon drive or a carpet dance.

When at last G. suddenly declared that he seemed to have something wrong with his nose and perhaps he'd better see a doctor, Etta was most sympathetic, and recommended immediate fomentation, applied inside, until the doctor should come.

The doctor came and gave penicillin, and on the next day the boil was opened. G. appeared with an extraordinary kind of plaster on his nose which caused him to resemble a poodle, a white poodle. His eyes especially had the look of a nice poodle who has just had a lump of sugar from a kind mistress.

And in fact, Etta's advice about the fomentation had had a very powerful effect on G.'s feelings. He perceived what he had never suspected, that she was not only exceptionally sympathetic, but thoughtful and responsible beyond her years. Who would expect a girl of eighteen to know so much about domestic medicine, much less to realise that a man of forty-six would prefer on the whole, if he had to have a boil on the nose, that it should burst inside rather than outside and leave his nose unscarred. It was not a thing he had cared to admit. In a man of his age and appearance it might have seemed a little absurd. Men are not supposed to trouble about their appearance. But he had been troubled, though, of course, he could not mention it, especially before these young girls. And then Etta, with marvellous sympathy, had saved him from the need. He was a sensible fellow, he was not going to build too much on such an indication. And the boil unfortunately had come outwards—it would leave an enormous scar. Fate had indeed given him every reason to break the furniture. But he was not merely reconciled to existence, he felt a mysterious happiness, as if, after all, he had had a revelation of some rational order in things, a Compensating Principle. Fate was cruel, but women could be angels. And it was the cruelty of fate that gave them the opportunity.

He knew, of course, that he was in danger of falling into an absurd passion for this young girl.

'I'm a shy man,' he said, 'and rather a lonely one—yes, definitely lonely. That's why I romanticise girls. I'm inclined to think too well of women, especially pretty girls.'

But this wasn't why he proposed, or tried to propose. He had no idea of such a thing. Neither had Etta. She was simply interested in this lover, who was not only a possible husband, by possible meaning a bachelor with complete limbs and enough funds to support a wife, but one whom her mother, so wrongly, considered unsuitable. She observed him, she asked after his nose, she brought him his whisky at seven precisely, which was his time for whisky. He would not have it earlier for fear of becoming too fond of it, or later in case of spoiling his appetite for dinner. She came and watched him shooting and congratulated him on a right and left at two very high birds, going fast. In fact, he was a good shot. W. had often congratulated him. But he had not cared for compliments from a man who did not know what good shooting was, and besides, was always ready to flatter a buyer.

Neither did Etta know what good shooting was. All the same, her praise enchanted him. And tho' he reflected that this, too, was due to nothing but psychology, still he talked with her all the way to the stand after luncheon, and the fact that she had no real interest in pheasant shooting impressed him even more deeply. Because she showed the most intense interest.

And some time during the night he faced the extraordinary idea that the girl might be thinking of him as a possible husband. 'After all,' he reflected, 'girls of that age are capable of anything—they are simply crazy. They get the most extraordinary ideas. It's nature. Like hares in March. And another thing, she may make fun of buyers, some buyers, but she knows very well a buyer is a buyer; she's been brought up in a business family. In this house, inevitably, a buyer, a large buyer, has a certain status. I don't want to make too much of this—it's a minor point. But it *is* a point. I'm not a snob, thank heaven, but I look at the facts. I'm not afraid of facts or I shouldn't be where I am—in the fifteen thousand a year class. I've

F

done every job in my business, from sweeping the factory floor, and I did it because it was the only way to learn the facts, about myself as well as the business. And the fact is that, in this house, a buyer is a buyer. Etta might well have a certain special feeling of respect for a large buyer, quite apart from his age, etc. And why not?'

And, in fact, next day, finding Etta alone in her mother's sitting-room, he suddenly advanced upon her and said, 'Do you remember when you were nine—however, that's a small point—only I've always had a feeling—and you've been so good to me that I've just wondered whether you have ever—I'm afraid you will simply laugh at me.'

Etta then shot out of the room just in time to shut the door behind her before she exploded into uncontrollable shrieks of laughter, rather hysterical laughter. She was even surprised at her own want of control.

In fact, she had not had time to get out of earshot. G. heard the explosion. He turned very red. He was most agitated. But he took the thing very well. He said to himself, 'I'm well out of that—she was playing with me. It's what I thought—she's utterly reckless and unbalanced. And I'm a fool. Yes, I've made a fool of myself. But I mustn't be too depressed—it's natural—a natural thing. Due to sex on both sides. Thank God I've had the sense to see it in time.' And he went to tell W. that he must go at once. He had had a phone call. Very urgent business.

However, W. knew that no phone calls had come in and he was surprised. And then Mrs W. came to inform him that Etta was weeping in her room, that that odious G. had upset her with some sinister indecency. She was prepared to take a good deal from buyers, however savage, but not this. W. must get the brute out of the house as soon as possible. Etta could not face him and it wasn't fair to a child of that critical age to inflict such an ordeal upon her. In fact, she had undertaken already that G. should go.

Just then, however, G. and Etta came in, holding hands, and confessed that they were engaged. They offered no explanation. It appeared later that Etta had suddenly dried her tears, gone to G. and assured him that she was no longer a child, that, in fact, she took a rather serious view of her responsibilities as a woman. The W.'s were, of course, delighted and said that they had expected the news for the last year. And they assured each other that a steady husband like Robert G. was just what Etta needed, she was the most feather-headed of girls.

In fact, they were a good deal surprised that she stuck to the engagement. And it is pretty certain that she would not have done so if she had not known that they expected her to change her mind. She was a fond daughter and followed her parents' reactions very closely.

However, after the marriage, when she found herself mistress of Robert's large, ugly house in the Midlands, she was bored to madness. She complained that there was no one to talk to—that is, no one to flirt with. And Robert's adoration no longer made her laugh, it filled her with horror and disgust. He was more than a bore, he was an incubus. There were rows. There had been rows on the honeymoon; for instance, when Etta threw a diamond ring into the Trevi fountain and refused to have it brought out. Robert was a generous man but he had a respect for good jewellery and considered that Etta should also respect it. 'That was a beautiful ring,' he said.

'Well, you can get the insurance and buy another,' said Etta, who was in her most troublesome and incomprehensible mood.

'But, my dear, that's just what I can't do. It wasn't lost.'

'Oh, how stuffy you are, Robert—of course it was lost. You've lost it, anyhow.' And then she began to giggle. 'Yes, you've lost it,' and she added rather sharply, 'why do you always look such a sheep?'

And this was the kind of question which always threw Robert into confusion. It had no connection whatever with the subject in hand. But he had discovered in the first hour of marriage that Etta had no idea of logic—her mind, if you could call it a mind—seemed to proceed by a series of flea-jumps. The effect was stupefying, how can one talk rationally with a flea? What answer did Etta expect to such a question? It didn't seem to have an answer and yet Etta seemed to expect an answer. She sounded most impatient for an answer. And all at once he responded, 'Why did you marry me?'

An answer which startled him—shocked him. How had he come to say such a thing, so wildly off the point? Was he, too, condemned to think like a flea? Was he to lose his natural human senses? He added hastily, 'But never mind.'

'But I do mind—I want to know, too.'

Robert said nothing to this. He didn't know what to say.

'You're sorry you married me,' she said then.

'Oh, no—of course not, my dear.'

'Yes, you are. And you think I am too. But you're quite wrong. I'm very *glad* I married you—you're so funny.'

They returned to G.'s family place, known simply as the Farm, with relief. Both wanted a change from the honeymoon, any change. G. was glad to see his pigs and cows, and especially his poultry. He knew where he was with cows and poultry. Their psychology was simple compared with young wives. And Etta at once set to work to change everything in the house, to get builders, plumbers, electricians, engineers and decorators. For six weeks she was gay, happy, charming; at a thousand pounds a week. Especially on the day that her sister Nora came to call and envied her the new bathrooms, she was so affectionate that Robert was completely reassured. He told himself that all was well, the difficulties that notoriously infect honeymoons were forgotten, and his marriage, his real marriage had begun.

But on the very next day, Etta complained of the awful boredom of life in B.shire, and went off to pay three weeks' visit to Nora. She came back only because Nora wanted her bedroom for a visiting Primitive—that is to say, because Nora had thought it time she went back to her husband.

The decorations were now complete and she hated them. But said it was not worth doing them over again—no one in B.shire knew a Regency wall-paper from a Morris. Her boredom was so awful that she would cry even before breakfast.

And then, quite suddenly, young men began to appear at the Farm. This was a great surprise to Robert and to everyone but Etta. No one had seen a young man at the Farm before, even the labourers were all well up in years. Young men were not thought to exist in this remote part of B.shire. But suddenly they appeared, not just one or two, but in flocks, droves. Like those male moths described by Fabre, who will discover a female of their species in an hermetically sealed case, locked in a bank vault, several hundred

miles away. And these males were in fact precisely the same species
as Etta. You might have been puzzled at first to give them any exact
definition. But when you saw them talking, with all their features
at once, and not only their features, but their knees, elbows, necks,
backs, even their behinds, when you noticed the way they sat with
their noses poked forward a foot in front of their knees, the way
they crossed the room, as if coming on the stage to loud applause,
the way they threw back their heads when they laughed, the way
they ate chocolate éclairs, like starved hyenas tearing at a corpse,
and, above all, the way they looked at Etta, you said at once,
'Simply male Ettas.'

The first to arrive were five young pilots from a training camp
about a hundred and fifty miles away. Robert came home one day
from shooting, with a buyer, and found these young creatures, all
in blue, swarming round Etta in the hall. As he entered, she was in
the act of flapping at them with a handkerchief and saying, 'Go
away, you horrid boys.' But her tone was far from minatory, and
the handkerchief was about four inches square.

What shocked Robert in this scene was more the vulgarity than
the mysterious arrival of five pilots as if out of the air. He had not
realised that Etta could look so much like a floozy, or say, 'Go away'
in just that tone of invitation. He was especially disturbed because
the buyer, S., one of his biggest buyers, was a thoroughly vulgar
fellow who, though over sixty and as fat as the fattest Yorkshire
White in G.'s sties, burst out laughing and at once began to treat
Etta as a floozy.

It is always exquisitely embarrassing for a wholesale merchant
when a buyer takes liberties with his wife. For, contrary to the
general opinion among cynics, it is only among some of the more
primitive and unsophisticated tribes that buyers are allowed this
privilege. In Europe generally, there is a kind of understanding, a
sort of *jus gentium*, acknowledged among the very largest buyers,
those who will give an order for twenty million pounds worth of
aeroplanes before breakfast, that they cannot, positively, expect
wives to be thrown in. The whole question as between buyers, and
sellers' wives, is, in fact, left open and entirely at the discretion of
the parties concerned. Wives, in short, even of millionaire manu-
facturers, are regarded almost as free agents. They have room for

manœuvre. They can, as devoted helpmeets, decide to lend their weight at a decisive moment, or they can stand aloof, and simply offer charm, flattery, Christian names, kind glances, shaded lights and intimate confessions.

But here was S., in Robert's very presence, thrusting himself on Etta with greedy eyes and dripping jaws. And Robert could not blame him. For the same law that enjoins self-discipline on buyers, assumes virtue in their hostesses. A wife may or may not clinch a deal, but it is understood that this dignity has its obligations. She must be a good woman. If she proclaims herself a mere floozy, all bars are down. Robert could not blame the brute S. for behaving like a brute. He could only rage at Etta.

As it happened, Etta treated S. with such contemptuous rudeness that he left next morning and did not give an order. She had called him a pig and this was his weak side. He had noticed the resemblance himself.

And, though Robert did not even tell Etta of the loss of the order, he was still more deeply wounded by this shocking treatment of a man who had bought so largely and generously from his firm, who had been a faithful supporter through slumps, wars and Japanese competition.

He was deeply relieved and deeply upset; he was like a man who has been saved from bankruptcy by being wrecked on a desert island. He did not know what to do, or what to think. And he was a man who, from youth, had always needed to have very clear ideas in both departments. He was one of those people who, in that larger part of the world which still lacks signposts, motor roads, bridges, are quite unable to find their way about. He had no sense of direction. He needed maps clearly oriented and plainly marked. Such men, of course, are easily bewildered in marriage, even in a love affair. They are always getting out their maps and compasses and finding that no map has any relevance. None of the chief features of the landscape is even marked. And the compass simply turns round in circles as if the magnetic pole had suddenly located itself in the lady and was even more disinclined to stay in one place.

Where was the poor fellow's psychology now, that guide in all the affairs of life? As far as he could see, this young woman had none at all. Today she was charming, she sat on his knee like a kitten and purred to be stroked; tomorrow, she could not bear the sight of him and locked her bedroom door. Did she love him or did she hate him? Was he, as she said sometimes, her dear old Baldy, or was he, as she said another time, a bore and a pest?

After the visit of those pilots, and some more pilots, she did seem to settle more on the last opinion. And after the pilots were reinforced by fifteen or twenty agricultural students from a county college (seventy miles away), by a reading party of undergraduates from Oxford (ninety miles), by seven cadets from Sandhurst in a jeep (a hundred and ten miles), she showed such hatred of the poor man that he was embarrassed even to be in the same room with her. And he was actually glad that the bedroom door was now permanently closed to him. He had lost his way, but at last he had come up against a dead end. And a dead end is definite. It gives you a position. You stay there or you go back.

After a few weeks' reflection, Robert perceived that his marriage was at an end. And he set himself to find a way back towards nonmarriage. But just when it seemed to him that he should consult a lawyer, Etta came to him one evening and implored forgiveness. She said she had been mad, she had behaved abominably. 'But it's because I love you so much, darling.'

Robert hardly believed this. For the last six weeks Etta had spent almost every hour of the day with her cousin Billy, just back on leave from Malaya. True, she had been away in London for three of those weeks, staying with a school friend, but, according to a friend of Robert's, that is to say, a business acquaintance from whom he bought large quantities of dye, Billy had stayed there too. And the school friend was away on a tour round the world with the husband of the dyer's wife's half-sister, who had been at the same school. The upper rank of the British merchant world is, in fact, quite small, and has a strong sense of propriety. Even a millionaire can be turned off a board simply for getting into the wrong papers in the wrong way.

Robert's dyer felt it his duty, both as a rich man and a seller, to give Robert warning that Etta and Billy were occupying the same flat.

Robert, therefore, answered rather coolly that Etta had a strange way of showing her love and asked her if she would divorce him, for, if not, he would divorce her. She could then marry her Billy.

'But, Bob, what do you mean? What awful nonsense. Billy is in Malaya. And I hate him—I always have hated him. Oh, Bob, I didn't know you could be so horrible—yes, horrible.'

And she cried. Then she was furious, and had a fainting fit. G., alarmed, sent urgently for the doctor. G.'s doctor was one of the old school of country doctors. He drove an ancient Ford, but he wore breeches and hunted with the B.shire in a black coat. Yet he was not horsey, and, though he fished and shot, he did not value himself on these pastimes. His attitude towards sport was slightly disillusioned, only less so than his attitude towards people. When he felt a pulse, he raised his eyebrows as if to say, 'Really, what nonsense.' When he sounded a chest, and said, 'Say ah,' the 'ah' came out like a sigh of self-pity. Everybody was rather afraid of him. He had an immense reputation, especially with the farmers. He could drink level with the largest. He was always called Old Doctor, not to distinguish him from any young doctor—there were none in B.shire—but simply as a term of respect.

Old Doctor asked what urgent meant. Had the patient broken her neck or was she bleeding to death? Informed that she was only gravely ill, he said, 'I'll be there,' and arrived next morning at breakfast time. He was in hunting kit and remarked that it was lucky that the Farm was on his way to the meet. He gave Etta ten minutes. He came then to G. and said, 'Pregnancy in an early stage, I should think. Your wife says it can't be. But time will show. Meanwhile she's all right. No cause to worry,' and he glanced at the decanter on the sideboard. G. gave him a neat whisky and said that it was impossible for Etta to be pregnant unless she was at least three months gone.

Old Doctor was drinking. He raised an eyebrow, put his glass down and said, 'She's not that—the question is if she's pregnant at all. I may be wrong. Time will show.'

'You're certainly wrong.'

'D'you think it's going to rain?'

'I happen to know you must be wrong.'

'If it rains, I'm going home. Arthritis. I went to a specialist and he said, "You're a doctor, you ought to know there's no cure for arthritis." I said, "Yes, but I was hoping," and he said, "And there's no cure for that either." But I didn't laugh. Why, damn it all, I heard that crack first in hospital, forty years ago. Only Harley Street would dare to try it now.'

G. said nothing to Etta of this discussion. But a month later, it began to appear that the doctor might not be wrong. G. at last found courage to ask Etta a question. She answered that, indeed, it seemed that she might, possibly, be pregnant.

'But it's not possible,' said G. 'If it were you would be in your fourth or fifth month.'

'I know—it's very funny. But Nora didn't show much either.'

'But it can't be me.'

'But Robert, what are you suggesting?'

Robert suggested Billy. Etta was insulted, furious; she had always hated Billy. Then she began to cry, and said she wanted to go home. Then she said that she couldn't go home because her mother would misunderstand, because her mother would never forgive Robert. Then she grew furious again and asked Robert how he dared to have such suspicions of her virtue. Robert saw, in fact, that she was trying to make a fool of him, and he was not prepared to be made a fool of. He mightn't be a genius but he knew it to be impossible that the baby was of his making. Besides, having reached a dead-end, having discovered a position, he was not prepared to be thrown once more into bewilderment and lunacy. He answered briefly to this effect and said that he would take steps. Etta answered that if he was thinking of divorce, her family would never forgive the disgrace and she would fight the case and expose his horrible cruelty. Robert left the house next day, ostensibly on tour. But stayed away for seven months.

He was waiting for the baby to be born. Then he could prove dates by the evidence of maids and Etta would have to agree to an uncontested and quiet divorce. For, above all, as Etta certainly guessed, he dreaded a court case. He saw himself in the witness box, the bald old husband of a young girl, and a husband that had been deceived, a jealous, a revengeful husband. A ridiculous husband. And not only ridiculous but somehow contemptible. Would not people say serve him right for marrying that poor young thing? No, he could not make up his mind to face the court.

Then the W.'s intervened. Mrs W. wrote to tell him that Etta was in despair. What had she done to be treated like this, in her condition? She was making herself ill. Did he realise his responsibilities?

G. decided to lay his evidence before the W.'s. He wrote to his lawyer and the lawyer answered by phone. Had he any evidence? Oh, merely maids' evidence about dates of cohabitation. But that was worthless. Did he not know that in English law it was almost impossible to bastardise a child, so long as it was born in wedlock? See the case Blank *v.* Blank, Blank intervening, not to speak of Roe *v.* Roe, Doe and Hooper.

G. had not known. He was amazed and still more confused. Could the law be so silly? He lost weight, his cheeks sank in, his eyes bulged out. He even accepted a large order for carpets, for a hotel company, at a losing price. He consulted a doctor who told him he was heading for a breakdown and advised a nursing home.

Then suddenly he flew into a rage against the injustice, the disorder of this wicked world. He made for home. He would turn Etta out. At least Billy's child should not be born under his roof. Afterwards, he would insist on a separation.

But he had cut it too fine. He arrived to find Etta in labour. All the W.'s were there, including Nora, and the youngest daughter, now eighteen, who received him on his own doorstep and told him that she would never forgive him. He had broken Etta's heart. If she died, as was highly probable, he could consider himself her murderer.

This girl, Susy, after a rather giggling adolescence, had lately taken to Greek and politics. She was cramming for an Oxford scholarship. Her moral standards had taken a severe turn and she considered that the woman was always right.

But Nora came out hurriedly to interrupt her sister while Robert was still struggling to find words for his indignation. She embraced him warmly on both cheeks. Nora, at twenty-five, looked almost as old as her shipowner. She was exceedingly plump and wore her hair in the Primitive style, drawn back to a small and tight bun. She used no make-up whatever, and dressed in what her sisters called garments. She was, in short, the extremely intelligent and successful wife of a rather difficult but high-minded egotist, who not only worshipped, but even, to a certain extent, appreciated her.

And, having greeted her brother-in-law with a warmth which astonished him, and also, so to speak, slightly tenderised him, as they say of a dry steak, she took him by the arm, drew him aside, and told him that he need not worry about Etta, she was doing very well considering her rather nervous temperament.

'And, Robert, I want to take this chance of saying how grateful—how immensely grateful—we all are to you in this rather horrible business. Yes, I know about Billy—we all knew that he was a danger. And we all feared the worst when he came on leave and Etta so madly insisted on seeing him. She always was mad about Billy—even though she couldn't really stand him. No, really——' Nora, feeling a certain resistance developing here, hastened to affirm this surprising fact, and then at once, like an experienced wife, hurried on, 'No, really—but what I wanted to say was how wonderfully you have behaved. No one could have understood poor Etta better or managed her more wisely. And believe me, she knows it. She realises it. You'll never regret your goodness to the poor child. You've absolutely saved the situation. I'm afraid,' she said, smiling affectionately, 'I used to rather laugh about your psychology but, believe me, I thank God for it now.'

Robert was just about to answer that Nora had got hold of the wrong end of the stick, that he had by no means forgiven Etta, much less accepted the baby. But suddenly there occurred in him a shift of ideas, much like that shift which takes place among piled and tangled logs when a lumberman breaks the jam. First one goes floating, and its neighbours begin to swing inwards towards the current, then they, too, move, and twenty more begin to swing. Great baulks whose heads have been sticking up at all angles, like stranded crocodiles, suddenly slide full-length into the water. And now the whole mass is proceeding smoothly and rapidly downstream, in parallel lines, as neatly ordered as a battle fleet.

So, in a period of half a minute, while Nora discreetly observed, from the side of the eyes, the effect of her intervention, G.'s ideas, for the first time in nearly two years, gradually assumed order and direction. The effect was immediate and striking. Like the lumberman who, having safely regained the bank after some ticklish moments, looks at his work and knows how good it is, he felt hard ground under his feet, he perceived that he was safe, and he enjoyed the dignity of one who has exhibited his skill, his mastery.

He answered Nora, with the modesty of a man of breeding, 'Really, I haven't done so much—I don't know if I could have done anything else in the circumstances.'

'You could have ruined Etta's life,' said Nora drily, 'and that's just what most men would have done. And believe me, she knows it very well, and won't forget it. Neither shall I. It's really been— well, noble is the only word.'

'Oh no, Nora, really. If you look at the thing from a psycho-logical point of view——'

It was the first time he had used that word for two years. But now he used it with a confidence quite new, even to himself. It really did seem to him that he had played not only a noble but a wise part, the part of a master of life. He was a sensible man, he did not want to exaggerate his foresight or his penetration, but there was no doubt that he had refrained from divorcing Etta, as most men would have done, or even separating himself from her. And that had been the psychological master stroke.

'Yes,' he said, 'psychologically speaking——' and Nora did not laugh at him.

Other people, neighbours, laughed a good deal when the baby was born. They knew the dates, as country neighbours always do. And the boy was the image of Billy, with brilliant blue eyes and a mole by his left eye.

But that was five years ago. Etta G. has had two more children, undoubted G.'s, poor things, taking very much after their father, in the usual way of daughters, and their mother is not only a devoted if rather slapdash mother, but a loyal wife. She is, indeed, almost too fond of showing her affection in public. She will suddenly throw her arms round her husband's neck and kiss him, on the most inappro-priate occasions. And, as she does so, you see on her still rather childish features that same expression, half mischievous, half enquiring, with which she used to kiss the pink nose of her grey pony, her kittens, her dolls, and the old pug.

She has a Jaguar of her own, but young men no longer swarm at the Farm. Etta doesn't encourage them, and besides, at twenty-five she is too old for pilots, or even military cadets.

And no one laughs at G. any more, except those failures in life who laugh at everybody. He is very obviously a big man, master of his own house, master in his business, Chairman of the Bench and an authority on Rhode Island Reds. His letter on Modern Business Management and a New World Order was not printed in *The Times*, on account of a Middle East crisis, but it is coming out next week in the *Poultry Breeder's Annual*. It is certain of respectful attention among informed circles.

A HERO OF OUR TIME

THE afternoon sun made a white ray like a searchlight through the dust and fell in a crooked oblong on the nursery floor. A bluebottle caught between the window-panes, buzzed for a moment like a circular saw; stopped; and buzzed again; but on a different note as if the saw were cutting a softer plank. A small boy with bronze hair and a thick round body was squatted on the floor, building a wall of blue and red bricks round the diamond of sunlight.

The room was full of a warm dusty silence. With its bare floor and wooden chairs it felt like a waiting-room at some small country station. A thin tall boy of twelve was making chemical experiments at the table. He dipped a test-tube into a jam-jar full of water, poured in some acid from a small bottle, and then looked round the room as if for some further ingredient. Noticing the small boy close to his feet, he said, 'Get out of my way, Moore,' and added scornfully, 'you don't think the sun will stay there, do you?'

Moore made no answer. He was holding a brick in the air and closely watching the sunlight within the enclosure. The tip of his tongue showed between his lips. He knew, of course, that the sun usually travelled across the floor. He had tried before to catch it, with his old wooden blocks, and failed. But these bricks were made of imitation stone, and quite new. He had had them only for two days, since his seventh birthday party. He had not yet tried them out.

The chemist went to a drawer and brought out a crooked nail which he dropped into the test-tube, then with a hasty movement like one getting rid of a bomb, he propped the tube against two books on the table and stepped back. Nothing happened. He looked at the tube, through his round spectacles, with gradually increasing surprise. At last, muttering to himself, he leant across the table

towards the box of chemicals opened upon it. This caused his leg to
press against the ear of the small boy who did not, however, notice
the pressure. He was absorbed in his own affairs. His tongue was
now half an inch beyond his lips.

The chemist, having read the directions pasted inside the lid of his
box, went thoughtfully out of the door. But immediately his head
reappeared and he said with an important tone, 'Don't you touch
any of my chemicals.'

The small boy made no answer.

'They're not safe unless you know chemistry—you might blow
the house up.'

Moore, with a quick stealthy gesture, as if to avoid giving alarm
to a sleeping enemy, put the brick into the last gap of his wall. Then
he sat holding his breath.

The chemist reappeared carrying a brass screw. He selected
another bottle of acid, poured it into the test-tube and added the
brass screw. Nothing happened. The boy was astonished. Obviously
he could not believe his eyes. After staring for half a minute, dumb-
founded, he picked up the test-tube and held it towards the light.

A bell rang just outside the room and from far below a voice
called, 'Moore, Moore, hurry up, aren't you ready yet?'

It was time for Moore's walk. He heard the voice but he did
not notice it. He did not even know that he had been called. Suddenly he jumped to his feet and cried, 'Charley—Charley.' He
stared breathless at the bricks and the sun. Then he said gravely,
triumphantly, 'It's stopped, Charley.'

Charley did not hear him. He shook the test-tube impatiently and
then prodded the nail with a pencil. At once the bottom of the tube
fell out and the acid poured over his blue shorts.

'Oh damn, damn it all——' he rushed out of the room and into
the night nursery next door. He banged both doors behind him,
causing Moore to blink twice.

But Moore had not forgotten his triumph. He took a deep breath,
swelling out his whole front, and looked down again, with a proud
smile, at the captive sun. At once he ceased to smile. He squatted
hastily down and looked more closely. The sun had jumped over
the wall at one side, towards the table. Probably, he thought, it had
taken the opportunity while his eyes blinked. He drew in his tongue.

He stood up. He let out his breath with a sigh. His figure ceased to be important. He put his foot slowly through the bricks.

'Moore—Moore.'

Moore glanced desperately round the room. He felt as if only a minute of life remained to him. Suddenly he noticed Charley's box of chemicals and the jam-jar.

'Moore, do you want me to have to come up?'

At these words, Charley rushed from the night nursery, in grey flannels, and hurled himself downstairs. Moore darted at the table, seized Charley's bottles and pill-boxes and poured a few drops, a few grains from each, into the jam-jar.

The water at once began to turn pink. Moore, on tiptoe, retreated quickly; looking over his shoulder. But before he had gone three steps, the nurse entered, seized him by the arm and jerked him towards the door, with cries of indignation.

He made no protest. Moore, after a lifetime of nurses, relatives and parents, was used to being handled. He was able to submit his body to any treatment without the least effect on his mind. His eyes were still fixed on the jam-jar as he was whirled through the door, into the night nursery.

'Why aren't you ready?' The nurse, a tall middle-aged woman in a blue uniform, was red with irritation. 'I sent you to get ready, didn't I?'

'I did get ready,' the boy murmured in a dreamy voice. He had given up hope of an explosion, and was looking at a crack in the floor. He had never noticed it before.

'But you weren't ready, Moore.'

Moore heard this but did not notice it. He had just had an extraordinary thought, that under the floor must be a ceiling. He was standing over a ceiling.

'What do you mean, ready?' the nurse said.

'I was just getting ready.' Moore gazed up at her with a candid expression. He jumped suddenly with both feet and then looked downwards with a smile.

'It's time you went to boarding school,' the nurse said severely. This was a threat. But Moore did not hear it.

She whirled him back into the day nursery and said, 'You stay there and don't you dare to move.' She went into the bathroom.

Something glittering and bright with colour caught Moore's eye from the far end of the table. The jam-jar now in full sunshine. But its contents had turned purple. Moore tiptoed round the table and touched the jar. It was quite warm. He darted from the room and flew downstairs. The nurse, still more indignant, did not catch him until she reached the park gate opposite the house. He was standing in the middle of the gate staring towards the roof of the house with such intensity that the nurse also turned to look in the same direction.

'What are you looking at, Moore?'

'Nothing.' He turned and ran along the path with a peculiar step, lifting his knees high. This movement usually meant that he had been up to something.

'That's why you take such a lot of interest in it, I suppose.'

The boy turned round again to stare, but the nurse at once caught him by the arm and jerked him round.

'Come on, do—I'm getting a bit tired of your antics.'

Moore followed slowly, looking back over his shoulder. Suddenly he heard a shrill cry. A small boy in green knickers was rushing towards him across the grass. In the distance, a nurse with a pram could be heard screaming after him, 'Come back, Richard—come back this minute.'

Moore left the path and ran towards Richard. The two small boys seemed about to rush into each other's arms; but at a yard's distance both stopped as if surprised by their own enthusiasm, and not quite sure if, after all, they knew each other very well. In fact, they had met but once before, at Moore's birthday party.

Richard was a dark child with small brown eyes and dark full lips, pushed forwards. These lips seemed to quiver with sensitive feeling, like a dog's nose. He pushed them out now at Moore and said, 'Hullo, Moore.'

Moore threw out one foot and put one hand to his head in a position which would have seemed affectedly lackadaisical in any-one but a small child. He said, 'What's your name?'

'Dicky.'

'Yes, I know. I thought you were Harry at first.'

'No, I'm Dicky.' Richard seemed about to cry. His enthusiasm had sunk to dejection.

Moore suddenly changed his pose from careless languor to animated confidence. He leant forward, 'Do you know what?'

'No, what?'

'It's a secret, of course.'

'I won't tell anybody.' Richard flushed with pleasure.

'I've made an explosion.'

'Is it a bonfire?'

'No, it's chemicals. It's getting hot—it will go off in a minute.'

'Can I see?'

'Yes, of course. It's in my nursery.'

'*In* the house?' Richard's dark thin eyebrows disappeared beneath the fringe of hair brushed across his forehead. This gave him an appearance of the utmost amazement.

'Yes, it's going to blow up.'

'The house?'

'Yes, it's in the nursery and it's chemicals. Look.'

He put his arm round Richard's waist and turned him round. Both gazed at the house. From the two paths the two nurses uttered loud cries. They did not, however, approach in order to seize their victims because they did not know exactly how to speak to each other. Richard's nurse was in a grey cotton dress and a hat like a maid, whereas Moore's was in uniform like a real nurse.

'Look, there it goes,' Moore said. 'You can see the smoke now—out of the roof.'

'Out of the roof,' Richard murmured. He screwed up his eyes and exclaimed suddenly in a new astonished voice, 'There *is* smoke coming out of the roof.'

'That's not from a chimney,' Moore said, confidently.

'Oh no, it's blue.'

'Yes, it's blue—it's just going off—it's just going to blow up. Blow the roof up.' Moore gave a hasty jump of excitement. 'I told you it would—it's chemicals. It was absolutely boiling.'

'Is anybody in?' Richard asked.

'Moore, Moore, come here this minute.'

'Richard, Master Richard—you wait till we get home.'

'Everybody, except Daddy.'

'But they'll all be killed,' Richard said, opening his eyes wide.

'They're not in the nursery. They're underneath.'

Richard reflected a moment. Then he said, 'But that doesn't matter—they'll be killed all the same.'

'But they're underneath,' Moore cried loudly.

'That doesn't matter,' Richard answered in an impatient tone. An argument had begun. 'Don't you *see*—when anything blows up, it falls down.'

The angry expression disappeared from his face and he remained with open mouth, much startled. He could not understand how the word down had come out of his mouth in such close relation with the word up.

'It *does* matter,' Moore shouted furiously. He had not noticed that his friend had already stopped arguing. But when Richard did not answer, he took notice of his last remark and said in a mild and doubtful tone, 'Mummy's in the drawing-room.'

An expression of delight came into Richard's face. He cried suddenly, 'But don't you see, Moore—when anything blows *up*, it falls *down*.'

'The house?' Moore gazed at the house with raised eyebrows.

'Of course, silly.' Richard chanted his gospel, self-proving by its own mysterious contradiction. 'When anything blows *up*, it falls *down*. Why, anyone could see that.'

'It's a very strong house,' Moore said. 'It was built at a good time.'

'But it will fall down. Don't you *see*, it must fall down, and everyone will be killed. Everyone. Your mummy and everyone.'

Moore, staring at the house, looked suddenly frightened. His lips parted. He seemed about to scream. Richard, who in the pleasure of his epigram, had forgotten all other issues, gazed triumphantly at his friend and cried, 'When it blows *up*, it will fall *down*. Of course.'

Moore turned very red and frowned at the house. Then he said, 'It's not going to blow up.'

'But you just said it was.'

'No, it's not,' Moore said firmly. He clenched his fists and frowned. 'It's not——'

'But the smoke.'

'That's nothing—that's a—it's a chimney.'

'Richard, *are* you coming, or aren't you?'

'I warned you, Moore.'

The children were jerked violently apart and dragged away. The air was full of angry women's voices. Richard, whirled across the grass by one arm, called back, 'When it blows *up*, of course it falls *down*.'

Moore, shaken until his head swam, was being driven towards the path. 'I've had enough of your disobedience,' the nurse was saying. She was very angry. 'You'll go straight in to your father as soon as we get home. If you're not old enough to behave yourself, you're not too old to be smacked.'

Moore, trotting forward, with flushed cheeks and guilty air, muttered to himself, 'It's *not* going to blow up, it's *not* going to blow up.' He was making it not blow up.

A moment later, as he trotted at the nurse's skirts, he looked nervously over his shoulder at the house. It was still there. He gave a thoughtful solemn skip, then ran forward, throwing out his legs in a proud manner, and pushing forward his stomach. He was pleased with himself. He had saved his mother's life.

THE TUNNEL

FOR instance, you're going out to supper with Alice, you've written that you'd love to come; but you'd much rather have stayed at home. It's raining frosty fog, and you're tired out. How will you face those awful stairs? Alice lives at the top of a decayed family mansion in West Kensington, with peeling stucco pillars and a long flight of cracked steps. It has the special squalor of imitation magnificence in its old age, like rabbit-mink going bald, and rolled gold showing the nickel. The stairway inside reminds you of the old pictures of the bad man's road from luxury to hell. The first flight has a pile carpet; the next two are cord carpets; the fourth, a worn oilcloth; and the last is quite bare. What's more, it's stained all over with mysterious chemicals, jaundice yellow, gas green, and a kind of mouldy blue; they look like poisons, and on the top landing there is a great dark red splash, like blood. Alice's door, too, is more sinister than that of any jail; low, black, and crooked. It squints as if it hated you, as if it had murders to hide.

If Alice hadn't sent that note, one of her last-minute notes which give you no time to invent an excuse, you'd be at home in front of a nice fire, eating a chop from your excellent landlady. She knows how to cook—Alice can't, but you couldn't tell her so. Even though you've been engaged for a fortnight; that is, re-engaged since that last breaking off about—what was it about? But what's it matter. Now we're fixed; we're sensible, we don't expect too much, and all the surprises are out. Yes, of course, a tender soul, but how cross when she has a conscience, and what terrible colds. The rain is getting heavier and colder—that right shoe is leaking again through the hole, and your corn is beginning to shoot, like toothache. The pavements are jammed with people looking at the Christmas shops; and how? They see nothing, they say nothing, they don't know what they want, they only get in your way and their own. They drift along in the wet like rubbish down a drain—their faces are like yesterday's newspapers. What do you care? Not a damn for a damn thing. You always go this way to supper with Alice, you don't need to think or feel. You just flow along in the drain—and all at once she's there, out of nothing. The presence of Alice. She's breathing about you, she's blowing her nose within you—you discover suddenly that Alice is special. Even with her most exasperating cold, even with a red nose. Especially then. You adore her. In fact, for the first time in your life, you know what it is to be in—how can you say it. No word can describe this sensation, this extraordinary—— For instance, if you had a gun and could fire it off, all six shots, not for her—Alice wouldn't understand it, she'd be terrified for you in case you hurt yourself, or got into trouble with the police—but for yourself. Or better, you think, as you dodge the umbrellas in a rather dirty Burberry and your wet weather hat—suppose you could just spread out your arms and float over the people, and while they gazed upwards in absolute amazement, you explained, 'This is because of Alice.' But of course, these lumps, these cabbage stalks wouldn't notice you at all—they'd simply go on brooding at the shops, or if they did look up they'd only say, 'What nonsense—I suppose it's some advertisement,' and they'd be disgusted, not only with you, but with everything. That would be the last straw.

To hell with them; to hell with everybody. And you dash along the road at the risk of your life, and when you arrive you leap up the stairs like spring-heeled Jack. And now the stairway is like the soul's ascent to heaven, at every turn it throws off another temptation of the devil, another materialist illusion and gets nearer to that noble austerity which belongs to the lives of the saints. And in fact, Alice is a saint. She's poor enough, God knows, her usual lunch is a bun, but what's the betting she's spent half a week's pay on this supper. Nothing is too good for you, and what have you done for her? What has anyone done for Alice? She's had to fight every yard from birth, but now things are going to be different—a new era begins. At last you can make her realise that she's appreciated at something like her real worth. You shout, knock, ring. You hear a step, and your heart pauses; you think, now you're going to see her,

Alice, your Alice. The door opens, and a young woman is standing there, a stranger—for twenty seconds at least you don't know her. You don't realise it's Alice. This isn't only because the landing is dark, and the light behind her is dazzling in your eyes, but because she has a different face, a new smile, and wears an enormous apron you've never seen before, an incredible apron from her chin to her feet. Your lips mutter at last, 'Am I too early?' And she answers with the same extraordinary smile, 'No, of course not; do come in,' but you know already that something is wrong, fearfully, catastrophically wrong. What can it be? You walk into the room, the only room, in a kind of daze as if you had been sandbagged. Alice has disappeared into the cupboard where she cooks. Her frock is hanging on a chair, her make-up things are on the chest of drawers. She hasn't yet done her face or dressed. You look at your watch and discover that, in fact, you *are* early—by twenty minutes. So that's the trouble. And you're shocked. How can the girl be so silly, don't she know how plain she is? Of course she does. She's often remarked that hats are her big problem because of her queer face, so why be upset at being caught with a shiny nose? What does she think you come here for? To gaze at her ridiculous nose and admire last year's frock, that doesn't suit her anyhow? Don't she realise that the only reason anyone could ever love her would be for her character, her gaiety, her intelligence, her self, her soul? That is to say, if and when he did love her, really and truly, without romanticising the thing.

You'd like to go away and come back at the proper time, but of course that's impossible just because of that smile, that apron, of this whole ridiculous situation.

Alice reappears with a proud indifferent look like a princess challenged by a cockroach, snatches the dress from the chair and vanishes again into the cupboard—you hear sounds as of a wrestling match and a bottle falls down. But you don't hear Alice say, 'Bother the thing,' as usual, and the tension increases. She brings in supper and only then does her face, with deliberate and brazen elaboration; but when at last she comes to the table you see her mouth is crooked and her nose is as white as chalk, a frost-bitten nose.

The silence is now unbearable, and you cast about wildly for a remark. But, as all the interesting subjects, that is, anything about furniture, flats, gas versus electric stoves, crockery or bedding, are impossible, you find yourself talking about the news—as neither of you takes the least interest in the news, the conversation at once reaches a very high level.

By the time you reach the customary veal Alice is growing animated about the atomic bomb, the terrible times we live in, and you are saying that civilisation is done for. The sort of thing you read in all the best modern authors, not because they believe it, but because they said it years ago when it was the right thing and they can't say anything else now, or perhaps because they want to frighten people, or simply because they're annoyed about the income tax.

Both of you know that all this is nonsense, that you don't believe a word of it. What if some bomb did kill you tomorrow, you wouldn't know anything about it. It might be a good deal better to die that way than in the way you will die. It's not just cowardly to fear wars and bombs, it's simply stupid, and perhaps bogus too. You look at Alice and think, 'I don't ask that she should throw herself into my arms; I don't expect anything exceptional; Alice is not a genius at self-expression. Far from it; she couldn't bring off the grand gesture if she tried; I should have been quite satisfied if she'd been glad to see me.'

You reflect, 'And why couldn't she welcome me? After coming down that horrible road in the horrible rain. Do I really know Alice? Aren't I deceiving myself about this very ordinary girl. I think her so modest, so affectionate, a shy and innocent creature who simply doesn't know how to hide her most trifling reactions. But isn't this the very disguise that cunning girls take to catch a man. I don't suggest even that she does it deliberately; to say that every woman, yes, from the age of one year, is a born actress is to repeat something so trite that it isn't worth saying. That's why I was forgetting it.

And if Alice isn't an actress then what did that horrid grin mean, that haughty step? What does she mean now by talking about Egypt and Russia and Chinese Imperialism—stuff only fit for suspicious-looking strangers chance-met in a bus queue. It can only mean she wants to insult me. I don't want to be unfair to the girl. Naturally she is touchy about her looks—with such looks. But it is perfectly clear that if she is not at least slightly deceitful—then she has certain flaws, deep flaws, in character and temper, that will have to be set off against her charm, if that's the right word for whatever it was that got me into this embarrassing relationship.'

Meanwhile you are remarking with the air of a Prime Minister, 'Of course the United Nations is a step in the right direction, or perhaps you don't agree.' And Alice makes a solemn face (but her face as well as her voice, her whole attitude, with a flat back, and her neck bent on one side, is completely false, and also, as it were, tense with the knowledge that the evening is becoming more and more disastrous) and says, 'But if Russia really has all these complexes, then you can hardly see how——'

'Oh yes, Russia is terrified, there's bound to be a war.'

'On the other hand if she isn't terrified——'

'Oh, if she's not afraid of war, we're absolutely done for, I agree.'

'Though we weren't done for last time there was a war.'

'No, but this time——'

And then we're back at the hopeless dilemma of the modern world, and the impossibility of enjoying life, especially for the young, like us. But both of us know perfectly well that life is not merely enjoyable, it is moments of such bliss that——

But it is impossible to describe that bliss; that compound of devotion and gratitude, and amusement (because you want to laugh at yourself for being in such an exalted state) and the sense that all this is understood, is shared, that you aren't alone (of course, nothing is really understood, but at this level you get away from words, you enter on the intimate, the real, the divine), that you are, in short, blissful—and not only blissful but happy.

For that is there too, happiness; a quite different thing from bliss, a kind of—what would you say—if bliss is slightly drunk, champagne drunk, happiness is just the opposite, it's a feather bed, a vast tranquillity, enormous contentment, entire confidence. Small babies have it when they sit on their mother's laps, you can see it in their eyes, but they don't know it, they don't know anything and you know too much; yet you can recognise happiness at once, you feel it and greet it. And such moments are not so rare either; they may crop up once, even twice a week; they can be got at even by art, when both parties are gifted with some talent for the thing, when they can laugh, for instance, at the same bad joke.

'So, in fact, you don't think life is worth living,' Alice says. And her voice is an accusation. What she means is, 'You don't love me.'

And the correct answer, of course, is to agree, to be, if possible, a little more pessimistic, a little more grand in despair. But for a moment you hesitate, you rebel, you ask yourself if it's really necessary for you to make this answer. Have you not control of your tongue, and your imagination? You resolve to break out of this tunnel down which you are being conducted by invisible forces, and you open your mouth to say, 'What awful nonsense you're talking,' but what you hear yourself say, quite lost in despairing astonishment at your own words, is, 'Logically speaking, and if one isn't afraid to face the facts, I don't see why any sensible person doesn't cut his throat pronto.'

Ten minutes later you are in the street; you are full of misery and rage. That good-night kiss, cold as bacon, how did she dare? What hypocrisy, what spite; and you say to yourself, 'This is the end, I'll never see her again, what an escape. She is a block, a lump, an automatic machine; no, she is worse, she knew that I was longing to be nice to her, but she wouldn't allow it. She was determined to spite me because I caught her with a shiny nose; what pettiness. What a small, mean creeping creature, what a scorpion, a bug, a vampire!'

You wake up next morning with a stomach ache, cramp in the right leg, black spots in front of the eyes, and feeling as if you had been but half resuscitated from a deep and muddy grave. Your mouth tastes of dirt. You are full of despair and self-satisfaction; at least you've escaped from ruining your life. How crazy you were to think you ever liked that girl, that pug-nosed, green-eyed, pigeon-toed, tittuping lop-lolly, that butter-fingered, small town, high school throw-out. Her mouth is bigger than her mind is small. Oh, how she drops things, cups, pens, ear-rings, saucepans, hairpins, and handkerchiefs. Oh, how she leaves her gloves in churches and her handbag in the ladies'. How she lets the kettle boil over and cries, 'What a fool I am,' and then does it all over again. Oh, how she gazes at you with intense interest while you tell her a new story from the office and interrupts in the middle with the question, 'Did you remember to get your shoes mended?' How she apologises for each new cold and won't take anything to stop her colds, and don't care either. Oh, how she says, 'You know what I mean,' when she hasn't the faintest idea what she means and is too lazy to find out.

You sit down at once to write, to make your getaway. 'Are we absolutely sure we're really suited to each other?' That's the tone; you'll post it on your way to the office.

You'll be late for the office but you don't care; if they sack you, you can always go to Australia, get right away from Alice—twelve thousand miles is not too much. A note in the letter-box. Alice's writing—to break it off? So she saw it coming. Just like last time. And just like her to rush in first. No date, as usual, and no beginning —she won't even write, 'Dear Dick.' But what's this—'I can't go to bed without writing, I feel so wretched. I can't even honestly say I had a headache or the blight. It was a kind of a horrible thing that got hold of me; I can't describe it—it was a sort of devilish thing— and you were such an angel. My darling, I don't suppose you will ever want to speak to me again. I couldn't blame you, and I've no excuse. But if it is for the last time I do want to tell you what a great and exciting thing it has been to know that you have sometimes wanted to be with me—the greatest thing in my life.'

And you don't go any further, you don't wait even to look at the second page. What do the words matter? The point is that if you are to see Alice before she goes to her office, you must fly. You'll be scandalously late at your own office but you don't care a damn, you don't care if they do sack you, though you can't go to Australia, though you can't get another job anywhere. You must make Alice understand that nothing, nothing, nothing, was her fault, that you were deliberately torturing her.

Look at that old colonel, or perhaps a banker. Certainly an important person, old and important, poor old chap, old, important, and ridiculous. He's absolutely furious with you for running your eye into his umbrella. What a liberty! And it *was* a liberty—you didn't even notice him. You wish you could stop and explain, for instance, that you're blind on that side, or that your foot slipped. It wouldn't be any good telling him the truth and why you have to be in Kensington by half-past eight. He'd be still more furious. He'd think you were laughing at him. Nobody, nobody, could under-stand what's happened to you. You don't understand it yourself—it never happened to you before; no, never before have you even begun to understand what Alice is to you—the miracle of her goodness, of that true soul which forgives everything because it only knows how to love. My darling, at last I can make you understand what I feel—what I mean when I say that at last I am really and truly in—but how flat that would be—how stupid, how absolutely nothing.

NEW WOMEN

SAMUEL THOMPSON, civil servant, was the only child of Athenia Battersby, the famous feminist leader. She is said to have been the original inventor of the plan for burning letter-boxes. She designed the suffrage hat, and wrote a book proving that Shakespeare was Queen Elizabeth. But it is a shame for the modern generation of women to laugh at Athenia. They owe her a big debt. She had courage and character, she really did a great deal to get them votes and sacrificed much of herself in the process—her sense of humour, for instance.

She forbade marriage to her followers, as a degradation, but after women's votes were granted, she married Sandy Thompson, a feminist as enthusiastic as herself, and taught him to cook; in fact, made him a modern husband thirty years before his time. He would do the washing-up while she dashed out to meetings.

Not that Sandy was put upon. He himself proposed to do the washing-up and learned how to sew. He was a man of pugnacious temperament who loved any excuse for a fight. If he had not been brought up a Christian pacifist, he would have made a first-class thug. As an organiser of suffrage demonstrations, he loved to bash policemen, and he hemmed dusters to show how much he considered women a superior sex.

Their marriage was very happy in its own way. But dedicated parents are bad for children, whose imaginations, like their bodies, cannot bear to remain fixed in any one position. Samuel had an austere upbringing—both parents taught him from his earliest years that boys were little better than brutes. But, as friends later pointed out to him, he had no right to complain of anything, he was lucky to exist at all, and had almost certainly been an accident. Athenia was even more against motherhood, at least for feminist pioneers.

than marriage. She held that responsible educated women should devote themselves to the professions, in order to take a commanding place in the life of the country.

Samuel took the point and was humbly grateful for life, such as it was. He grew up a modest and retiring character. Even in his office in the Ministry of Energy, he was hardly known, except as a signature, by anyone outside his own staff. He belonged to no clubs and played no games except Patience. His hobby was collecting stamps, but he also took an absorbed interest in the latest scientific developments, as recorded in his morning paper, an old Liberal daily which, by tradition, gave at least half a column a week to general culture. The theory of the expanding universe occupied him for months and drove his acquaintances distracted. He was also extremely concerned in nuclear physics and the possibility of the disappearance of the world one morning owing to an accident at Harwell.

He especially avoided the company of women; he appeared a confirmed old bachelor. But at forty-six, to everyone's astonishment, he fell in love with one of the secretaries at the office and married her. Aminta was a very smart young woman direct from college and right up to date. She condescended to Picasso and was completely bored with the subject of homosexuality. She wore a Victorian cameo in her hat and had two fine drawings by Millais in her flat.

The wedding was in church. Aminta was a keen churchwoman. This was slightly embarrassing to Samuel, who had never even been baptised. Athenia Battersby had strong views about religion. As a scientist, she called it nonsense; as a feminist, a man-made device for the subjection of women. But Aminta pushed him through the service and he did not disgrace himself.

They settled in a charming little villa at Kew, Ruskin Gothic, and furnished it with some good mid-Victorian mahogany. Aminta was lucky enough to find a Clarkson Stansfield sea picture in a junk shop and to get it for ten pounds. This fine work gave great distinction to their sitting-room. Aminta's treasure was a gilt clock under an original glass dome, which required and received a draped mantelpiece.

Aminta now proposes to entertain Samuel's friends and is surprised to find he hasn't any. She has dozens of both sexes and all ages, especially friends from college. All these young women are in jobs or just married or both. They arrive every day to see Aminta, bringing small babies or bottles of claret. All of them want to see Samuel, and gaze curiously at him, tell him that Aminta will make a very good wife in spite of her intelligence, and, when they go away, say to each other, like all friends of a new-married person, 'But how extraordinary—how on earth did it happen—can it last?'

They suspect that their dear but reckless Aminta has acquired Samuel as a collector's piece.

Samuel is embarrassed by all these young people, especially the girls. They shock him by their conversation about the most intimate details of their love affairs and the complexes of their lovers; they startle him by their strong views on the subject of marriage, and especially the duties of a wife and mother. They have no patience with a girl who can't cook, clean, wash, drive any make of car, mend linen, put in a fuse, do running repairs on household gadgets, choose, store and decant a respectable wine, and pick a smokable cigar at a smokable price.

As for children, they all want six apiece and take the view that if any child does not turn out a perfectly integrated and responsible member of society, the mother will be entirely to blame.

When Samuel dares to murmur that there can be bad fathers, they gaze at him for a moment and then say that no doubt mothers sometimes make that excuse, but it's not really an excuse. They obviously think that any woman ought to be able to cope with any kind of man, including the worst of fathers. Cope is their great word. Though polite to Samuel, they don't take him very seriously. When he raises the question of the expanding universe one evening, he is assured by two girls at once, of whom one has taken a first-class in mathematics and is a Fellow of her college, that it is a stunt for the tabloids. The universe, they say, can be made to dance the polka with a suitable equation; it depends only on which system you use. The mathematician, who is in the eighth month of her second child, then returns to the subject of lyings-in. Is it better to have a monthly nurse at home or go to hospital? Either way things can go wrong, and then the party discusses some cases that have gone wrong, with the technical elaboration of experts. It is, for instance, quite wrong to suppose that the widest hips are a guarantee of safety. Samuel listens with horror, and breaks into cold sweats. Aminta is small, with an eighteen-inch waist and hips of that rare type that look slim even in jeans.

Aminta, after two months of marriage, is already expecting. She has been decided on six children from the age of ten. She, too, has had a feminist mother.

Samuel mutters in his sleep and wakes up with a moan. Next day he begins to flutter about Aminta like a nervous hen. She must not lift that chair, she must not use her arms, she must not run on the stairs, she must not go out this morning, it is too hot or too cold. Aminta laughs at him and obeys till he has gone to the office. Luckily, at this time his newspaper brings out some articles on painless childbirth, and Samuel rushes out at once to buy all the books. Aminta is commanded to do exercises, to learn how to relax. And she obeys. For Aminta herself has been a little apprehensive, even if she says nothing about it. What girl doesn't have some anxiety in her first pregnancy?

Aminta has lost her parents young, and her family was small and scattered—Service people. A naval cousin dropped in from Hong Kong one day with a real Chinese jar of the genuine ginger. An elder sister, an Anglican nun, brought her an original Negro carving from Central Africa. A great-aunt from the Midlands, who had sent her, for wedding present, a plated muffineer dating from her own wedding, asked herself for a week because she could stand anything except modern hotels.

She was a little thin woman of seventy-six with the complexion of a sea captain. Her nose was Atlantic blue, a dark fierce blue like the middle of a storm cloud. Her mahogany cheeks were as dark as a cabin door. Her forehead, a sharp line above her eyebrows, was dead white, like that of an old sailor. But she had not the suave and ingratiating manner of the liner captain; she was bluff and gruff. She had got her complexion from sixty years in the hunting field where she had made a distinguished career as the first woman M.F.H., at least of a smart pack.

Even in town she wore the mannish dress affected by pioneer women of the late 'eighties; a Tyrol felt, a double-breasted reefer, a man's hard collar and four-in-hand tie.

She was amazed and disgusted by the furniture, especially the gilt clock and the draped chimney board. 'Good God,' she said. 'Just like my granny's, and *she* was a stuffy old relic even for Dawlish. All that dusty rubbish went out with moustache cups.'

She thought the Stansfield equally out of date. She herself possessed a seascape, a Boudin: 'But of course, I know this modern French stuff doesn't appeal to everyone.'

She brought a brace of pheasants and two bottles of port, Croft '26. She instructed Aminta to cook the pheasants, an anxious job for so particular a gourmet, but she allowed no one but herself to decant the port.

And over a second glass that evening, she unbent so far as to say she could forgive Samuel everything but his mother.

'My God,' she said, 'what a disaster—that vote. When I was young, women ran the civilised world, let's say, France down to Longchamp and England up to Newmarket, but they don't run anything now, except those ridiculous nylons. My generation were people; we made ourselves respected, but you girls are just a sex. Look at the advertisements.'

When she heard of Aminta's relaxing exercises, she snorted, 'There you are—just what I said—as if women were all the same size and shape, just lumps of sex stamped out from the same batch of cake mixture and served up in the same frills.'

She poured and savoured her third glass, accepted a cigar, glanced at the name on the box, said, 'How do you afford Havanas? You young ones today spoil yourselves.'

'They were for you,' said Aminta.

'I thought so,' said she with the grim smile of an M.F.H. 'Getting round the old fool on her weak side.'

Suddenly she became extraordinarily genial, in the way of so many gruff old people who seem astonished and overwhelmed at the least mark of affection. Probably the old woman paid for her local glory in loneliness. All at once she couldn't do too much for her dear Aminta and Sammy. She would send them game every week and her own recipe for bread sauce. She would order a dozen of burgundy at once—that was the stuff for breeding gals, nothing like it to make blood. As for the lying-in, there was only one man in England—one that a woman could trust—her own man, Dr McMurdo.

'He's delivered all the Hunt children for forty years, and he's set my collar-bone five times. He's been retired since the war, but he'd do anything for me. I'll bring him up at once to look over the ground.'

And she wired the next morning. She belonged to the generation before phones.

Samuel swore that no Blankshire bone-setter should come near his Aminta. But Dr McMurdo came the next day. It was apparently true that he would do anything for a lady so distinguished in history as Aminta's aunt. He was also in his seventies, an enormous man with a huge, round purple face and a great swag belly. He was dressed in a shaggy yellow tweed with four-inch blue check and a duster-pattern white flannel waistcoat. He ate and drank with all the gusto of a Falstaff. To see him at table would have been an inspiration to Stratford. He, too, was an expert on port. His manner with the patient was less fatherly than familiar. He did not exactly slap her on the behind after his examination, but it was more than a pat.

When she talked about her relaxing exercises and painless childbirth, he grinned like a satyr and answered with more affectionate pats, 'Leave it to me, dear. That's what I'm here for. Just you relax.'

And he winked at Thompson—a wink combining all the genial villainy of a Falstaff with all the cynicism, as Thompson put it, of an abortionist. And, as soon as Aminta had her first real pain, out came the chloroform mask. She knew nothing more till she waked up feeling beautifully flat and heard, as in the far distance, a baby crying somewhere, and gradually realised that this was her baby.

After that, it somehow came about that McMurdo attended also for the other two children. They are brought up in the new style, to mind their manners, and to get up when their papa comes to table— just as Aminta promised to obey, so she says a house must have its head and supports the authority of the father. The result is that when she threatens them, 'I'll tell Papa,' they become instantly as good as gold and amenable as lambs. They are happy, lively, and reasonable; they have no moral problems and always know the right thing to do even when they don't mean to do it.

The Thompson family, in short, is a very happy one—Aminta's friends, who assured Samuel that her intelligence would not prevent her from making a success of marriage, were right. Samuel adores her. Their only subject of occasional difference is the vote. As a son of his mother he thinks Aminta takes the vote too lightly.

Not that she despises it. 'Of course, it's a thing one has to have,' she says, 'like mumps. But why do they always have elections on wet days and put the polling booths in back-yards among municipal dustbins? What do votes *do* after all?'

Though Aminta makes a great deal of Samuel's authority as master of the house, it is noticed that she runs everything; looks after all the money, pays all the bills, even at Samuel's new croquet club, drives the car and chooses the family holiday. What's more, when in that frantic fortnight before Budget Day, Samuel, like all senior Government clerks, brings back memos in the evenings and even for the Sunday, she will sit down and knock up a quite masterly report on the Calorific Value of Brick Dust, or the Profitable Utilisation of Factory Smoke.

In this happiness, Samuel has bloomed in a late florescence. He has given up stamps and collects glass paperweights. He wears a bowler and fancy waistcoats. His trousers grow narrower and narrower. He says that nowadays there is so little difference between political parties that old Liberals like himself might as well vote blindfold. And last election he very nearly did vote Conservative. The only reason why he refrained at the last moment was because he discovered that the Liberal candidate was a strong supporter of Sunday observance, and he has become a devoted churchman with a leaning to evangelism. In short, he is nearly a new man.

PERIOD PIECE

TUTIN, married sixteen years, with three children, had an affair with his secretary, Phyllis, aged eighteen, and wanted a divorce. His wife, Clare, with her usual good sense, was resigned. 'If you feel you must make a break,' she said, sadly but without bitterness, 'there's no more to be said. It would be stupid to try to hold you against your will. You'd only hate me and that wouldn't help either of us.'

But when her mother in remote Yorkshire heard of this arrangement, she wrote and said it was preposterous and wicked, she wouldn't allow it. Old Mrs Beer was the widow of a canon. She was a short, stout woman with a red face and a heavy jaw—a pugnacious and indomitable face. Yet there was something defeated about it too. The little faded blue eyes especially seemed to confess that the old woman had long given up hope of any serious attention from anybody.

You see such faces in boxing booths among the seconds and backers, men who have been in the ring all their lives and lost all their fight, but still follow the game as bottle holders, training partners, punching bags for young champions.

Her son-in-law laughed at her when she didn't exasperate him to madness by her sudden raids and arbitrary commands. Each time a child was born she planted herself in the household and took charge of every detail—laying down the law in an intolerable manner and flatly contradicting everybody from the doctor to the monthly nurse.

Now, at this talk of divorce, she excelled herself. When Clare wrote her explanations she came south without any warning whatever, broke into Tutin's office and, marching up to his desk, umbrella in hand as if about to beat him, demanded, 'What's this nonsense about a divorce?'

This in the presence of the secretary who was taking dictation—not Phyllis, of course—Phyllis was no longer a secretary. As the future Mrs Tutin she had to think of her dignity. She had a nice flat in a new building in Mayfair and spent her time shopping. The new secretary, on promotion from the general office, was a widow of fifty, Mrs Bateman, with a dark moustache and a strong cast in one eye. Phyllis had chosen her as a thoroughly reliable person.

All the same, Tutin was not anxious to have his most private affairs discussed in front of her. He opened his mouth to tell her to go but Mrs Beer had now come between. She planted her umbrella on the desk and shouted at him, 'But there's not going to be a divorce——'

'My dear Mamma, all this has been discussed between Clare and me and we are completely agreed that it's impossible to go on.'

'Of course you can go on—if you *had* to go on you'd go on very well.'

Mrs Bateman was still folding up her notebook, now she dropped her pencil. Tutin, a thoroughly good-natured man, hating to quarrel with anybody, answered patiently, 'Of course, these things are not so simple.'

Frank Tutin was a humane, a kindly man. He was extremely upset by this crisis in his family life. He realised how his wife was suffering, how much the children were concerned. He did not forget for a moment, he said, the danger to them of a broken home. Divorce was a very serious thing.

For days he had discussed it with Clare, analysing all the complex factors involved: Clare's feelings, his feelings, the children's feelings, Phyllis's feelings and everybody's right to consideration. Sometimes he had thought that there was no way out—divorce would be as bad as the present unhappy situation. But gradually he had found confidence; certain large principles detached themselves in the confusion—that the children of divided parents in an unhappy home were, according to a psychiatrist consulted by Frank himself, just as likely to suffer in character as those left with one or the other, alone but devoted, after divorce; that the Tutin's home life was growing every day more distracted, tense and impossible, that the one guiltless person who must not be let down was poor little Phyllis, that Frank and Clare had had many years of happiness together and could not fairly expect to go on for ever.

Clare in this crisis lived up to all Frank's expectations of her. Like the highly intelligent woman she was she took all his points.

And now, just when the divorce had been arranged in the most civilised manner, when Clare had agreed to ask Phyllis to the house to discuss the whole affair—Clare had been charming to Phyllis, so young and so worried, so terribly in love, Phyllis was already quite devoted to her—and when she had agreed to accept a reasonable alimony and allow Tutin to have free access to the children, Mrs Beer comes charging in like some paleolithic monster, hopelessly thick-skinned, brutal, insensitive. Comes and calls him selfish.

One could not blame the poor old woman. She was simply out of touch—she belonged to a rougher, cruder age where psychology was practically unheard of, where moral judgments were simply thrown out like packets from a slot machine, where there were only two kinds of character, bad and good, and only one kind of marriage, with no problems except the cook's temper, the drains or, in extreme cases, the monthly bills.

He could ignore poor old Mrs Beer—but suddenly he felt a strange uneasiness in the middle of his stomach. What was this? Indigestion again. He had had a touch of indigestion for the first time during these anxious weeks—Clare had been worried about him and sent for the doctor who had warned him strongly against worry. But how could he help worrying—he wasn't made of stone. It was worry, a new worry, that was working in him now. Had the old woman yet seen Clare, and what would she say to her? Clare didn't take her mother too seriously, but she was fond of her. And Mrs Beer had never before been quite so outrageous. The uneasiness grew to a climax; and suddenly he jumped up and made for home. He drove far too fast and beat at least two sets of lights. He had an extraordinary fancy that Clare might have decided to walk out and take the children with her. He rushed into the house as if his shirt-tail were on fire.

What a marvellous relief—Clare was in her usual corner of the sitting-room doing her accounts. She looked at him with mild surprise, blushed and asked, 'Is anything wrong? Do you want me for anything?'

'No, my dear,' Tutin caught his breath and gathered his nerve. 'It's nothing—by the way, your mother is in town. She turned up just now in the office.'

'Yes, she's been here too.'

'Oh, I suppose she's been telling you that I'm a selfish brute.'

Clare was silent, and Tutin's irritation rose. 'Selfish—spoiled—a mummy's boy.'

'Of course, Mamma is always rather——'

'Do you think I'm a selfish brute?'

'Of course not, Frank, you know I don't. You've been most considerate from the beginning. You've done your best to be fair to everyone.'

'Yes, but especially to myself, the mummy's boy.'

'What do you mean—I never said——'

'But you didn't contradict.'

'Mamma is so upset.'

But Frank knew his Clare. He could detect in her the least shade of criticism and he perceived very easily that she was not prepared to say that he was quite free from a certain egotism.

To himself he admitted that he had acted, partly, in his own interest. But so had Clare in hers. He was the last to blame her. To do anything else would have been flying in the face of all the best modern opinion; everyone nowadays was bound to pay attention to his psychological make-up, quite as much as to his physical needs. A man who did not, who took no trouble to keep himself properly adjusted in mind as well as body, was not only a fool but a selfish fool. It was his plain duty, not only to himself but to his dependents, to look after himself, and only he could tell exactly what was necessary to keep him in health.

They had agreed that Phyllis was the key to the problem. In fact, the matter was decided and now he could not do without Phyllis—it was impossible. She adored him. The poor kid simply lived for him. This new exciting love coming to him now in his early fifties had transformed his life.

He had simply forgotten what love and life could mean, until Phyllis came to him. Since then he had been young again—better than really young, because he knew how to appreciate this extra-ordinary happiness.

And he exclaimed to Clare, in a furious, even threatening voice, 'She's got round you, in fact, but I don't care what you think of me. If you refuse a divorce I'll simply go away—Phyllis is ready for anything, poor child.'

'Oh, but of course I'll give you the divorce. Mamma doesn't understand about—well, modern ideas.'

Tutin didn't even thank her. He had been profoundly disillusioned in Clare. Apparently she took very much the same view of him as her mother. In this indignant mood those sixteen years of happy marriage seemed like sixteen years of deceit. He could not bear the thought that during the whole time Clare had been regarding him with her critical eye. He was too furious to stay in the house.

He went out abruptly and then made for Phyllis's flat. It had suddenly struck him that Mrs Beer in her rampageous mood might even attack Phyllis, and he was at the moment particularly anxious to avoid the least chance of any misunderstanding with Phyllis on account of a slight difference of opinion between them about a mink coat. Phyllis considered that, as the future Mrs Tutin, it was abso-lutely necessary to her to have a mink coat. Tutin was not yet convinced of the absolute necessity.

As he came in Mrs Beer came out. And Phyllis was in an extra-ordinary state of mind. Red, tearful and extremely excited, even, as he had to admit, unreasonable. For she flew at him. What did he mean by letting her in for that old bitch? She'd been here half an hour—she'd be here still if he hadn't turned up, bawling her out as if she were a tart. She was damned if she'd take it.

'But Phyll, I didn't even know she was coming to London.'

'Where did she get my address?'

'Well, the office perhaps——'

'It's never you, is it—what are you gaping at? I tell you you'd better do something. She called me a common little tart. She said I'd put my hooks on you because you were meat for a floozy.'

'But you needn't mind her—she's only a silly old——'

'Not mind her,' shouted Phyllis; she advanced on him with curled fingers. 'Why, you fat old fool——'

For a moment he had the awful expectation of her nails in his face.

But she did not claw, perhaps she was afraid of breaking a nail; she only shrieked again and went into hysterics.

Even after Tutin gave her the mink coat she still considered that she had been cheated of her case for damages against Mrs Beer.

Phyllis had very strong ideas about her rights. She asked Tutin several times if he didn't agree that this was a free country and he agreed at once, very warmly. He could not forget those awful words, 'a fat old fool.' He did not wish to offend Phyllis again. He even had some gloomy doubts about his future bliss with this darling child.

But he did not change his plans. He was too proud to creep back to the treacherous Clare.

And Clare was a woman of her word. The divorce went forward, and Mrs Beer, defeated again, trailed back to her bear's den in the northern wilds. Three weeks later, and before the case had come to court, Phyllis met a young assistant film director who promised to make her a star. They went to Italy on Tutin's furniture, and got a house within a hundred yards of the assistant director's favourite studio on the mink coat.

Tutin did not go back to Clare; he felt that confidence between them had been destroyed. There was no longer sufficient basis for a complete and satisfactory understanding, without which marriage would be a farce; a patched-up thing. It was Clare who came to him and apologised. In the end she succeeded in persuading him at least to let her look after him while he was getting over the great tragedy of his life.

He was, in fact, a broken man. He felt ridiculous and avoided his friends. He neglected to take exercise and ate too much. He went quite grey and in an incredibly short time developed the sagging figure of middle age. But under Clare's care his sleep and digestion greatly improved.

All this was seven years ago. The other day a visitor, a new acquaintance, who had stayed a week-end at the Tutin's, congratulated him on his happy family life, his charming wife, his delightful children. And in his B and B letter he declared that he would never forget the experience.

The young fellow, who wanted to join Tutin's firm, was obviously anxious to be well with him. Tutin was amused by his compliments. But suddenly it struck him that there was some truth in them.

After all, most of his happiness was in his home, and it was a very considerable happiness. How and when it had begun to re-establish itself he could not tell. He had not noticed its arrival. He had not noticed it at all. It wasn't romantic—it had nothing exciting about it. It was not in the least like that matrimonial dream of young lovers, an everlasting honeymoon agreeably variegated by large and brilliant cocktail parties for envious friends; it was indeed the exact opposite—a way of life in which everything was known and accepted, simple and ordinary, where affection was a matter of course and romantic flourishes not only unnecessary but superfluous, even troublesome. As for parties, they were perhaps necessary, but what a bore, really, what a waste of time, that is, of peace, of happiness.

And it seems to Tutin that he has made a great success of life in its most important department, at home. How wise he had been to make all those subtle adjustments in his relation with Clare, necessary to render possible their continued life together.

As for Phyllis, he has seen her once in a film, an extra in a crowd scene. It is a night-club and she is a hostess—he is entranced—he feels his heart beat double time—he thinks, 'I might be her husband now, and living just such a life as those roisterers.' He shudders all down his spine and an immense gratitude rises in his soul. He thanks his lucky stars for a notable escape.

Mrs Beer is seventy-eight and has shrunk down to a little old woman with a face no bigger than a child's. The angry red of her cheeks is now the shiny russet of a country child's, and its look of the defeated but still truculent pug has turned gradually to a look of patient surprise. The high arched eyebrows in the wrinkled forehead, the compressed lips seem to ask, 'Why are young people so blind and silly—why does the world get madder and madder?'

She rarely comes south, but when she does she gives no trouble. The Tutins cosset her and keep her warm; she plays a great deal of patience. Once only, after her good-night kiss from the children, and possibly exhilarated by getting out two games running, she murmurs something to Frank about how things had come right again as soon as he had given up the idea of a divorce. Frank is startled—he has forgotten the old woman's excitement seven years before. But, looking at her as she lays out a new game, he detects in her expression, even in the way she slaps down the cards, a certain self-satisfaction. It seems that she cherishes one victory.

For a moment Frank is astonished and irritated. Had the poor old thing really persuaded herself that her ideas had had anything to do with what no doubt she would call the salvation of his marriage? Did she really suppose that people hadn't changed in the last half-century, or realise that what might have been sense for her contemporaries in the 1890's, before psychology was even invented, was now a little out of date? Had she the faintest notion of the complex problems that he and Clare had had to face and solve, individual problems quite different from anyone else's, in which her antique rules of thumb had no more value than a screw-wrench to a watchmaker?

The old woman is still slapping down her cards and for a moment Frank is inclined to tell her how little he agrees with her on the subject of divorce, but he thinks at once, 'Poor old thing, let her enjoy her little illusion.'

Mrs Beer puts a red ten on a black jack, gets out an ace, looks up and catches Frank's eye. She gives a smile and a nod, quite openly triumphant.

Frank smiles as at a child who dwells in a world of phantasms.

THE SHEEP

Tomlin, having come in from the garden, settles down by the fire with his pipe and a paper. He has round him all the comforts of an old bachelor retired from business on savings, who understands exactly how to please himself, chiefly by limiting his desires. His health, carefully nursed, his digestion, are perfect; at sixty-five he is still able to eat anything he likes. He does not, however, indulge himself in such things as lobsters, mushrooms, or elaborate savouries, because, although he likes them, he suspects that they might be bad for him. He intends to enjoy his leisure for a long time still.

He opens *The Times*, ready for the keenest enjoyment of his day. He never reads *The Times* until evening, in order to have all day the pleasure of this anticipation.

Suddenly the phone rings. Like all old bachelors' phones, it is within reach from his armchair. He picks it up and hears a hoarse voice, 'Willie, this is Peter.'

'Who?'

'Peter—Peter. Don't tell me you've forgotten Peter.'

'Peter?'

'Yes, Peter—Peter, P for pee, E for eats, T for tight, E for more eats, R for racket—Peeeter. Now, look here, old boy, there's something you can do for me. And you're the only person who can do it.'

'Excuse me—but are you sure you've got the right number?'

'Right number? You're Willie, aren't you? Willie Tomlin. Damn it all, old boy. This is PETER—Peter Blew, of the Somme. We were wounded on the same day. I must be your oldest friend.'

Tomlin, casting his mind back forty years, to the front line of the '14–'18 war, does now recollect a Peter Blew, but with uncertain feelings. The vision that springs from some cavern of the past is of a young second lieutenant with a great deal of hair, a great deal of swagger, and a great line of blarney. According to himself, he can beat the bookies at their own game, and have any woman he likes, on sight. He is, however, not very popular among his brother officers, being given to sponging, lying, bragging, cheating and disappearing when there is work to be done.

It's true that they were both wounded on the same day. He remembers very well the base hospital where they lay in the same ward; Blew with a slight arm wound, picturesque and painless, Tomlin with two holes in his stomach, extremely ill. Blew is the darling of the nurses in a day, he keeps them in fits of laughter with his wonderful tales. Especially about little Willie at the war. Little Willie in this case is Tomlin. And Tomlin, out of pure self-respect, must laugh also at these legends. To laugh, for him, is agony. And when he laughs Peter Blew makes a bleating noise and says, 'Hear the dear old sheep.'

This word sheep, as Blew knows, enrages Tomlin. It has pursued him from his childhood when, in a large family, he was always the one to be ordered about, to take the part of Boer in a war game or horse in a bull-fight. In those days he had never been without bruises, and his black eyes were so rich and numerous that they became a family joke.

His mother would say, 'Poor Willie is so good-natured.'

Willie himself did not accept this explanation. For he resented his fate. He longed to be the fierce hussar, killing people with a sword, the ruthless cold-eyed matador, the wild bull. But he never got a chance.

And here is this four-letter man, Blew, a shyster if ever there was one, pinning him with the same tags.

It's not true and it's not fair. Why should Blew get away with it, with everything? It can't go on.

But when both come out of hospital, Blew gets a job at the base. His Colonel, a prejudiced old regular, thinks he is better out of the front line, that for all his swagger and his trench knife, he lacks the offensive spirit, that he is deficient in something called leadership. Everyone has noticed that in the actual presence of bullets, Blew becomes modest and self-effacing.

Tomlin, on the other hand, is returned to the trenches as soon as he can stand on his feet. He is not very adventurous but his men will follow him anywhere. And he is wounded twice again before the end of the war.

He remembers even more vividly a meeting years after the war, with a red-faced fellow of thirty or so, who calls on him at Hammersmith. Tomlin is still living with his widowed mother in the family house, a small terraced house in a street just one step removed from the squalid. All the same, it has been a hard fight for Tomlin to keep this house for his mother. He is her only support. His father, a curate in this same parish, has died young of T.B. and general overwork at fifty-two, leaving nothing but debts, themselves pitifully small.

His elder brothers and sisters, all prosperously married, are extremely sorry that the expenses of their families prevent them from affording any help. He is lucky, they say, to be a bachelor and free from this terrible burden of modern family life for the professional man.

Tomlin resents their meanness—even though he does not particularly want to marry he does not see why he should be deprived of the possibility. But, with this sense of injustice, he is all the more proud of his neat little house, so cleanly kept.

All the same, life is dull and he is flattered when Blew comes to call. He has forgotten his hard feelings of war-time and is pleased to see an old comrade, especially in such fine form. Blew is driving an enormous new shining Bentley, and has with him three lovely girls in the latest summer frocks. He himself is in white flannels and a straw hat with the pink ribbon of a famous rowing club. It is Saturday afternoon, and the party is on its way to Henley. Blew, however, is apparently not in training. He is smoking a cigar and as he approaches Tomlin he breathes a strong flavour of whisky.

Mrs Tomlin, a small, rather shy woman of sixty, has also come to the door. She is eager to welcome this rare visitor, a friend of her dear son's. She suspects that his life is dull, that he is sacrificing for her more than she comprehends.

Blew introduces himself, 'Major Blew—how do, Mrs Tomlin,' but at once turns to Tomlin and grasps his hand, 'My God,' he cries, 'dear old Willie—just the same as ever. What a bit of luck to find you. I knew you were somewhere round here and the milkman did the rest. I was sure he'd know—you always liked milk, didn't you?' And he goes into a shout of laughter and slaps Tomlin on the shoulder.

Tomlin is confused. What's this about milk? Then he remembers his diet at the hospital, and is confused by his own confusion. He feels himself growing red.

The three ladies, gazing from the car with the most intense appreciation, burst into giggles and one of them cries, 'Oh, you Pete, you are a one.'

Tomlin now perceives that these ladies are very much made-up, probably very far from ladies—also that Blew is swaggering before them at his, Tomlin's, expense. But he says to himself, 'After all, we were comrades in arms,' and says, 'Do come in and have something —all of you.'

'Milk,' murmurs one of the girls, and the whole three explode into helpless giggles.

'Thanks, old chap,' says Blew, 'I'd love it—but the fact is we're late already. We had a bit of trouble at the start—argument with a bobby at a crossing, and now, damn it all, I find I've left my wallet on the piano. If you could cash me a cheque——'

The girls are now once more silent and gaze at the scene with fascinated eyes; the expression of spectators who wait to see a conjurer produce a gold watch from the ear of some country hick selected from the audience.

Tomlin is now growing embarrassed, not so much by Blew's bad manners, as by the mere presence of the man. There is something in Blew that not only disgusts but makes him feel uneasy, as men feel when they read of parcel bombs, and are suddenly reminded of how much spiteful meanness there is in the world, and how easily it gets away with every kind of malicious evil-doing. He sees that Blew despises both himself and his mother who stands ignored and equally embarrassed in the doorway, uncertain whether to stay or go away. He wonders how Blew has become a major, he had only been a lieutenant at the end of the war. And he wonders also how he has become a member of Leander—he doubts very much if he knows one end of an oar from the other.

He is very ready to cash a cheque for five pounds to get rid of

Major Blew, and he is not greatly surprised when the cheque is promptly returned to him from his bank marked 'R.D.'

But now, after all these years, having identified this oldest friend, he is not so patient. He answers him in a very cool voice, 'Yes, I do remember you now—and also a cheque you gave me for five pounds.'

'No doubt of it, old boy. I don't remember the cheque but I've always been a good friend to my friends—my real friends. Now, look here, my dear old fellow, it's about Florrie—I'm terribly worried about her——'

'Florrie?'

'My daughter Florrie, my only daughter. My only child. Dash it all, you were devoted to Florrie. Don't you remember how she used to sit on your knee to say her prayers?'

'No, I'm afraid I don't. I didn't even know you were married.'

'Married—who said I was married? What are you getting at? And what about that cheque? What cheque?' Blew is suddenly truculent. Tomlin remembers that when caught at cheating or lying, he was always extremely noisy and pugnacious.

He says, 'I wasn't getting at anything—as you mentioned a daughter, I thought——'

'Well, that's it, old boy,' Blew has decided to overlook the offence. 'The poor little thing has no one but me—you can understand a father feels a special responsibility in a case like that. And I've done my best, God knows. But a man has his work, he can't be around all the time—and this is it, Willie, Florrie's bolted. This very day as ever is. Gone off with a chap from the village. A complete crook and welsher. But I've just found out where they're going—London. To Paddington by the 9.30. And if you get along now you'll catch 'em easy. You've forty minutes.'

'But really, Blew—I never met your Florrie——'

'Wait a minute, old boy. Here's a kid of seventeen been got at by a crook—a real crook. He's a known bigamist. Did time for it under the name of Caffee. He's not only a crook but a stinker—owes money all round, and he drinks. If she goes with him she's finished for life, imagine a kid like that—as simple as a new-born kitten. And all you got to do is go to Paddington and tell Florrie I'm coming up by the night train and will she just wait to see her poor old daddy before taking the high jump. Just wait a few hours, that's all. For Daddy's sake. And without prejudice, no commitments either side. Just put it to her. And if she says no, well, it can't be helped. It'll break my heart but I'll just have to take it. But she won't say no, old boy. You can rely on that. She's a good kid—she loves her old daddy like he was her mother, too—it's just this bastard has got round her or she'd never have done such a thing. She'll wait for me and thank you afterwards—thank you all her life. You can't mistake her. She's a light little thing—fair hair, bright blue eyes. Looks younger than she is—just a kid. And she's wearing a long, green coat and a green hat. I don't know what he's wearing but he's a regular spiv type with a black moustache, and look here, my dear old chap, if he says a word, all you've got to do is call the police. You won't see his arse for dust——'

And Tomlin, not wishing to argue with the fellow, answers, 'Sorry, but it's too late, I couldn't make the train. I've no car and this is a rather primitive kind of suburb—I doubt if I'd even get a taxi.'

'No car and no taxi—that's a pretty thin tale. Do you realise you're the only man in the world who can do this for me—save this poor kid from misery and shame? My God, Willie, if you're really going to quit on me I'll just chuck my hand in—cut my bloody throat. I haven't so much to live for—I've had a hard time in this life—but I still had some faith in friendship. I've said to myself, "Damn it all, it's a rotten world but there are one or two decent souls left among the stinking dirt, there's Florrie and there's Willie Tomlin." And now it seems I was wrong there, too. Oh, to hell, what's the good.' And he rings off. Tomlin sinks back in his chair. He thinks, 'I'm well out of that. What a fantastic idea.' He relights his pipe, reopens *The Times* and seeks that evening bliss which has been interrupted.

But it has gone. His nerves are upset. He is deeply uneasy. He is ready to write off ninety per cent of Blew as cant, but he can't help feeling that the other ten is really in distress. After all, he is obviously fond of this daughter of his, and even crooks have hearts. He hears again that cry, 'I haven't so much to live for.' And he feels a pang; he is more and more shocked by his own selfishness. Here is a fellow creature in the midst of a desperate crisis, and all he does is to bring up against him a dud cheque, forty years old.

He is quite astonished at himself. How has he grown so callous, so small-minded?

He wishes now that he knew Blew's address. He would ring him up and offer at least to make the attempt. Almost certainly there would be no taxis available, and if there were, it would be too late to intervene at Paddington. But he would like to show good feeling. Also he would like to do something to appease his nagging conscience.

Ten minutes later the phone rings and his hand stretches out automatically. Again the oldest friend's voice, 'Hello, hello—Willie? Are you there? I've got you a hire car—it's coming for you now. A thoroughly reliable man. Drives like an ace. Don't forget to wrap up, old fellow. I remember your colds in the old days. And remember—soon as you set eyes on that chap Caffee and mention my name, he'll be off like a pickled rabbit. You've nothing to do but appear and say, "Colonel Blew's friend——" '

'Colonel?' Tomlin says; and then hurriedly, in case he may be hurting Blew's feelings, 'Right you are—I'll be there.'

He is actually relieved. His soul is at peace. He feels like an heroic soldier going over the top.

But even before the car arrives, he begins once more to see the difficulties of this undertaking. And they seem rather more formidable than German machine-guns.

With a deep sigh, he puts on his heaviest overcoat. He reflects that, after all, the whole affair will be over in an hour, and he'll sleep all the better for having done his duty.

Five minutes later he is on his way to Paddington in an ancient car, with all the doors rattling and a strong petrol leak somewhere, driven by a ruffian with a cigarette glued to his lip. Draughts blow in even through the floor, and Tomlin, who is indeed subject, not to colds but to lumbago, wonders where on earth the oldest friend has managed to hire such a miserable vehicle.

At the station the ruffian gets out and says to him, 'You looking for Miss Blew?'

'Why, yes, I was. Do you know her?'

'From a baby. *And* her guvnor. Used to drive for him. Did the Derby with him five years running—as an amateur—down the course to beat the book—needs a quick getaway at times. Too quick for *my* liver and lights. Got a fag?'

Tomlin gives him a cigarette, he lights it with a thoughtful air, humps his shoulders and says, 'A sporty boy—you might say.'

In the next five minutes, while they wait for the train, which is late, he breaks the silence only once with a loud and peculiar laugh, something between a crow and a snort; and throws the butt of his cigarette, with some violence, across the platform on to the down line.

Tomlin offers him another cigarette from his pack; he makes a slight movement of his forefinger, the sketch of a salute, and takes the pack.

The train comes in, the ruffian plants himself by the exit gate, Tomlin hovers in the background with a wild idea—an idea he knows to be impossible—of losing himself in the crowd and going home by the underground. But there is no crowd. About thirty or forty people only come from the long train and at once he sees the ruffian approaching a couple walking rapidly down the platform.

The girl is hanging on the man's arm; the man is carrying a large brown suitcase. She is a very stout girl with a large snub nose, red cheeks and small green eyes. She appears about thirty. The man is a large and heavy thug with a purple face and a black moustache.

Tomlin, seeing nothing for it, goes up to the girl and says politely, 'I beg your pardon. Miss Blew, I believe. I had a phone call from your father.' The man answers for the girl, 'Who the devil are you?'

'Colonel Blew phoned me and asked me to meet his daughter.'

'I asked who the hell are you? What right have you to speak for Colonel Blew?'

'My name is Tomlin. I tell you Colonel Blew requested me to speak for him, as a friend.'

The girl says, 'Never heard of you.'

The man makes as if to push Tomlin aside, 'Here, you clear out.'

Tomlin ignores him in a dignified manner and addresses himself to the girl.

'Your father asks me to say that he is coming to Town tonight and will see you tomorrow morning. He begs you most earnestly to take no irrevocable step until then.'

'I don't believe a word of it,' the girl cries. 'Irrevocable step.

What stuff. Daddy don't talk like that. What the bloody hell, any-how. I know your sort—pestering respectable girls at railway stations.' And the man pushes up against Tomlin saying through his teeth, 'Are you getting out or aren't you?'

Tomlin, determined not to have trouble, ignores this provocation and appeals again to the girl, 'You must have heard of me—Willie Tomlin. Your father's friend—his oldest friend.'

Caffee pushes Tomlin a yard, 'Here, what's your game, you ponce? Do you want me to dot you one?'

Tomlin, more and more irritated by the idea that he has been let in by Blew for this ridiculous affair simply because he is Tomlin, pushes back vigorously and says, 'Come now, don't be silly.'

'Silly—we'll see who's silly.'

'We don't want the police, I imagine.'

'The police,' bawls the other. 'What you mean about the police?' and he tramps heavily on Tomlin's foot with his heel.

Tomlin loses his temper, loses it suddenly and completely. His whole infuriated soul demands why these spivs and crooks should make a fool of him and despise him at the same time, simply because he has some decency. He shouts at the top of his voice, 'What do I mean, Mr Caffee? You ought to know that better than I do. I haven't a record.'

'A record—you bastard. What you mean, record?' He aims a blow. Tomlin thinks, 'I'll show 'em who's a sheep,' hits him flush on the nose and gets a punch in the ear. The girl shrieks, porters and a station policeman come running up and tear the pair apart. Caffee is bleeding from the nose and claims justice. Miss Blew never stops swearing that Tomlin has started the whole thing and struck the first blow.

Tomlin is arrested. But he declares that Caffee is abducting this child, daughter of his oldest friend—he has reason to suppose that he is a bigamist. And the two men are taken to the cells, while Miss Blew shouts after them that they are beasts, brutes and crooks, she never wants to see either of them again.

Next morning Tomlin, bailed out by a friend, goes home and finds the girl in possession. The ruffian has driven her to his address. She has spent most of the night in hysterics and is now drinking brandy to strengthen her nerves before getting up.

But she complains that if she gets up now she will not be able to eat—that scoundrel Tomlin has wrecked her health as well as her life.

Tomlin telephones for Blew and he arrives at three. He enters bellowing Tomlin's name and slaps him on the back so hard that he makes him stagger.

He is now an extremely bloated person with a face mottled like new-cut brawn, a lilac nose, and little bloodshot eyes. He is dressed in an old tweed coat, with leather elbows, and extremely tight and dirty twill trousers. When he causes Tomlin to stagger he also staggers, shouting with laughter. He is in the highest spirits. He has been celebrating on the way and is in a fine glow of triumph. He claims full credit for the masterly scheme as carried out by Tomlin.

'Didn't I tell you it would be as easy as a Derby mug. I knew that rotten crook had no guts. You'll see, we'll hear no more from him.' And he adds with deep satisfaction, 'That'll teach him to welsh on the old Colonel.'

Then he borrows a pound to pay his taxi, takes two more double whiskies and goes upstairs to see his little darling. Immediately the door closes behind him a noise is heard like a dog fight between a mastiff at its last wind and half a dozen small neurotic terriers. The terriers yap, scream, howl without cease; the mastiff roars, moans and gasps.

Finally Colonel Blew descends, rather redder and more swollen than before, exclaims at Tomlin, 'Christ, you've made a proper mess of things, haven't you?' falls in a chair and asks for a whisky, which he takes neat.

'A proper bloody muck up,' he says. 'Poor Florrie—that poor child. Well, I suppose you didn't think. You're not a family man—you dodged out on all that too. How could you know how a girl feels in a jam like this—all her life's happiness down the plug. And as for me, as for my feelings—but no one ever thinks of this poor old soldier. I'd be a fool to expect it. My trouble is I wasn't born your sort—with insides like a fish and no sense of responsibility. What do you care if she's been crying her eyes out all night, poor little lamb? But all I can say is, keep away from her if you value your bits and pieces—she's all out to cut you off with a blunt bread knife.' He

catches his breath, takes another gulp of whisky, throws up his arm
and cries, 'Good God in Heaven, man, what got into you last night?'

'When—how——'

'Hitting that chap and calling names. Ker-rist, you must have been
mad unless you were tight. But I might have expected it. It's always
the same with you half-alive chaps that stand from under. You're so
keen on watching out for a drop of rain that you fall down the first
open manhole.'

'You told me he'd been in gaol.'

'Je-sus, that wasn't any reason to tell *him* so. That's libel—
criminal libel. Don't you know your law? And what's more, old
boy, it seems he didn't exactly do time—neither.'

'You said he was a bigamist.'

'And so he was,' the Colonel shouts. 'So he was—in the eyes of
God. But it seems he didn't marry the girls—neither of 'em. And as
for gaol, he should have got there years ago but Florrie swears he's
not actually been inside. I'm sorry, old boy, but how did I know
you'd rush in like that without smelling out the ground. And now I
really don't see how you're going to come off without a pretty stiff
sentence. Criminal libel is a serious thing and so it ought to be. You
can't go calling chaps crooks all over the place—not in England, and
quite right, too. No, not even if they *are* crooks, as you ought to
know. In England, the public has protection. Of course, you could
go and apologise, but the question is, would he take it? Why should
he? He holds all the aces and then some.'

'You seem to have changed your ideas about Mr Caffee.'

'Bill Caffee! There you've got me wrong. I always liked Bill—
we've been in several little things together. He has a wonderful eye
for a horse, win or lose. A fine chap—all I worried about was would
he make a suitable husband for my Florrie. Would he be able to
meet his engagements and support her in the way she's been
accustomed. And I admit I doubted it, old boy. But it seems he's
just brought off a double at Leicester—he's prepared to pay off all
debts, debts of honour, anyhow, and offer her quite a nice little
home. And as for being suitable, well, it seems he's been suiting her
already. The sooner they get hitched the better—it's urgent.'

And within the next ten days, Tomlin, having been censured and
fined in court for an unprovoked assault on an innocent citizen,

thinks himself lucky to escape a further action for criminal slander by the humblest apologies to Caffee and a hundred pounds damages.

The Blews then forgive him. Blew borrows a hundred pounds to pay for the wedding, and Caffee another hundred for the honeymoon. Miss Blew suggests that a silver tea service would be appropriate as a present, and, in fact, deserved, since Tomlin has so nearly wrecked her happiness. He compromises with an electric kettle, and is not asked to the wedding at a register office or the party afterwards. But Mrs Caffee thanks him from Monte Carlo for the kettle, which she spells kettel, and sends a formal card for a flat-warming after the honeymoon, on the third of September, in a suburb forty miles away; the kind of invitation that expects immediate rejection. Tomlin answers with polite regrets that in September he will be away on holiday; and he adds that he always takes his holiday in September, after the crowds, for peace and quiet.

He writes this twice in draft and leaves it out again. He feels that it may sound like a reproach, even a dig. But finally he says, 'Damn it all, why be so sheepish? If they take it wrong, let 'em, they deserve it. And after all, it does show why I can't come to the party, that I'm not just dodging their damn party.' And he posts the letter, with dig.

There is no retort from the young couple. If they have understood his note as a dig they have taken it lying down. And he gets a certain moral satisfaction from his dig—at least he has not let those undisciplined savages get away with everything. He has vindicated morality and now he can really enjoy his peace again. He has paid heavily for it.

And he doesn't intend to take any more risks. On the day, five weeks later, when he is to leave for his annual fortnight at Brighton, he tells his housekeeper when she brings his morning tea, to give no one his address—not even if he says he's a particular friend.

Suddenly there is the noise of a taxi at the gate, a loud and prolonged ring at the door. The housekeeper pulls an astonished face and goes downstairs. A moment later Mrs Caffee charges into the room and cries, 'Thank God—you've not gone yet.'

She throws herself on Tomlin's chest, conveying to him a strong smell of gin. 'That brute,' she cries, 'that liar and crook—he hadn't any flat—he hadn't any money—he hadn't any job—and he hit me. I've left him for ever. I told him so. I said, "You think you can treat me how you like because I've no proper home and nowhere to go. But you've forgotten Willie." '

Tomlin, appalled, mutters, 'Your father——'

'Oh, Daddy—you know what Daddy is. You saw him. I phoned him last night and he told me to go to hell. All he wanted was Bill to pay him that ten quid. But I never expected anything from Daddy and I never got it either. Daddy's a hog. Besides, I shouldn't wonder if he wasn't my daddy at all. Mum only picked on him because he was tight——'

The housekeeper comes in with a still longer face, 'Excuse me, sir—it's the taxi man, he wants his money.'

'Oh yes, I forgot,' says Mrs Caffee, 'I haven't any money.'

Tomlin, in dressing-gown, goes down to pay the taxi man. As he passes his spare bedroom, he hears a small baby crying. He stops in surprise and looks in. The baby, a very wet and dirty one, is lying on the silk eiderdown, lately re-covered. Seeing Tomlin, it screams still louder.

And suddenly Tomlin is again embraced. Again he gets that breath of gin. 'Yes, it's little Peter. What else could I do—and I knew you wouldn't mind—you're so good——' And she sobs loudly, 'A true friend—my only friend in the whole world. Just while I look round—just for the next day or two——'

But six months later she is still looking round. Tomlin has appealed to Blew but the Colonel has disappeared into Eire after some trouble about a horse that has changed its colour from all black to brown, with three white socks, in a thunderstorm immediately after winning a race. All he has had from him is the bill from the ruffian for the drive to Paddington and back, forwarded with the note, 'Why have you kept this poor chap waiting for his money? You're lucky he didn't sue.'

There seems nowhere in the whole world for Mrs Caffee and little Peter to go except the Institution or the streets. And though she seems likely to do well on the streets, though she knows already a great many men who call on her at odd hours to share Tomlin's whisky, Tomlin can't make up his mind actually to throw her out.

He knows that if he did so he would never have another hour of peace.

The housekeeper has left, he keeps with difficulty an occasional char, the house is filthy, the bills are awful. Tomlin has aged ten years, he takes pills before and after every meal. And he hasn't even the satisfaction of a good opinion of himself. For he has quite failed to like Mrs Caffee.

He doesn't even take to the baby which grows more and more like Caffee every day, even to the impudent loudness of its voice. What depresses him most is the feeling that the whole thing is ridiculous, and it wouldn't have happened to anyone else, and that anyone else would know how to put an end to it.

But one afternoon when Tomlin, sunk in such gloomy thoughts, is waiting for tea, already half an hour late, a taxi stops at the door. Tomlin is sitting in the window to put himself as far as possible from Florrie who, having at last come downstairs, is about to ring the bell. For Florrie demanded all the privileges of the house mistress and Tomlin found it advisable to give Florrie exactly what she wanted. She was an expert in making life intolerable for anyone who did not.

From the taxi emerges a little old man in a blue suit and bowler, who looks like a bank manager or perhaps a retired sea captain. Tomlin is gazing at him in dull surprise, wondering what he can want, when he hears a strange exclamation behind him and looks round. Florrie is up on her feet and is also looking out of the window. Her eyes are jumping out of her head, her cheeks are blue-white, her mouth has sagged open. Tomlin has never seen anyone so completely and utterly terrified. For a moment she does not move, probably cannot, only the slack mouth twists as if she were going to scream.

But she does not make a sound. She shifts her gaze to Tomlin, puts a shaky finger to her lips as if to implore, 'Not a word,' and just as the front door bell rings, she tiptoes out of the room.

A moment later the char flings open the sitting-room door and flaps away back to the kitchen. She is a scrub-woman by nature and resents answering bells.

The little old man walks in, hat in hand, and presents himself, 'Mr Smith.'

In address and manner he is more like a captain than a banker. His glance seems to say, not 'What sort of an account are you?' but 'What sort of a man have we here?'

'I don't think I——' Tomlin stammers. Florrie's mysterious panic, her last imploring gesture, have thrown him into confusion. Here is some kind of crisis and he isn't used to sudden crises.

'No, you don't know me,' says Mr Smith, 'and I don't know you, but I'm not selling anything and I shan't keep you a moment. I believe you know a friend of mine called Blew, one of my oldest friends. I hear his daughter Florrie has been staying with you quite recently.'

'Yes.'

'Is she here now?'

'I'm sorry but she's——'

'Do you know her present address?'

'I'm sorry but I'm afraid——'

'Well, then, Blew's address. He's the man I want.'

'I'm sorry, but I think——'

'No idea where he is?' Mr Smith keeps his little blue eyes fixed all the time on Tomlin's face with an unwinking stare which would have been rude in a detective examining a suspected murderer.

This look is as disconcerting to Tomlin as that of a maniac whose whole way of thought is alien. But Mr Smith has an even more alarming habit. His mouth, which is absurdly small, a mere pucker under his rather thick nose, is in perpetual motion. After each of Tomlin's remarks he will chew for several moments as if tasting the flavour, and after each of his own he will purse up his lips as if to whistle. He purses them up now and pushes them forward till they resemble the sucker on an octopus.

Once Tomlin has caught sight of this mouth he can't look any-where else. Neither can he give any real attention to the man's questions. There is a kind of block in his mind.

He is not in the least afraid of this man. He is only confused before him as in the presence of something incomprehensible. Just as in face of his elder brother's delight in humiliating him he had felt more discomfort than resentment—a kind of sick bewilderment at such a phenomenon, and was ready to do anything to put an end to it—so now he does not know how to deal with a creature so mysterious and evil to his feeling. He is anxious only to get him away or to get away from him.

'Well,' he stammers at last, 'I did have a letter.'

'Where from?'

'I—I rather think it was Eire.'

'Eire,' Mr Smith is suddenly interested. His eyebrows rise high into his bulging forehead. 'What address?'

'He didn't give an address but the stamp was Eire.'

'What postmark?'

Tomlin, gazing at the man's mouth, actually does not take account of this question till Mr Smith, raising his voice, as if to a deaf person, barks, 'Postmark?'

'Postmark—oh, the postmark—I don't think I noticed the postmark.'

'Got the envelope?'

'No.'

Mr Smith whistles silently and takes a last hard look at Tomlin. His expression is not so much contemptuous as enquiring. He seems to be asking himself, 'What is this thing, this object?'

Then he dismisses him with a chew. He is once more animated.

'Eire—so that's the idea is it. I hadn't thought of that one.' He adds to Tomlin, 'Thanks a lot, Mister——' and makes off to his taxi. Tomlin falls into a chair.

'I wonder,' he thinks, 'what goes on inside that chap.' He gives a deep sigh and reflects, 'At least I didn't put him on poor Florrie's track.'

The char appears in great indignation which she aims at Tomlin. She is indignant with everything and everyone, but especially Tomlin. 'What have you done with the baby?'

'What baby?'

'Why, the baby,' bawls the char, who has a certain feeling for Florrie's baby because Florrie gives her gin and complains to her of Tomlin. 'It was in the garden, but the pram's empty.'

And in fact, not only the baby, but Florrie herself has disappeared. The only news of them to be had is from the milkman who has seen Florrie, hatless and coatless, with the baby, running down the back lane. 'I asked her if anything was wrong, but she didn't stop,' the milkman says.

That is two years ago, and Tomlin has heard no more of Florrie.

And as of an evening, alone in his shining house, beautifully kept by one of those excellent housekeepers always available to house-proud bachelors of quiet habits, Tomlin toasts his muffins and unfolds his *Times*, he feels a gratitude beyond expression. At last he admits it to himself. 'No doubt about it, I'm a sheep, a born sheep. And what luck that is, what marvellous luck.'

GOVERNMENT BABY

'SHE's coming, Caffin.' Two grinning faces appeared outside the mosquito house. The wire mesh gave them the look of early press photographs, grey and blurred.

Caffin, a pale fat young man, lying on the bed in a singlet, glared savagely at them.

'Can't you let me sleep?' he growled. 'I got a head like a sore tooth.'

'But you told us to tell you—it's that mish girl that brought the tracts yesterday.'

'Damn it all, why does she come now?'

'Oh well, it's all right, it's only because you said to tell you.'

They smiled at Caffin and Caffin glared at them. The smiles were now a little doubtful and Caffin felt the doubt. He got up slowly, swearing to himself, dressed even to a necktie, drank a hasty gin to steady his legs, and stepped out into the afternoon sun.

His two hosts peering out of the top windows of the store bungalow across the glaring earth of the station, watched him intercept the girl at the opening of the mission road.

He took off his hat, she jumped off her bicycle with a quick eager gesture. Caffin stooped forward, hollowing his back and wriggling his behind in a Chaplin pose. The two men in the store laughed, and Billson, who was the agent in charge, a man of fifty who did not laugh easily, said in a tone of surprised pleasure: 'That chap—he really is——'

Caffin accosted the girl. He gave another wriggle and raised his hat high into the air. The two watchers suddenly exploded with laughter. They could not contain themselves. Billson did not seem the same man. The tall dignified agent, with his thick grey hair and reserved critical expression, fell back into a chair, kicked up his legs and crowed. He clasped himself. He could not bear it. With a violent effort he controlled himself, sat up and wiped his eyes.

'You couldn't believe it unless you saw it—what a nerve——'

Meanwhile Caffin, his head swimming, played his part.

'I read the tract you left at the store, Miss, and I was wondering if you had any more of the same kind.'

'Oh, I'm so glad you liked it.' She was a short thick-set girl with a snub nose and round chin. She was neither plain nor pretty; an ordinary girl, but Caffin liked her skin and her expression. The first told him that she was young and new to Africa, the second that she was full of life and enthusiasm. He leant towards her giving his bottom another wriggle for the pleasure of his admirers, and said earnestly, 'You don't mind me speaking to you like this, Miss.'

'Of course not——'

'Well, Miss, I only thought you might have heard something——'

The delighted watchers, now including every white man in the station, saw Caffin's modest air of repentant sinner, the girl's eager and encouraging glances and gestures while he led her slowly towards the deeper shade of the bush road down which they disappeared. The bicycle left leaning against a tree was the only relic of the episode. Billson stared at it as if at something solid left over from a dream. 'You couldn't believe it,' he murmured. 'What a nerve.'

This was Caffin's first visit to Dabbi. He had been sacked from some temporary job further down the river and had invited himself to stay with Billson who had once met him on a boat. Caffin was a well-known character. There were many stories about him and all of them created the idea of a complete liar, soaker, coward and thief. But Dabbi thought them a little too good.

Saxby, the district officer, had used these very words at the club, 'Perhaps a little too good, Billson.'

'Oh, of course, the chaps pile it on,' Billson agreed.

All the same Caffin had a gratifying reception at the club that night. At least he had shown unusual gifts.

'And where's the lady friend?' Saxby asked him.

'She had to go back to her Bible class. She asked me to go along, but I said I was shy.'

The club which was held that night in the store compound down by the river, laughed heartily. Caffin didn't laugh. He was a post-war hero and his pose was the hard-boiled, the bored, the victim of fate.

'She'll change you yet, Caffy.'

'You bet,' he said. 'Back to the fold.'

There was another laugh but Caffin said gloomily, 'I can't keep off 'em.'

Saxby, who had been as generous as anyone in his appreciation of the artist, said, 'You're a wonderful chap, Caffin—how do you do it?'

'There's only one thing to tell a girl—that you're bad—rotten bad.'

'You tell 'em the truth, Caffy,' said a young soldier.

'Yes, they won't believe it—not a really nice girl.'

Again the club laughed; Saxby, good husband, good father, laughed more than anyone. 'I see—that's the idea.'

After this Caffin met the girl every day, although, of course, he complained bitterly of the necessity, saying in a disgusted voice, 'Why do I do it—it's just silly—and me feeling rotten too.'

In the evening he reported to the club, imitating the girl's voice, 'Oh, Mr Caffin, you mustn't think so badly of yourself.' Then in his own voice, 'Miss Smith—Martha—I may call you Martha, mayn't I—you're so kind, too trustful.'

The club roared with laughter. Caffin said in a mournful voice, 'It makes you tired.'

Another night he described his first attempt at a kiss. The lady, it appeared, had been greatly shocked.

'What did she do, Caffy?'

'All the usual things.' Caffin sighed. 'She said I was a disgusting beast.'

'She believes in the truth, too.'

'And she said she didn't see any need for that sort of thing.'

'Do they all say that?'

'All of 'em. I don't know why I go on.'

'And what did you do then?'

'Oh, the usual. I told her I couldn't help my feelings and that she was a crool hard-hearted girl.'

'And then?'

'Well, then, of course, I did it again.'

'What, kissed her?'

'Yes, God knows why. There's no kick for me in green apples. But it was the next move.'

'Did you though?' Saxby strove to call up the idea of this unconventional act. 'And what did she say to that?'

'Oh, the usual thing—she asked me to forgive her.'

'To forgive *you*?'

'For being so crool and hard-hearted. And, of course, she wanted some more, a lot more.'

'A lot more what?'

'Why, kisses.' Caffin said this word with such concentrated misery and disgust that the club burst into a shout of joy. 'It makes you sick,' he said, 'but I suppose it's my own fault—why do I do it, why?'

The next night he arrived in such extreme depression that the club actually cheered him. The whole circle broke into laughter and cries of encouragement as soon as he came into the firelight. He accepted his triumph with a gesture of despair, fell into his seat and sat bent forward for about five minutes gazing at the ground with his head between his hands.

'Come on, Caffy, what's the latest? Did she propose?'

He shook his head slightly but he did not groan. He never overacted a part; it is quite probable that he did not act at all. He played the part, modelled no doubt on some hero of the post-war magazine, some Huxley neurote or coffee-stall philosopher, so often, that it was himself.

'Spit it out, Caffy—we'll hold your hand.'

Caffin took a drink. 'It's only something she said tonight—but you wouldn't believe it.'

'Now then, Caffy.'

'Well, you know what sort she is—she gets her feelings in a big way,' and he sighed. 'She wouldn't be a mish if she didn't—I can't blame her—I just asked for it.'

'Go on, Caffy, what did she say?'

The club implored. Even Saxby gave his official encouragement. 'Now then, Caffin, you mustn't disappoint us.'

'She said, "God sent you to me." '

'No, no, Caffy.'

'Try another, Caffy.'

'No, Caffy, a thin tale.'

Caffin sat up. 'Damn it all, don't you understand anything—a girl like that—it's the shock of their lives—they don't know any-thing—I bet you that one never had a doll, not a real baby doll—teddy bear's the style, don't raise any awkward ideas or nasty feeling—they're brought up in a bag and when a chap tickles 'em a bit through a moth 'ole, it's like a revelation from 'eaven—if they 'aven't been smothered already——' in his excitement Caffin began to drop aitches. But the club repeated from all sides, 'No, no, Caffy.'

The joke was that Caffin took the thing seriously, it appeared that he valued himself as an expert on seduction and female psychology. He had a weak side; a faith, almost a religion. 'No, no, Caffy,' everyone cried, and he shouted, 'Damn it all, I tell you—that's nothing—lots of girls—it's just the natural thing—give 'em a chance, that's all.'

'No, no, Caffy, that's a bit too good.'

At last Caffin got up and went away. He was huffed.

The club was surprised and a little conscience-smitten. The Dabbi staff at that time were thoroughly good fellows, all of them, sociable and good-natured. Saxby had the name for making happy stations, and he deserved it. He was an excellent district officer, hard-working, conscientious with a strong natural sympathy for the natives, and he had never stood on his official dignity.

He took his pipe from his mouth, looked after Caffin with a startled air and said, 'He isn't wounded in his feelings, I hope.'

They reassured him. 'It's all right, sir, he had to go.'

'I'm afraid he was hurt. I must drop in tomorrow and say some-thing.' He put back his pipe and reflected. Gradually a chuckle rose through his huge form. 'Funny sort of chap.'

'Shouldn't believe everything he tells you,' Billson said.

'Well, I don't know.' Saxby puffed and reflected. A serious expression appeared on several faces. The Dabbi club was accus-tomed after sunset now and then to hear some thoughtful remark from Saxby, on politics or religion, and it received these always with respect and appreciation.

There was a slight pause. A boy pushed inwards the faggots burning beside the circle of chairs and blew on their red points. They burst at once into a bright high flame in which the features of Saxby,

Billson and even the young soldier suddenly acquired striking light and shade. They seemed like a circle of deep-eyed philosophers, pondering the nature of things.

'Well, I don't know,' Saxby said again, 'about that girl, for instance.'

There was a respectful pause.

'Some people do have extraordinary ideas,' Saxby said, puffing. He looked round with impressive gravity. 'Extraordinary.'

'It's the religion,' Billson suggested. 'I been to chapel myself and you wouldn't believe how some of them talk.'

'H'm yes, but it's not only the talk—it's—well—it's a different kind of—well—almost outlook.'

There was another long pause while everyone contemplated the bottles glistening in the firelight.

'And then, of course, they really do believe in God,' Billson said.

'Why not?' the young soldier asked in a surprised voice.

This startled everyone. Saxby cautiously turned his big face towards the young man, Billson opened his mouth to speak and then thought better of it.

The subaltern was a perfectly ordinary young man from an excellent school, neither tall nor short, dark nor fair, with brown eyes and a neat little brown moustache. He had never done anything to make anyone even suspect that he had any ideas about anything except drill, polo and beer.

There was a pause. Billson's mouth remained open. Saxby was pondering. He knew by experience that you had to be careful with soldiers. They not only picked up the most extraordinary stuff but sometimes they believed it, really believed it. It could be most embarrassing, especially in a mixed company. He glanced at Billson and slightly moved an eyebrow. Billson shut his mouth. Saxby said in a thoughtful voice, 'I see that Robert Lynd wants to change the law about maidens.'

At once everyone began to discuss the future of cricket. This was a favourite subject with Saxby, who took a sensible and serious view of the state of the game. He was never content to say, 'Let it alone.' No better subject could have been suggested to take discussion away from a dangerous subject. Saxby had that excellent tact which does not appear like tact. The young soldier and Billson both had strong views on cricket and when the philosopher's circle broke up for dinner an hour later, everyone felt that kind of gratification which follows upon an expansion of feeling and imagination.

Saxby called at the store next afternoon to ask Caffin to tennis, but the young man was out. For a while he was not seen even at the club. Billson said that he was spending all his time at the mission. There was even a rumour that he had attended the mission chapel.

All the same, the announcement of his engagement to Miss Martha Smith caused surprise in the station and a kind of confusion. It was discussed in Caffin's absence, during the whole of one evening, and no one could fail to notice the flat and disappointed tone of the speakers. Even Saxby was a little put out.

'I'm afraid friend Caffin has lost his character,' he said. 'He can't be such a blackguard as they say.'

'Nature's been too much for him.'

'Or the climate.'

'Perhaps he was tight,' the young soldier suggested.

But no one would accept this whitewashing. 'Caffy's always more or less tight—but it never affects his form. No, she's caught him—another good man gone.'

Caffin himself was not seen at all until one evening Saxby met him on the town road going towards the mission. He was whistling in a particularly lively manner.

But as soon as he caught sight of the district officer, his shoulders drooped, his forehead wrinkled. He lived up to his ideal. Saxby congratulated him and he answered in a tone of gloomy despair, 'Just when I got nicely settled in with old Billson—but what can a chap do?'

Saxby told the story at the club which agreed that Caffin was a bit of a fraud, that he had always been a poser. The next day Caffin took a lift in the company car to railhead. Miss Smith saw him off at the store. She was obviously in bridal spirits; everyone who saw her described her as quite pretty in her excitement. Billson, who had lent Caffin ten pounds for his trip and necessary expenses, said that after all Caffy had done pretty well for himself.

There was no more news of Caffin for two months. He was then said to be in Spanish Muni with a high yellow señorita. Billson was furious. 'The dirty little swine,' he shouted. 'He's bilked me.'

The others were sympathetic but much amused. They were also, of course, sympathetic with the poor girl at the mission who was said to be suffering a good deal, but there was a ring of pleasure even in Saxby's tone when he said at the club, 'So after all there was something in those stories about Caffin.'

'I wonder what he got out of it.'

'Probably everything she had.'

'Did you ever hear how he bought an ejaw girl for fifteen shillings and hired her out?'

'No, but I can well believe it.'

Everyone began to tell stories about Caffin's mean tricks and the meanest gave the most pleasure.

The station had been a little surprised at Caffin's disappearance, but everyone was astonished when the rumour went round that the girl Smith, though ill with unhappiness, was growing plumper every day.

Saxby spoke of it to the missionaries, a couple called Beatty, who said there was nothing in it. The Beattys in fact could not believe their own eyes. It was the nursing sister who had to make them understand that the symptoms had exactly the same meaning in Martha Smith, though she was white, as in any of the pagan girls who disturbed the mission every year with unexpected babies.

'It's incredible,' Beatty said to Saxby, 'quite incredible—a most respected family in the West Country.'

Beatty was a small fair man with very blue eyes. He had a habit of bending towards you while he talked, as if asking for your sympathy and understanding. Probably he knew by experience that missionaries could not expect fair judgment. He was plainly in distress about Martha Smith.

'And do you know her explanation—the only explanation she vouchsafed to give us?'

'No.'

'That he thought she couldn't really love him.'

'My God, what a blackguard Caffin is,' Saxby pondered. 'Seemed quite an ordinary sort of lad—it's really astonishing——' Suddenly he caught Beatty's eye, whose pained expression warned him that he was smiling. He became at once grave. 'Poor girl, I suppose you'll send her home?'

'She won't go home.'

'Oh, I see—yes—naturally—in that state.'

'But I can't turn her out, can I?'

'No, I suppose not—certainly not.'

Beatty went away quite stooped with anxiety and perplexity. However, a few days later, Miss Martha Smith suddenly turned up at the station rest-house. It seemed that Beatty had solved his problem after all. Little Mrs Beatty explained that matter to Billson who, although he no longer went to chapel, had once belonged to a congregation. 'Poor, poor girl,' she cried. 'We didn't know what to do—my piccaninnies are so sharp and quick, even the quite, quite little ones, poor neglected darlings. But we brought it all to prayer and really, we were wonderfully answered—the poor girl softened at once. She saw what harm she was doing us.'

'I suppose she hasn't got a ring or anything?'

'I don't think so, Mr Billson, why?'

'Well, Mrs Beatty, that chap Caffin took ten pounds off me to buy things for the wedding—and so of course, if he did send her a ring, it's really out of my property.'

'Oh, I'm sure she'll give anything back—she's really a very nice girl. She's been accusing herself of selfishness towards us and really, it was a little selfish of her not to think of the mission sooner.'

'Well, if you would just mention about the ring. I wouldn't like to intrude myself.'

'Of course, Mr Billson—that's six tins of tomato soup, isn't it, and you've made an allowance for the flour with the weevils. Of course, I was sure you had.'

Miss Smith was very retiring. None saw her at all except in the late evening, when a short figure, in a cloak which gave it almost a conical shape, was sometimes seen moving quickly towards the garden by the bush road.

No one troubled her. It was supposed that she was waiting for her steamer ticket. Saxby took care that regular supplies of wood, water, chickens and yam were delivered at the rest-house, and gave his cook-general orders to keep an eye on her commissariat.

After a month, however, even Saxby began to wonder how long the girl would stay. He sent a discreet note asking when she would need transport. When did her boat sail? She wrote back to say that she had no boat and she did not mean to sail.

Saxby was uneasy. He felt that the girl was suffering and that she needed help of some kind. He appealed to the Beattys who came at once to the office.

'But what can I do, Mr Saxby? She ought to go home, of course. But I can't turn her out into the bush, can I?'

'No, but couldn't you persuade her?'

'Terribly, terribly obstinate,' Mrs Beatty said. 'I always said she was the difficult type—poor thing. I noticed it at once—especially her neck.'

'Her neck?'

'Terribly, terribly short. Poor girl, nothing could ever teach her. What are we to do, Mr Saxby—it's such a dreadful anxiety for us at the mission—and the poor girl must be suffering so terribly too. Even though it is her own selfishness.'

'I was told you had a little meeting with her,' Saxby said.

They gazed at him. Suddenly Mrs Beatty understood and with a little smile for the layman's ignorance of terms, she murmured, 'He means when we brought it to prayer, dear.'

'Oh yes, but it's no good. We tried—we've tried everything, Mr Saxby.' His blue eyes implored Saxby to believe him, to understand his difficulties.

'Poor, poor, girl,' Mrs Beatty murmured. 'I feel so terribly sorry for her. I wonder, Mr Saxby, is this a good sixpence?' Mrs Beatty had taken advantage of the visit to cash a cheque. 'Yes, I was sure it was—some of the new ones are so yellow, aren't they?'

Beatty said in a tone unexpectedly decisive, as if, having given up hope of sympathy, he fell back on his rights. 'Besides, we have no jurisdiction—since she left the mission.'

Saxby understood this very well. The Beattys did not intend to do anything further. Having been successful by the aid of prayer in removing Miss Smith from the mission, they were leaving her to providence. Saxby was indignant and alarmed.

But he was a conscientious man. He put on a tie, took an early whisky, and went across to the rest-house and knocked on the side of the doorway with his stick. 'Excuse me, it's Saxby.'

'Come in.'

The hut was in twilight, and at first he could see only a dark bundle of shawls or cloaks in the middle of the bed, under the looped-up net. Then he perceived a white face, thin and small, projecting from the top of this bundle. He could not recognise this face, thin and hollow-cheeked, and for some reason this increased his confusion: as if he found himself confronted by something altogether beyond his expectation.

Perspiring, he murmured another apology and began to make his little prepared speech of sympathy and encouragement. He meant to explain to the girl that she must not feel ashamed or shy, that everybody knew how badly she had been treated. But he had barely uttered three words before it struck him that the girl resented his interference. There was an awkward silence. Then with an inspiration, he said, 'I just called to know about the chickens.'

The girl said nothing.

'You're getting them all right? You're all right for supplies? Because if there's any difficulty—the least difficulty, I hope you'll let me know at once,' Saxby said firmly. He then wished her good night, stepped quickly out into the compound and made his way home at speed. He was distressed, but on the whole pleased with himself. He had got out, he thought, with the least damage to anybody's feelings.

But he was still anxious about Miss Smith and, as her case was not official, he put it to the club that evening. He wanted popular support, so to speak.

'The best thing you could have done, sir.'

'Well, I thought, as she obviously wanted to be left alone——'

'Of course she does.'

'Better not seem to notice her at all—that's the kindest thing,' Billson said.

Saxby was reassured, and had just put up his feet on the foot-rest when the young soldier arrived from the polo pit, sweating and crying out for drink. He said at once, 'Has anyone seen that girl lately? Why doesn't the parson come to see her?'

'She won't have him,' Billson said. 'She's got some funny notion, you know, that she disgraced the mission and that there oughtn't to be any connection. Besides, they say she ought to go home and she won't.'

'I don't care, he ought to come and pray with her at the least. Hi, boy, where's that cold drink?'

Everyone looked with new interest and curiosity at the young soldier. Billson opened his mouth, hesitated a moment and then asked boldly, 'You think it would do her good?'

'Oh, I don't know about that, but it's his job I should think. Cheeroh, sir.' He raised his glass to Saxby.

Saxby was pondering. Everyone was pondering. Now and then someone looked doubtfully at the young man. At last Saxby said in his most thoughtful voice, 'Prayer, that's an interesting question.'

The club continued to ponder, but with rather a blank expression of eye as if faced by a huge bare wall. Saxby and Billson finally looked at the subaltern. Saxby's expression was at once enquiring and a little apprehensive. He was both curious and alarmed. Probably he regretted already his impulsive plunge into a subject so tricky.

The young man with a most cheerful and knowing air was holding up his glass to the firelight. He closed one eye and said, 'It's not too bad, this beer of yours, Billson—to look at.'

Every expression at once showed relief, and Saxby said, 'If you can call lager, beer. Now, real beer——'

Meanwhile one would suppose that there was a tremendous scandal. The Beattys expected it. So did the station.

But there was no scandal at Dabbi. For some reason no one was particularly shocked about this case, and nobody talked about it very much. It did not strike the imagination. Visitors to Dabbi might be there for half an hour before they heard of it and even then they seemed unable to get any definite flavour out of it.

'At the rest-house, you say—seven months gone——'

The rest-house at Dabbi was a round hut with a broken thatch set a little crooked on the walls. It looked as if, slightly fuddled, it had dozed off in the sun a year or two before, with its hat on one ear. The visitors might gaze at it with hopeful interest but this interest faded quickly; they found it like any other rest-house in any of a hundred rather dull little bush stations where there was no butter, no potatoes, no ice; where newspapers were a fortnight old, the library consisted of two Edgar Wallaces and somebody's *Auction Bridge* with all the middle pages torn out, and nothing ever happened except in the native town which was a perfect nuisance in any case.

'Seven months gone—and Caffin's in Patagonia.'

'A bit tough on the girl—how's she taken it?'

'Well, of course, we don't see much of her.'

'Keeps herself to herself?'

'That's it—in fact she don't show up at all.'

By this time interest had entirely disappeared.

'But he's in Patagonia, is he? What do they do there?' and they talked sheep or currency or revolutions.

It was tax time and Saxby was extremely busy. He liked, however, to be busy, and he always made time to see that the rest-house was looked after. He would inspect it twice a day to make sure that the prison gang had swept the compound and brought the water. He built a neat private way to the latrine, of straw mats, from the back door. Saxby was not called 'dear old Saxby' for nothing. He was a most good-natured man. Also he felt a real admiration for Miss Smith. He would say, 'She might have made it damned awkward for everybody, but she's been no trouble at all. That girl has real guts.'

Some time before, he had written complaining that the station doctor had not yet returned from leave; and pointing out that a station with half a company of troops was entitled to a doctor.

For six weeks this had no effect. The wires were not even acknowledged. Then in May, when Saxby had given up all hope of a doctor, just before six o'clock in the evening of the fourth, a telegram came from headquarters: 'Clear the line M.O. Bing due Dabbi fourth. Stop. Resdt.'

'Good God,' Saxby said, and then he began to laugh. He went down to the club with the wire in his hand. 'Do you know who they're sending us for M.O.?—Bing.'

'No, sir.'

'Not really.'

'Not old Bing. Good Lord, what a joke.' The young soldier gave a shout of laughter, and two people began simultaneously to tell a story about Bing. The rest were smiling even before they heard it. The very idea of Bing made them smile. Bing, or Major Bing, as he preferred to be called, was then one of the biggest jokes in the service.

'A perfect terror,' Saxby said smiling. 'He tried to diet me once. In fact, he did put me off my palm oil chop.'

'Did you ever hear how he wanted to cut my liver out—well, part of it——' Billson laughed heartily at the recollection and having told the story, said, 'My God, Major Bing is really——'

'And due today,' Saxby said.

'Today. By Jove.'

There was a thoughtful pause. Then the young soldier got up. 'I think I'll just have a look round the barracks,' and ten minutes later Billson refused a third gin.

'It's not because of old Bing,' he said, but the club laughed.

Yet next morning, when the lorry arrived at last with Bing's loads, there were groans from all sides. Bing was a joke to the imagination, but in fact he meant trouble for everyone, insults, contempt and hard work.

Bing's car was close behind the lorry. He was a short plump man with a purple face and a curled-up moustache, like two little rolls of barbed wire; who leant so far backwards as he walked, or rather strutted, that he seemed likely every moment to fall on his own spurs. He always wore uniform, with his war ribbons; sometimes major's uniform, but usually a khaki coat with shoulder straps which looked like army uniform from a little distance. No one more military than Bing could be imagined. He ought, of course, to have been in the Ram corps, and, like many Ram corps men, he was a student of tactics. He used to cross-examine company commanders about Napoleon's battles, and prove to the whole station that they knew nothing about war and oughtn't to be soldiers at all.

Bing's first visit was expected by the soldiers, and two fatigues had been cleaning up barracks from dawn. Saxby, too, having sent him an invitation for breakfast, ordered an unusually light meal. But Bing did not begin on Saxby's diet, or Billson's liver, or the company latrines. He was one of those men who had an infallible nose for the place where the most trouble was to be found, the biggest stink, and, of course, it was usually a place quite unnoticed or long overlooked by the inhabitants. Bing always took his victims unawares, on their exposed side, in flank or rear, and having engaged battle, he massed his artillery and blew a hole in their line before they knew what was happening.

He stopped his car at the rest-house and charged through the doorway. For twenty minutes his loud voice volleyed from within.

While Saxby, in great surprise, was still wondering what the noise was about, he came marching across the station, already hot as a griddle, to the divisional office.

'Look here, Saxby,' he bawled, without greeting, 'what the devil do you think you're playing at with this woman Smith?'

Saxby nearly fell out of his chair. 'Playing——' he said.

'Playing—playing—damn it, I said playing—by God,' he stared at Saxby with amazement, 'I don't believe he realises it now——'

'Realises what?'

'The situation, man, the very urgent and critical situation—dammit, right under your nose for about six months—but I suppose you've been absorbed in chasing an odd sixpence through the cash book——'

'My dear Bing, I know that Miss Smith was—ah——'

'And do you know the regulations of your own silly department? No, dammit, he don't! Talk about the efficiency of our civil services. Do—you—realise—that it's absolutely impossible for that woman to have her baby here—that she ought to have gone home two months ago, as I damn well told her.'

Saxby was now perturbed as well as astonished.

'But, Bing, I don't think she wants to go home. Naturally, she rather shrinks from it.'

'What's that got to do with it? When it's laid down in black and white that no white woman is allowed to have babies except in a station on the schedule. Perhaps you can show me Dabbi on the schedule, or perhaps not.' Bing spoke this with an ironical inflection which had, during the war, thrown regimental sergeant-majors into confusion.

'But white babies have been born in Dabbi. Mrs Beatty had one last year.'

'What? Where? Oh, in the damn mission.' Bing hated all missions, which he considered to be a military necessity, like rum and No. 3 pills. 'I'm talking about civilian babies,' he said with hearty contempt.

'But this is a civilian baby. Miss Smith was a missionary.'

'Not at all. They drummed her out of the mission. She's in a Government rest-house, in a Government station, and she's in my charge. She's in exactly the same position as an official wife, and her baby is a Government baby.'

'But, Bing, think of her feelings, going home in that state!'

'Feelings be damned.' Bing had no more sympathetic imagination than a mule, and much less than a horse. 'Do you understand the nature of an order?' he snapped.

'Really, Bing.' Saxby was growing slightly annoyed. He thought that Bing was making unnecessary trouble. Bing grew redder. He could not bear the least opposition. 'I know my duty,' he said; and no one but Bing could have said such a thing with the same dramatic air. He swelled up his chest, bringing the medal ribbons into great prominence. The ribbons no doubt meant something to Bing, his religion, his idea of things, including himself and his duty, and he entered into that idea with great enthusiasm and energy—an energy overwhelming to Saxby. Saxby, a most dutiful man, was embarrassed by the very word duty. He said mildly, 'All the same, we have to be careful.'

'Careful be damned. There's the regulations. The woman's in my charge, and I'll thank you to arrange for deporting her by the next boat. That means leaving here this afternoon. I've told her to be ready for an examination at nine, so you'd better go now. And I'm reporting to the P.M.O. by the next mail.' He made for the door.

Saxby, heavy and slow-moving as he was, rushed after him. 'But, my dear Bing, I can't absolutely order the poor girl to——'

'You'll have to. She told me she'd rather shoot herself than go.'

'What!' Saxby, with a look of horror, rushed for his hat.

'You needn't be alarmed.' Bing looked his military contempt of a civilian panic. 'She hasn't got a gun. I asked her.' He marched off.

Saxby fell back in his chair and cursed Bing. Then he laughed, and mopped his forehead. 'My God, what a—really—Bing is——'

But he knew he would have to act. Bing was an autocrat by nature and education. All doctors tend to autocracy, and Government doctors are tyrants. Ram corps doctors are also tyrants. But Major Bing was worse than any Ram corps doctor, because he was not a real major; he was the dictator who must always act the tyrant because otherwise people will remember his lowly origin.

Saxby sighed and pondered. What was he to do? What could he say to that unlucky girl? Really, it was a terrible position for anybody. He reflected deeply for some time. A bugle sounded from the barracks for the guard-changing; five minutes to nine.

Saxby remembered that at nine Bing was going back to the rest-house. He suddenly felt a deep sense of alarm, so urgent that he was half-way to the rest-house before he had decided what to say.

As he knocked at the door, he was startled to see the girl move quickly across it, as if in flight. He went in at once, but she was already seated on the bed. She glared at him, panting.

'What do you want?' she asked furiously.

'I'm awfully sorry if I seem to intrude, but Doctor Bing came to see me just now.'

'I'm not going home.'

'But Bing tells me——'

'I'm not going home like this——' She made a gesture full of rage, throwing out her hands, like a leper who says, 'See my horrible body.' 'Why should I? You can't make me——'

Saxby was startled by this passionate violence. What had happened to that nice little mission girl? It was incredible that she should have changed into this excitable woman with huge, furious eyes. He stood astonished while she declared in the same dramatic manner that she would do what she liked with herself, that she didn't belong to anybody now.

'Of course not,' Saxby murmured. 'I don't want to interfere at all—but Doctor Bing——'

She made as if to spring up from the bed, and Saxby hastily stepped back. His bald head knocked upon something dangling. He looked up and saw a rope hanging from a rafter. It was thrown loosely over the palm rib, and it had a running noose at the lower end. A box stood below, slightly to one side.

Saxby stared at the rope, and then at the girl. His mouth opened. He was shocked out of his discretion.

'But you didn't mean——' Saxby said. 'It's too——'

The girl sat motionless, staring at him. She did not blink an eye, and Saxby faltered into silence. They gazed at each other, shocked. It was as though a mutual discovery, flashing through the air, had turned it into a heavy medium in which neither could move.

Suddenly the girl's face twisted, her eyes turned aside, and she said in a faint voice, 'I was just putting up——' She looked round, as if for inspiration. Saxby found one before he realised it. 'Oh, yes, very convenient—hang things up.'

'The lamp,' she said.

'Yes, of course—the lamp,' and his face relaxed. He put a hand to his forehead.

'Hullo,' said a voice outside. 'It's Bing.'

The girl sprang up. She and Saxby together grabbed at the rope. Saxby's long arm reached it, tore it down and jerked it behind his back. He heard the girl's voice in his ear, full of contemptuous rage: 'No one can stop me. I'll do what I like.'

Bing was already in the doorway. The girl sank back suddenly on the box.

'Hullo.' Bing stared at her suspiciously. 'Got your orders?'

'Not from me,' Saxby exclaimed hastily. 'I'm not taking the responsibility.'

'I'm not going,' the girl said.

'What do you mean, responsibility?' Bing glared at Saxby.

'The patient must be consulted.'

'The patient,' Bing snapped. 'But all that is decided. What do you think service regulations are for?' His tone might have referred to Holy Writ. 'I suppose it means nothing to you, miss, where your baby is born, but it's my duty to see that you don't have it in a place already scheduled as unfit for babies.'

'Nothing to me?' she looked at him in amazement and rage. Then suddenly her expression changed in a manner very surprising to both the men. It was as though something had escaped from behind the girl's hard, furious mask, by eyes and lips and even cheeks, so that the eyes looked beyond Bing and the rest-house wall, the compressed lips softened and stood open, the cheeks were coloured with life. 'Mine,' she said.

Saxby, as well as Bing, stared uncomprehendingly while the girl's colour deepened, her lips trembled, and her eyes, a moment before as hard as agate, sparkled with tears. Suddenly she made that gesture, common in the pregnant woman, as if to clasp her womb between her hands. 'Oh, how wicked I have been—how ungrateful.'

'Now, now,' Bing said sharply. 'No hysterics. Please control yourself, and answer my question. Do you understand that you must go home? Do you understand the nature of an order, a Government order?'

Saxby, still perspiring, terrified of Bing's roughness, said hastily in a cajoling voice, 'You see, Miss—ah—in Major Bing's view, you are to a certain extent, in Government charge.'

The girl gazed at him as if through a window at a new discovered sky. 'Yes, yes, in Government charge—of course, I'll do anything.'

Suddenly she caught Bing's hand and kissed it. 'God sent you to me.'

A TOUCH OF GENIUS

THE general agent, after an exhausting journey of three days, arrived in Gwanki at five o'clock. He was a large man with legs like a billiard table, and in Africa he always wore a white silk coat and tweed plus fours to show that though he was a bloody trader he was still an English gentleman. He was astonished to hear that there was no club in Gwanki.

'Can't understand it, doctah,' he said to Doctor Pagnum. 'It don't take much to organise a club. Now, the new chap I got for the store —this new chap Robbins,' he made a vague gesture towards the river, 'he's a wonder at organising—that's why I rather jumped at him—sociable sort of chap, too.'

Doctor Pagnum opened one eye and peeped at the silk coat with malignant disgust. He himself was dressed in a very dirty khaki shirt. There was two days' beard on his fat chin and a strong flavour of gin drifted from him.

'What's the new swindle?' he muttered. 'Organise your ass, you bloody British gent.'

Bolsover was disgusted. He toiled across to the district officer's bungalow, lifting his huge feet like a patient sportsman in a turnip field. But young Sharp, the district officer, saw him coming and hastily put on a hat. They met on the stoop.

'I thought you were closing this branch.' Sharp looked at him keenly, turning his thin beak to one side like a watchful bird. He was dressed in very neat bush kit with bright steel chains hanging in loops from his belt to his pocket. All Sharp's belongings, his official keys, his box keys, his knife and pencil were separately chained to him.

'Well, of course, we haven't had much luck in Gwanki—seems like a sort of hoodoo on the damn place. But this new chap is keen as mustard—and he certainly has a flair for jobs like this—reorganising a business—really a touch of genius. I'm only rather afraid he may be too lonely. He's a bit rough of course, but quite a decent sort.'

'That's very nice.' Sharp seemed to close a lid on the subject. 'I hope he'll do better than the last one.'

Bolsover glanced past the officer into the cool house. He was longing not so much for a drink as company, talk. A little crease between Sharp's brows deepened. He was tired of Bolsover. Sharp was quickly tired of anybody just then except a superior officer who might be able to tell him why he had been sent to Gwanki and if he was condemned to stay there. What had he done? What hadn't he done? How should he get out again?

To Pagnum Gwanki was a hospital or asylum; but to Sharp it was a road-house where he had stuck for a few days and where it was waste of time to know anybody. He was waiting, so to speak, for some rich relation to call and sweep him away in triumph to the grand hotel.

'I've never been in a station before where there wasn't some kind of a club,' Bolsover complained.

'Sorry I must go along,' Sharp said. 'The mail, you know,' and he hurried away to the office. He really had letters to write. He believed in keeping up with people; that is, senior officials.

Bolsover went back to the rest-house but later on he was seen sitting by himself in his long chair, next the parade ground, with a lantern boy, a box for his whisky and even a fire. He had made a little club for himself. No one joined him. The O.C. troops, Captain Colley, passed, but did not seem to notice him. Colley was usually absorbed in his own thoughts. Sharp was busy in the office, and Pagnum gazing at his light from the door of the native hospital, with a dirty bandage in his dirtier hand, said loudly so that the dresser might hear, 'Look at'm, the bloody little tapeworm, who's he hooking on to now.'

Pagnum, a man with very good degrees and a hard worker insulted everybody except his dirtier patients, and hated anyone who was polite to a superior officer. That, perhaps, was why he found himself in Gwanki.

Bolsover went off next day. But he made a last appeal to Sharp from the car. 'Might ask him up for a drink—a bit hairy about the heels, of course, but a real good sort,' and as the car moved on, he shouted out something about a real go-getter.

The business genius turned up a week later. He came by river with a large load of cut timber for the new store, bales of cloth and boxes of trade goods. He was a little dried-up hollow-chested creature about five feet high, with pale tow-coloured hair rising straight up like hay from a very large head on a very long neck. His face also was long and hollow, dried up by sun and yellowed by fever. In fact, as Pagnum discovered, he was just out of hospital. This greatly pleased the doctor. 'He'll die on 'em—another triumph for the bloody British business man, bless 'm.'

Meanwhile it was reported that all the blackguards in Gwanki had been engaged by the new district agent, at the highest wages, and he was starting them at work from dawn. Rumours of his odd appearance, manners, and language also went round. Sharp, on his usual route to the native prison, stopped a moment to see him at work on the new store. He was certainly energetic. Fifty men were unloading the barges amid a tumult of yells and songs, and a carpenter's gang had already set up two corner posts and a cross beam of the new store. Robbins himself, looking like a mummified monkey dressed in remarkably dirty cotton shorts, was hopping about on the beam in bare feet, waving a hammer at the crowd which was roaring with laughter at his antics. Sharp looked on for a moment with casual interest.

Pagnum's surly voice sounded in his ears. 'The fool's drunk, by God—I thought he looked like a soaker.'

This was the first time Pagnum had spoken to Sharp for three weeks. Sharp replied with official politeness, 'The company has a high opinion of him.'

'Yah,' Pagnum said, with indescribable contempt. 'That bloody company is a bloody good judge of agents.'

In fact, of the last three agents in Gwanki one had bolted with the cash, a second had eloped over the French border with an Arab girl, and the third, a hard worker, after doubling the business, set the store on fire one afternoon and stayed inside. The servants had seen him pouring kerosene on the bed. He was a capable man and he had made a great success of the fire. The store burst like a shell. Afterwards it was found that he had done away with the cash. He had not embezzled it but hidden it; fifty pounds in a biscuit tin under the company wharf, another twenty on top of the window frames and fifteen odd in sixpences down the barrels of his gun. Six hundred pounds were still missing, and he had been seen dropping bags into the river; but nothing more had been found.

Pagnum looked again at the little man jumping on the beam and said, 'Lucky for the looby if he breaks his bloody neck now—it'll save a lot of trouble.'

But Robbins continued to perform feats on the beam and he did not fall. It appeared that he had been a sailor. On the next afternoon when Sharp, stopping to see the odd performance, found Pagnum there already, he bawled at them, 'Excuse me langwidge, gentlemen —if I josh 'em a bit. It's just an idea of mine—makes work a pleasure as you might say.'

Pagnum growled to himself and walked on with his dresser. He was going to some patient in the town. Pagnum delighted in attending to some old leper in a Gwanki slum, especially when the sick parade from the fort was waiting for him. He used his very virtues as a weapon against authority.

Sharp went off in the opposite direction. He had even less time for Robbins than Pagnum. But Robbins, as they soon discovered, addressed everyone he saw, at any distance, in a very loud voice, like a bo'sun hailing the yards. Neither did he seem to expect any reply. He had made half a dozen speeches to every member of the station before one of them spoke to him.

Meanwhile he certainly got work out of his blackguards. On the fourth day the trade goods were all unloaded into temporary grass huts and the whole lower frame of the store was complete. Robbins, springing about the beams, directed a gang in fitting together the first roof principal on the ground.

A girl walked up from the river with water. It was the regular path. Dozens went that way. But Robbins happened to notice the girl. He revolved slowly as she passed, balancing himself on his bare crooked feet, and staring without a blink; then suddenly, as she turned towards the town, he pointed his hammer at her and bawled, ' 'Ere, you.'

The girl walked on. She was a southern girl, coffee coloured, with big round arms.

' 'Ere,' Robbins called. 'You with the pot—'ere, yaller girl, 'ere, arf a minute, Topsy.'

The girl disappeared among the huts. Robbins gave a yell, dropped his hammer, jumped from the beam to the ground and rushed after her.

This was seen not only by Pagnum, who was taking his usual stroll past the store, but by Colley who had been gazing at Robbins for some time from the other side, in the native market.

Colley had a habit of staring in this manner. He was a tall skeleton of a man, with the head and appearance of a smart soldier. His greyish hair was always neatly parted down the middle, his shirts, shorts, ties, boots, were of the finest quality; he carried about him a faint smell of expensive soaps and hair wash. But his face, especially his forehead, was deeply wrinkled, and his eyebrows were fixed in a high permanent arch. Such an arch and such forehead markings are seen only in men of Colley's type, rather simple-minded unambitious men who have received a shock, or several shocks, in their course through life, strong enough to fix them in a kind of permanent surprise.

Colley, so far as people knew, had not suffered any unusual misfortune, except that his wife had bolted during the war with a friend. He had run through a good deal of money as a subaltern, backing horses; but many subalterns have done that. He had not been a successful soldier; but then, he had not aspired to the staff college; he was not one of those unfortunates who are at once stupid and ambitious. Colley had never had any ambitions for personal glory. However, if he wasn't clever, he was obviously a man of strong feeling, or such common treacheries as a turf swindle, a weak wife and an unreliable friend would not have stamped his face and mind with the shape of tragedy. Total strangers always had the same respectful or curious glance when they met Colley. They recognised in him something unusual, a capacity for generous feeling which is after all much rarer than its cause.

Colley, like all such people, was absent-minded, preoccupied no doubt with memories which would have been trivial enough to describe, but were to him still astonishing and mysterious. He would be found often enough beside the parade ground or on the river, gazing into the air, with his high eyebrows still higher and his little forehead still more deeply wrinkled, in a kind of trance.

He was gazing in this manner at the place where Robbins had been, when Robbins emerging from the huts, panting and sweating but empty-handed, shouted at him, 'You see that one, sir—I got an idea she'd suit me—nice expression she 'ad. I'll 'ave to look out for 'er.'

To which Colley, inexpressibly startled, replied with a gaze of wonder and a deep 'Er-r-r.' Having focussed Robbins and perceived him, so to speak, as the source of communication, he said 'Er-r' in a tone which was almost a question. But Robbins had once more rushed among the huts.

However, he had no trouble in finding the yellow girl.

As soon as it was understood that his intentions were serious, about twenty were proposed for him. But he was faithful to the original. A bargain was struck at once; five pounds for the parents, and a couple of blue cloths for the bride.

'I got an idea she's cheap,' he told Sharp. 'It's the expression—I always go by a girl's expression. You take a tip, sir, when you want a permanency—go by the expression—the 'abitooal expression.'

'I see,' Sharp said smiling, amused in spite of himself. 'I must make a note of that,' and he hurried away on his important affairs.

Robbins was a generous bridegroom. He gave a feast to his new relations, and a set of silver bangles to Mrs Robbins; he offered the station free drinks.

Mr E. Robbins presents his humble comps and would be honoured to present to the gentlemen of Gwanki station (1) case gin in celebration of his marriage to Mrs Bamu Robbins of Gwanki. Mr E. Robbins regrets unable to be present himself owing to domestic duties, so wine is without prejudice.

Nobody knew what to do with this gin. Sharp wrote a note of thanks. Pagnum, who was in the middle of some violent quarrel with his own department asked angrily, 'Does he take me for a bloody British snob like himself?'

He even went to the wharf with some idea of telling Robbins to take the gin away, but when he got there, he found Colley fixed in a trance before the company bungalow. This was a temporary mud hut with a large stoop. At the edge of this stoop a square framework like that of a hut, about ten foot each way, in unusually stout timber, was being erected by a gang of company labourers.

Robbins, in rather dirtier rags than usual, and with a much dirtier face, was standing within a yard of Colley and bawling up at him. 'It's a bed, sir.' He turned to include Pagnum. 'I got an idea for a bed, sir—a real bed—with room to move about in. That's what you want in the tropics. Mind you, I know wot fellers say—keep your mammy in her proper place and that's on the floor.' He waved at Bamu squatting behind him, and the three visitors stared downwards at the girl who, feeling shy, pushed in her chin and giggled. 'But the way I look at it, gentlemen,' Robbins looked round at the party, 'if you want 'appiness, you got to take a chance and 'ave a real wife—and that means a real bed.'

It took him four days to complete the bed. There was, of course, timber at hand; four of the store beams had made excellent corner posts, and four rafters the frame, but he did not want to cut them because, as he pointed out to all visitors, they would be needed for the store as soon as the hides began to come in.

He had plenty of visitors. It was something to do in Gwanki to visit the wharf and see what Robbins was doing. For he was always doing something.

'Wonder what he's up to,' Pagnum would say, 'or is he just a bloody idjit.' Pagnum had no sense of humour. His idea of a joke was a clerk in clean trousers falling off a bicycle. But Sharp, relaxing a moment from the cares of an officer who wants to catch his Resident's eye from a division completely uninteresting and insignificant, would smile and say, 'I suppose he knows which side his bread's buttered.'

Colley was the most regular visitor of all. He would gaze at the bed and listen to Robbins for half an hour at a time. No one knew what his thoughts were, but one evening, walking back to the station between Pagnum and Sharp, he said, 'Strornary chap, that.' Suddenly he stopped in the path, opened his death-like jaws and uttered a loud ha ha. The sound was appalling. It threw a deeper shade on Pagnum's savage gloom, but Sharp smiled again and said, 'I wonder.'

'Killing himself,' Pagnum said. 'He's been out four years. But what's the good of talking to the bloody fool—he's no sense.'

But Robbins still refused to die and the marriage was a great success, especially after the birth of a son in the following March. Robbins introduced all visitors to Mam Robbins as she was called by the natives, and little Alfred; and as Robbins was now an established joke for a hundred miles round, no visitor refused the invitation. It was the thing, that year, to visit Gwanki store and the Robbins family; and men in distant stations would ask laughing, 'Have you met Mam Robbins?'

Robbins made no secret of his pride as a father and his gratitude as a husband. Of course, as the station had found some time before, he never made a secret of anything. He took the whole world into his confidence, generally at the top of his voice. 'It's a bit of luck for a chap like me,' he would bawl, standing beside the famous bed after presenting a deputation, two French officers going north or a couple of Catholic fathers on their way south, 'to get a wife like that. A real bit of luck, especially as I'm not wot you call a beauty spot. But mind, you, I 'ad a 'unch she was a good un as soon as I set eyes on 'er. It was the expression. Why, with a nice girl, it comes out all over 'em. Furst time I saw Mrs Ar, it was her backside, and I didn't 'ardly need wait for her phiz—I knoo it would be a real 'ome maker.'

'Ha ha,' Colley would laugh, staring with intense pleasure, and afterwards Pagnum would ask with angry surprise, 'D'jever hear such stuff and, by God, I believe he believes it. S'no good telling him that mammy is taking on half the town.'

'But does she?'

'If she doesn't now, she will—they all do. But he's only got himself to blame. A born mug.'

If Robbins showed off the bed, the station showed off Robbins. Sometimes all three would take visitors to the wharf where Sharp with his precise voice would say, 'Here are some visitors for you, Robbie,' or 'How's business?' And Pagnum would ask, 'How's the bed today, Robbie,' or 'How's little butter scotch?' grinning round like a keeper who stirs up the monkey cage.

Pagnum, of course, had attended Mam Robbins in her labour, and so he had a kind of right to chaff them all. But Robbins never seemed to notice chaff. He would answer quite seriously, 'Well, gentlemen, I got an idea that if you want to settle down with a mammy, you better treat her like a real yuman wife and give 'er a real bed. After all, gentlemen, she's a female woman and wot more do you want. It's your own fault if you can't make yourself 'appy with a nice lil gurl like that.'

Visitors and owners would go back to the station and dine together in order to tell stories about Robbins. Gwanki at this time was looked upon as a sociable station even by its own staff. The club had been flourishing for so long, at least five months, that no one could remember when or how it had started. It frequently entertained Robbins himself, and it often met again after dinner at Colley's or Pagnum's house. For now that the club had started itself, it appeared that Pagnum and Colley were men who could not bear to break up a party. If anyone prepared to go away Pagnum would say, 'Aw, you're not going yet—g'wan, have another one—have one on me. There's only one life and this is the only bit that's worth living.' And when Sharp agreed to sit another half-hour, he would approve him in the words, 'That's it, damn the bloody job. To hell with Jelly-Belly.'

Jelly-Belly was Pagnum's name for the Resident, an energetic rising official whom he loathed as much as Sharp admired.

Sharp never sat very late. But the fact that he was prepared to sit up half an hour and drink more whisky than was good for his head next morning had a surprising effect on Pagnum. He treated Sharp almost with deference and used to bounce up and wish him good night as if he were a governor. He reminded one of those farm dogs on a chain who rush at all-comers with their hair turned the wrong way and every tooth showing, and then, for some insignificant piece of consideration like a pat on the head or simply a 'good dog,' crawl at one's feet, and lick one's boots in the effort of showing their appreciation. At the same time, of course, he redoubled his abuse of the Resident. 'Let him sing for his bloody assessment. Don't you put yourself out for that bloody old ass creeper—I'll give you a medical chit if you like.'

Sharp thanked him politely but did not accept the offer. When he had taken his one extra whisky, he went to bed. But Pagnum and Colley could still be seen at the fire till two in the morning when Colley's ha ha would inform everyone for half a mile round that they were talking about Robbins.

Colley and Pagnum laughed together but their laughs were quite different. Colley's ha ha conveyed, in some way, the highest admiration; whereas Pagnum's was full of impatient pity. He would say, 'They'll do for'm, these Gwanki apes—you can't teach that kind of hoddy-noddy.'

But Colley was one of those whose ideas, though painfully acquired, stick like nails in the best oak. He spent hours at the company wharf, listening with a serious expression to Robbins' views on the world, and gazing at Mam Robbins and the baby Alfred. Every evening before dinner one saw the same group; the plump little woman sitting in the state bed nursing the baby, and the two men seated alongside, Robbins with that natural air of benign triumph which belongs to all male parents from cocks to tigers, and Colley the typical family friend, admiring, a little embarrassed, and extremely respectful. One could almost write reverent.

Pagnum would roar with laughter at Colley's expression and say, 'The bloody British bachelor and the mystery of bloody nature.' He warned Robbins every second day, 'Look out for the bloody British soldier and your piece, Robbie, he's got his eye on her.'

In fact, Colley and Mam Robbins never exchanged a word. Their friendship did not go beyond a beaming grin from the woman and a sudden rather embarrassed smile from the soldier which, however, would remain for about ten minutes afterwards, in violent contrast to the painful fixed surprise of the forehead.

'The old dog,' Pagnum would say, 'the Piccadilly pointer.'

'Ha ha,' Colley would laugh. 'All the same, strornary kid that.'

'Little butter scotch—pity they didn't drown it.'

'The way it looks at you—strornary cute,' Colley would murmur and he would add after ten minutes' reflection, 'Strornary see Robbie with 'em—Mam and the kid. Y'know he really couldn't think more of 'em if they were a—well, a real family.'

'More fool Robbie.'

'Of course, I suppose any of these women——' Colley would ponder, pursuing his idea like a beagle after a fox, already miles away and getting further every moment, 'any young one, anyway——'

'Go on, Colley, get a Mammy of your own.'

But Colley was still in pursuit. 'But then Robbie's such a strornary——'

'Five bob down and the rest at lady day—I'll give you a diagram of the works——'

'Ha ha.' Colley had grasped one new idea at Gwanki, that Pagnum was an amusing fellow and a good chap.

It was about this time that Robbins was noticed to be unusually depressed. Pagnum's chaff produced no response; Sharp, who was used to smile, in an indulgent manner, at everything he said, found him silent. He said at last, 'What's wrong, Robbie?'

'Well, sir, now you arsk, it's this 'ere annual inspection.'

'Does the company have an annual inspection?' he asked, as if enquiring into the primitive customs of a savage race. He was greatly amused.

'Yessir, and it took me a bit by surprise, as you might say. It didn't seem mor'n a week since I came and began to put up the store.'

'A week—it's eleven months,' Pagnum said. 'You don't mean to say that bloody British gent is coming to inspect you?'

'Not Mr Bolsover, doctor—it's the provincial agent—he's due next month.'

'And no store,' Sharp cried, laughing.

'Why no, sir, and no 'ides either, you see. I couldn't very well start getting in the 'ides with nowhere to put 'em.'

'No, no, of course not, Robbie.' Sharp spoke in that kind tone used by a nurse to a backward child. Sharp had used this tone ever since it began to appear that Robbins was making a mess of his business. For some reason this not only amused the young man but excited his sympathy. He would say sometimes in a tone almost of commiseration, 'Poor Robbie, I'm afraid he's a muddler.'

'Yes,' Robbins said thoughtfully. 'I'll reely 'ave to get on with that store. Luckily I'm a quick worker.'

Sharp and Pagnum looked at each other and burst into a loud laugh.

Robbins himself did not laugh or even smile. No one can tell to this day whether Robbins ever saw anything funny in his own proceedings. He made jokes sometimes but they were all of the old-fashioned type, usually puns, at which no one else could laugh.

'Ony thing is,' he said thoughtfully, 'I'll 'ave to cut it down a bit
—I can't exactly take Mrs Robbin's bed from under 'er, as you
might say—she 'as the right to 'er own marriage bed.'

'Of course not, Robbie,' Sharp said, still smiling. 'No one could
expect that.'

It was agreed at once that Robbins must not touch the famous
bed. But how was he to deal with the agent? Everyone made
suggestions. Pagnum, with a roar of laughter, advised making the
agent drunk and putting him into bed with Mrs Robbins; Colley
offered a fatigue to knock him up the store.

Robbins gratefully accepted the last suggestion. 'I've sent out for
some 'ides so we can't 'ave the store too quick. But as for putting
'im into bed with Mrs Ar,' he shouted, 'wy, I'm afraid, you know,
that she'd get out on the other side—she's got a surprising lot of
feeling, Mrs Ar—very sensitive, gentlemen; if you didn't 'appen to
be noticing 'er face, you'd think she wasn't different from a real
lady—not inside. But if you could praps let me 'ave a few nails
sir.'

Sharp, red with laughter and full of good nature, cried, 'I've got
some nails on charge to the Post Office—they're at your service,
Robbie.'

'The bloody British business man,' Pagnum said. 'It's a duty to
bamboozle the bastard.'

'All hands to the rescue,' Sharp cried. 'What about the station
carpenter? Would he be any help?'

The last offer apparently took Robbins' breath away. He drew a
long inhalation and shouted even more loudly than usual, 'Well,
sir, that's a joke that is—if anyone told me last year, that 'is Majesty's
own magistrate was sending 'is own carpenter to 'elp Ted Robbins
out of an 'ole, I'd 'ave said somebody was being funny. Makes a
chap proud to be English.'

Pagnum growled, wishing to damn the English, and Sharp smiled.
Robbins sent for the carpenter next morning. Robbins had no false
shame; no false anything, perhaps. He didn't mind asking for things.
During that day he borrowed tools from Colley, galvanised nails
from the Post Office department, and a tarpaulin from the hospital.
Colley also sent the fatigue and his company storeman. A passing
veterinary officer remarked afterwards that the whole political

medical and military staff of Gwanki district seemed to be at the disposal of the Mosi Company.

But the station was delighted with itself. Sharp, having sent his carpenter, went down after breakfast to see him at work. On the way he picked up Pagnum.

'That man of mine will soon knock up the store.'

'Damn good scheme of yours.'

'Just as well the Resident didn't turn up instead of the vet.'

'Oh my Gawd, old Jelly-Belly.'

At the wharf Robbins and the station carpenter were found perched on top of an enormous packing-case, at least eight feet cube, which was planted at the water's edge. It was patched here and there with raw cow hides. Robbins was on all fours putting nails into a hide. His mouth was full of nails, and as he hammered in one nail with his right hand, he spat out another into his left and put it into position for the next blow. The hammer was moving so fast all the time that it was simply a blur, like a fly's wing. The noise was like machine-gun fire.

Colley and half the town were standing below, admiring; Mrs Robbins with little Alfred could be seen in the royal bed on the stoop.

'Hullo,' Pagnum roared.

'Hullo, Robbie,' Sharp cried, smiling already in anticipation. 'What's all this?'

Robbins looked over and bawled down in his usual cheerful and serious tone, 'It's a noo idea of mine—a diving bell.'

'A diving bell?'

'A diving bell, gentlemen. It was the 'ides give me the idea, soon as they came in.'

Robbins, who was dressed only in a pair of ragged trousers and a broken straw hat, scrambled to his feet, looked thoughtfully at his work and then shouted, 'I suppose you're going to say, wy not a cassoon?'

'Why not, indeed?' Pagnum cried, poking Sharp in the ribs. 'Why not a what d'you call it, Robbie, though God knows what it is.'

'It certainly seems to need an explanation,' Sharp said.

'Well, gentlemen, I'll tell you wy I didn't make a cassoon—it's like this—the river's seventeen foot deep and the largest planks I got is only fifteen foot, just the length of the store, and there's another thing——' he began to explain in detail how difficult it was to make a caisson waterproof at the bottom. 'So, gentlemen, as you'd 'ave to pump any'ow, I got the idea, why not a diving bell with 'ides on the outside?'

'That's a damn fine notion, Robbie.'

'A good idea, Robbie.'

'Ha ha—strornary good—strornary.' Colley stared at his friend fascinated. Sharp and Pagnum had the delighted and expectant expressions of aunts when the child is doing something unexpected.

'Very nice indeed,' Sharp said, 'and what's it for?'

'For sir, wy sir, there's six 'undred pounds at the bottom of that river.'

Two days later the bell was actually ready. The station joyfully attended to see its first trial. It was found supported on two dug-outs in mid-river. On one side, at the bottom, a door had been cut. A long rubber hose from the top was joined to a small pump in one of the dugouts.

The box was pushed overboard amid cheers from the station, almost turned over, wobbled and rolled from side to side, and then gradually sank. Laughing and shouting natives jumped upon it to drive it down and then dropped stones on it. The pump was set going. Enormous bubbles burst on the surface of the muddy water.

Robbins was dancing with excitement and delight. 'It's arf full of air now,' he shouted, 'you can see by were it's coming through the sides.'

'And are you sure the money's there?' Sharp asked.

'Wy, sir, just you arsk yourself, if you was balmy and thought someone was going to steal all your dibs, wot bit of river would you choose to drop it in—the deepest 'ole you could find.'

'I see.'

'I don't say if you was you,' Robbins shouted politely. 'But if you was balmy—in a balmy funk, as you might say.'

'I see, Robbie.'

'That's the idea, sir.' Robbins was peeling off his trousers. 'Excuse me, gentlemen, not 'aving a costume.'

'You're not going to get into that contraption yourself?'

'Well, gentlemen, if I don't, no one else will. These Gwanki chaps won't go under water—they think it's full of devils.'

'Look here, Robbie,' Pagnum said, 'you can't go playing the bloody fool with a heart like yours.'

'That's all right, sir, I ain't taking risks. Wy, wen I get in the bell, I'll only 'ave water up to me navel. It's no more'n a walk in the Mile End Road, as you might say, on a wet morning.' He paused and reflected. He was about to make a joke. 'Being an old naval man, you see, gentlemen, I won't feel out of my depth.'

He looked round for appreciation, gave one loud 'haw' and dived into the water.

The men at the pump turned the handle with furious energy, the surface of the water above the packing-case burst into a froth of bubbles.

There was a long silence. Pagnum said angrily, 'It's suicide.'

Sharp said in a surprised voice, 'I say, do you think he's all right?'

'Trust Robbie,' said Colley with loyal confidence. 'He's a real——'

Another half minute passed; the water foamed, the pumpers sweated. The three white men gazed solemnly at the water. Colley said suddenly in a voice of protest, 'I say, damn it all.'

At once all deportment was lost. The doctor jumped into a dug-out and seized a paddle; Colley shouted at the pumpers; Sharp stretched out his arm and commanded, 'Turn it over, damn you. Turn it over. Pull the ropes.'

Ropes were pulled; the packing-case tilted; a long pale object like a dead bream, pink and silver, was seen floating just beneath the water. Colley and three boatmen jumped in simultaneously. Robbins was hauled into the dugout, emptied of water, filled with whisky and rushed to hospital in a stretcher. As they put him down on the bed he opened his eyes and asked, 'Wot 'appened?'

'You damn nearly passed out, you bloody lunatic.'

'Yes, but look 'ere.' He opened one hand and showed a fistful of mud with a two shilling piece embedded in it. 'I knoo a bell would do the trick. Wy, the air down there is better than wot you get up 'ere—cooler.'

He was put to bed. An attempt to get up the next day brought on a fainting fit so that he was obliged to obey the doctor's prohibition on diving.

He was greatly depressed when on the third morning he was let out of hospital; he sat all day on the quay looking mournfully at the floats which marked the bell's position.

Even at the club, which was held that evening by unanimous agreement at the company's wharf to celebrate his convalescence, he was depressed.

'This is a hhonour, gentlemen, to see you at my 'umble abode,' he said sadly, 'and I only wish I could say 'ow much I appreciate it.'

Robbins always spoke of his humble abode, not in a joking manner, but seriously. His manners and ideas were extremely old-fashioned. 'But you must take the act for the word, gentlemen, wen I say welcome and thank you. Boy, bring gin one time.'

A dirty little naked up-country girl of about fourteen with a face eaten by smallpox came running out of the mud shack behind the famous bed, stared at the visitors and ran away again.

'Boy,' Robbins shouted. ' 'Ere, 'urry up, Geeser, wot you playing at?'

There was a loud squeak as if a puppy had been trodden on and the girl staggered into sight again in front of a large black foot, belonging, no doubt, to Robbins' cook. Rubbing herself behind, and twisting herself into various shapes, she came to the chairs.

'Get small chop,' Robbins commanded, and said mournfully, 'excuse my staff, gentlemen, I tell 'er to put on a cloth every time I see 'er, but she's not up to it yet, are you, Geeser?'

The dirty child, now holding out a plate of fried yam to Sharp, looked over her shoulder at the sound of her name, with a scared expression, and then, catching Robbins' eye, grinned nervously. The display of her teeth, gleaming and regular, in the midst of her ruined face, was somehow touching, and Sharp said, 'She's been unlucky with the smallpox.'

'You may well say it, unlucky all round. Look at the marks on her be-hind, if you'll excuse me, gentlemen—turn round, Geeser.'

Robbins turned the girl round and showed deep grey weals cut into her buttocks and hips. 'That was 'er mama did that,' he said, 'and then she turned her out into the bush.'

'What for?'

'She says she was a thief, but I shouldn't wonder if it wasn't jealousy. You see, in a country where any man may 'ave any girl in a manner of speaking—all right, Geeser, run along and wash yourself.' He gave the girl a push and a slight slap, the kind of caress which a man gives to a young daughter, and Jiso, grinning, withdrew from sight.

'What does Mrs Robbins say?'

'Delighted, sir—it was Mrs Robbins suggested putting her on the job here.'

'She thinks you ought to afford a two-wife harem.'

'Wy no, sir. Mrs Robbins isn't out so much for swank—she's got a real European's affections, she 'as—you'd be surprised——'

'Jealous of you, Robbie.'

'Fond of me, sir—it's a funny thing, love, especially in a woman.'

'You're bloody right there, Robbie.'

'I suppose it's a natural thing, too—dogs 'ave it very strong.'

A voice from the shack, which was now hidden in the dark, called Jiso, and there was a sudden commotion behind Robbins' chair. The dirty small girl shot out and vanished into the shack. Apparently she had been squatting almost under Robbins' chair, but he did not notice her sudden eruption. He pursued his idea. 'I suppose nobody loves so strong as a dog—and that's a funny thing, too,' his voice rose into a kind of song of amazement. 'Why should a naminal love a yuman being?'

'Why indeed?' Sharp said, smiling.

'Shows what I always say that animals have no real sense,' Pagnum said.

'Ha ha.' Colley laughed but checked himself suddenly and looked at Robbins to see if perhaps a laugh was out of place.

Robbins in fact was serious. Robbins in all the numerous discussions at Gwanki about love, women, God, dogs and famous sporting feats, was always serious. He shouted now, 'Well, sir, I got an idea that a dog doesn't know a lot of difference, except of course the trousers—it only likes a man better'n another dog because 'e's more interesting.'

'You think the dirty dogs are laughing at us, Robbie.'

'Well, sir, I wouldn't say that—dogs 'as more respec——'

'Happy dogs.'

'You may say so, sir.'

'Would you like to be a dog, Robbie?'

'Wy, that's a funny idea—going round on all fours among a lot of smells. Haw.'

'Depends on your master,' Sharp suggested.

'No, no, sir, I wouldn't be a dog, 'appy as they are. A man 'as more scope and 'e 'as 'is regular job.'

'You like a regular job, Robbie?'

'Wy, sir, a man 'as 'is duty—all you gentlemen got your duties to 'is Majesty, and I got my duty to Mrs Robbie 'ere and little Alfie and the Company.'

'The Company—did you say the Company, Robbie?'

There was a shout of delighted laughter, in the middle of which the doctor's house-boy suddenly appeared before his master and said in a severe tone, 'They put that girl Jiso for water——'

'What's that?'

The police orderly now sprang forward and saluted Sharp. A policeman in Nigeria never interferes with the course of events unless somebody else has done so. He then hastens to make an official report. 'I beg to report, sah, they put the girl Jiso for dive for money in river. She no come back.'

Robbins jumped up, waving his long arms and shouted for his canoe men, for lights. He then made a dash at the water and would have jumped in if Pagnum had not seized hold of his shirt.

'Not on your bloody——' Pagnum said ferociously.

Robbins paid no attention to this grip behind, but continued to jump up and down like a small boy attached by a leading rein. 'Go on—get under,' he bawled, 'arn't you ashamed of yourselves—one pore kid beats the lot of you—turn it over, you doolies.'

Suddenly he gave a gasp and fell. He had fainted. This added very much to the excitement. There were shouts for brandy as well as for Jiso; and in the middle of the confusion, a young man in full uniform, with a neat little moustache, was seen on the wharf, looking about him with the air of one ready for anything.

This was a new assistant district officer, sent to help Sharp with tax assessment. He had been sent to Gwanki because he needed, so the Resident said, experience of a bush station. He was beginning at once to acquire that experience.

He addressed Pagnum politely, 'Can I do anything?'

'Get out of my way, damn you.'

He turned to Sharp. 'I beg your pardon, sir, but——'

Sharp thrust him aside with a brandy bottle and Colley, galloping up with Pagnum's little bag, nearly threw him into the river. All then stooped over Robbins.

The young man, much embarrassed, stood a little apart and assumed the air of an official mourner at a state funeral.

Robbins opened his eyes, gave a deep sigh and said, ' 'Ere, wot's this? Wy, gentlemen, this is 'ardly wot you 'ave a right to expect.'

Just then Jiso poked her head between Pagnum's and Sharp's and made a noise like the mingled whine, howl and squawk of a frightened and conscience-smitten puppy.

Robbins stared at her and said in a lazy voice, 'Wot you want is a blooming good 'iding. Wot you do it for?'

Jiso, with an anxious look, held out two florins.

'Oh, so you got there, did you?'

He reflected for a moment, gave an immense grin which was always the warning, like the distant head-lamp, of a joke coming.

'You wouldn't think her much in the bell way, gentlemen,' and in case no one saw the point, he added, 'not with a face like that.'

But this did not satisfy him. He frowned and half closed his eyes. Pagnum said impatiently, 'Now, Colley, let's put him bye-byes.'

They stooped and took him carefully up and carried him towards the bed towering in the background. With its vast muslin mosquito nets, and the hurricane lamp slung from the front post, it looked like some mandarin's house-boat floating in the dark.

The new A.D.O., joining the procession at a slow march, found himself next Sharp and asked in a low tone, 'Who is he?'

But Sharp, carrying the brandy bottle and closely watching the patient, made no reply. The young man, abashed, fell back a step. He did not venture even to offer any assistance while Robbins was being put to bed. He felt, no doubt, like a new courtier without privilege of entry to the royal presence.

Mrs Robbins peeled the shirt off the thin wasted body, which looked like a famine child's, while Colley carefully aimed the dirty feet at the legs of the pyjamas. Robbins himself was still thoughtful. Once he began a sentence about bells and belles, and everyone, even Mrs Robbins, who perhaps knew the tone of voice in which her husband made jokes, stopped to listen. But he frowned again and was silent.

He was put to bed at last with the baby in its usual place on his left hand, and Mrs Robbins sitting up on his right in her chemise. She had taken this place to give him a supper of egg nogg, prescribed by Pagnum. He was still very weak.

The party took its leave. He looked at it open-mouthed, anxious, forgetful of his politeness, and then suddenly he uttered a loud, 'Haw. Wot you might call a diving belle. Geeser, I mean—a diving belle, gentlemen. Haw.'

The party smiled, and Robbins sank back contented on the bosom of his wife.

The A.D.O., still smiling respectfully at the joke, now introduced himself to Sharp and as the party strolled back along the shore, asked, 'Who is that?'

'Who's who?'

'That—ah—gentleman?'

'Robbie,' Sharp said in surprise. 'Oh, he's—what is he, Pag?'

'A perishing maniac, blast him—jumping about like that.'

'Might have killed himself,' Colley said. 'Frightened the missus— did you notice her face?'

'Oh yes, is the—lady—ah—his wife?'

'The lady,' Sharp said, and suddenly the whole party gave a shout of laughter. The young man looked surprised. But after a moment, he realised at last that Robbins was a joke and joined in the laughter. He was delighted to find himself on firm ground.

'Damn funny.'

'Oh, damn funny,' Pagnum said, glaring at him and already beginning to hate him.

'Always something new with poor old Robbie,' Sharp said, laughing quite as innocently as the A.D.O.

'A bit of a character, what?'

'A bit of my ass,' Pagnum said, turning his own on the youth. 'Come on, Colley, come and have a short one.'

Colley looked down mildly on the young man and said, 'Robbie, you know, he's a most strornary good chap.'

The A.D.O., who felt already that mysterious respect which belonged to Colley's presence, was crushed. He actually turned red. He fell back with the resolve, very obvious in his expression, not to jump at conclusions, until he knew his way about Gwanki.

Robbie was advised to stay in bed for a week, but when Pagnum and Colley went to see him, he was directing a diving party. Jiso was in the bell, the men were pumping, the water was frothing and half the population of Gwanki was watching from the Company wharf.

Sharp's mild suggestion that as the provincial agent was due in less than a month, it might be wise to finish the store, was badly received.

'You see, gentlemen, to finish the store, I'd 'ave to break up the bell——'

'But won't the agent prefer a store to the bell?'

'Well, gentlemen, 'e's got both. The bell is the store as you might say—and 'e's got six 'undred pounds, too, practically speaking.'

Jiso's black face broke surface and she held up a florin. Robbins turned with a shout. 'See that—she's got two pounds already this morning—I knoo we could do it. We'll 'ave the lot in a week— six 'undred—and I tell you wot, gentlemen, I got a noo idea. Bridges.'

'Bridges?'

'With this 'ere bell. Wy, I could build you a bridge anywere— in concrete blocks.'

'Cement is expensive—you'll want some capital, Robbie.'

'Well, gentlemen, it'll be a bit 'ard if I don't get a commission on six 'undred pounds—out of the hair, as you might say.'

Unluckily he did not get the six hundred. At the end of a week's diving, he had only gathered another three florins and a few odd shillings. Jiso dived twenty times a day but she brought up nothing but handfuls of mud. Meanwhile Robbins had a new anxiety which, like all his troubles, he confided to the station. The provincial agent was coming a fortnight early. ' 'E's 'eard something,' Robbie said, 'you can tell by 'is letter. 'E 'opes that my suggestions to the central office 'as worked out, and that there's plenty of 'ides ready for transport.'

'We'd better get that store up at once.'

'But the bell's workin' wonderful—just look at it—since I put those twenty new 'ides on the cracks there's 'ardly any air gettin' out.'

'The agent will prefer a store.'

' 'E'll prefer six 'undred pounds.'

'How much have you got?'

'Two pounds seventeen and six to date.'

He was walking up and down the quay in nothing but a dirty straw hat and a pair of dirty grey trousers. His thin body was burnt chocolate brown and as usual he looked, in spite of his protruding bones, his flat chest and panting breath, full of energy and life. 'And two teresa dollars,' he shouted, 'and a bloody cold in the 'ead.'

Sharp laughed all the way back to the station. 'Poor old Robbie—his two pounds seventeen and six. Talk about go-getters——'

'The bloody calf has done for himself.'

'But we can't,' Colley muttered. 'We ought to be able, between the lot of us—a subscription or something.'

'Poison the bloody agent,' Pagnum said. 'If there's anything poisonous enough.'

'The fact is,' Sharp said, 'that poor old Robbie is not fit to look after himself. We'll have to take complete charge; put up the store, get in the hides—and keep them away from him till the last minute.'

'Yes, but how?'

'Suppose I get the hides and put 'em in the rest-house till this agent is really due—the chiefs will take my word they'll be paid—and suppose you put up some kind of a store, Colley.'

'That's a damn good idea of yours.'

'Sharp, you're a bloody Bismarck.'

Sharp himself was very pleased with his scheme. He had never looked so Napoleonic as on that evening, sending off messengers to chiefs, and bustling across to the rest-house where he devised a kind of framework to keep the skins out of reach of ants.

Colley, for his part, was on the wharf at dawn with twenty men in fatigue dress, carrying matchets. The bell was down, Jiso was already diving, and Robbins, in carpet slippers and part of a pair of drawers, was directing a tall Nupe boatman at the pump. 'Go on, wot you think you're doing, you silly great long bleeding addick, playing the horgan?'

Robbins refused to bring up the bell. 'We've 'ad a lucky turn today, cap—she's brought up something every time.'

'Well, Robbie, you know it's—how much have you got?'

'A two shillings, a sixpence and a dollar, sir, but she felt a bag, too. Just one more day, sir.'

Pagnum came rolling up scratching his hairy chest and frowning. He said, 'Robbie, d'you know what—you're certifiable. Up with that bloody bell, Colley, I'll hold'm.'

Just then Jiso climbed ashore and Robbins rushed to the edge of the wharf. She gave him a muddy sixpence and made for the compound.

Pagnum said, 'Hi you, Jiso.'

The girl began to run, whereupon Robbins, shocked by this lack of manners, shouted, ' 'Ere, 'ere, come 'ere, Geeser. Didn't you 'ear the gentleman.'

Jiso came back reluctantly; Pagnum took her by the chin and pulled down her lower lip. 'Open your mouth, you ape.'

'Why, what's wrong with her, doc? Go on, Geeser, open your mouth for the doctor.'

The mouth slowly opened and Pagnum, putting in a finger, hooked three florins out of each cheek. Robbins was astonished. 'Coo,' he said. 'Wot you do that for, Geeser?'

Jiso stood with an air of embarrassment, scratching her left ankle with her right toes. Her mouth still hung open, so that the lower lip showed its wet lining.

'There you are,' Pagnum said in triumph. 'Didn't I tell you all your apes were a lot of bloody thieves.'

Robbins, looking at Jiso with astonishment, shouted, 'Wot were you going to do with it?'

Jiso looked still more foolish. Robbins raised his thin eyebrows into his tow hair and bawled, 'Making yourself a bottom drawer, is that it?' He seemed equally amused and surprised. Robbins could not understand jokes, but on the other hand he found something funny in almost everything that happened in life; especially his own misfortunes. 'Layin' it up were moth and rust don't corrup', ay, Geeser? I say, were d'you think you'll go wen you die, Geeser—robbing pore master like that? Hi, you thief, you.'

Jiso understood this word. She shook her head and muttered something about cuku.

'She says she gave it to your cook,' Pagnum said. 'I shouldn't be surprised. All coast cooks are bloody robbers.'

'Tom.' Robbins' voice was full of laughter at this mounting story of treachery. 'It was Tom, was it?' He turned towards the store and bawled, 'Hi you, Tom.'

But Tom had already disappeared. Enquiries in the compound showed that he had left almost as soon as the coins fell out of Jiso's mouth. He took nothing with him but no money was found. The canoemen explained that Tom for the last week had kept his box somewhere in the bush. Sharp put out a warrant for him, but he was not found in the town. He had simply walked into the bush which at Gwanki begins fifty yards from the town wall.

Nothing could describe Robbins' appreciation of Tom's cleverness and his own defeat. At the Scotch club, when he came to drink, he kept shouting out every five minutes, 'Well, that Tom made a proper fool of me, didn't he?'

Once he gave a loud laugh, full of delighted appreciation, 'Haw, that bastard Tom had the proper laugh of me.'

The police sergeant came to report to Sharp his failure to catch Tom. He said that the last person to see him had been an old woman gathering firewood who met Tom and Mrs Robbins, each carrying a box, pushing rapidly towards the west; that is, the French frontier.

'The missus,' Robbins said. 'What's that?' He started up and ran off into the darkness. After half an hour, since he did not come back, Pagnum also got up and exclaimed, 'It had to happen.'

He made off for the wharf at top speed cursing all the way. Sharp followed at leisure. Robbins was found sitting on the bed. The curtains were rolled up. Under the enormous canopy he looked out of proportion, like a small boy.

He received his visitors with a hollow roar of despair. 'It's true, gentlemen—she's gorn—she followed 'im as soon as I was out of the way and, wot's more, she's took Alfred.'

Pagnum flew into a rage. 'And didn't I tell you that all these women were bitches——'

Sharp patted him on the shoulder like a grandmother, 'Poor old Robbie—you're well rid of her.'

'Well, am I?' Robbins asked. 'I don't feel like that, gentlemen. Losing your family all of an 'eap like that—it's a bit of a knock.'

Just then the A.D.O. arrived. He had been arranging for the transfer of three hundred hides from the rest-house to the wharf. Though at first he had been mildly surprised to find the Government in the skin trade, he was already used to it. Obviously such things were done in the bush. He greeted Robbins with a smile and a query, 'How's fishing today, Robbie, any luck with the bell?'

'The bell,' Robbins said. 'We've broke it up.' He waved his hand towards a pile of splintered planks lying in the shadow, 'and I'm broke up, too.'

'I say, what a shame,' the A.D.O. humoured him in just the right tone, with just the right expression of sympathy established by usage.

'The bell don't matter,' Robbins said bitterly. 'Anyone can make a bell, but oo's going to make another woman like my Bamu or another Alfie. Wy, I feel like I been murdered alive. It's a fair knock-out, gentlemen.' His voice roared like an organ pipe, throbbing in the air, and suddenly they saw the tears on his cheeks. The A.D.O.'s face altered with ludicrous suddenness. He looked at Pagnum and Sharp in wonder and saw there expressions which instantly changed his own to the profoundest sympathy and dismay.

The party did not break up till a late hour. The scheme, tacitly agreed upon, was to make Robbins drunk. But drink did not seem to affect him. Pagnum at last filled up half a glass of whisky with gin instead of water and offered it with these words, 'Here's hell to bloody everything, goddamn its dirty soul.'

Robbins drank it in two or three gulps, opened his mouth again and sang out for the tenth time, 'You see, gentlemen, I bin 'appy, I'm a family man, gentlemen—it's natural.' Suddenly he rolled off the bed and lay like a corpse.

'Come on,' Pagnum said. 'Put the corpse to bed—pity he'll ever wake up, poor sod,' and while the party walked thoughtfully home under a sky like a blue-black ocean full of phosphorescent eyes, he shouted up in a fury of disgust, 'What's the good of telling anybody anything—they'll still smash their bloody skulls on the same old bloody walls.'

All this time Colley was in the bush with every available man. Half a company of the Nigerian Regiment spent half the night tumbling among thorn scrub in search of the Robbins family, which was probably ten miles over the French border before it left barracks.

But Colley did not give them up till next morning when, exhausted and full of thorns, he turned up at the native hospital. Pagnum was with his out-patients and still in a very bad temper. 'Serve him right, the cretin—didn't I warn him?'

'You don't understand, Pag.' Colley turned his mournful face towards the doctor. 'A thing like this—it's what Robbie says—it's a knock-out.'

Robbins himself could not be seen because the agent had arrived. He was a short pale man with polished black hair and a serious expression. Even his clothes were serious. He wore a dark worsted suit with a pin stripe and a dark satin tie. His shirt-sleeves were long and carefully buttoned at the wrist. He rode about the station in trousers and shoes like a serious man who takes a pony as in London he would take a taxi or a train to the office.

Everyone expected an explosion which would blow poor Robbins to fragments. But the agent obviously separated business and pleasure, and he came to the station for pleasure. He never mentioned business. He was extremely affable in his grave way, informed the party at lunch, given by Colley, that he had heard of Gwanki's reputation for hospitality, drank eight whiskies, and spoke seriously of politics. It was his considered opinion, he said, that the Great War wouldn't be the last, because of all this currency chaos.

He pronounced chaos chass to rhyme with bass, and for some reason this made everyone, already depressed, look pensive and remote. Sharp was preoccupied anyway, for that morning he had received a most alarming wire from the provincial office. Urgent. Explain immediately report Government collection hides. Stop. Resdt. Sharp looked like a man upon whose head, at some dignified ceremony, the chandelier has fallen with a crash. In his bewildered injury, looking for sympathy, he had even showed the wire to

Pagnum, but Pagnum had growled only, 'Good for you—tell'm collect his own bloody hides for hell.'

The lunch party broke up early. Robbins was not spoken of or seen. He had, of course, already been sacked.

But about half-past five, when Colley in a gloomy trance was riding about the parade ground with the embarrassed A.D.O. who had come out to practise polo with him, Pagnum came rolling up and said, 'He's gone, they've just chucked the poor doodle in the bush.'

Colley continued to gaze into the air as if enquiring of a blank wall what was behind it all. 'I thought I'd better keep off the grass,' he said at last.

'Oh, I wasn't intruding on any bloody funeral,' Pagnum said. 'But if Robbie's going to follow the precedent, I hope, he won't set fire to the bloody shop till the bloody agent's inside.'

'You don't really think——' the A.D.O. was shocked.

'I don't think, because it bloody well won't bear thinking about; you don't think because you can't, and he don't think because he isn't built that way, he just lays himself out for every bloody hog in the world to chaw a dinner off him. But if Robbie cuts his bloody neck, he'll cut a bloody better neck than the one you've got to laff at him.' Pagnum said this with a tone and look which startled the young man but which he did not understand. For all his Piccadilly air, he was slow in the uptake, and he had neither seen hatred before nor realised from what trivial causes, in men of a certain passionate energy, it can arise; so sudden and powerful as their love, and made of the same materials.

There was a short embarrassed silence, interrupted by a distant shout from the road.

'*Good* evening, gentlemen.'

They turned and saw Robbins' long neck and celebrated straw hat projecting over the scrub by the town road. He approached with a beaming grin, showing all his teeth which, in his very brown face, had always an effect of surprising gaiety. When he had cleared the bushes, Jiso was seen, following at a respectful distance of two yards, and carrying on her head a net full of yams, a white enamelled chamber-pot on top of them, and a thermos flask in her hand.

'I was just looking for you, gentlemen,' Robbins said, 'to say good-bye.'

Colley dismounted, staring all the time with his eyebrows at their highest; Pagnum muttered something inaudible except for two terrific curses in the middle.

'I'm sorry to go, gentlemen, but I wanted to thank you first.'

Colley suddenly grasped an idea. 'Look here, Robbie, come and stay with me—long as you like.'

'As for that,' Pagnum said with an air of hearty disgust, 'he can't clear out like this. See here, Robbie,' he caught him by the arm, 'come along to the house and we'll send all the bloody shirt collars to where they belong. Not a word out of you. You can't go. Haven't we done you well—not to say we saved your rotten life about fourteen times. I think we have, and damn well. You can't go. You can't play us a dirty trick. You owe us to stay,' and he ended with an angry shout, 'You can't go, Robbie.'

Robbins was astonished. He looked round with open mouth. He bawled in his loudest voice, expressive of the strongest feeling, 'Wy, gentlemen, I reely don't know 'ow to speak—it's like the doctor says—thanks to you gentlemen and Mr Sharp, Gwanki's been a reel 'appy station and after all, a nappy station is the 'appiest place on earth. But wot I say is, give me reel gentlemen like you gentlemen are and they'd make any station 'appy. Ony thing is I got to get to the plateau and I 'aven't too much time.'

The plateau is the tin mining area of Nigeria about three hundred miles south-east from Gwanki.

Pagnum dropped his arm. 'The plateau, how the bloody hell are you going to get there?'

'Wy, walk.' Robbins was amused by this question.

'Have you got a job on the plateau?'

'Not essactly a job, gentlemen. I wouldn't take a job—the fact is, gentlemen, 'as it ever struck you that tin-mining, the way they do it, is a funny business?'

'What's funny about it?'

'Wy, you know wot they do. Dig up the mud in the bottom of the river and wash out the tin dust—it's like washing for gold on the Klondike. But gentlemen, I bin thinking, were does the tin come from in the first place—it must come from somewere—and it must come down the rivers—it couldn't go up. Now, you see my idea—I'm going to find were it comes from—were it's at home, as you might say—the microbe of tin.'

'The microbe of tin.' Colley was once more in a trance. His eyes, fixed on Robbins, seemed to have a new cause of wonder. But he certainly had not yet reached the idea of tin in any form.

'That's it, sir, and I got an idea where it is, too—I could put my finger on the place—well, gentlemen, I got to get along—I'm in a bit of an 'urry, as you might think, to get there before anyone else 'as the same idea. So if you'd excuse the liberty, I'll be saying good-bye, gentlemen, and God bless you one and all. Say good-bye to the gentlemen, Geeser.'

Jiso, startled by this sudden glance of the party, hung down her lip and dodged behind her master, who bawled at her, 'Go on, where's your manners. Say sanu, you silly kipper.'

Jiso, understanding this word, bobbed down on one knee and looked idiotic. Robbins gazed at her with the pondering expression one sees sometimes on the face of a dog owner. 'She ain't much to look at,' he bawled then, 'and of course she ain't got no manners, but you'd be surprised wot sense she 'as—she's as good as a clurk, better.'

'You're taking her along.'

Robbins looked round them with his most amused expression. He shouted at last, 'Well, I arsk you, gentlemen, am I taking 'er or is she taking me—I arsk you, gentlemen.' He took off his hat and walked down the road, but ten yards away he turned and shouted back, 'I arsk you, gentlemen.' He pointed at Jiso who, at once, like a dog which has learnt a trick and performs it on all inappropriate occasions, went down on one knee. But this time, sure that she was doing the right thing, she grinned broadly.

'I don't believe she's more than fourteen,' the A.D.O. said, 'I wonder is she safe with him?'

'I should bloody well hope not,' Pagnum said, as he stumped away towards his house.

Colley was silent. He was staring after Robbins. Suddenly his brow wrinkled with the beagle look, he had scented the idea again. He turned to the A.D.O. who was holding the two ponies, and said, 'You know, the real thing about Robbie is——' he frowned. But after all, even if Colley had caught up with the ideas suggested to him by Robbins' unexpectedness, both in triumph and defeat, he could not have put them into words. Colley was a man of feeling, but his feelings had to remain his feelings, walled away, slowly accumulating in their cut-off intensity.

'At any rate,' he said after a few minutes while they were riding side by side along the road, 'that chap Bolsover was all wrong about him.' The A.D.O. always had a profound respect for Colley, but he was unaccountedly shy of him. Besides, he had begun to realise that Pagnum was annoyed with him and he was wondering why. 'These bush stations,' he thought, 'certainly need experience—the Resident was quite right.'

They had reached Pagnum's house where usually they stopped after a polo practice, to call out that they would be at the club. Pagnum could be seen on the stoop, under a hurricane lamp, drinking what looked like neat whisky, in his old style. Colley drew rein. But Pagnum's head was turned towards the district office where a light showed that Sharp was working late.

'Look at 'm,' he said, 'the bloody little ass crawler—stewing up some eye-wash for Jelly-Belly.'

The two gazed at his large dark cheeks which seemed to be sweating hatred against all the world, and rode on. Colley's face, as he turned towards the company bungalow, struck the young man unpleasantly, gave him a shock, as they say. 'But,' he reflected, 'after a twenty-one-month tour any man might look hollow in cheek and eye.'

He himself was preoccupied. He could see his small boy on the circular road, with his new green chair marked with his initials in large black letters, and a new bottle of whisky, wandering about in an uncertain and embarrassed manner. He had ordered him to place chair and whisky by the parade ground, but though it was past club time, no other chair had yet appeared there.

He gave the pony to the groom and went to fetch the small boy back. 'Better wait,' he thought, 'till I see what's the order of the day. I haven't really got the hang of this place yet.'

Suddenly in the growing dark he came across the agent, in spotless white with a black bow tie, followed also by a boy with chair and a bottle.

'If you are looking for the club,' he said, 'there isn't one. I've just seen the doctor.' And he added in a savage tone, 'I was told Gwanki was a friendly station but I've been seriously misled.'

He pronounced misled mizzled to rhyme with drizzled, and for some reason, this caused the young A.D.O. to be still more cautious and reserved. He murmured only, 'Good night.'

The agent made no reply. He seemed to be deeply disappointed. He hadn't found what he expected in Gwanki.

THE REBEL

THE market had been full and busy, a summer market, but now, at three o'clock, the stalls were packing up. All along the alleys between them were barrows and boxes full of goods, dustbins full of rubbish.

Because the crowds had gone, the dusty market place seemed hotter than ever—stall-holders, sweating and crimson, staggering slowly out from the shade of their awnings, embracing slippery rolls of calico and American cloth, threw them into rusty, battered cars, with gestures which were like curses, 'Hit or miss, I've done with you.'

A vast woman in black, with a bag pulling her crooked in the left hand, and two children dragging at her skirts, waddled a few yards across the open, glared at a cheap-jack who was still spieling from his stand, then turned her back on him and sat down, or rather collapsed down in a box.

The little girl, of about five, stood leaning against her knee with a sympathetic expression; the little boy, about three, in a thick wool suit, with a pirate's stocking cap cocked on the side of his head, turned away and was about to make for the cheap-jack, when his mother grabbed him by the back of his jersey and planted him in her lap.

'There you are, lovey—I'm sure you could do with a rest.' But the boy was already wriggling himself slowly downwards under her arm. The pirate cap worked itself off, revealing a head clipped so close that the hair glittered all over as pale as barley stubble, the jersey gradually rose displaying a body unexpectedly thin in continuous snake-like movement.

'Oh, do leave off, Billy, didn't you promise to be a good boy if mum let you come?'

The more you looked at the woman, the more enormous she seemed, from the huge head, the great shoulders, thick as an ordinary body, to the vast hips spread out as she sat so that they completely hid the box, each diameter enlarging on the last so that her general shape was that of a mountain, a British mountain, like Snowdon; not so much cleft, precipitous like some Himalayan peak, tortured by lightning, glacier and avalanche; as chipped by June frosts, and worn down by eons of half-gales, millions of driving showers. The top of her head, a rounded summit of black streaked with a light rime of grey, showed a bald patch like a piece of dry rock, polished by dusty mornings. Her long stringy hair, falling on her enormous shoulders, joined the rocky summit to the thick body in a continuous declivity, the short neck was hidden from behind, where she seemed like a hunchback, and in front, entirely swallowed up in the great hanging chins. From this, in easy but massive slopes, fell breasts, belly, the vast foothills of the hips, the huge thighs. Her lap was like that broad deep valley half-way up Snowdon where there is room for a lake, a mill, and a thousand sheep.

Her vast white face, with its falling nose, cheeks, and chins, was like one of those cliffs, so eroded by falling streams, that with its knobs, lumps, cracks, chimneys, it looks like easy climbing, but is in fact so soft and friable as to be exceedingly dangerous.

Billy, crimson and slowly strangling, made a sudden corkscrew twist, and turned over on his face, thus unfastening his chin from his mother's grip and offering to her purchase only the smooth back of his head. She tightened her arm, but it was too late—he jerked out his head, as one pulls a cork out of a bottle, and then with fiery shining cheeks, a nose purple from friction, turned round to run off.

'Come here, Billy. Why can't you behave. Don't you have no consideration—don't you love your poor mum.' The woman was outraged.

But Billy, having taken one long look at the cheap-jack, was making for the stalls, the boxes full of tins and bottles, the barrows stocked with buckets, brushes, kettles, saucepans, and glittering objects of all kinds.

The little girl, leaning against her mother's knee, yearned upwards towards her and said in a voice of deepest, of maternal sympathy, 'Isn't he *ba-ad*, Mummy.'

The woman turned her head towards Billy and uttered a weary prayer, 'Oh no, Billy is a *good* boy—aren't you, Billy? He always does what his mum asks him. He's coming back now. You'll see.'

Billy disappeared round the nearest stall, and a loud clatter was heard as of falling pans. The mother quivered, swelled and rolled on her seat; a kind of shudder or earthquake agitated hips, belly, shrugged-up shoulders, chins, cheeks. A deep rumbling sound was heard. 'Oh, the little bitch—what's he up to now. Oh, I'll give him such a smack in a minute.'

Billy suddenly reappeared from behind the stall and stared at his mother with an air of calculation. The rumble, probably the word 'smack,' had reached him. The little girl caught up the cap from her mother's lap, ran to him, and fitted it back on his head with the gestures of a modiste selling the latest thing to a film star. 'There, darling—there's your nice cap.' She took his hand, 'You see, it's time to go home—it's *tea*-time. We *have* to go home for tea, haven't we, Billy?'

Billy, his eyes still fixed on his mother, allowed himself to be drawn towards her. But suddenly, within a yard of her knee, he baulked.

'That's it, lovey, come to mum,' said the woman.

Billy was taking a last long look. His head gradually inclined sideways until the pirate tassel touched one shoulder. The broad forehead, delicately wrinkled, the set mouth, the small pointed chin, the large wide-open grey eyes expressed the highest concentration— for the moment, the child showed the face of an old man—one long experienced in the world where anything can happen, where no one and nothing is to be accepted at its face or word value. Then his features changed, not to a smile, but to a look of cheerful amusement. The grey eyes, especially, creasing beneath, sparkled with laughter. He looked now like the soubrette in a French comedy.

'Mummy's boy.' The woman dived forward and swung out her huge arm, thick as a leg, to scoop him in.

Billy dropped his sister's hand and made for the boxes at full speed.

'Oh, *Mum*.' The little girl was full of alarm as well as sympathy. 'I'll get him——' and she started to run.

But the woman was struggling to her feet. The mountain was

heaving like a volcano before eruption. 'All right,' she bawled towards the market alley where Billy was now trotting. 'All right, don't then. Go on and lose yourself.' She turned her back on the stalls and laboured away across the square, walking as a mountain might walk if its legs were in barrels. Each step was a convulsion, and at each step she jetted out roars of fury. 'I don't care—if you won't pay attention, then don't. Go on and get your legs broke under a lorry—go on and fall in the river. It's nothing to do with me.' She lifted her great head and threw up her enormous right hand, in the gesture of one who defies Heaven, who has finished with God and man.

'I'm only your mum.'

The little girl, having run three steps after Billy and two back after her mother, stopped on one leg. Her face wore a look of despair—the agony of a sensible and civilised member of society among impossible people.

Billy vanished among the dustbins.

FIRST LOVE

THE little girl, aged five, circled for a long time round the visitor's dog, an old black retriever. She had never seen a dog so big and black.

'Nice dog,' she said doubtfully. 'It's nice, isn't it, Mummy?'

Her mother and the visitor broke off their gossip and gazed at the child with the blank eyes of topers interrupted in a debauch. Then the visitor, a square, pale woman, said to the hostess, 'It's all right—Rover is good with children.' The little girl approached within a yard of the dog, then jumped quickly back.

'He's a darling dog, Mummy, isn't he?'

But her mother was in mid-speech '. . . cruelty and desertion. It was made absolute only last month. And now to seek him out like that——'

The little girl tugged at her mother's arm.

'He's a darling dog, Mummy, isn't he?'

'Yes dear—run along now.'

The little girl carefully put out a hand and patted the dog's ribs. The dog wagged his tail once. 'Look, Mummy,' she cried, 'look at me.' Her mother did not answer. The visitor said in a thick firm voice, exactly like her figure, 'She was always a bit unaccountable.'

'Yes, she was, wasn't she? Still!'

The thick woman said nothing. There was a pause. The hostess said in a tone of forced excitement, 'Some people are *extraordinary*.'

But the thick woman did not answer. There was another pause. The hostess cleared her mouth to speak but no word came. A look of panic appeared in her eyes. Was the afternoon to be a failure after all. And it had begun so unexpectedly well. She had dreaded the visitor, so hard to move, but she had seemed to find the right note at once. Somehow there had emerged a really delightful harmony of excitement and morality, a perfect little world in which anything said created satisfaction and self-esteem for both parties. But now this second pause! And already it was a gap. A gap like a yawn—a chasm over which no words could pass. The thick woman moved awkwardly in her tight stays and crossed her feet. She, too, was aware of uneasiness. But what was to be done. There was, so far as she could tell, no more in the bottle.

The child was now patting the dog's head. She looked up at her mother to see if this boldness was recognised, to find out exactly what she had accomplished. But the mother was repeating with the same exaggerated emphasis, 'Think of it, after her——'

The child watched the dog while she patted with an enquiring expression as if to ask, 'What does *he* think of me?' The pats gradually became harder.

Suddenly they turned to smacks. The dog gave a yelp, got up and walked away slowly, looking over his shoulder, out of the side of his eyes, with an apologetic air. The little girl ran after him and gave him another smack. The two women looked round with their glazed eyes. Their faces were blank with a different blankness, like those of topers who have reached the bottom of the bottle and begin to wonder what on earth they shall do next.

The mother jerked up and seized the child.

'Don't be so naughty, Annette. Do you want him to bite you?'

'Why didn't he bite me, Mummy?'

'Because he knows you're only a silly little girl. See, he wants to be friends even now.' She petted the dog, who at once wagged his tail with vigour, elevated his behind, threw out his paws in front and gave a short foolish bark, which obviously meant nothing. It was the ejaculation of a perplexed but well-meaning creature trying to do the right thing.

The little girl imitated her mother and stroked the dog.

'Dear Rover.'

The thick woman had now gathered all her forces. She said in a flat voice like one repeating a commonplace, 'It isn't as though she wanted to go back to him.'

The little girl put her nose within an inch of the dog's and said with gradually rising pitch, 'Darling—darling, DARLING ROVER.'

'Of course one mustn't say so—but what can one think when she goes to stay in the same house—alone.'

They looked at each other; after all, it seemed that there was something left in the bottle. The little girl was pulling the dog's ear, and punching him in the neck. 'Nasty, nasty, nasty,' she cried, 'nasty old Rover.'

The dog, unable to escape and suffering acute pain, snapped at the child's hand. Then, with hanging head and tail between its legs, slunk like a criminal beneath the table. The little girl burst into tears. The two women turned towards her their blank eyes and exasperated faces.

You see such faces at the ring-side, when, just before a third round which promises to be bloody, somebody calls from the back that Clifford So-and-So of the Board of Control has an announcement to make. The mother glared at her. 'It's your own fault. You silly girl—let him alone.'

'But I wasn't doing nothing,' the child screamed.

'You must have hurt him or he wouldn't have snapped at you.'

The dog-owner said in her flat voice, which seemed to go with her pale thick skin and large feet, 'It's all right, Helen. He won't bite her. I thought they were dividing the furniture.'

'Yes, but it didn't need a week—besides, there was always something about Nellie, you know, even when she was quite little. Well, that time when she wanted to be a nun and starved herself—and then immediately afterwards she ran away for a whole day with those awful boys, and half the night—of course nothing was proved.' She lowered her voice and leant forward. The little girl gazed round the room in despair—was this a party? Pictures, wall-paper, furniture, grown-ups, all appeared utterly senseless. Her glance came back to the dog. She crouched under the table and reached out her hand towards him, 'Nice doggie—nice Rover.'

The dog beat the floor with his tail, opened his mouth, lolled out six inches of tongue and looked imploringly at his mistress's back, solid and thick as a sack of flour.

TASTE OF GLORY

WHEN twelve o'clock struck from a dozen great bells, Antony, aged nine, sat up abruptly like a clockwork figure released by a spring. He had been keeping himself awake for three hours only for this moment. In two minutes he was dressed in shirt and blue school knickers. Then he opened the night nursery door and looked down the well of the stairs, dimly illuminated by a pale bluish square of skylight. He held his breath and began to descend. A stair creaked and he flew, terrified, through the drawing-room, and unlatched a window. In a moment he stood at the end of the back lane.

A broad street stood before him, lined with trees and houses; and in the middle a church with a low tower. He gazed at the bright sky, the moving leaves, the quivering stars, as if astonished to find a living world. The church, too, seemed sleepless, and the grave-stones in the churchyard which he saw every day as he ran to school, or the sweet-shop, now filled him with wonder. Their foreheads, tipped with moonlight, some bowed towards the church tower, like listeners towards a pulpit, others inclined to one side or the other, seemed like a congregation, waiting for some important announcement.

He ran across the street on tiptoe, like a small animal whose muscles of themselves make a dance to express the tension of pleasure.

At the tall house behind the white gate, the dining-room window was already open. Antony, standing beneath it, looked back quickly at the sky, the trees, the stones, as if expecting that they might have turned to watch him. But they were still meditating their own private affairs, in sleepless patience.

A high voice hissed from the window, 'Iss that you, Tony?'

'Hullo, Bob.' He put his hands on the window frame.

A long pale face, topped with a thick mass of dark hair, appeared in the window opening. 'I ssay, don't make ssuch a noisse—there'ss been a plessman.' Robert's spluttering whisper quivered with excitement. 'He'ss jusst been passt—he looked over the gate. Don't push,' the voice rose to a squeal, 'the window ssqueaks.'

Antony, wriggling through the window, was silent. He was irritated by Robert's undignified excitement, but the irritation was trifling. He was used to Robert's nervous manners and had long learnt to put up with them.

Having reached the floor of the room, he said in a low voice which disdained to whisper, 'Did the policeman see you?'

But Robert had already forgotten his remark about the policeman. He had spoken only to express his excitement. He said now, 'What *were* you doing, you idiot—I thought you were never coming.'

Antony said nothing. He was gazing round him at the moonlit room.

'I say, aren't you glad you came?' Robert exclaimed, scratching himself through his pyjamas. He grinned broadly and stared at Antony who stared at him gravely. Neither spoke. They did not know what to say, or to do, next. They had forgotten their plans. Antony's eye, passing along the streak of moonlight which crossed the floor to the hearth-rug, fell upon a candle stuck to a cup bottom, a bottle of orangeade, a large tin of fruit, a soup-plate and two spoons. Robert, following his glance, broke into new splutters, 'The feasst—there you are—I got everything—come on, what are you waiting for?'

He drew the curtains together, lit the candle and took his seat on the hearth-rug. 'We better hurry up—we've got a lot to eat. It's a two-pound tin.'

Antony silently took his seat on the opposite side of the candle. Robert gazed at him with little sparkling black eyes and cheeks darkened with excitement. He was trying not to laugh, but every time he stopped speaking, his lips parted and twitched. Then quickly he spoke again, with a careless abrupt tone, like a tough used to midnight debauchery, 'Have some booze.'

'Thanks.'

'I ssay, it was a good idea, wassn't it?'

'What?'

'Having a feasst.'

Antony said nothing to this. He felt that the adventure was too serious, too grand, to talk about.

Robert intercepted another bursting grin. 'Come on, what about the booze—I ssay, where's the corkscrew?'

'What corkscrew?'

'I ssay, dassh it all, I asked you to bring a corkscrew.'

'You said you had one.'

'No, I didn't—it's in the dining-room and the floor creakss like mad.'

'Oh well—we'll have the pineapple—you got whole slices, didn't you?'

'No, I couldn't, you can't since Christmass—itss peachess—I ssay, did you bring an opener?'

'What opener?'

Robert, with the tin in both hands, looked round at the floor. He frowned angrily but his lips were still trying to smile. 'Dassh it all, you idiot—we can't do anything without an opener.'

Antony was gazing at the brass fire-irons, shining by themselves in the candle-light. He put out his hand and touched the knob of the poker with the careful gesture of one who caresses a strange dog.

Suddenly he looked up and saw Robert grinning from ear to ear. Robert's feelings had overrun his sense of what was correct for a night-rover. He exclaimed, 'Rather glorious idea, don't you think—a feast?'

Antony raised his brows slightly. The word glorious struck him, with surprise, as exactly right for the adventure. That was why he didn't choose to talk about it. He gazed thoughtfully at his friend across the bottle and the tin, the clean soup-plates and the spoons. 'Not bad.'

A ring at the door thrilled on the air. Robert flew out of the door, Antony darted for the window. Three minutes later, Robert's father, in dressing-gown and slippers, was standing in the hall interviewing a young policeman, who grasped Antony by the arm.

The boy was extremely pale, his eyes were round, but he seemed more absent-minded than afraid.

'Ran right into me, Professor—just at the gate—thought you'd better have a look round.'

The professor stroked his bald head with a slow thoughtful movement from front to back. 'But Tony—I don't understand—what were you doing with Robert—why did you come here at this time of night?'

Antony said in a dreamy voice, 'We wanted to have a feast.'

'A feast.' The professor suddenly dropped his hand and asked, 'You've not been drinking cider, have you?' And turning towards the stairs where Robert's pyjama legs could be seen through the landing balusters, he called, 'Bobby.' The legs disappeared. The professor said, 'Robert is much too fond of cider.'

'Stronger than beer, some of it,' the policeman said, with the air of an expert.

'So I tell them, officer.' Both looked severely at Antony.

'We didn't have cider.'

'What did you have?'

The small boy slightly raised his eyebrows. He could not remember what he had had at this feast, so long prepared, so gloriously achieved.

'A tin of fruit,' he murmured at last, doubtfully.

The professor smiled and once more his little plump hand went to his bald head. He gave it a circular rub of amusement. 'Heavens, are you boys in the habit of breaking into houses at midnight, to eat tinned fruit?'

Antony was still gazing out of the window. He was lost in that indescribable experience of the midnight world; where even the sky and the familiar stars, had a strange look; a new still world full of something he had never felt before, and the word 'grand' came to his mind. But the very word had a new meaning.

'A tin of fruit,' said the professor.

'Yes, it was—pineapple.'

The professor laughed; and even the policeman smiled.

'Pineapple,' he said, 'the taste of glory.'

Antony, suddenly recalled to this world, gazed at them and opened his mouth to say that the pineapple had not been important. But he closed it again and said nothing. He realised that nothing, nothing he could say would make them understand. Because they had already decided the whole thing was fancy.

THE EXPLORERS

THE children were playing weddings. The parson was a red-haired girl who broke into giggles as soon as she began to read. She was at once bitterly reproached by a boy in school uniform, sitting at the nursery table with a wireless set in front of him, from which the back had been removed.

'How can I hear where it rattles while you make all that noise?'

'We were only playing.'

'This is a job of work and a pretty tricky one, too—to mend a wireless.'

'Shall we stop?'

'No, of course not.' The boy, having asserted the dignity of his task, was at once good-natured, 'As long as you don't play the ass.'

The girl, whose broad freckled face expressed a placid good nature, began again to read, 'Wilt thou take this man——' the boy, screwdriver in hand, twisted his head sideways to examine the under part of the chassis, and frowned like a public character conscious of the interested stares of a large crowd but determined to take no notice of them.

The bridegroom scratched himself with sudden impatience, behind the knee. He was a small boy of about six, and his dark eyes wandered continually about the room. The bride, however, a very fair little girl, rather older and taller than the boy, held tight to his hand and gazed at Phil with an anxious face. She was wearing for veil an old muslin curtain and carried a bouquet of cowslips.

'Wilt thou have this woman to be thy wedded wife?'

The red-haired Phil stopped, she was again on the verge of giggles. The little girl turned towards the boy and cried, 'But she mustn't, must she, Reggie, it's real, isn't it?'

He made no answer. He had just discovered that his screwdriver was too large for the wiring connections, which he had meant to tighten. He was therefore uncertain what to do. His frown became more important.

'Reggie, tell her not to—tell her to do it properly.'

'It's no good telling her anything,' the boy said gloomily. 'She always behaves like a kid.' With careful precision he brought the screwdriver against the back of the chassis, as if some delicate mechanism were beneath its edge. But there was nothing there except a blank space of vulcanite.

Red-hair made another effort. 'Wilt thou have this man to be thy wedded husband. Wilt thou obey him and serve him, love' (here she paused to control a giggle) 'honour and help him in—so long as you both shall live?' The little girl grasped the boy's hand firmly and said in a loud voice, 'I will.'

The little boy suddenly jerked away his hand and made a dart at the cat which was just about to take her seat in a patch of sunlight. As he swooped upon her, she sprang as if through his hands, and with tail erected, every hair on end, but with a calm expression and easy unhurried movement, bounded towards the door. The small boy rushed after her. The red-haired Phil cried, 'Don't, Davy—let her alone,' threw down the book on the table and flew to rescue the cat.

The little girl, still in her muslin veil and grasping her bouquet, sat down in a chair and gazed at the wall with an enquiring frown. At last she gave a sigh exactly like a sigh of happiness, and said, 'I'm so happy.'

The boy, Reginald, having found a screw which would fit his screwdriver, got busily to work and took it out, whereupon a valve tumbled suddenly off the face of the chassis; in trying to catch the valve, he dropped the screwdriver and the screw rolled on the floor. But he remained calm and thoughtful as if all this had been foreseen and expected.

'I'm so awfully happy, Reg,' said the little girl. 'It's simply lovely to be married.'

The boy was working upon another screw of the same size. He had decided to change his plan of operations. Since his screwdriver fitted the larger screws, he would take the wireless to pieces instead of putting it in order.

The little girl sat motionless for another two minutes. Her gaze was still fixed on the wall. She said again, 'It's lovely to be married.' But there was enquiry in her tone as well as her eyes.

A condenser fell suddenly with a crash on the table causing the valve to roll to the floor where it exploded loudly. The boy cast an angry glance at the little girl, but she did not move. She had not noticed the accident. His face at once became again calm and important. He picked up the condenser, which was now bent and unworkable, and said, '*Just* what I expected.'

The cat came winding round the door and advanced, licking its whiskers, towards the patch of sunlight. The little girl went up to the table and gazed for a long time at her brother. At last, in a pleading voice, which asked for support, for encouragement, she said, 'It's nice to be married, Reg.'

The boy, who was looking at the ruined wireless set with surprise and anxiety, as if he could not imagine how it had reached such a condition, murmured, 'Don't interrupt, you might make me do something wrong.'

The little girl drifted round the table and saw the cat. She stooped over it and said, 'Are you happy, Topsy?'

The cat yawned and curled itself up in the sun; a bell rang from the street; it was the ice-cream man. The little girl dropped her bouquet, tore off her veil and flew out of the door; but the engineer was already leaning out of the window. 'Hi,' he shouted, 'hi, there.'